Now the Day
is Over

Now the Day is Over

a novel by

Jennifer Wixson

BOOK 6 IN THE SOVEREIGN SERIES

White Wave Publishing
P.O. Box 4
Troy, ME 04987
whitewavepublishing@gmail.com

ISBN 979-8-9942403-0-4

10 9 8 7 6 5 4 3 2 1

For Dad,
who, after putting us kids to bed at night in Winslow,
used to sing to us from the bottom of the stairs

"Now the day is over,
Night is drawing nigh,
Shadows of the evening
Steal across the sky.

"Now the darkness gathers,
Stars begin to peep,
Birds, and beasts and flowers
Soon will be asleep."

Excerpt from: *"Now the Day Is Over"*
by Sabine Baring-Gould

Table of Contents

Who's Who in Sovereign, Maine?

*A Guide for Those (Like the Author) Who Need Help
Keeping the Characters Straight*

Main Characters

Maggie the Minister and Her Family

Maggie Walker Hodges Faulkner – the seventyish long-time minister of the Sovereign Union Church, currently on sabbatical to write a book. Her place in the pulpit has temporarily been taken by the new young pastor Sabine Burbury. (See *Maggie's Friends and Neighbors*.) Maggie is the mainstay of all six books in the Sovereign Series.

Duncan Faulkner – Maggie's second husband, a retired Presbyterian minister. A steady, good-natured man, Duncan and Maggie's romance is featured in Book 5 of the Sovereign Series, *Maggie's Dilemma*.

Nick Faulkner – Duncan's unmarried son (Maggie's stepson), a bohemian woodsman who earns his living selling wild mushrooms. Nick came to Sovereign about ten years ago passing himself off under the pseudonym of **"Walden Pond,"** as featured in Book 4, *The Minister's Daughter*. Nick lives off-grid in the Sovereign Woods in the old Nutt place.

Nora Faulkner – Duncan's unmarried daughter (Maggie's stepdaughter), who resides in North Dakota.

Nellie Walker Lawson – Maggie's daughter, who lives in the neighborhood and is married to Doctor Bart (Metcalf Bartholomew Lawson). Nellie and Doctor Bart run a free medical clinic, Songbird Medical Clinic, out of their home. They are expecting their second child in early fall. Nellie and Metcalf's love story is told in Book 4, *The Minister's Daughter*.

Metcalf/Doctor Bart – **Metcalf Bartholomew Lawson**, Nellie's husband. Metcalf is known by all (except immediate family) as Doctor Bart. He and Nellie run the free Songbird Medical Clinic. Metcalf's mother Jane Metcalf Lawson and Maggie were childhood chums.

Jana Lawson – Nellie and Doctor Bart's seven-year-old daughter, currently Maggie's only grandchild. Jana was named for the beloved former music teacher of Sovereign, Miss Jana Hastings (whose poignant story is told in Book 3, *The Songbird of Sovereign*.) Upon her death, Miss Hastings willed her home to Doctor Bart for his medical clinic.

Maggie's Friends and Neighbors

At the church:
Sabine Burbury – Sabine is the young unmarried daughter of a minister with whom Maggie attended seminary. She was named for the nineteenth century Anglican priest and hymn-writer, Sabine Baring-Gould. Sabine is the romantic lead in *Now the Day Is Over*.

Courtney Gilpin – accompanist, who is married to Gray Gilpin, manager of Gilpin's General Store.

At the old Russell homestead:
Rebecca Russell – the widow of **Wendell Russell**, who passed away in January the year the book opens. Wendell was perhaps the most beloved old-timer in Sovereign. While the story of Wendell and Rebecca's romance is told in Book 1, *Hens and Chickens*, the couple has played a major role in every one of the six Sovereign Series novels. Wendell inherited the old homestead from his grandparents, **George and Addie Russell**, whose story is shared in Book 3, *The Songbird of Sovereign*.

George "Tad" Russell – Rebecca and Wendell's nine-year-old son.

Amber – Rebecca's grown daughter from her first marriage. Amber is now married and living in Winslow. Mentioned only briefly in this book, Amber's love story with Bruce Gilpin is told in Book 2, *Peas, Beans & Corn*.

At Scotch Broom Acres:
Leland Gorse – octogenarian woodchopper and owner of Scotch Broom Acres, although the farm is now run by his daughter Trudy and her husband Ryan. Leland, an independent Old Fart who like to tell tall tales, is one of Maggie's oldest friends.

Trudy Gorse MacDonald – Leland's daughter, who is a part-time librarian at the Sovereign school. In addition, Trudy and her husband Ryan now manage her father's dairy farm, Scotch Broom Acres, and are known for their quality organic butter, cream, cheeses, and other products.

Ryan MacDonald – formerly a high-powered attorney from Boston, Ryan was first introduced in Book 1, *Hens and Chickens*. He returned to Sovereign to court Trudy in Book 2, *Peas, Beans & Corn*. Ryan does most of the legal work for Sovereign residents, in addition to helping Trudy with their butter and cheese business at Scotch Broom Acres.

Alice Rose MacDonald – Trudy and Ryan's eleven-year-old daughter, who is a bit on the bratty side.

Hope MacDonald – Trudy and Ryan's sweet nine-year-old daughter.

Up the road from the old Russell homestead:
Henry Trow – an elderly retired history professor from New Hampshire. Henry purchased the significant Lovejoy property (from which Maggie's schoolhouse lot was cut) about a decade ago. Then a recent widow, Henry, in Book 4 (*The Minister's Daughter*) courted and married Doctor Bart's great-aunt Hannah. They live in the gracious

nineteenth century brick house built by the Lovejoys, which is situated up the road from the old Russell place.

"Aunt Hannah" Trow – Henry's wife and Doctor Bart's great-aunt. Noted for her cooking, Aunt Hannah still prepares meals for Doctor Bart and Nellie three days a week.

Stephen Danforth – seventy-plus-year-old parttime truck driver. Danforth is a good friend and neighbor of the Russell family. His home is situated beyond Henry and Hannah's house on the Russell Hill Road.

Nadine Danforth – Stephen's wife, who has been friends with Hannah Trow since Kindergarten.

Gerald Danforth – Stephen and Nadine's wild, red-headed grandchild, about twelve or thirteen years old. Although Gerald is supposedly homeschooled by his mother (who lives in neighboring Thorndike), he spends most of his time running wild in the Sovereign Woods or helping Nick Faulkner with his mushroom business.

Other Characters

Robinson Crockett – solar farm developer from Away, who comes to Sovereign.

Miss Helen Crump – an eccentric centenarian who loves chickens and owns an extensive gravel pit. She is a large benefactress of Doctor Bart and Nellie's free Songbird Medical Clinic. Miss Crump first appears in Book 4, *The Minister's Daughter.*

John Woods – longtime First Selectman of the town of Sovereign. His wife **Ruth** is also briefly mentioned.

Betty Peabody – Sovereign Town Clerk.

Gray Gilpin – Thirty-year-old manager of Gilpin's General Store, now that his grandfather has retired. Gray was first mentioned in Book 1 and has played a minor role in several Sovereign Series novels. He is one of the three selectmen in town. Gray's wife **Courtney** is also the accompanist at the Sovereign Union Church.

Bob Jessup – the third Sovereign selectman.

Frank Whitehouse – elderly sexton of the Sovereign cemeteries.

Jarod Palmer – newspaper reporter for the *Morning Sentinel.*

Mike Hobart – a romantic lead in Book 1, *Hens and Chickens*, Mike is mentioned because Sabine has rented the off-grid cabin he built years ago.

Maynard Nutter – Nonagenarian former Sovereign selectman who appears in several Sovereign Series novels and who makes a brief appearance here. He was once in love with **"Ma Jean," Mabel Jean Brown**, however, she married another man, as told in Book 2.

Jenny Dalton – old dairy farmer and longtime moderator of all Sovereign Town Meetings.

Jacob Nutt – early nineteenth century settler of Sovereign. Nick Faulkner bought and fixed up the old Nutt place, which is situated in the middle of the Sovereign Woods.

Chapter 1

The Yellow Moccasins

Morning dew still dripped as they picked their way through the sylvan shade of the Sovereign Woods.

"You *do* know where you're going, Maggie, I hope?" called out Duncan Faulkner, in a tone of voice that suggested his own confidence was diminishing. The retired Presbyterian minister halted momentarily to allow the half-dead pine branch displaced by the disappearing figure of his wife to return to position, thus not whacking him in the face. "We've been off the main trail quite a while now."

"Of course I know where I'm going," Maggie called back. "At least, I have a good idea," she amended honestly. Maggie paused in a clearing on the deer trail she had been following so that her husband could catch up to her. Three or four mosquitoes rose up from beneath the hay-scented ferns to greet her. "Dang it. I forgot the fly dope."

Duncan parted the silken tassels of several closely-growing young pine trees to enter the clearing behind her. "I'm beginning to think I'm the dope for agreeing to come on this little adventure." He pushed back the brim of his Red Sox baseball cap. His handsome, age-lined face displayed a teasing smile, however.

"I thought you wanted to see the yellow moccasins, too?" Maggie challenged, hands on hips. Despite the fact she was closer to seventy than sixty, gardening and hiking combined with wood splitting and stacking had kept the long-time minister of the Sovereign Union Church in good physical shape. She used the tail of the light blue Oxford shirt she was wearing (one of her husband's castoffs) to wipe the perspiration and dirt from her face.

"I do want to see your special wildflowers—the name is so alluring. Yellow moccasins! But I might not fully enjoy the experience of your rare wild orchids if we spend the night lost in the woods of Sovereign, Maine. How will we ever find our way back out?"

"Oh, good heavens, Duncan! Don't tell me you haven't been tossing out bread crumbs behind you?" Maggie joked.

"What? You can't think I'm going to sacrifice one of the sandwiches! Surely you know me better than that after eight years of marriage?"

It was true. Maggie Walker Hodges Faulkner had been married to her second husband for nearly eight years. Where had the time gone?

How the decade had flown since her first husband and childhood chum Peter had keeled over from a heart attack while folding laundry at the kitchen table! Those had been dark days, but since then much sunshine had come into Maggie's life, including a second husband and a granddaughter, with another grandbaby on the way. In addition, her family and most of her special friends were healthy and happy, the younger ones producing offspring so that Jana, Maggie's seven-year-old granddaughter (named after the late beloved music teacher of Sovereign), had plenty of playmates in the neighborhood.

Some days, like today, Maggie wished she could take hold of Time and slow it down. The world—and her life— were moving much too fast! Instead, she inhaled deeply the fecund scent of the May forest, mingled with the fresh astringent scent of pine and balsam fir. "Ah, I could live on this smell forever! Isn't this Paradise? Listen! There's an oven bird."

"Paradise with a few caveats, such as the mosquitoes and black flies," Duncan grumbled, swatting at a whining mosquito. "Somehow you forgot to mention them when you sold me on this hike today."

"Did you expect only sunshine and blue skies? It's springtime in Maine, remember?" Maggie felt a bead of sweat rolling up between her breasts. In a flash, she realized her mistake. Sweat did not roll *up*. She yanked the tee-shirt she was wearing under her Oxford shirt away from her chest in a very unfeminine fashion, and stuck her hand down her front.

"No, but ..."

"Excuse me," she interrupted her husband, "personal grooming." Maggie nabbed the tick between the fingernail of her thumb and forefinger, halting its forward progress. She hauled the intruder out triumphantly. "Gotcha, you little devil!" Maggie held the tick out for her husband to see.

"Great!" Duncan exclaimed with disgust, examining the arachnid. "Please add ticks to my list of caveats. I hope it's not a deer tick. I would prefer that neither of us get Lyme disease."

"Wood tick, worry wart." Maggie crushed the body of the offending tick with her fingernail and brushed the remains from her hand. "Besides, it didn't even latch on. We'll have to check each other carefully when we get home, though. The ticks are mighty hungry this time of year."

"That's something to look forward to, at least," Duncan said, brightening up. He regarded his wife thoughtfully for a moment. "You know, that's what I love about you," he continued. "You see the world through rose-colored glasses—and it's a beautiful world. Yet I know underneath those roses you also see the reality of the situation."

"I just try to focus on the good. I'm not crazy about the bad, but I know it's part of life. Like black flies and ticks."

"Ah, the Problem of Evil!"

"Ticks aren't evil, silly. That implies intent, as you well know. I've never witnessed evil intent outside of a human heart. Ticks are just trying to get on with their lives, like every other living thing on this planet, including us."

"I was speaking of God's intent," Duncan clarified. "What was the Divine purpose in creating ticks, and black flies? Paradise with a few caveats, as I said."

Maggie laughed. "I'm not even going to try and answer that question, because I know when you go all theological on me it only means you're hungry. Don't worry, we'll eat soon."

"Not a very flattering portrait of me, but probably accurate." Duncan glanced hopefully around the small clearing, peopled by the sweet-smelling ferns in assorted sizes and shades of green. "Is this our picnic spot? It looks very serviceable. And the sun feels nice after the dampness of the woods?"

Maggie shook her head. "If we set up here, I'm afraid we'll have to share our lunch with your caveats, those creatures looking to get on with their lives." As if to highlight her point, a cloud of black flies swarmed in. Maggie attempted to disperse the flying insects by waving a fern switch. "We need a high spot to eat, where the wind will keep these blood suckers at bay. Argh! I just swallowed one. Well, that's one less black fly to worry about. I was planning to eat on top of the Millett Rock. There's always a nice breeze up there." The Millett Rock was a huge glacial erratic left over from the last ice age. The colossal flat-top rock was a popular picnic spot.

"So eminently practical! Lead on, milady—if you know the direction to proceed."

Maggie reconnoitered the woods surrounding the clearing. "I think we're almost there. I remember this clearing from last year when Nick brought me to see the yellow moccasins." Nick Faulkner, Duncan's son and Maggie's stepson, was an expert woodsman, and probably the local person most familiar with the two thousand-plus acre swath of wilderness between the Cross Road and Route 9 in Sovereign, Maine. Many Sovereign residents knew where to find pink lady's slippers; however, Nick had discovered this patch of the rarer yellow lady's slipper—Maggie's favorite—only the prior year. "Hush a moment, please."

Her husband obliged obediently. Maggie cocked her ear. "Yes! That's running water. We must be close to the brook. That jives with the directions Nick gave me on the phone the other night."

Duncan, who also had been listening intently, but had heard nothing but the irritating whine of mosquitos, was skeptical. "I don't suppose you would consider abandoning our quest and heading straight for the Millett Rock?" he suggested. "Nick said he'd be home soon. He can show us the yellow moccasins, then." For the past ten months, Duncan's thirty-four-year-old son had been hitchhiking around the United States on a personal mission of self-discovery. Nick worked off his room and board by performing odd jobs for individuals and small businesses. When the young man had arrived in Sovereign a decade ago (two years prior to his father's arrival), introducing himself as "Walden Pond," he supported himself by harvesting and selling wild mushrooms. Since then, Nick Faulkner—who marched to a different drummer like his idol, the naturalist Henry David Thoreau—worked as a carpenter to pay the bills in addition to selling mushrooms, and had become an important part of the fabric of the eclectic farming community that comprised Sovereign, Maine. Everyone loved this big, gentle, bearded man, especially the local children, with whom Nick shared his affinity for the natural world.

"And have me confess to my stepson that I couldn't follow his directions? I think not. Besides, yellow moccasins only bloom for a few weeks. I don't want to miss them. We don't know when Nick will get back."

Duncan scratched at a bug bite on his neck. "That's true," he admitted. "Where did Nick say he was? At a truck stop outside Hartford?" Without waiting for his wife to reply, Duncan continued on. "I certainly didn't expect when he left last July he'd be gone nearly a year." He shifted his backpack, trying to find a more comfortable position to carry their picnic lunch, the blanket, and other accoutrements. "I'm surprised how much I've missed having him pop in at inconvenient times."

"I've missed him, too. Nick always has something interesting to share. He certainly has a singular way of looking at the world."

"My son didn't get his outlook on life from me."

"You didn't need to tell me that!" Maggie stepped close to her husband and adjusted one of the straps on his pack so that the bag hung evenly. "Nick notices every little change in the woods, whereas you don't even notice the sunset. Is that better?"

Duncan jiggled his shoulders. "Much better, thanks."

"Let's just hope he's found what he was looking for on this journey of self-discovery."

"Amen to that. If Nick hasn't found his place in life at thirty-four, I'm not sure he ever will."

Maggie was about to retort, "O, ye of little faith!" But prudently remembered that it was safer when discussing Nick with his father to let Duncan have the last word.

Within ten minutes, Maggie and Duncan had found what they were looking for—a patch of yellow lady's slippers, *Cypripedium parviflorum*, thriving in a moist, but well-drained grove about three hundred feet from the brook. The orchids occupied one corner of the grove, protected by a mixed forest canopy that was interrupted in a few places where older trees had fallen or been blown over by adverse winds. The breaks in the canopy allowed streams of sunlight to poke through, warming the rich black soil and highlighting the delicate-looking lady's slippers. Eight or nine of the wild orchids were in bloom, showing off their bright yellow moccasins.

"Oh, aren't they gorgeous!" Maggie exclaimed, dropping to her knees in front one of the plants. She reached out and gently touched the soft, silken toe of one of the yellow moccasins. "There are more blooming now than last year when Nick brought me here."

Duncan examined the bevy of yellow lady's slippers that brightened the small secluded patch of woods. "Remarkable! They do look like miniature yellow moccasins." He shrugged out of his backpack, set the pack on the ground, and scootched down beside his wife to net a closer look. "Mother Nature has outdone herself, I'd say. If I didn't know these were real plants, I'd think the little boots were made from yellow satin ribbons."

"Mother Nature's design is clever, as well as beautiful. The boots aren't just for show—they're designed to trap insects. Once caught, the bugs have to climb up past the anthers to escape, fertilizing the flower on the way out." Maggie pointed out two fertile anthers hidden beneath the yellow lady's slipper's showy staminode.

"Eminently practical! Just like my wife."

"Thank you, dear." Maggie sat back on her haunches. "I've never seen so many yellow moccasins in bloom at one time! My grandmother had three or four that grew at the farm. Her brother transplanted a yellow lady's slipper there decades ago. Of course, that was before collecting wild orchids was discouraged. Ours managed to survive and multiply, though."

"Why would anyone discourage transplanting them? I would think transplanting lady's slippers would help increase their numbers, like what happened at your family's farm."

"You would think so, but the opposite is usually the case," replied Maggie. "Lady's slippers are quite a challenge to grow. The plants require a very specific fungus—a beneficial fungus—that enables the lady's slippers to uptake the correct nutrients from the soil. Transplanting the plant not only damages the eco system from which the lady's slipper is taken, but also generally spells the death of that plant because most people don't have the beneficial fungus in the soil where they put them. It's a lose-lose situation for the orchids. That's why both the state of Maine and environmental groups discourage transplanting lady's slippers, although only the showy and ram's head lady's slippers are considered rare and have protected status. The ram's head is listed as globally rare, I believe. "

"I thought you said the yellow moccasins were rare? You mean there are others that are rarer? That's hard to believe." Duncan closely examined one of the delicate blooms, admiring the boot's crimped edge set off by light green leaf-like petals with rust-colored mottling. Protective, cupping leaves similar to those of lily-of-the-valley rose up from the base of the orchid's long stem.

"Yep. I've never seen a ram's head lady's slipper. Couldn't even tell you what it looks like. But when I was young my mother pointed out a showy lady's slipper to me once when we were hiking. I wish I could remember where we were! But I was just a kid, and didn't care that much about flowers, then. But I do remember the blossom—the boot or pouch was pink and the petals surrounding it were white. Very showy, indeed! It's well named."

"Are there any other colors?"

"Plain pinks. But pink lady's slippers are fairly common in Maine. I know several locations where they grow, and I bet Leland knows half a dozen spots to find the pinks, if not a dozen." Leland Gorse, an octogenarian woodchopper and one of their special friends, was nearly as familiar with the Sovereign Woods as was Duncan's son. "But I bet even Leland doesn't know about this patch of yellow moccasins."

"Probably not," Duncan agreed with a wry smile. "If my ole buddy Leland knew these beauties were here, we could have followed a well-worn path through the woods."

Maggie chuckled. "Leland isn't big on keeping anything a secret, that's for sure." She retrieved her phone from the back pocket of her jeans and snapped several photographs of the yellow moccasins. To her surprise, Duncan also took out his phone to photograph the lady's slippers.

"Sending some pics to Nick?" Maggie asked, as her husband knelt awkwardly in front of one of the yellow moccasins to capture a better photo.

"Nope. Sending them to Nora." Nora Faulkner was Duncan's daughter, Nick's younger sister. "She likes flowers, especially unusual ones."

"Ah! Still trying to lure her back to Maine, I see." Since graduating from Colby College in Waterville Nora had lived and worked in North Dakota. Her last visit to Maine had been during the Christmas holidays.

"You're onto me," Duncan said, sitting back. He squinted at his phone to review the photos, then selected two of the best images and texted the pics to his daughter. "These probably won't go through. Can't imagine we have cell service this far out in the woods."

Maggie looked at her phone. "One bar."

"Oh, well! Nora wouldn't answer me, even if the photos did go through. You know how young people are."

She smiled. "I think that's what young people say about us—'You know how old people are!'"

"You think I'm over the top?" he asked, slapping at a mosquito.

"Just a little."

Duncan sighed. "You're probably right. But at least my intent is beneficial, like your fungus. Now that Nora has dumped what's-his-name, I don't see why she needs to live out west. North Dakota is his home, not hers."

"Spoken like a true meddling parent!"

"Nora wouldn't even have to quit her job because she's worked at home since COVID. Some days she says she doesn't even bother to get dressed," he groused. "What kind of a life is that?"

Before Maggie could form her usual assuaging reply to her husband's concerns about his daughter, Duncan's phone pinged with an incoming text message. "That was fast," she spoke cheerily. "That's a good sign, dear."

Duncan's face fell, however, as he read the text message. "It's not from Nora—it's from the bank. Remind me when we get home to figure out how to stop these advertising messages. Better yet, remind me to switch banks!"

Maggie, understanding her husband's frustration, wisely chose not to reply. Instead, she stood up, brushed herself off and checked her shirt and pants for ticks. Finding none, she retrieved the backpack from the ground. "Let's go eat our picnic lunch. Shouldn't take us more than twenty minutes to get to the Millett Rock from here."

At the mention of food, Duncan's thoughts were immediately diverted from his daughter's life (or lack thereof). "Music to my ears!" He arose and allowed Maggie to slip the pack onto his back. "Good thing this will be lighter on the way home—I'm not as young as I used to be." He shifted the pack. "By the way, who owns this section of woods? "

"Henry does, I think. He owns five or six hundred acres altogether, a hundred or so next to the brook." Henry Trow was Maggie and Duncan's nearest neighbor. About a decade earlier the retired history professor from New

Hampshire had purchased the homestead of one of the town's original nineteenth century settlers. The ten acres upon which Maggie's little house stood—formerly a one-room schoolhouse—had been cut from that extensive property.

"Henry certainly owns some beautiful real estate," Duncan mused. "I'm almost envious, although I probably wouldn't be once I opened his tax bill."

"He doesn't pay much tax on his woodlots. Most of Henry's land is enrolled in the tree growth tax program. It's the brick house that costs …what the heck?!"

Rambunctious snapping and cracking sounds rent the quiet of the glade, arresting Maggie mid-sentence. She cocked her head and listened to the crashing noises emanating from the woods, now growing louder. Whatever the creature was, it was obviously approaching. A nosy bluejay, which had been keeping an eye on Maggie and Duncan, screeched out a warning and flew off in a flutter of panic, deeper into the forest. It was an ominous sign.

Chapter 2

"Ain't This Henry's Land?"

"Something is following us," Duncan said, quietly.

Maggie nodded, without offering a reply, her mind intent upon identifying the gate-crasher to their yellow moccasin party.

"Do you think it's a moose?"

"Maybe," she whispered. Maggie was not normally fearful in the Maine woods; however, whatever was approaching was larger and louder than any creature she had ever heard in the forest before. Her brain ran the course of dangerous possibilities: tick-crazed moose? Mama black bear with cubs? Axe murderer?

Suddenly, a distinct whistle pierced the air. The whistling expanded into a few musical notes. Recognizing the popular fifties melody, Maggie relaxed. Only then did she realize she had been holding her breath.

"Phew," Duncan exhaled, visibly relieved. "I'm surprised that bird is so loud."

"Ha! That's no bird," Maggie responded. "Unless it's a parrot who likes Rosemary Clooney. I happen to know 'This Ole House' is one of Leland's favorite songs."

"Leland? Here!"

Sure enough, Leland Gorse, their elderly woodchopper friend, popped out of a thicket into the grove. The scrawny man was carrying a dented tin pail in his left hand and in his right hand he wielded an antiquated Snow and Nealley kindling axe, with which he was hacking away tree branches and puckerbrush. "Figgered I might find you folks here," Leland said, a broad smile on his wrinkled, weathered face. "I widened the trail for ya," he continued, stomping down an obstinate maple sapling with his steel-toed leather boot. 'Twill make it easier for you to git back to the main path. I know how squirrely you are in the woods, Duncan."

"Very considerate of you, Leland," Duncan replied.

"What are you doing here?" Maggie demanded, suspicious of her friend's sudden appearance in the remote grove.

"I come to see the yeller moccasins, jest like you, I expect. Ain't they purty!"

"You knew the lady's slippers were here? And you never told me about them!"

"Now, don't git yer back up, Maggie," Leland enjoined. He hitched a thumb into one of the belt loops on his tan work pants, the kind worn by old-time Maine dairy farmers. A wrinkled, long-sleeved work shirt, also tan, completed his ensemble. "I didn't know nuthin' about 'em, leastways not 'til lately."

"How did you know the yellow moccasins were here, then?"

Leland dropped the pail, which hit the ground near his feet with a plunking sound. He pushed back the brim of his ratty ballcap and grinned at Maggie, enjoying her perplexion.

Duncan, on the other hand, put two and two together with no difficulty "Looks like Nick isn't good at keeping secrets, either," he said, drily.

Leland chuckled. "Thet's right—yer boy called me t'other day. Walden 'n I had a real good conversation, too. Glad to hear he'll be home soon." Leland was one of the many in Sovereign who continued to address Nick Faulkner by the nom-de-guerre the youth had assumed when he first arrived in town.

"Of course! I should have known Walden—Nick—would tell *you* about the yellow moccasins," grumbled Maggie. "You two are as thick as thieves."

"Ayuh." Leland leaned his axe up against a nearby pine tree, then gingerly knelt down onto one bony knee in front of the cluster of yellow lady's slippers. "Course, 'twould have preferred Walden had told me about 'em last year." He withdrew a trowel from his rusty pail.

Before Maggie could fathom Leland's intention, the old woodsman inserted the pointed trowel into the rich black soil and dug up one of the wild orchids. He dropped the trowel and cupped the prize in his blue-veined hands. Leland carefully placed the fragile plant into his pail. Maggie was shocked by her friend's brazenness. "What are you doing?" she demanded.

Leland retrieved his trowel and used the point to push himself back up. He stomped the excess dirt into the hole. "Takin' one to Hannah. She ain't never seen a yeller moccasin afore." Hannah was Henry Trow's wife. "She cain't walk this far."

"But … you shouldn't dig them up!"

"Says who? Ain't this Henry's land?" Leland cocked his head and gave Maggie an innocent, quizzical look.

"You don't fool me, Leland. You know that collecting lady's slippers is discouraged by the state."

"Whoopy-do!" he snorted. "'Tain't agin the law."

"That isn't the point! What are you going to do with the plant after you show it to Hannah?"

Leland lifted the pail by its wire bale, clasped the bucket to his belly, and reached inside. He gently tucked the moist black soil around the plant to ensure the fragile roots were completely covered. "She wants a yeller moccasin fer her flower bed."

Maggie was miffed. "You know that plant probably won't live." She rarely called out her non-conforming friend on any of the rules he broke. After all, Leland had helped care for her during her battle with breast cancer ten years ago. But this transgression against the yellow lady's slipper was too much for the minister's plant-loving soul. In her book, plants, birds, and children were sacred. "Don't you even care?"

Leland shrugged and gestured around the little grove. "Plenty more yeller moccasins here, jest like Walden said."

"That's a fine excuse," Maggie scoffed. "'Plenty more where these come from.' Do you want yellow moccasins to go the way of Maine shrimp?"

"Thet's a stretch, ain't it, de-ah?"

"Or clams? Or lobster? Pretty soon, thanks to attitudes like that—and climate change—we won't have anything left in Maine that makes Maine—Maine."

"Now, don't be so dem self-righteous, Maggie! I'm only takin' one to Hannah. And she 'n Henry own the dem plant—not you—'n sure 'nuff not the state."

Maggie felt a hot sense of wrath, as though she had been betrayed by a sibling or best friend. She was about to come back with a scathing retort, when Duncan, who had been quietly observing the testy exchange between the two close friends, stepped in. "What about that lunch you promised me?" he said to his wife. "It's after eleven. I'm famished!"

Maggie bit her tongue. It was hard for her to back down from a fight, especially when she believed she was in the right. Why couldn't Leland see that digging up the yellow moccasin was wrong? Surely, Leland knew better! What was he thinking?

"'Tis drawing nigh to dinnertime," Leland allowed, willing to have the disagreement defused.

Maggie harumphed. Still nursing her anger toward her old friend, she turned her back on him, leaving Leland clutching his rusty pail. Without a word to either of the two men she began hiking back, perversely setting a new course rather than following the trail that Leland had hacked out.

Of all the stupid, thoughtless things that Leland had ever done, digging up a yellow moccasin crossed the line! This time he had gone too far. Magge wouldn't automatically forgive him for this transgression, like she had all the others!

Duncan wordlessly fell in behind his wife. As Maggie strode along, castigating her old friend silently in her heart, she heard Leland whistling "This Ole House" and knew he was bringing up the rear.

"Leland ain't gonna need this ole house no longer," Maggie thought snarkily, "'cause *he's* getting ready to meet the saints!" As soon as this thought crossed her mind, however, her conscience smote her. Maggie realized how probable it was that their elderly friend might soon be moving on to claim his Great Reward. They had already lost Wendell Russell this year, in January. Was Leland next? Even if he lived another ten years, was an argument over digging up one yellow moccasin for Hannah worth jeopardizing their decades-old friendship?

Fifteen minutes later when Maggie reached the main trail leading through the woods from the Cross Road to the Sovereign Union Church, she was somewhat cooler headed. She paused to allow the two men to catch up to her. Feeling twinges of guilt, Maggie invited Leland to join them on their picnic to the Millett Rock. "I'm sure we have plenty of food," she added, rather ungraciously.

"I'll take a rain check, deah," said Leland, patting his pail. "Want to git this yeller moccasin in the ground. You knows how sensitive they is."

Maggie opened her mouth to retort, then closed it abruptly with a snap.

"Probably a good idea," Duncan remarked.

"You goin' to the May Breakfast?" Leland asked, prior to heading south down the trail in the opposite direction of the Millett Rock. The May Breakfast, a popular spring church fundraiser, was scheduled for that up-coming Saturday. "Or you gonna let Sabine git all the glory this year, Maggie?"

The long-time pastor's wrath was immediately rekindled. Did Leland—godless heathen though he was— really believe her ministry was an opportunity for personal glorification? Or was he deliberately trying to goad her because she chastised him for taking the yellow moccasin? Well, if Leland was trying to get her goat, she wasn't going to fall for it.

"Sabine is in charge of the May Breakfast," she responded cooly. "But I'll still be there—for the food and the fellowship." Sabine Burbury, daughter of one of Maggie's friends from her seminary days, had recently been hired by the Sovereign Union Church as an interim minister—after Sabine's successful six-month pastoral internship under Maggie—to cover while Maggie was taking a well-deserved sabbatical. Technically, Maggie was utilizing her paid time off to complete a writing project, but the truth of the matter was she was trying on retirement to see how it fit. Today was the first Sunday Sabine had been in the pulpit on her own, and Maggie had purposefully absented herself from church.

"Good 'nuff," said Leland. His hands being full, he nodded a courteous farewell to Duncan. "See ya." Then the woodchopper ambled off southward on the pine needle-covered path toward Maggie's abode, where he had left his pickup. Although his stooped shoulders pronounced his advanced age, Leland carried himself well. He naturally balanced the axe in his left hand and held the pail in his right, swinging it lightly like a ten-year-old boy. He resumed his whistling mid-tune.

Duncan watched the older man disappear around a bend. "That Leland is amazing! He cut a trail out to us and barely broke a sweat. He's got a good ten or fifteen years on me, too. I certainly can't keep up with him."

"Oh, he's amazing alright," Maggie replied sarcastically. "Leland thought he could sneak in today and grab a yellow moccasin without me knowing it! He thought I'd be at church."

"I don't know that you can say he snuck in. He certainly wasn't trying to cover his tracks," Duncan pointed out.

"You're right! Leland wouldn't bother to cover his tracks. He's shameless."

"Was he telling the truth when he said digging up the yellow moccasin isn't against the law? Or is that another one of his tarradiddles?"

"Technically, he wasn't lying. But collecting lady's slippers goes against a certain code of Maine conduct."

Duncan pondered Maggie's words a moment. "Perhaps in Leland's code, bringing a yellow moccasin to Hannah is more important. And Henry does own the land the yellow moccasins are growing on…?"

"Don't you side with Leland, too! It's bad enough Nick always takes his side."

"Seems to me you've sided with Leland and his misadventures many times in the past."

"Not this time," Maggie declared. "He's on my 'no pie' list."

"Ouch! That seems harsh." Duncan, like Leland (and most others in Maggie's orbit) was fond of her fresh blackberry and raspberry pies.

"Be careful what you say next, or you might find yourself on that list, too," she warned her husband.

Duncan mimed zipping his lips. Despite her anger and frustration at Leland, Maggie laughed.

Into the lull, a red-eyed vireo began trilling out its monotonous slurred notes. The birdsong grew louder as the vireo became more and more enamored with the sound of its own voice.

"Now, that I *know* is a bird," Duncan said. "Which of our little feathered friends is it?"

Maggie glanced upward at the noise emanating from a tall pine tree, but the small songbird was well-hidden. The red-eyed vireo continued its unflagging sermonizing for a minute or two without seeming to take a breath. "It's a red-eyed vireo."

"Ah, a vireo! He's quite a virtuoso. Such a big voice for a little bird."

"They're remarkably persistent, too." Every time Maggie heard a red-eyed vireo, she recollected that the annoying creature was known in birding circles as "the preacher bird" thanks to its unflagging vocalizing. She hoped her sermons weren't as tiresome and monotonous as the proselytizing of a red-eyed vireo.

Listening to the vireo, Maggie forgot all about Leland and the yellow moccasins. Her mind wandered off in an altogether different direction.

Duncan noted his wife's abstraction. "I know what you're thinking," he said, after observing her for several minutes.

"I doubt that!"

"You're wondering why Nick decided to tell Leland about the yellow moccasins this year."

"Not even close."

"No?"

"No. I was wondering what Nick would think of our pretty new preacher when he gets home. Don't you think Nick and Sabine would make a good couple? They have a lot in common."

Duncan raised an eyebrow. "A lot in common? Are we talking about the same Nicholas Faulkner?"

"Be serious, Duncan."

"I am serious. I can't see what Nick and Sabine have in common, except that they're both human beings under the age of thirty-five."

"They're both preacher's kids."

"OK, I'll give you that, although I'm not sure being a PK is much of a commonality."

"Probably more than we realize. And they're both sensitive, spiritual people."

"Nick? Spiritual?"

"Yes, haven't you noticed? He's read every book in my library, and he's always been very respectful of my ministry."

"Because you're his stepmother, Maggie. Let me know the next time you see Nick at church."

"The Maine woods *is* his church," Maggie parried. "Spirituality isn't only about little white churches, Duncan, as you well know. Nick has obviously been wrestling with something over the past couple of years. What if he's been wrestling with God?"

"Then God might have met another Jacob," retorted her husband.

"If so, Nick will be well and truly blessed."

"Don't try and play matchmaker, Maggie," Duncan cautioned her. "Even if what you suggest is true—that they have a lot in common—I can't think of anyone less likely to appeal to a level-headed young woman like Sabine than my irresponsible, irreligious son."

This time Maggie did not hold back. "O, ye of little faith!" she opined.

Chapter 3

Sabine

"Thanks for the ride, man," said Nick Faulkner to the driver of the semi who had given him a lift from Portland. He retrieved his internal-frame backpack and hopped down onto the wide pavement in front of the Sovereign Union Church. Nick waved a salute as the truck driver pulled back out onto Route 9 and worked the transmission of the inline-six diesel engine back up through its gears. Nick tossed his hefty dark ponytail over his shoulder and turned to face the church. He noted several cars in the side parking lot by the banquet hall attached to the church, which reminded him that it was Sunday. He glanced at the sun. Midday. Church was definitely over. "I wonder if she's still here?" he pondered, stroking his wiry black beard with his right hand while his left balanced the overstuffed pack against his thigh.

The "she" was Nick's stepmother Maggie. He had meant to hike out to his remote nineteenth century post-and-beam house and get cleaned up prior to seeing anyone; however, why not take the opportunity to talk to Maggie without his father being around? Somehow, Nick always felt tongue-tied with his father, as though his brain was disconnected from his vocal cords. With Maggie it was a different story. Nick felt he could talk to her about anything—no judgment. Nick left his backpack leaning against the railing of the handicap ramp and proceeded into the little white church.

The Sovereign Union Church is much larger than it looks from the outside, since it encompasses mostly one large room with an expansive cathedral ceiling and elongated leaded windows stretching nearly from ceiling to floor. The initial effect upon entering is one of uplifting brightness, most likely the effect intended by the town's hope-filled early settlers. A plush burgundy carpet covered the aisle separating two long rows of pews. The white wooden pews were covered with soft, wine-colored seat cushions running the length of each pew. Up front, the elevated altar bore the traditional empty cross of the Protestant faith. Beneath the altar was the mahogany lectern where Maggie preached every Sunday.

Without understanding why—or even feeling the need to understand why—Nick felt his spirits rise as he entered the church. A single pillar candle burned on the alter. He paused at the back of the church; a feeling of hopefulness encompassing him. The flame of the candle flickered as the moving air from his entrance reached it, and he marveled at this one small example of cause and effect in the universe.

Nick had been in Maggie's office many times, but this visit would be different. Her office was small, having been cobbled onto the back of the church around the turn of the twentieth century. He loved his stepmother's study because it was lined floor-to-ceiling with shelves of books, some of them eighteenth century texts bound in tan calf's leather, which had been left at the church by Maggie's pastoral predecessors. She also had brought into her office her theology and Biblical textbooks from her time at Bangor Theological Seminary and to these had added her favorite classical novels and poetry, including works by

William Makepeace Thackeray, Anne Ritchie Thackeray, Robbie Burns, Sir Walter Scott, Jane Austen, Anthony Trollope, and Nick's personal favorite, Emily Dickinson. Nick knew his stepmother's library well because over the years he had borrowed and read most of her books.

Nick made his way to the back of the church. The door to Maggie's office was open. He heard her shut a drawer in her desk revealing she was still here. He paused, anticipating the joyful welcome he would receive from Maggie after having been gone for nearly a year. Boy, it was great to be back home!

"I'm back!" Nick proclaimed, stepping into the office with a theatrical flourish. Stupefied, Nick stopped dead in his tracks. Rather than espying the congenial face of his short, gray-haired stepmother, he beheld a tall woman with dark-blonde hair in her twenties standing behind Maggie's oak desk. She was dressed as a pastor in a white flowing robe and had been in the process of untying a braided gold cord from around her waist.

"Whoa! You startled me," she said, her right hand flying to her throat. "I didn't hear you come in." Rather than exhibiting fright at his bold entrance, however, her smiling, chestnut-colored eyes telegraphed the welcome he had expected to receive from his stepmother.

Nick blinked in confusion. He quickly scanned the shelves—yes, the books were still there. He noted, however, that a dozen or more new volumes had been added to the library since his last visit. "Where's Maggie?" he asked, somewhat rudely.

"At home, I suppose. Today was my first day alone in the pulpit." The young woman stepped from behind the desk and held out her hand. "Welcome back, Nick. I'm Sabine. Sabine Burbury. It's great to finally meet you. I've heard a lot about you."

Nick hesitated, then stuck out his hand. "Hey," he said, using the opportunity of the handshake to take her measure. She was big and large-boned, but carried herself with assurance. Proper seminary training, no doubt. She had a firm handshake, too. Her name, "Sah-BEAN" (as she pronounced it), was unusual. Nick had never heard the name before.

Sabine withdrew her hand. "You don't have a clue who I am, do you?" she asked, laughing.

"Not a clue," he admitted. "I was expecting my stepmother."

"Maggie never told you I interned with her over the winter?"

"If she did, I wasn't paying very close attention. Why are you still here? Sorry, that came out wrong," he added hastily. "I mean, winter's over."

"And I'm still here? The church hired me as interim pastor while Maggie's on sabbatical. I'm officially graduating from Iliff—Iliff School of Theology in Denver—on June 6th. But I won't be there for graduation."

"Maggie's on sabbatical? But I just spoke with her a few nights ago!"

"I guess you weren't paying close attention, then, either. She hasn't gone anywhere. She's working on a book project while she's on sabbatical." Sabine moved back behind the desk. "Sit down," she said. "I'm not used to having someone tower over me." The tall young woman placed herself purposefully in Maggie's desk chair and pointed at two gothic-looking mahogany chairs, each sporting matching plush burgundy seat cushions. "Those are ancient, but better than anything you'll get from Wayfair. They'll hold your weight, too. I know, because they hold me."

Nick appropriated the chair nearest the desk, curious about this interesting female. Although normally guarded with other adults, he felt comfortable with Sabine. He appreciated her frank and direct nature. In addition, she had a natural grace and ease of manner that inspired confidence and trust.

Subdued light from the one elongated leaded window illuminated the room. Nick noted—and also appreciated the fact—that Sabine had been using the room without having switched on the electric lights. Nick's old house, which he had been bringing back to life since buying the property in the Sovereign Woods from Wendell Russell, was off-grid. No sense adding more harmful greenhouse gas to the atmosphere. A good chunk of the electricity used in the United States still came from coal-burning power plants.

Nick clasped the mahogany arms of the chair with his hands, enjoying the smooth feel of the polished wood. The old-timers sure knew how to make things! "How did you know who I was?"

"I stayed with Maggie and your Dad when I was here for my internship. There are pics of you all over their house, almost as many as there are of Jana on the fridge."

"I've sure missed my niece. Cute kid!"

"Now I'm renting Mike Hobart's cabin."

Nick nodded in satisfaction. "No wonder you don't have the lights on. Mike's cabin is off-grid, too."

"I have solar panels and battery backup at the cabin, but I still try not to waste electricity. You don't even have solar at your house, do you? Maggie pointed your place out to me when she took me to the Millett Rock last fall."

"Nope. It's beeswax candles and a wood stove for me. I've only renovated two rooms so far—the kitchen and living room—so I don't need much heat. Probably the mice have taken over the place since I've been gone."

"Better mice than porcupines," she joked.

"For sure!" Nick absently fondled his beard, wondering what to say next.

"I've heard a lot about your cross-country trip," Sabine continued. "Sounds like an amazing experience."

"It was. It's good to be home, though."

"I'm sure. Your Dad and Maggie will be thrilled to see you. When I lived with them, every night at dinner it was always, 'Nick is in Red Wing' …

"I was in Red Wing. Lots of great birds!"

"… or, 'Nick is in San Diego, now' …

"Amazing Safari Park. Only the park is actually in Escondido. I worked at the park for a while."

"In fact, I thought you were an only child until one night Duncan mentioned Nora was coming to Maine for Christmas."

Nick dropped his hand and leaned forward. "Have you met my sister?"

"Nora and I bunked together over the holidays. We shared Nellie's room." Nellie was Maggie's daughter, now happily married to the local doctor. "That was fun. I've always wanted a sister."

"Sounds like a tight squeeze in Nellie's old room?"

"We managed. Your poor father had to wait to use the bathroom, though, with three women in the house."

"I bet! Has Nora been home since Christmas?"

"Nope. Much to your Dad's disappointment."

"Yeah, that's what I figured. Her North Dakota boyfriend is the jealous type."

"Her *ex*-boyfriend," Sabine corrected Nick.

"Ex? That's good news! Dad must be happy about that. Maybe Nora will come back east now." He gazed thoughtfully at the young minister. "What about you? Are you a native Mainer?"

"Ayuh," she quipped. "Born at the big hospital in Bangor. My mother and Maggie attended Bangor Theological Seminary together. That's where my parents met, too. After graduation, my parents co-pastored a Methodist church in Dover-Foxcroft. I started school there, but when I was ten my parents divorced, and Mom took a pastorate in Fairbanks. I went with her."

"Must have been hard to leave your father behind?"

Sabine shrugged, and toyed with a pen on the desk. "He never asked me to stay. He took up with the church organist. They live in Florida, now."

"Bummer!"

"When I was a kid, I used to feel badly for Nellie, until my parents got divorced." Nellie, who was illegitimate, had grown up without a father. "After that, not so much."

Nick examined the pulpit robe Sabine was wearing. The white cotton robe flowed over her ample curves and accentuated her blooming completion. He could see what appeared to be a hand-carved wooden cross half-hidden by the folds of Sabine's robe, hanging from a colorful cloth braid. She must have removed her stole prior to his entrance. That's probably what he heard her put in the drawer. "Aren't you young for a minister? You must have gone straight from college to seminary?"

"I took a year off between high school and college, but after college I did go right to Iliff. By then, I knew I wanted to be a pastor."

Amazed, Nick shook his head. "How did you know? At that age! I can't wrap my mind around it."

Sabine's eyes narrowed. She regarded her visitor closely. "You're hearing the Call, aren't you?"

Nick felt the young woman's dark eyes boring into his soul. Was it so obvious? He licked his lips, fearful of not finding the right words to reply. What could he say? Wasn't this why he had stopped in to see Maggie? Sabine was a minister, too. Could he talk with her about his situation?

Nick clutched the solid arms of the chair for physical support. "I…I think so."

Sabine nodded knowingly, but said nothing.

A gulf of quiet opened up between the two young people. There was a natural rhythm to the stillness, like the steady progression of the ocean tides or the breathing of someone at rest. Nick felt his heartrate slow. Angst, anxiety, and frustration drained away. Outside the window he could see a white-breasted nuthatch slowly foraging down the sap encrusted gray bark of an ancient pine tree.

After five or six minutes of companionable silence, Sabine spoke first. "At our church in Alaska one of our members was a retired minister—Beverly, she's dead, now—who took me under her wing. Mom was usually busy so Beverly became my second mother and mentor. One day, when I was about fourteen, she said she wanted to talk to me. I thought it was going to be the sex talk, but it wasn't. It was the God talk. She said she had seen me visiting some of our elderly parishioners and said they were pre-pastoral visits. Beverly asked if I had heard the Call. I pretended I didn't know what she was talking about, but I really did. She wanted to know how I was going to answer it. 'Who says I'm going to answer it?' I said, defiantly. 'Oh, you're gonna answer it,' Beverly replied. 'You can do it the easy way—or you can fight it—but sooner or later you're gonna answer God's call.' I thought then about my parents and their difficult journeys. I also recollected what I knew about the spiritual journeys of some of the pastor friends of my parents, like Maggie. When I was in college, I decided not to fight it any longer, but to answer the Call the easy way."

Sabine folded a very capable set of hands upon the desk. She fell silent, looking expectantly at Nick. He intuited what the young minister had left unsaid as clearly as though she had said the words aloud. "And I took the hard way," he finished. "That's probably why my father doesn't understand me."

"And vice versa?" she suggested.

"And vice versa," he acknowledged. "Dad always knew he wanted to be a minister."

"That's why you came here first to see Maggie—to speak with her about your calling? She took the hard way, too."

"Guilty as charged. It's easier to talk to Maggie than my father. But I'm not sorry Maggie wasn't here."

"Me either." Sabine relaxed in her chair and unconsciously found and fingered the wooden cross hanging around her neck. Another stretch of comfortable quiet ensued before she spoke again. "I feel as though we're kindred spirits, Nick. Even though my journey was more like your Dad's than yours. But we all ended up in the same place, didn't we? Answering the Call."

"So much for free will!"

"God has a plan for each human life, to be according to the Divine's will. To that end, God is constantly calling us."

"Immanuel Kant?"

"Sabine Burbury, and probably thousands of others who've come to the same conclusion. But don't get me started on free will, Nick, or we'll be here all night. We've got some practical business to take care of first. What kind of minister do you want to be? Apostle? Pastor? Teacher? Prophet? Evangelist?"

Nick grinned, showing a set of white teeth through his bushy dark beard. "You mean—I get a choice?"

Chapter 4

May Breakfast

As Nick tramped out to his house in the Sovereign Woods following his meeting with Sabine, he reran their conversation through his head, feeling more hopeful than he had for years. She understood him. He was not going crazy. He wasn't sure who or what he was being called to be or do, but Nick was energized knowing he was finally moving in the right direction. He had been flailing about seeking answers, looking everywhere—everywhere, that is, but within himself. With Sabine's validation, however, a burst of understanding had illuminated his soul, as brilliant and thrilling as the flash of a brook trout leaping up out of dark water to catch mayflies. As he hiked along Nick heard the flute-like song of a wood thrush. With his heightened sensibility, he felt as though the music was the advance herald of an angelic "Welcome home!" He spied a young doe peering at him through a thicket of raspberry canes. The flora and fauna of the forest was turning out to greet him! He was one with the woods.

Nick put off his reunion with his father and Maggie until the following day, not knowing that if he had taken the side trail to the Millett Rock he would have found them enjoying their picnic.

His first meeting with Maggie and Duncan on Monday morning was as joyful as he had been expecting when Nick had popped into Maggie's office. His stepmother hugged him and hovered over him like a mother hen. Nick's father even shook his hand, obviously pleased to see him.

Over a second breakfast, Nick brought his parents up to date on the final leg of his journey home. But he decided not to share with them—the two people most closely concerned with his life—what occurred during his accidental meeting with Sabine or tell them anything about his own Divine calling. At the moment, that seemed too sacred to share. Besides, Nick felt as though he needed time to chart his own spiritual course without the influence (and interference) of the two ordained clergy. He was also fearful that, after hearing of Nick's calling, his father might fail to take him seriously. Nick was aware that he had lain the groundwork for his father's disbelief and lack of faith in him by deriding his father's vocation over the years. He realized now that he had attempted to diminish his father's calling so that he would not see or hear his own.

Nick's omission about the meeting with the interim minister had been one of prudence, not guilt; however, he realized he had made a mistake—too late!—soon after his arrival at the Sovereign Union Church for the May Breakfast on Saturday. Maggie had been keeping an eye out for him and spotted Nick from the back of the room when he walked into the attached banquet hall. His stepmother took him by the elbow and steered him up front to meet Sabine. Until that moment Nick had not considered the ramifications of his omission. What would Maggie think when she found out he and Sabine had already met? And that he had not disclosed that fact? In his confused mind, he jumbled up his omission with disclosing to his parents the very personal conversation he'd had with the young pastor.

Nick felt sweat break out under his armpits. He could tell by Maggie's enthusiasm and praise for Sabine that she had been looking forward to this moment for months. How could he have forgotten his stepmother's penchant for matchmaking? What a dolt he was not to have casually mentioned he had stopped by the church Sunday on his way home! Was it too late to tell Maggie now?

The banquet hall was crowded with attendees, giving Nick a moment in the confusion and mingled noise of voices and clattering plates from the kitchen to think about how he would greet Sabine. The smell of bacon frying, however, further muddled his senses.

Fortunately, Sabine picked up on his discomfiture. "Hello, Nick," she said, at Maggie's beaming introduction. She shook his hand as though he was no more than a stranger.

The young minister was not wearing her pastoral robe today, but rather a long-sleeved burgundy dress and black flats. A black belt accented her waist, neatly delineating her tall, robust frame. Nick was glad to see Sabine was not ashamed of her large size. "Hey," he replied, not knowing whether he should allude to their prior meeting. He noted that she did not lie—she did not say, "Nice to meet you!" Sabine merely smiled and squeezed his hand with her reassuring handshake. The knowing twinkle in her brown eyes telegraphed: "Don't worry—your secret is safe with me."

Nick, who was six-foot-four, hadn't realized just how short his stepmother was until she was standing next to Sabine. The younger minister towered over Maggie by eight or ten inches. Sabine chatted with them for a minute or two and then excused herself. "I better make the rounds," she said. "I'm supposed to be the hostess with the mostest."

Maggie patted Sabine's arm with obvious affection. "Come sit with us when you're done," she suggested. "We'll save you a seat, won't we Nick?"

"Absolutely," he said. The eagerness of his reply pleased his stepmother.

"I'm sorry," said Sabine. "I promised Henry and Hannah I would sit with them."

"Of course," Maggie replied, feeling disappointed. For the first time in her life, the long-time pastor of the Sovereign Union Church wondered how many people she had disappointed over the years by preferring to sit with her special friends, rather than with other members of her congregation. Sabine was doing the right thing. Henry and Hannah Trow were important members of the community, donating freely to the church and other local organizations.

"We'll talk soon, though," added Sabine.

"I'd like that," responded Maggie. Nick suspected, however, that Sabine wasn't replying to Maggie, but rather was signaling to him.

The May Breakfast was an annual fundraiser for the Sovereign Union Church. This year the event was to raise money to repair the church's original cast-iron bell. The historic bell had been out of commission for decades. The bell had been cast at Paul Revere's foundry in Boston in 1827. Although the famous Revolutionary War patriot had died in 1818, the foundry continued operation for another decade. The last bell cast with the Revere name had been manufactured for the nearby Benton Falls Congregational Church in 1828. The bell belonging to the Sovereign Union Church was therefore one of the last with the Revere name, and the townspeople—even those who did not attend church—were anxious to repair the historic bell. In the old days, the clanging of the bell, which had resounded throughout the Sovereign hills, had not only summoned the people to religious services, but also (prior to the advent of the telephone) alerted residents to emergencies, such as approaching forest fires or lost children.

Leland Gorse was holding court at the kids' table when Maggie returned to her seat at the neighboring table with Nick at her heels. Although Maggie had not seen Leland (who only appeared at church to eat or for funerals) since their confrontation over the yellow lady's slipper, she did not believe her old friend was deliberately avoiding her today. She knew the inveterate storyteller simply preferred the adulation of the children to the company of adults. Before sitting down, Maggie eavesdropped on the conversation at the kids' table.

"There's a few pickles missin' in thet crock!" Leland said, obviously concluding a story. Maggie wondered if Leland had been telling tall tales about her. Few pickles short of a crock? Probably!

The children, ranging in age from seven to eleven, hooted with laughter—all except Hope. "What's a crock?" asked nine-year-old Hope, Leland's sweet and serious granddaughter.

"You know what a crock is, stupid," replied Alice Rose, Hope's older sister. At eleven, Alice was the bossy matriarch of the neighborhood playmates. "It's the big stoneware container Mom makes sauerkraut in."

"It's not nice to call Hope stupid, Alice," said Jana, Maggie's granddaughter. At seven, Jana was four years younger than Alice. Jana was fearless, however, and felt duty bound to chastise her naughty friend.

"Thet it ain't, Miss Major," affirmed Leland. (He had nicknamed his eldest granddaughter "Miss Major MacDonald" and his youngest, "Miss Minor.") "Don't let yer Ma hear you call yer sister stoopid. She'll take you out to the woodshed fer shore."

"But why are there pickles in Miss Crump's sauerkraut?" Hope persisted, ignoring Alice's snub. She was used to her sister's mean remarks.

So, Miss Crump was Leland's victim today, thought Maggie. Not me!

Leland tapped his finger to his head. "Cause she ain't got no pickles up here."

"He means brains," Tad Russell explained to Hope. Carroty-top Tad was the only boy in the bunch. At nine, he was same age as Hope, and had already set himself up as her champion. "Not pickles."

"That's not nice, either," declared Hope, pursing her rosy lips.

"Geez, hard crowd here today," Leland complained, making a face. Alice laughed.

"You shouldn't make fun of Miss Crump, Grampa," Hope scolded him. "I like her."

"Me too," said Jana. "She's good to her chickens."

"Want me to make fun of you instead, Miss Minor?" he teased Hope.

"Yes, please."

Maggie smiled to herself. The kids could keep Leland in check without any help from her. She turned away from the children's table and sat down next to her husband with the other adults. Nick, however, pulled up a chair with Leland and youngsters, where he was energetically welcomed.

The little group of friends and neighbors at the adult table with Maggie and Duncan included Leland's daughter Trudy, a librarian in the Sovereign schools, and her husband Ryan MacDonald, the local attorney. Trudy and Ryan had taken over the running of Scotch Broom Acres, Leland's family farm (where he still resided) and were known throughout the state for their quality hand-crafted butter and cheeses. They were the parents of Alice and Hope. Also present were Maggie's daughter Nellie and her husband Metcalf (Metcalf Bartholomew Lawson, "Doctor Bart"), who were Jana's parents. Nellie and Doctor Bart were expecting their second child in early fall. Rounding out the group was Rebecca Russell, the next-door neighbor to Nellie and Doctor Bart on the Russell Hill Road. Rebecca was the mother of George "Tad" (short for tadpole), the only boy in the neighborhood. Tad's birth was a surprise and a blessing for the menopausal Rebecca and her older husband Wendell Russell, who had not expected children at their advanced ages. Sadly, Wendell— a mainstay of the Sovereign community—had experienced a heart attack in January while shoveling heavy snow after a blizzard. He died in Rebecca's arms before the ambulance arrived. The wooden folding chair next to Rebecca remained empty, a poignant reminder of the group's loss. Nobody—not even young Tad—dared to sit in Wendell's chair yet.

"What did I miss?" asked Maggie, scuffing her chair closer to the table.

"Apparently, Miss Crump is a few pickles short of a crock," Ryan MacDonald informed her.

"I heard that. What did I miss for *adult* conversation?"

"You mean gossip?" quizzed Doctor Bart, Maggie's son-in-law.

"I prefer the term 'local color'," replied Maggie. She smoothed her cloth napkin in her lap and glanced around the table expectantly. Her gaze ended at her husband.

Duncan shook his head. "Don't look at me. I can't remember what we were talking about. Everything flew the coop when I heard Leland tell the kids Miss Crump brings her chickens into the kitchen on cold nights."

"I wouldn't count on the veracity of that statement," interjected Trudy. "You know my father."

"Poor woman!" said Rebecca. "I can't imagine how she manages to take care of herself at her age, let alone all those chickens." Miss Crump, a local eccentric who had recently passed the centennial mark, had become wealthy over the years from the sale of gravel from her gravel pit. Despite her wealth, she lived in a small, wood-frame house situated across from the entrance to her gravel pit, where she raised a motley menagerie of chickens. Anyone in Sovereign looking to dump their played-out hens—or get rid of a troublesome rooster—knew to take the birds to the elderly spinster, who had a soft spot for poultry.

"I don't think Miss Crump is missing many pickles," said Doctor Bart, toying with his empty coffee cup. "She keeps a close eye on the trucks that go in and out of her gravel pit every day. She sits in her rocking chair by the window with a tally counter and pushes the button every time a loaded truck comes out. At the end of the week, when the guys come to pay up, Miss Crump knows exactly who's hauled gravel and how much."

"I remember when she first came to the clinic," said Nellie, who with her husband ran the free Songbird Medical Clinic from their home. "When she left, she gave Metcalf one of her chickens as payment. Henrietta, I think it was. Miss Crump had the hen in a cage in the back seat of her old Dodge Dart. Remember, Metcalf? Thank God she's finally given up driving!"

"Aunt Hannah drives Miss Crump to her appointments now," added Metcalf. (Hannah Trow was Doctor Bart's great-aunt.) "I'll never forget my first appointment with her. I thought I'd stumbled into Mayberry RFD."

Nellie leaned forward. "Can you imagine? Miss Crump had never seen a doctor before! And she was ninety-two, then."

"Oh, my!" said Rebecca. "She must have the constitution of an ox."

"Or one of her Bantam roosters," Maggie joked.

"Miss Crump is now one of our favorite patients, as well as one of the clinic's biggest donors," said Doctor Bart. "By the way, that chicken immediately laid an egg."

"How was it?" asked Ryan.

"The chicken?"

"No, the egg!"

"Fresh. Very fresh. And tasty."

A waitress came over to the table carrying a steaming pot of coffee. Several cups were immediately pushed forward for refills. "The buffet is open," said the waitress. "Better go get your scrambled eggs before they're gone. We cut back on eggs this year because the price is so high."

"Oh, dear!" said Rebecca, standing up. "I'll get the kids headed in the right direction."

"Sit down," Trudy urged Rebecca. "Once my father sees movement at the buffet table, he'll make a rush for it. The kids will all follow him." Rebecca regained her seat and watched as the children's table shortly emptied out.

"My wife the clairvoyant!" chortled Ryan, observing the short legs of the children scramble to keep up with Leland's loping stride toward the buffet. "There goes the Pied Piper of Sovereign with his retinue."

"I'm not clairvoyant. I just know my father—and the kids."

Maggie was happy to see Nick helping her granddaughter fill up her plate from the buffet. Little Jana was Nick's niece by marriage and the two of them shared a special connection.

"I regret eating that egg," continued Metcalf, assuming a demeanor of melancholy. "If I'd hatched the egg—and the eggs that *that* chick laid—I'd be almost as rich as Miss Crump by now. We could certainly use the extra cash at the clinic!"

"You wouldn't have gotten very far without a second co-payment from Henrietta," Maggie pointed out. "You'd need to hatch out at least two eggs."

"Is Henrietta the chicken I brought over to you, Trudy?" Rebecca asked. "If we're talking about the same hen, Doctor Bart, I drove into your driveway after Miss

Crump left and offered to take it to Scotch Broom Acres. I was with you when it laid the egg."

"The very same bird!"

"I remember Henrietta well," recollected Trudy, tidying a salt-and-pepper shaker. "She was a White Leghorn and a very good layer—jumbo eggs, too. I'm sorry, you can't have her back Doctor Bart, because she's unalive, as Hope would say."

"And not to put a damper on your pipe dream, Doc," added Ryan, "but the second egg would have had to hatch out the opposite sex, too."

"Marplots, all of you!" Metcalf joked, pushing back his chair. "Speaking of eggs, I'm not waiting until the Pied Piper and our kids clean them out." He stood up. "You coming MacDonald? Duncan?"

"You bet," replied the lawyer. "Right behind you," added Duncan. The men departed for the buffet, leaving the four women seated at the table.

"What's a marplot?" Trudy asked Nellie, assuming the younger woman would know what her husband meant.

"Not a clue. You know Metcalf—it's probably his Word of the Day."

"A marplot is a spoil sport," Maggie answered. "Someone who ruins things by meddling. I know, because Metcalf called me a marplot once." The regular minister of the Sovereign Union Church was known for her penchant for matchmaking and meddling.

"Quaint," adjudged the librarian. "I'll have to remember that—marplot."

Rebecca, who had lingered in the prior conversation, now spoke up. "I'm almost sorry Wendell and I didn't carry on with the egg business after Bruce and Amber were married," she said. (Amber, Rebecca's daughter by a prior marriage, had been the linchpin of the Russell's egg business, as told in a prior tale.) "I do miss the chickens."

The other three women exchanged glances. They empathized with the recent widow, understanding well that Rebecca was grieving for Wendell. Still, her friends had been worried lately that Rebecca was exhibiting unhealthy symptoms of wallowing in her grief.

"They were good eggs," said Maggie, somewhat lamely.

"Weren't you losing money with the eggs back then?" Trudy reminded Rebecca. "Remember how cheap you sold them? Organic eggs, too!" When Rebecca and Amber had folded the egg business, Trudy had purchased a few of their hens. Amber had also taken some to Oaknole Farm in Winslow, her husband's family farm. But most of the chickens had been sold to a stranger.

Rebecca shuddered in recollection. "Yes, Amber scared me when she showed me how much money we were losing! She kept the books. Wendell and I never had much money between us, and after seeing our monthly losses I was afraid if we kept going, we might lose the farm. We had to sell the chickens, although Wendell would have kept going, if that's what I had wanted. I wonder how much we could get for a dozen of our eggs today?"

"Ten or eleven dollars, I bet," said Maggie. Her remark netted a warning look from Trudy.

"Ten dollars a dozen! No wonder the church is cutting back on scrambled eggs. We always used to provide eggs for the May Breakfast—remember, Maggie? But I don't suppose the church could afford to pay ten dollars a dozen, and we'd have lost another customer." Rebecca sighed.

"Ten dollars a dozen is too rich for our blood," Nellie agreed. She was a recent addition to the church's board of trustees. "We couldn't raise enough money to repair the bell at that price. We only ask for a ten dollar donation for the breakfast, although some people give a lot more, like Henry and Aunt Hannah. Some can't even afford the ten dollars, especially the elderly."

"Of which there is a plentiful supply in Sovereign," said Trudy. She was keeping one eye on the children and the other on her mischief-making father.

"Oh, well! Wendell and I couldn't have carried on the egg business anyway once Amber left. She did everything." Rebecca sighed again. "And I certainly couldn't have carried it on now—without Wendell." Tears filled the widow's eyes.

Maggie was about to arise to go around the table and comfort their grieving friend, but before she could get out of her chair Rebecca straightened up and resolutely brushed away her tears. "Enough of feeling sorry for myself. This too shall pass!" she proclaimed. "In the meantime, I'm giving a dinner next Saturday night and I want you all to be there. I've got something important to announce, and I want my friends to be the first to hear it."

Chapter 5

"Doing the Cemeteries"

"What do you think Rebecca wants to tell us at her dinner party Saturday night?" Maggie asked her husband Tuesday afternoon, while shopping for geraniums at Longfellow's Greenhouses in Manchester. The upcoming weekend of Rebecca's dinner was also Memorial weekend, and Maggie always decorated her family's graves in remembrance of ancestors loved and lost. While "doing the cemeteries" (as the tradition is known in the Maine vernacular) is not as commonplace as it once was, the task remains the springtime duty of a few certain women (and even fewer men), usually one volunteer per extended family.

When she was a girl, Maggie's grandmothers had taken her to help decorate the cemeteries for Decoration Day, as the day of remembrance was then known. (Decoration Day was initiated by the Grand Army of the Republic after the Civil War, and changed to Memorial Day in 1971.) By taking Maggie along, both matriarchs were laying the groundwork for their eventual replacement. Maggie recollected that together her grandmothers had purchased thirty-seven geraniums. Now, Maggie's geranium tally, which included the lists of both progenitors plus her own family and a few friends, totaled fifty-eight plants. "There's no end to it," she said to herself, picking out five of the best-looking white geraniums and schlepping them onto the top shelf of her cart.

"I haven't a clue what Rebecca has to tell us," Duncan responded. He was pushing a matching cart along the aisle opposite Maggie and noted with some little pride that he was the only male among the two dozen shoppers in the mammoth geranium greenhouse. "Hopefully not that she's getting married again."

Startled, Maggie looked up from picking dead leaves off a plant on her cart. "Don't even think that!" she chastised him. "Wendell's only been dead four months."

"Relax. I was joking. What color geranium does he get? Or isn't Wendell on your list? I don't know the etiquette of this cemetery decorating business."

"If I followed cemetery etiquette, I wouldn't do Wendell. Decorating the grave of a recent Dearly-Departed is the sole provenance of the widow—or widower. But in Wendell's case, I asked Rebecca if she minded if I planted a geranium or two for him and she was pleased."

"Very thoughtful of you."

"Rebecca is going to take a fresh bouquet of lilacs up to Wendell every day, But the lilacs will only bloom for another week or so and the geraniums will bloom all summer," Maggie explained. "That is, if we remember to water them." Dissatisfied with one of her selections, she removed one of the white geraniums from her cart and replaced it with a more appealing plant. "I'm getting two geraniums for Wendell—a red one and a white one."

"Why two?"

"Sentimental reasons. The red is for love—Wendell was loved by everyone in Sovereign. And the white is for innocence. He was as innocent as a child. Wendell never had an unkind word for anyone. There's wasn't an evil bone in his body."

"He was the kindest man I ever met," Duncan agreed. "Jesus might have been the only perfect human, but Wendell ran a close second."

"It will be strange not to have him at the dinner table. Rebecca is brave to have us all over so soon. I don't know how we'll get on without Wendell." Maggie pointed to a large collection of deep violet geraniums on the table beyond Duncan. "Pick me out two of those New Hampshire purples, please. I always put those on my mother's grave. Purple was her favorite color."

Duncan moved his cart ahead and paused next to a sea of purple blossoms. "Which ones should I get?"

"The best two you see."

Duncan hesitated. What constituted the "best" geranium? Number of blossoms? Up and coming buds? Nicest-looking foliage? The greenhouse was warm and humid and he felt himself beginning to perspire.

Maggie, seeing his hesitation, read her husband's mind. "One or two stems of full blossoms with a couple of stems of healthy buds," she directed. "No dead foliage, please."

Duncan carefully made his selection and placed the two violet geraniums on his cart to accompany the seven pinks for the female ancestors on Maggie's father's side. (The men in his wife's family were allotted white geraniums.) "Who's going to do the cemeteries when you die? Nellie?"

"Ha! Not likely." Maggie peered at her list. Her mother's ancestors were next and they required red geraniums. She needed twenty-seven for them, plus there was the one extra red geranium for Wendell. "If it was up to Nellie, she'd put my ashes in an urn and keep me on the mantle. That's what Millennials do, I think."

"I promise I'll put you in the ground, if you die first. 'Ashes to ashes, earth to earth'," Duncan quoted.

"That's what I'm counting on."

"Dying first? I hope not. It's easier when men die first—at least it would be for me. I've already buried one wife."

"And I've buried one husband, so we're even."

"Let's try to go together, shall we?"

"Can't, sorry. If we die at the same time, Nellie will put me on the mantle for sure!"

Duncan noted that the older woman in the aisle across from him was smiling, probably she had overheard their conversation. "Good thing our kids aren't around to hear us joking about death," he said in a lower tone of voice. "I'm not sure they'd appreciate the humor of it."

"They'll understand when they get to be our age," Maggie stated. "And to answer your question, I'm counting on my granddaughter to take over the cemeteries."

"Jana? I should have known."

"That's why we're not going to do the cemeteries in Norway until Sunday—which is a bit late. We can't go during the week because Jana is still in school and we can't go Saturday and get back from western Maine in time for Rebecca's dinner party."

"You've got it all planned out."

"I do. We're going down to Albion after school on Thursday to do the cemetery there, and I told Nellie I'd pick Jana up from school this afternoon so we could do Wendell and Miss Hastings today." Miss Jana Hastings was the former Sovereign music teacher and child singing prodigy for whom Maggie's granddaughter was named. The vivacious little woman had been buried at the Russell Hill Cemetery in Sovereign, where her parents and childhood sweetheart (who died young) had also been buried. "Speaking of Miss Hastings," Maggie continued, looking up from her list, "I need a hot pink for her—those prudent pinks in your cart won't do for Miss Hastings."

"Seems fitting," Duncan replied. "My ole buddy Leland says Miss Hastings was a hot ticket."

"She certainly was!"

"Does Jana know she's your cemetery decorating replacement?"

"Of course not! She's only seven. I'm not sure Jana even knows about death yet."

"Probably not."

"I started going to the cemeteries with my grandmothers when I was about Jana's age and I didn't have a clue—not until my grandfather died. Even then, it took me quite a while to understand he wasn't coming back."

"I never spent much time in cemeteries when I was young," Duncan mused. "Burial grounds seem like such a sad place to me."

"Now, there we differ," said Maggie, pushing her cart ahead toward a table of bright pink geraniums. "I've always found cemeteries uplifting. I enjoy chatting with my grandfather when I'm in Albion."

"Kind of a one-way conversation, isn't it?"

"No, because I know what Grandfather would have said—or think I know, and that's all that matters." Maggie picked out a hot pink geranium for Miss Hastings and added it to her cart. "And when I'm at Norway Pine Grove I have a good conversation with Gram. Doing the cemeteries brings back a lot of happy memories from childhood. Sometimes I even talk with the Wentworth ancestors—those are Gram's ancestors—when I'm in Norway, and I never knew any of them. There's a lot of interesting history in a cemetery."

"That's certainly true."

Maggie pushed ahead to the first table of red geraniums, Duncan following in his aisle. Fortunately, red was a still a popular Memorial Day color and there were several tables of different varieties of red geraniums to choose from. The first table where they stopped featured Calliope, a medium-dark red geranium that Maggie preferred. She studied the dozens of individual plants and began picking out those that passed her suitability test. Maggie loaded up the bottom shelf of her cart, counting as she worked. "Eighteen, nineteen, twenty—I need eight more. You'll have to put them on your cart. I don't have any more room."

"That's a lot of red geraniums!"

"Gram planted twenty-seven and we need one extra red one for Wendell."

"Shouldn't you get twenty-nine, then?" Duncan queried. "What about your grandmother? Doesn't Gram get a red geranium?"

"She would if she were alive to tell me what to do," answered Maggie, laughing. "I always plant a peach-colored geranium on her grave."

"Sounds like apostasy to me. Why peach and not red? Your Gram's geranium must stand out among all those reds on your family's graves."

"Peach reminds me of the dress Gram bought me when I first moved in with her. I needed a dress for a wedding we were invited to, but I didn't own a dress and didn't have much money, so she bought me one—a beautiful, peach-colored silk! I loved that dress. I probably still have it somewhere."

"So, the peach-colored geranium represents your grandmother's love," he guessed.

"Ha! Wrong again. Gram didn't love me then—we hardly knew each other. I wasn't her favorite grandchild. She bought me the dress because she was afraid I'd embarrass her by wearing bell-bottom blue jeans to the wedding. The peach geranium reminds me how much Gram and I matured living together, how we came to love and respect one other over the years."

"So peach is a symbol of personal growth?"

"Exactly. For both of us."

"Interesting. So, there are no hard and fast rules in Maine about 'doing the cemeteries' like there are with collecting—rather, *not* collecting—lady's slippers?"

"Only one rule, and it's sacred," Maggie stated.

"What's that?"

"The person who assumes the financial, physical, and spiritual burden of doing the cemeteries gets to make the rules—at least until she's dead."

That afternoon, while Maggie and her granddaughter were tending Miss Hastings' grave—and the minister was telling Jana the story of the Songbird of Sovereign—Duncan wandered around the Russell Hill Cemetery reading the old gravestones.

As Duncan moved along, he became more and more despondent realizing how young some of the early Sovereign settlers had died. Two or three women had passed away in their thirties, probably from complications related to childbirth. American flags fluttering in the breeze identified soldiers, some of whom died during the Civil War. But saddest of all were the gravestones of children. Two nineteenth century monuments featured an angelic cherub perched beside the headstone. A third child's monument had a lamb resting peacefully on top. Duncan knew that the mortality rate for children in the United States prior to the advent of antibiotics and vaccines was very high. The young often succumbed to diseases such as diphtheria, measles, whooping cough, and tuberculosis. He paused to read aloud the inscriptions on two of the children's gravestones—sisters who had died within days of each other. The inscriptions revealed the depth of their parent's grief: "A moment in our arms, a lifetime in our hearts" and "Sleep, darling sleep."

"I don't know how she can find cemeteries uplifting," Duncan thought to himself. "I'll never understand it!"

An ancient purple lilac bush in full bloom dwarfed the northeast corner of the cemetery, its scent perfuming the moist May air. On the far side of the lilac Duncan came upon an old-timer methodically cutting squares of grassy sod out of the ground with a flat-edged shovel and stacking the sod upon a tarp in preparation for digging a grave. Duncan recognized the man as Frank Whitehouse, the town sexton. Frank lived alone on his old family farm near Miss Crump's house and gravel pit. Whitehouse was humming snatches of a tune and Duncan, rather than interrupt the sexton at his work, seated himself on the rising ground and waited for the older man to take a break. A perky flycatcher landed in the lilac behind Duncan, its brown tail bobbing. Whitehouse cut out several more squares of sod, then removed his ballcap and swiped his elbow across his face to sop up the sweat.

"Pretty hot afternoon for digging, isn't it?" Duncan remarked, standing up. If the sexton was surprised by his presence, he didn't reveal it.

"Yep, but I'm used to the heat," Whitehouse replied. He hitched up his pants.

"Who died?"

"Charlie Frost. Maggie didn't tell ya?"

"No. I don't think she knows about Charlie. When did he die?"

"T'other day. Thet's right—I forgot. Young Miss Sabine is doin' Charlie's funeral tomorrow, not Maggie. Sally wants to git him in the ground afore Memorial Day." Sally Frost was the widow of the deceased.

"I'm sorry to hear about Charlie," said Duncan. "Although I didn't know him very well."

"He was my best friend," Frank Whitehouse said simply. He leaned onto the handle of his shovel.

"Then I'm doubly sorry. It's hard to lose a dear friend, especially as we get older." Duncan absently scraped some orange fungus off the marble gravestone in front of him with his thumbnail. "Don't you find this rather lonesome work?"

"Lonesome?" the sexton repeated. He looked at Duncan and laughed in a quiet way. "Why would I be lonesome here? In town I don't hardly know nobody no more. Here, I knows nearly every single soul. There, they are strangers, or if I knows 'em it's only by name, like I knows you. But here are my parents, my grandparents, my brothers and sister. My friends thet I used to go huntin' and fishin' with are here—I dug their graves 'n lowered 'em into the ground myself. My wife is here—right over there." Whitehouse broke off to point out to Duncan the plain marble monument resting in the shade of the lilac. "I planted thet bush fore Doris. Cain't hardly believe she's been gone so long!"

"It's a beautiful lilac. I noticed it right away when we drove in."

"Maggie here doin' Miss Hastings?"

Duncan nodded. "With her granddaughter."

"Cain't start 'em too young!"

"That's what Maggie says. And we brought some geraniums for Wendell, too."

Frank Whitehouse tossed his shovel down and retrieved a canteen of water lying on the grass next to his jacket. "Now, thet's a big loss," he said. The sexton took a gulp of water and wiped his mouth. "Wendell always used to hep me keep the place mowed up. I gots to hire it done, now—when I kin find someone."

"Perhaps I could help?" Duncan offered. He surveyed the three-acre cemetery, which sprawled across the top of Russell Hill. "I noticed the back part still needs mowing."

"You got a push mower?" asked the sexton, scratching the white stubble of his beard. "Cain't use a ridin' mower here. She's mounded up bad on account o' the old graves."

"We do have a push mower. I use it at our place."

Whitehouse looked pleased. "I'll thank ye kindly, then, for yore offer. I been worriet 'bout gittin' this one done by Friday, what with Charlie's funeral 'n all."

"My pleasure," replied Duncan. The retired Presbyterian minister unconsciously straightened his shoulders, already feeling a sense of ownership and connection to the Russell Hill Cemetery. "I'll come back this evening and get that done for you."

Frank bobbed his head in gratitude. "You're a good sort, Duncan. Glad to have the opportunity to git ta know ya better."

"Lose a friend—gain a friend," Duncan said, smiling.

"Ayuh!" The sexton returned the canteen to the grass and picked up the shovel with his gnarled hands. Whitehouse seemed in no hurry to return to his labors, however. "There's Maynard, bringing flowrs to Ma Jean," he pointed out. "They was sweethearts when they was kids, but she married someone else. Maynard was well-nigh heart broke. He tends Mabel Jean's grave like they was married sixty years. He always brings a potted plant fore Harold, too."

"Harold?"

"Ma Jean's husband. He was from Away, but Maynard didn't holt it agin him that Harold won the prize."

"Very generous," said Duncan. The two men watched as Maynard Nutter, now in his nineties, removed a large cemetery vase of fresh-cut lilacs from the passenger seat of his pickup and carefully set the vase in front of Mabel Jean's gravestone.

Whitehouse leaned onto the shovel again and scanned the balance of the cemetery with pride and affection. "When I'm here diggin' a grave, like today," he continued, "or tendin' the flowrs, I sees 'em all jest like 'twas yestiddy."

"You do?" Duncan's eyes followed the sexton's gaze around the cemetery. He spotted Maggie and Jana planting the two geraniums for Wendell. The seven-year-old had her own little trowel and was industriously digging a hole for the plants. Maggie tousled her granddaughter's brown locks, and Jana looked up with innocent affection. The two presented an idyllic tableau.

"Yep. Sometimes I talk with 'em 'bout the thoughtless things we did when we was young, and didn't know no better. We larnt soon enough, tho. Remembering those days sort o' cheers my heart. And I'm comforted to think that soon—quite soon, probbly—someone will kindly hep me down into the ground to sleep longside o' them. No, I ain't never lonely here!" the sexton declared. He thrust the flat edge of the shovel back into the sod, commenced his humming mid-tune, and went back to his work.

The May breeze on the hilltop shifted direction and Duncan inhaled the fresh floral scent of the lilac bush that Frank Whitehouse had planted for his wife. He gazed again upon his own wife tending Wendell's grave, with her eager replacement at her side.

Duncan's heart overflowed with love. He thought he finally understood Maggie's affinity for cemeteries.

Chapter 6

The Forest Cathedral

Thursday afternoon, after Sabine's office hours were over (during which she had received drop-in visits from two parishioners), she changed out of her skirt and blouse into jeans and a white-and-blue Iliff School of Theology sweatshirt. She slipped on thick cotton socks and a pair of stout leather hiking boots, and pulled her dark-blonde hair back into a jaunty ponytail.

At the May Breakfast Nick had offered to give her a guided tour through the Sovereign Woods, and Sabine had eagerly accepted. They had set today for their "date." Sabine was looking forward not only to seeing more of the woods, but also to spending time with this modern-day Thoreau. Nick had suggested he meet her at the church; however, Sabine knew his remote house in the swath of wilderness was located closer to the other end of the Sovereign Woods trail. She proposed instead that they both depart around three o'clock and meet on the trail along the way.

A little after three she set off down the slight hill behind the church, where the trailhead was located. The trail soon leveled out. The scent of warm pine needles rose up from the forest floor. A black-capped chickadee issued a spring mating call, "fee-bee."

What a glorious day! Sabine thought. God is good.

A red squirrel followed Sabine for the first twenty or thirty yards, leaping from tree branch to tree branch, all the while scolding her for trespassing. Sabine laughed at the tiny creature's pertinacity. "I'm not leaving," she informed the squirrel. "No matter how much you jabber!" The red squirrel abruptly shut up.

Sabine and the squirrel parted ways at the bridge that forded Black Brook. The thirty-foot wooden span was built and maintained by the local snowmobile club. In winter, the bridge was also utilized by snowshoers and cross-country skiers. During the other three seasons the bridge was used by hikers, bird watchers, picnic goers, and horseback riders.

Sabine paused mid-way across the bridge to gaze downstream where the water divided the two parcels of forestland. Rounded gray boulders in varying sizes hugged the shorelines and dotted the dark water of the brook. The boulders impeded the water's natural course, causing frothing white spray to splash up against the rocks. She wondered if the neighborhood kids—Rebecca's son Tad and his three young girlfriends—ever hopped rocks when the water was lower? Or perhaps the children fished off the bridge?

Sabine moved on, knowing Nick was headed to meet her. She felt excitement at the thought of seeing him again. Over the six months she had resided with Maggie and Duncan, her mentor had spent a good deal of time chatting about her stepson. Sabine had been intrigued by what she had learned about him and now looked forward to getting to know Nick in person.

The main trail followed the east side of Black Brook. This trail, which ran north to south through the Sovereign Woods, followed the meandering course of the brook.

From the church on Route 9 to the turnoff to the Millett Rock was about half a mile. From there, it was another mile out to Maggie's house on the Cross Road. In total, the Sovereign Woods encompassed two thousand acres. The marshy ground on the west side of the brook, however, was rarely penetrated. There, beaver activity had flooded the brook in sections, creating an almost impassable myriad of rivulets and wetland.

The town of Sovereign owned the largest parcel of land comprising the Sovereign Woods (900 acres). The balance was owned by Henry Trow (more than 500 acres) and Rebecca Russell (since Wendell's death, about 300 acres). All the forestland on the east side of the brook was harvested intermittently, and Sabine soon came to an almost clear-cut section near the trail. The cut was sprinkled with wolf pines and a few oaks trees. The behemoth pines had been left for seed trees; the oaks had been left by the woodcutter to provide acorns—valuable winter food—for the deer, squirrels, and other wildlife. Since the clearing's harvest, it had been taken over by wild raspberry canes. Sabine made a mental note to return to the rambling patch of raspberries in summer to harvest some of the fruit.

When Sabine reached the turnoff to the popular picnic spot the Millett Rock, she spied Nick coming up the main trail towards her from the south. She waved, and paused at the intersection of the two trails waiting for him to catch up.

"Hey, Sabine," Nick said in greeting, as he reached her side. "Am I late? Sorry, I don't own a timepiece."

The woodsman was dressed in jeans, a red plaid flannel shirt, and LL Bean hiking books. Under Nick's arm was tucked a woven-willow fishing creel, which hung around his neck by a leather strap. Sabine noted with approval that his black bushy beard had been recently trimmed. She thought he looked as if he had stepped out of the nineteenth century Maine woods. Noting the creel, Sabine assumed that Nick had a rod stashed somewhere near a fishing hole and planned to take her fishing later. That would be fun! Perhaps they would cook the fish over an open campfire?

"What time do you think it is?" Sabine queried him, interested to test the woodsman's ability to gauge time by the sun.

Nick turned and gazed above the treetops at the bright orb in the sky. "Three-twenty."

Sabine removed her phone from her pants pocket and checked the time. "Three-twenty-six," she said. "You're six minutes late."

He grinned, yellow lights twinkling in his brown eyes. "I don't follow time much. Cramps my style."

Sabine smiled ruefully. "Time is a stern taskmaster. Unfortunately, some of us are bound to it."

"Not for life, I hope?"

"Only 9 a.m. on Sundays."

"When church starts?"

"You guessed it. But this is Thursday, so let's put the taskmaster away." Sabine returned her phone to her pocket. "Which way should we go from here?" She gestured toward the unmarked path leading up the hill to the east. "Where does this trail lead? I know the other one…" and she pointed at the west-leading path opposite, "… goes to the Millett Rock. Maggie took me there last fall."

Nick's eyes climbed the narrower eastward trail. "That goes to Wendell and Rebecca's house. It's how the locals used to get to the Millett Rock in the old days. People would park at Wendell's and hike down. Most people just walk in from the church now, though."

"Why? Did Wendell object to trespassers?"

"Wendell? Not hardly! He was the kind of a guy who'd give the shirt off his back to anyone, whether they needed it or not. No, a few years ago a local troop of Scouts cut this main trail from Route 9 through to the Cross Road, near Maggie's house. After that, it was much easier to hike to the Millett Rock from the church than it was to come down from Wendell's."

"Poor Rebecca! She'd probably appreciate the company now that Wendell is gone. I didn't know him well—Wendell died a few months after I started my internship with Maggie—but my impression of him was that he was a very special man."

"He was a brick," Nick affirmed. "I don't think Leland will ever get over his death. He told me once Wendell was like a younger brother to him."

"That's so sad. I'll never forget how welcome Wendell made me feel at their house the first time I had dinner with them. He pulled my hair—affectionately, you know—and told me I was his favorite song."

"His favorite song?"

Sabine nodded. "'Now the Day Is Over'—that's Wendell's favorite song. It's a hymn, actually. We sang it that night after dinner. At first, I thought it was in my honor, but Rebecca told me recently they sang that hymn every night before they went to bed. Isn't that romantic? Wendell had a beautiful baritone, too."

Nick was confused. "I don't understand what the singing has to do with you?"

She laughed. "Oh, you don't know, do you? I was named for Sabine Baring-Gould, the Anglican priest who wrote that hymn, as well as 'Onward Christian Soldiers.' I just expected you to know because your father connected the dots right away."

"My father's a Presbyterian minister," Nick pointed out. "He would know stuff like that. Besides, it isn't pronounced the same as your name."

"No, fortunately. My father loved 'Now the Day Is Over,' but he thought SAY-bean was too quirky a name for a girl, so I got Sah-BEAN. It's spelled the same, though."

"Boy, that was a close call!"

"Had I been a boy, I would have been stuck with SAY-bean. I can just hear all the other kids now: 'Say, Bean! Whatta ya up to? Jack-in-the-BEANstalk?'"

Nick's face clouded over. "I know what it's like to be picked on as a kid, and it sucks. Your father made the right decision."

Sabine glanced up at Nick's dark countenance. She reached for his hand. A spark of electricity passed between them. "Someday you'll have to tell me about your younger years."

"OK, but it's not a pretty story," Nick warned.

"What's that corny aphorism people say? 'What doesn't kill you makes you stronger?'"

"Yeah, I'm still waiting on that."

She squeezed his strong hand reassuringly, then released it. "Let's take Wendell's trail, shall we? Why don't you lead the way and I'll follow."

Sabine's choice of trail pleased Nick, bringing him out of his temporary funk. He might be able to harvest a few morels on the trail to Wendell's place. Due to the advent of the emerald ash borer, many Maine landowners had taken precautionary measures and harvested their ash trees, under which morels like to grow. But Wendell had not gotten around to cutting his ash before he died. In addition, there was something on Wendell's property that Nick particularly wanted to show Sabine. The only drawback, however, was that because this old woods road was so overgrown, the two of them couldn't walk side by side.

Nick started up Wendell's trail, being careful as he hiked along to hold back any branches and bushes for the young minister. Balsam firs, hardwood saplings, ferns, and weeds had sprouted up in the little-used woods road. These invaders, combined with thick clumps of grass hiding tree roots, necessitated careful attention to feet placement. Nick took care to point out the large roots to Sabine. Other than these occasional cautions, they hiked along in companionable silence, listening to the wind in the trees carrying melodious birdsong to their ears.

Suddenly, Nick stopped abruptly. "That's a yellow-rumped warbler," he said, looking up. He and Sabine were soon rewarded by a repeat of the sweetly-whistled trill, an answering call.

"He's got a girlfriend, too!"

"'Tis the season," Nick replied, feeling happy and content. Yes, it was the season for love! Why not for him?

He resumed his pace, recalling as he moved up the hill that the only other young woman he'd met in the Sovereign Woods was his stepsister Nellie—prior to her becoming his stepsister. He'd had a crush on Nellie when he'd first come to town, but she wouldn't give him the time of day. She was already in love with Doctor Bart. Nick and Nellie had become good friends since then. He hoped he and Sabine might become more than friends.

Nick had had lovers over the years, but those temporary relationships were never satisfying. He wanted a true partner, a woman with whom he could connect physically, emotionally, and spiritually. Someone with whom he could feel the kind of passionate, spiritual love experienced by Nathaniel Hawthorne and Sophia Peabody. Could Sabine be his Sophia Peabody?

"Are you a birder?" she asked, interrupting his train of thought.

"Sort of, although I've never formally studied birds. I've just gotten to know them from spending so much time in the woods. I once listened to a crow and a gray tree frog carry on a conversation for about half an hour." Nick stopped to hold back for Sabine the springy limbs of a balsam fir encroaching upon the trail.

"That must have been an interesting conversation!"

"It was. The crow made a regular barking sound, like an annoying dog." Nick mimicked a couple of short barks. "And the tree frog garbled back a reply. Sorry, I can't do a gray tree frog. Anyway, I sat next to the brook and listened to them for quite a while, the crow barking something and the tree frog answering back."

"What were they talking about?" asked Sabine, curious.

"Me, probably."

Sabine laughed merrily. "I bet you're right! Not many people would sit around and listen to a crow carry on with a frog. The two of them probably wondered what the heck you were up to."

Out of the corner of his eye Nick spotted a yellow morel pushing up from the forest floor. He instinctively unhooked his knife from his belt and scootched down next to the mushroom. He expertly cut the morel at the bottom of the stem with his curved knife. The woodsman flipped open his creel, brushed a few flecks of black soil from the sponge-looking mushroom, and carefully placed the morel into his cloth-lined creel. Nick shut the cover with a snap and stood up.

"That's for mushrooms!" exclaimed Sabine. "I thought we were going fishing later."

"We are—fishing for 'shrooms."

She thought a moment. "Jesus was a fisher of men; you are a fisher of nature. Is this part of your calling?"

Nick was momentarily disconcerted. Was she making fun of him? Then he realized Sabine was sincere. He shook his head. "Just a way to pay the bills and put food on the table."

Sabine seemed truly disappointed that he didn't elaborate. Instead, Nick resumed their hike. After he'd gone several minutes up the trail, however, he felt badly for shutting her down. How could he ever find the true love he was looking for unless he began to open up about himself? Allow himself to be vulnerable? Let someone in!

Nick also realized, with a dawning sense of shame, that love wasn't all about himself. Love was a two-way street. What about Sabine's hopes and dreams? Thoughts and feelings? So far on their "date" she had peppered him with two or three questions for every one of his to her.

"What's your sermon about Sunday?" he asked, turning sideways as he walked along.

"I'm preaching on Lydia's conversion in Philippi, from the Acts of the Apostles. I'm a good Methodist, so I follow the Revised Common Lectionary, unlike Maggie. I know she's U.U."

"Dad followed the Lectionary, too. Before he retired. Who's Lydia? I don't remember her. Forgive me, but I only went to Sunday school a few years."

Sabine paused to retie her hiking boot. "Lydia was a dealer in purple cloth from Macedonia. She was one of the Apostle Paul's important converts."

"Paul, I remember. Not favorably, either." Nick had stopped when Sabine stopped, and now waited patiently for her.

"You mustn't believe everything you hear about Paul," she urged, straightening up. "His words are often taken out of context and used as a tool for discrimination and repression. Paul had his issues, but he had his good points, too. He was an inspirational evangelist, for one."

Nick casually removed a spruce sprig from her hair and tossed it aside. "Not sure if you can change my mind about Paul. I might have to go to church Sunday to hear your sermon." He turned and continued up the trail.

"I'd like that," Sabine said, following along behind in her steady pace. "But what will your father think when he sees you in church?"

Nick's attention was claimed by a cluster of morels in the woods. He leaped over a decomposing ash tree and squatted down to harvest the mushrooms. He brushed off the mushrooms one by one and carefully placed the morels in his creel. Nick snapped the creel shut and stood up. "Dad will think I've got a crush on the pretty new minister. I haven't been to church since I was ten."

Sabine laughed. "Well, we won't disabuse Duncan, then, if that's what it takes to get you back in church."

Nick leaped back over the downed ash and they resumed their hike. The trail soon widened where Wendell had kept the old woods road clear and he moved to the right so that they could walk abreast. The May sun, well past the meridian, cast elongated shadows of the trees standing sentinel on the south side of the old road. Bunches of scented ferns unfurled at the base of a stone wall, which in the fullness of time had partially toppled over. On the far side of the wall, deeper into the woods near the little stream that flowed down the hillside to Black Brook, Nick spied a family of skunk cabbages. The large green mounds with their ear-like leaves were so bright against the dark of the woods the plants were almost startling to behold. He pointed out the unique plants to Sabine. "Do you have skunk cabbages in Alaska?"

She paused to contemplate the plant. "Not in Fairbanks, but I think it does grow up there. It looks sort of cabbage-y. Does it smell like a skunk?"

"Only if you crush the leaves, otherwise, the smell isn't discernable. But that's not what makes skunk cabbage unique."

"No?"

"Nope. Skunk cabbage has heat generating properties. The plant gets warm enough in spring to melt the snow around it."

"Get out! You're kidding me."

"I am not kidding. One of the first signs of spring around here is when you see skunk cabbage poking through the snow. I'll bring you back here next spring to show you, if you're still around."

The two resumed walking. "I'd like that," Sabine said. She stumbled over a loose rock in the woods road and Nick snaked his arm out to prevent her from falling. His heart leapt as their flesh connected. "Thanks," she said, gracefully pulling away from his solid frame. She adjusted her ponytail. "Maggie's taking a whole year for her sabbatical," she added. "My contract with the church ends next May."

"Cool! That gives me plenty of time."

"Time for what?"

"Time to get to know you better." Nick's dark eyes gleamed in admiration.

"I'd like that," Sabine replied, blushing slightly.

Nick moved forward along the woods road and Sabine easily fell into step with him. Not many women could keep up with him on a hike, but Sabine with her long legs appeared to have no difficulty. "You really think God is calling me?"

She thought a moment. "I think the proper question is—do *you* think God is calling you?"

This time Nick didn't equivocate. "Something's eating at me, that's for sure," he answered honestly. "There's a Voice inside me that wants me to listen. Every time I ignore it, something bad happens, and it hurts like Hell."

Sabine waved away a mosquito. "So, you've discovered God's electric fence?"

"Electric fence? It figures your Christian God would employ a torture device."

"It's hardly that—just a heads up, when we ignore the Voice and go in the wrong direction."

"OK, you'll have to explain that one to me—sounds deep."

"Oh, I think you can follow along easy enough. My theory of the Divine Will isn't that complicated. I began formulating my own theology when I was in my teens. I always spent my summers at my grandparent's dairy farm in Montville—my mother's parents farm—where I learned the hard way to stay away from electric fences, especially when the grass is wet. When I began to think about things like free will and the problem of pain, I thought about my grandfather's electric fence. Eventually, I came to see that God uses pain as a way of saying, 'Heads up! Don't go that way.' That's what I call God's electric fence. Pain is the clue we're heading in the wrong direction. Unfortunately, a lot of people—myself included, at times—don't pay any attention to the pain and barge on through the fence."

Nick was impressed with the simplicity of her exposition. "Are you talking about spiritual pain?"

"At first. Most pain starts as spiritual pain because that's what we feel when we separate from the Divine. But spiritual pain is easy to ignore, or wash away with drugs and alcohol."

"Yeah, you got that right."

"Then the pain devolves into emotional pain, which causes us to do stupid things and leads to heartbreak."

Nick wanted to ask Sabine if she had ever had her heart broken, but he didn't. "Been there—done that," he said, instead.

"Finally, if we continue to grab hold of the electric fence, we experience physical pain. That's a lot harder to ignore."

Nick reached down and plucked a tall blade of grass. He stuck the stem in his mouth and began chewing as they strolled along. Bitter juice oozed out from the crushed stem. He found the bitterness strangely satisfying.

"Did you follow me?" she asked.

"Oh, yeah. Just thinking it over." He removed the blade of grass from his mouth and tossed it aside. "And remembering all those times I ignored the Voices telling me not to do something. I think I'm a 'grab hold of the electric fence with both hands' kind of guy," he admitted. "At least, I used to be."

"You've let go of the fence, then?" Sabine stopped and anxiously surveyed his face. She was very serious.

"I think so." The relief and compassion radiating from Sabine's brown eyes was so powerful Nick looked away. He glanced up the woods road and noted they were almost at the place he specially wanted to show her. "Come with me," he said, taking Sabine by the hand. When they reached the rise in the road, he halted. In front of them to the east sprawled a majestic stand of pine trees. The woods road passed straight through the grove, giving one the impression of entering the nave of a church. Nick felt as though he was leading Sabine down the aisle.

Sunlight streamed through the gaps in the trees, saturating the grove with an ethereal glow. "It's a forest cathedral!" Sabine proclaimed, in awe.

"Something like that." Nick suddenly felt bashful. He was pleased that she, too, felt the same spiritual connection to the place that he did. "It's my happy place. I hitchhiked all over the United States this past year—searching for serenity—but I never felt at peace until I came back here."

"It's gorgeous! Did you plant this pine grove?"

"Nope. This is Wendell's handiwork. He's been thinning and pruning his pine stand here for years. He was very proud of it. I don't know what will happen to the stand now that Wendell's gone. Probably Leland will carry on."

Sabine turned to face him, eyes aglow. Excited, she clasped Nick's arm with both hands. "This pine grove is your temple, isn't it? I can see it! I can see you leading worship services here. Teaching people about the natural world. Revealing the goodness of God's creation. It's so natural—it's perfect for you!"

Serenity settled over him like a pastoral robe. For the first time in his life Nick knew what it was like to have a calling.

Chapter 7

Dinner at the Old Russell Homestead

Maggie and Duncan were the last guests to arrive at the old Russell homestead Saturday evening for Rebecca's dinner party. Maggie had been surprised when Rebecca issued the invitation at the May Breakfast, since recent widows were not generally known to throw parties. "I wonder what Rebecca wants to tell us?" Maggie cogitated, for the hundredth time, as her husband turned the car into the gravel driveway of the old Russell homestead. Peering over the voluminous blooms of the cut peonies in the quart canning jar she clutched, Maggie perused the vehicles parked on the side lawn. "Even Henry and Hannah are here! It must be important to bring us all together like this."

"I expect we'll find out soon enough," Duncan said, parking the car on the grass next to the crew cab pickup from Scotch Broom Acres. "Watch it! You're going to dump those if you're not careful."

Maggie thrust the slippery, water-filled jar of flowers at Duncan. "Here, you take the peonies. They'll mean more to Rebecca coming from you, anyway." She popped open her car door.

"I don't know about that," he demurred, but took the glass jar. Duncan lowered his nose into the blossom of a blousy white peony. He sniffed. "Nice fragrance! Not overpowering." He exited the vehicle, carefully cradling the jar of flowers.

Maggie came around the side of the car to meet her husband. She looked at him and laughed. "Cute!"

"Thank you, dear. You're just noticing how devilishly handsome I am?"

"You are with that yellow nose. You might want to wipe that pollen off before we go inside, though. Careful—don't spill my flowers!"

The old Russell place was a hulking set of white buildings and sheds set back from the Russell Hill Road. The main house was built around 1840 using post-and-beam construction with timber harvested from the property. The substantial barn followed the house, and the shed connecting the two came later. Last to be cobbled onto the connected mass was the hen pen, which Wendell's grandfather George "Pappy" Russell (for whom young Tad had been named) had built onto the south side of the shed. Here Wendell's grandmother, Addie Russell, housed her 300 laying hens. Wendell had lived with his grandparents as a youth, helping his grandfather with the cows and his grandmother with her egg business.

Maggie glanced at the empty hen pen. Now, there's only one chick left at the old Russell homestead, she thought. At least the Russell name would have the possibility of continuing with nine-year-old Tad. But how sad Wendell would never see his son grow up!

Considering the number of vehicles in the dooryard— and the number of children present—Maggie thought the place was unnaturally quiet. "Are we at the right house?"

she jokingly asked her husband. "I don't hear any kids. That's not a good sign. They must be up to something."

"O, ye of little faith," retorted her husband, smirking at her over the tall peony blooms.

"Good comeback! I don't have much confidence in the neighborhood kids. There's usually trouble when the four of them get together."

Maggie knocked on the shed's exterior door. Hearing no reply, she entered, passing through the shed, with its assortment of boots, jackets, and hats, and walked into the old-fashioned country kitchen without knocking. Duncan followed his wife into the house carrying the flowers.

Rebecca was tending various pots on the cookstove, but looked up with a smile when they entered. "Welcome, Faulkners! I was wondering when you were going to get here."

"Are we late?" asked Maggie, glancing at the red-and-white Sessions wooden wall clock. Rebecca had said dinner was at six, and it was only five-forty.

"No, just the last to arrive."

Duncan presented Rebecca with the jarful of pink and white peony blooms. "These are for you. Maggie just picked them."

"Lovely! Just what the doctor ordered, thank you both." Rebecca wiped her hands on her apron and took the jar of flowers from Duncan's hands. "Our peonies aren't in bloom yet," she added. "These smell heavenly!"

"Watch the pollen," Duncan said, smiling at his wife.

Rebecca placed the jar on the countertop and opened the cupboard above it. She gazed up at three stoneware pitchers on the top shelf and sighed. "Can you reach that big pitcher up there, Duncan? The largest one. I don't have a stepstool. Wendell always got the high things down for me."

"No problem," Duncan replied. Although he was six inches taller than Rebecca, he was not a tall man and had to stretch to reach the pitcher. Even then, Duncan had to move the container forward with his fingers to grab hold of the base. He set the heavy stoneware pitcher down on the counter. "Maybe it's time for that stepstool," he remarked.

Rebecca sighed again. "I guess you're right. I've been standing on chairs to get things, but that's not very safe." She took the pitcher to the antiquated slate sink and filled it with cold water. She placed the blooms in the container and gracefully arranged them.

A pot lid on the stovetop rattled, prodding Maggie into action. "I'll take that," she offered, stepping forward to take the flower arrangement so their hostess could focus on her dinner preparations. "Where do you want them?"

"Just set them on the kitchen table, please." Rebecca lifted the cover of the rattling pot, stuck a fork in the potatoes, and adjusted the gas under the burner. "The children picked me a wildflower bouquet for the dining room."

Maggie set the pitcher in the center of the oval oak table. She recollected that Wendell had once told her that his grandfather had been born on that table. "Speaking of the kids—where are they?"

"Out playing hide-and-seek. It's Tad's favorite game here because he knows all the best hiding places." Rebecca opened the oven to check on her pork roast, filling the room with the meat's mouth-watering fragrance.

"Mmmm," said Duncan. "That roast smells amazing!"

Rebecca closed the oven. "Thank you. Almost done." She laid the potholders on the counter.

Screams of laughter and high-pitched voices erupted on the back lawn. "Sounds like someone's been tagged," Duncan observed, glancing out the widow over the kitchen sink. "Correction, not yet. Alice is climbing the apple tree after Tad. He's high up in the blossoms."

"Goodness! He's going to make me old before my time," exclaimed Rebecca. She darted out through the shed to the back door. "George Scott Russell," she called. "You come down out of that tree right now! And you, too, Alice Rose."

Tad meekly began scrambling down from the upper limbs, sending a shower of pink-and-white apple blossoms down to the ground. Alice, on the other hand, waited in the crotch of the tree for her playmate to come within arm's length. She slapped Tad on the foot. "Tag, you're it," she shrieked, laughing.

"That's not fair!" Tad protested loudly. "Mama made me come down."

"Fair is for sissies," Alice replied. She stuck her tongue out at the younger youth and slid down the tree trunk.

Rebecca, when the children were safe on the ground, closed the back door and returned to the kitchen. "Sorry about that," she apologized. "I don't know what I'm going to do with that boy! Tad has been acting out at lot since his father died."

"I wouldn't worry about him just yet," said Duncan gently, putting his arm around the widow. "Tad is also acting like a normal nine-year-old boy."

"You think so?"

"I know so. I was a boy myself once—or so they say—and I raised a son, too." Duncan gave Rebecca a reassuring squeeze.

Rebecca daubed her moist eyes with the corner of her apron. "Thank you, Duncan. I needed to hear that. Poor Tad!"

The widow turned and gazed out the window at the apple tree, but Maggie knew she wasn't seeing the tree or the children, she was seeing Wendell, harvesting apples in years gone by.

"I forget what a good minister you are," Maggie whispered to her husband.

"Sorry if I stepped on your toes, but the spirit moved me."

"Step away! Who am I to fight the spirit?"

The pot lid rattled again. "What can we do to help?" Maggie asked, her eye on the stovetop where the potatoes were again perilously close to boiling over.

Rebecca moved quickly to the stove. She reduced the heat under the potatoes, and glanced anxiously at the clock. "You could fill the water glasses, please."

"How about me? What can I do?" said Duncan.

"Would you mind keeping an eye on the children? Alice Rose sometimes gets a little bossy with Tad. He doesn't like it."

"Perfectly understandable. I wouldn't like it either," said Duncan, heading for the door. "Especially in my own home," he added under his breath.

"Alice has a lot of her grandfather in her," Maggie commented, after the shed door closed behind Duncan. "Unfortunately, not Leland's finer qualities, either."

"She certainly does," Rebecca agreed. "Now, Hope, on the other hand, is such a darling! Tad dotes on her. He tolerates Alice because she's Hope's older sister—and Hope wouldn't like it if he was mean to her sister. He'd do anything for Hope."

"A true white knight! Just like his father." Maggie retrieved ice from the freezer, filled the two water pitchers with ice and water, and proceeded into the great room. The large room ran the length of the main house and served as a combined living-dining room. If the kitchen was the heart of the old Russell homestead, the great room was its soul. Maggie had attended many happy dinner parties there over the years. Wendell always sat at the head of the table in the spindle-back oak Captain's chair. She wondered who would take his place this evening. Henry? Ryan? Or perhaps Rebecca herself?

The table was set for a larger than usual dinner party. Maggie counted thirteen water glasses as she filled them, which meant twelve guests in addition to their hostess. The kids, she knew, would eat outside at the picnic table, as usual. Mentally she counted the friends who would soon be seated, devouring Rebecca's famous pork roast; mashed potatoes and gravy; fresh greens from Trudy's greenhouse; Rebecca's rhubarb sauce; and strawberry-rhubarb pie for dessert. There were Leland, Ryan, and Trudy from Scotch Broom Acres; neighbors Henry and Hannah Trow; Maggie's daughter Nellie and her husband, Doctor Bart; Duncan's son Nick; the new minister Sabine; and she and Duncan. With Rebecca, that would be twelve of them around the table. There was one extra water glass.

Who else was joining them? Wasn't thirteen an unlucky number?

Maggie shook off a sudden foreboding. "Where is everybody?" she asked, when she returned to the kitchen with the empty pitchers.

Rebecca pushed back a stray strand of her soft brown hair, which only lately had begun showing signs of gray. "Nick's upstairs rounding up some extra chairs, and Ryan and Trudy have gone to the store to get me some cream. They didn't have any extra—the farm had a lot of butter orders this week and some of their cows are dry."

"And Metcalf and Nellie?"

"Doctor Bart and Nellie have taken Sabine up to show her Wendell's bees."

"I forgot all about Wendell's honeybees!" Maggie exclaimed. "How are the bees doing?" She began icing and refilling the two pitchers for the dining room sideboard.

"His bees survived the winter, but that's all I know." Rebecca carefully removed the pork roast from the oven. She lifted the roast with two wooden-handle forks and placed the hefty saddle of meat on a large wooden cutting board to let it rest before slicing

Maggie admired the perfectly-browned roast. "That must have come from one big pig."

"It's one of Leland's corn-finished pigs."

"Probably one of his old sows," Maggie surmised. "But if the roast tastes as good as it looks, we won't hold that against him. Leland does have some good qualities—he can still cut firewood and raise pigs. Can I help you with that pan?"

"No, no. Just watch while I dump this and make sure the juice goes into the frying pan." Rebecca tilted the roasting pan and poured the pork drippings into the iron frying pan on the stove top. She set the dirty roaster into the black slate sink and ran some hot water into it.

"And where are Henry and Hannah? They're already here, too, I see."

Rebecca flicked on the front gas burner. "Getting a tour of the hen pen," she said, turning the flame to low. "Would you believe it? Henry has never seen where the chickens were kept. Robinson has never seen the hen pen, either, of course, and Leland naturally offered to show them around."

"Naturally, Leland would take charge, just like his granddaughter. Wait—who's Robinson?"

Rebecca stopped what she was doing. "That's right, you haven't met him yet, have you? Robinson Crockett is why I asked you all here this evening."

Maggie sucked in her breath. Was Duncan correct? Did Rebecca already have a replacement for Wendell? Could that be possible? She wanted to pepper Rebecca with questions about her mystery guest, but a quick glance at the drooping shoulders and the despondency of the widow's demeanor informed her that her interrogation wasn't necessary. Nobody could replace Wendell in Rebecca's heart.

"Why isn't anyone helping you?" Maggie asked, instead. "Usually, you can't get Hannah out of a kitchen." Then she remembered—too late—that Wendell always acted as Rebecca's sous chef.

The widow plucked an old-fashioned tin gravy shaker out of a cupboard and set the shaker on the counter. "I've never needed help in the kitchen before," she admitted. Then, to the minister's surprise, Rebecca sat down at the table and burst into tears. She covered her eyes with a white cotton dish towel. "Oh, oh! Wendell always helped me cook. I didn't expect him to die so soon," she wailed. "I thought I could host this dinner party by myself—that's what he would have wanted. Poor Wendell! He'll never get to see Tad grown up. Poor Tad!"

Maggie appropriated the chair next to her friend. She slid the chair closer so that she could drape her arm over the younger woman's shoulders. "Go ahead and cry," she urged. "Get it out!"

Rebecca wept uncontrollably for several minutes, then stopped as suddenly as she started. "I'm making a fool of myself, aren't I?" The widow wiped her eyes with the dish towel. "I never knew how much I depended on Wendell until he was gone. I can't even get a pitcher down from the shelf without him!"

"Let us help you," Maggie pleaded. "All your friends are here for you. You didn't need to do this today. I could have cooked dinner at my house."

"No, no. I *did* need to do this today. I signed the contract yesterday and I want to be the one to tell you all before you read the news in the papers."

"Tell us what?" An uneasy feeling gripped Maggie. Was Rebecca going to sell the old Russell homestead? The property had been in the family seven generations! Could that be possible?

"Oh, my gravy! It's bubbling already." Rebecca hopped up and returned to the stove.

Maggie rose up from her chair just as Henry and Hannah entered the kitchen. Accompanying them was a tall, dark-haired man in his mid to late thirties. Robinson Crockett—the mystery guest—proprietor of the thirteenth chair. He was a stranger to Maggie. Or was he?

"Smells heavenly!" said Hannah. "What a beautiful roast. Here's the cream. Trudy said you needed it ASAP. She and Ryan have gone to check on the kids."

"Perfect timing, thank you," said Rebecca, taking the carton of cream. She filled the bottom of the gravy shaker with cold cream and quickly dumped two tablespoons of corn starch into the cap. She put the cap and body together and gave the old-fashioned shaker a thorough shaking. Rebecca slowly poured the white liquid thickener into the bubbling pan of roast drippings, whisking briskly with a fork.

There was an awkward moment while everyone stood around watching Rebecca tend the gravy. Maggie knew that Wendell always carved the roast. Should she offer to carve?

The same thought occurred to Rebecca's elderly neighbor Henry Trow. "Get me a carving knife," he ordered, hobbling forward to the sink to wash his hands. "Carving is a man's job."

"Goodness! I forgot all about cutting up the roast. Wendell always does that for me."

Henry wiped his hands on the hand towel and rolled up his sleeves. "Ready to carve!"

Rebecca gratefully handed the knife to the retired history professor. "Thank you, Henry."

As he took the knife, Rebecca's stodgy, white-haired neighbor leaned close to her. "The first time for everything is always the hardest," he counseled. Henry had been widowed himself several years prior to meeting and marrying Hannah in Sovereign a decade ago.

"Take heart, my dear, it does get easier," added Hannah, coming forward. She affectionately patted Rebecca's shoulder. "Now, the rest of us will just stay out of your way until dinner is ready." The plump, motherly woman took a seat at the kitchen table and looked meaningfully at the others standing around. Rebecca moved to the stove to stir the gravy and tend the potatoes.

Maggie reclaimed her seat in the pressed-back oak chair. She studied the thirty-something stranger, who was leaning up against the door frame. Although thin, he was well-muscled, and possessed of a healthy tan that signaled he spent much of his time out of doors. The stranger's face looked familiar. Where had she seen him before? "Do I know you?" she asked the newcomer.

The stranger straightened up and stepped to the kitchen table. He held out his hand to Maggie. "Robinson Crockett. And no, I don't think we've ever met. You must be Maggie?"

The minister shook the newcomer's hand, her eyes on his face. "Are you sure we've never met?"

"Quite sure."

"He's my special guest, Maggie," Rebecca said over her shoulder from the sink. She drained the water out of the potatoes and set the pot on the counter on a pot holder. She began mashing the potatoes, adding a generous amount of fresh butter from Scotch Broom acres, salt and pepper, and the cream.

Robinson offered up a crooked smile. "I don't know that I'm all that special. I know who you are, Maggie, because Rebecca told me who of her friends would be here, and you and your husband are the only guests I hadn't met. You're the local minister, right?"

"Guilty as charged, but I'm on sabbatical at the moment."

"I met your husband—Duncan—a few minutes ago with the young people. He's a minister, too, if I'm not mistaken?"

"Was," Maggie corrected. "Retired Presbyterian." Maggie found it odd that the newcomer had focused on her and Duncan's vocation. Did he have a problem with organized religion? Or was there some other reason he seemed to zero in on their professional calling?

Leland, who had stopped to leave his barn boots in the shed, breezed into the kitchen. He spied the roast and sidled up to the counter where Henry was carving. Leland proceeded to pull a loose piece of meat from the roast and pop the pork into his mouth. "Mmm! Berla cooked up to be a dem good roast!"

Henry scowled at the woodchopper, waving Leland away from the roast with the carving knife.

"Berla?" Maggie exclaimed, with a grimace. "Honestly, Leland! Way to kill an appetite."

"Thet was her name."

"Thank you for the roast, Leland. Perhaps you'd like to wash your hands before dinner?" Rebecca suggested.

"Don't mind if I do," said Leland. He ambled out of the kitchen toward the bathroom.

After the old woodchopper disappeared around the corner, Rebecca faced the others in the kitchen. "Don't say it!" she warned, holding up the mashed potato serving spoon. "I know what you're thinking, but Leland is family in this house. He and Wendell were like brothers."

"Say what?" said Henry, resuming carving. But he quietly cut off a small section of pork near where Leland's dirty hand had touched the roast, and set the piece aside.

"That certainly is a remarkable pen for the chickens," Robinson spoke up, changing the subject. Taking Hannah's hint, he had joined her and Maggie at the table, making his lanky frame comfortable by stretching out his long legs underneath. "I'm interested to know how Wendell's grandfather designed the coop so the hens always had fresh air."

"His design got rid of the ammonia smell, too," said Rebecca, proudly. She dished the mashed potatoes into a large serving bowl. "That was a big help when Wendell and I had chickens, I know!"

Maggie found herself warming to the newcomer. "The natural convection system was genius in its simplicity," she explained. "The heat from all the laying hens on the ground level rose up through the air slats George Russell built on the sides of the hen pen. The ammonia-laden air went out and was replaced by fresh, colder air from outside, coming in from the bottom."

"Simple, but clever," adjudged Robinson Crockett.

Maggie regarded the young man's sun-wrinkled face. She was sure she recognized him, but from where? "Are you an engineer?" she asked, fishing for a clue.

Robinson leaned back in his chair. "Is it so obvious?" he said, with a self-deprecating grin. "I graduated from Northeastern, the College of Engineering."

Maggie was sure she had seen his quirky crooked smile before. An image of him in another setting briefly passed in front of her eyes, but disappeared before she could pin it down. Another challenge of getting older, she thought. Can't remember things.

Multiple voices and footfalls were heard from the shed and in a minute most of the other guests trooped into the kitchen. They were laughing, joking, and talking at once. Maggie wondered how Rebecca could stand the noise and confusion and still get dinner on the table.

The cheerful little crowd had the opposite effect on Rebecca, however. She perked up. "Dinner is ready," she called happily over the din. "Let's all gather at the table and give thanks for our many blessings, shall we? Don't worry about your kids," she added, when Ryan turned and headed for the door. "Nick and Sabine have offered to take charge of them."

"Sounds good to me," said Doctor Bart. He picked up the bowl of mashed potatoes and headed into the great room carrying the spuds.

"Me, too," said Nellie. "I'll take that platter of pork, if you're done, Henry."

"All set, my dear." Henry lifted the platter of sliced roast pork and passed the meat to Nellie, who departed for the dining room.

Henry retreated to the sink and cleaned his hands. Hannah had stood up upon Rebecca's announcement and Henry now took his wife by the arm and escorted her into the great room. To the elderly couple's surprise, Leland was already seated at the table—at the head of the table, in Wendell's chair! "Don't say it," Hannah cautioned her husband, squeezing his arm. "I know what you're thinking."

Henry harumphed in reply, but said nothing, nor did he look at Leland.

"Somebody wanting to feed our children? Sounds too good to be true," Trudy said to Rebecca.

"Quick!" Ryan chimed in, "before Nick and Sabine discover what they've gotten themselves into. Are those greens going in?"

Rebecca passed the bowl of greens to the farmer-lawyer. "Thank you. But that leaves me with nothing," said the widow. "The rhubarb sauce is already on the table.

Duncan held out his arm to Rebecca. "Then, may I?"

"You may!"

Before Maggie had time to wonder who would escort her into dinner, the newcomer had stood up and offered his arm to her. "Looks like we're the last ones. Shall we join them?"

"Why not?" Maggie replied, glancing up into Robinson Crockett's craggy, good-natured face. Somehow, he reminded her of a fisherman from Down East Maine. But she didn't know any fisherman, except for Joe the Lobsterman from Stonington. And he certainly wasn't Joe!

Whoever he was, Robinson Crockett was a gentleman, Maggie decided.

She liked him. But ... she was not yet prepared to accept him as a neighbor if Rebecca had decided to sell out. Maggie wanted the old Russell homestead to remain in the Russell family.

As Robinson led her to the table, Maggie prayed silently that Rebecca had done nothing foolish.

Chapter 8

Wendell's Legacy

Dinner at the old Russell homestead was consumed with the usual joking, jostling, and passing of serving dishes that accompanies family-style dining. After the pork roast and gravy, mashed potatoes, and other main dishes were consumed, Trudy and Nellie cleared the table and ferried in slices of strawberry-rhubarb pie, as well as cups of herbal tea and coffee. The Gifford's vanilla ice cream container made the rounds of the table on its own legs.

When Maggie had first entered the great room, she was dismayed—and a bit shocked—to see Leland sitting in Wendell's chair at the head of the table. But when Rebecca serenely took her seat in her usual position, to the left of the Captain's chair next to Leland, Maggie realized that their hostess must have asked Wendell's best friend to fill in for her husband. By the time the pie made the rounds of the table, Maggie had become accustomed to seeing Leland in Wendell's seat and gave Rebecca credit for her table arrangements.

Very generous of her, Maggie thought. Rebecca understands that Leland misses Wendell almost as much as she and Tad do.

Thanks to Trudy's careful management of her loquacious father, Leland had been confined to only one tall tale during dinner. But Leland was not to be cut short, especially considering his elevated position at the head of the table. He wolfed down his pie and ice cream before most of the other guests had even dished up their Gifford's. Wendell had always served as a foil for the storyteller, so today Leland sought out Duncan, who was sitting next to Maggie on the living room side of the table. "I knows how much you like outhouses, Duncan," he began, pushing back his dessert plate and throwing his forearm on the table. "Did I ever tell ya the story 'bout Amos 'n the outhouse?"

"Amos and the outhouse? No, I don't think I've heard that one before," Duncan replied, good-naturedly, forkful of pie half-way to his mouth.

Maggie pinched her husband under the table.

"Ow! Ah, but then again, maybe I have …?"

Leland disregarded Duncan's hesitation. "Amos went down to Phil Fernald's place in Troy to git his vehickle worked on. Remember Phil, Hannah?"

"Of course, I remember Phil, Leland. Everyone took their cars to him."

"Wal, Phil told Amos might take an hour or two to fix the vehickle. Amos said he warn't in no hurry. Phil didn't have no place to sit inside his shop, so Amos begun to walk 'round the place. Now, Phil had a huntin' camp out behind his garage—quite a ways back in the woods, where he shot deer out of—so Amos decided to walk out and look ovah Phil's camp, to see if 'twas legal, like. He hadn't no more 'n got to thet camp when he felt nature callin'—and 'twarn't the kind of nature thet makes a man feel comfortable jest steppin' upta a tree, if you knows what I mean."

"Father!" Trudy chastised. "Some of us are still eating."

"I think we all know what you mean, Leland," Ryan added, drily.

Leland ignored his daughter and son-in-law, confident that he had the rest of the table in his power. "Fortunitely, Phil had himself an outhouse behind his cabin. Jest a one-holer, but good 'nuff.'"

"Very handy," said Robinson Crockett. He had been keeping a low profile during dinner, but was amused by Leland's storytelling.

"Although not very sanitary," said Doctor Bart.

"Naturally, Amos availed himself of thet outhouse—'twas quite a relief, too. Only problem was—warn't no toilet paper in thet outhouse!"

"Now, that's a dilemma," Henry Trow pronounced, clinking his fork down upon his dessert plate in something like disgust.

"Boy, can I relate to that!" Nick chimed in. The young woodsman, after helping feed the four kids, had escorted Sabine into the house to join the other adults for dessert. The children were now quietly playing a board game up in Tad's bedroom.

"Bummer!" declared Nellie, making a face. "I always look to make sure there's toilet paper before I sit down."

"Even in an outhouse?" her husband asked.

"Especially in an outhouse!"

"TMI," Maggie interjected, shaking her head at her pregnant daughter.

"Go on, Leland," Nick encouraged his elderly buddy. "What happened next?"

"Wal, Amoses wife Muriel all-ways put a clean white hanky in his pants pocket every morning—he hardly ever used it, course. But while he was settin' there, wind blowin' up his arse …"

"Father!"

"… like wind does in a outhouse, Amos recollected Muriel's white hanky."

"Oh, dear!" said Rebecca. "I don't think I like where this is going."

"Amos stood up to get thet hanky outta his pants pocket. But when he was fishin' for his hanky—his pants was 'round his ankles, you see—..."

"Oh, we see him alright! Too clearly," said Ryan.

"... a fifty-cent piece was caught up in thet hanky. I'll be demmed if thet fifty-cent piece didn't drop down the hole." Leland splayed both palms against the table and leaned forward. "'Twas one o' them Kinnedy half dollars, too!"

"Oh, my!" said Rebecca.

Ryan threw his left arm across the back of his wife's chair. "Fifty cents doesn't sound like much of a loss."

"I was thinking the same thing," said Sabine, perplexed.

Leland glared at his son-in-law. "Recollect, son, 'twas 1964—when them fifty-cent pieces was *100% silver*. Course I don't 'spect you to know thet," he added kindly to Sabine. "You warn't even a glimmer in yer Pa's eye, back then."

"Actually, the Kennedy half dollars were 90% silver in 1964," Doctor Bart corrected Leland. "My grandmother Metcalf collected them. They were never all silver. In 1965 the percentage in the coins dropped down to 40%."

Leland ignored Metcalf's comment. He turned toward Duncan, awaiting the retired minister's observation.

"I take it the Kennedy half dollar was a big loss to your friend Amos?" Duncan asked, obliging the woodchopper. He was also eager to move the story along. "What did he do?"

Before Leland could respond, Henry Trow harumphed loudly. "Not much anyone could do, I'd say," the former history professor concluded with authority. He folded his hairy white forearms atop his modest belly and leaned back. "I cleaned out a good many outhouses growing up and half a dollar certainly wouldn't be enough to tempt *me* to do that scutwork."

Leland never missed a beat. "What did Amos do?" he repeated, surveying his audience with widened eyes. "Why, he took a ten dollah bill outta his wallet 'n threw thet bill down the hole after thet fifty-cent piece."

"What the heck!" exclaimed Nick. "Why did Amos do that?"

"To make it worth his while to go down the hole after 'em both!" Leland declared with a grin.

The table broke into gales of laughter. Even Henry, who disapproved of Leland and his tall tales, laughed heartily. "Good one," admitted Henry. "You led me right into helping you with that punchline."

Leland winked at his fellow octogenarian. "Much obliged." He preened himself as he enjoyed the fruits of his labor.

"Well, that certainly is a story I won't soon forget," Rebecca pronounced, setting her cloth napkin onto the table. "If everyone's done with their dessert, why don't we move over to the living room where we can be more comfortable? Robinson and I have something we'd like to share with you."

There was a period of bustling confusion while the guests regrouped to the west end of the great room. Doctor Bart had counted chairs and seeing that there weren't enough seats—even with the couch, which was large enough for four—began ferrying several of the straight-back chairs from the dining table into the living room to create what would have been a sewing circle back in Grammie Addie's day. While the others were getting settled, Trudy ran up to check on the kids, and Nellie and Sabine cleared the table, stacking the dirty dessert plates next to the slate sink.

"Should we wash these up now?" Sabine asked, reaching for the dish soap.

Nellie surveyed the messy kitchen. "No, we'll clean everything later. It sounds like Rebecca has something important to tell us."

"Hmm," said Sabine, adding a few more plates to the stack. "I hope she isn't selling out?"

"Me too! That's the first thing I thought of."

"Although Robinson does seem nice," Sabine added as an afterthought.

Nellie returned the butter to the Scotch Broom Acres container and set the wooden box back into the fridge. "Rob is quite good looking, too," she said, closing the refrigerator.

Sabine smiled as she rinsed her hands. "I see where you're going, Nellie, and I'm not interested."

"No? Could it be there's somebody else?"

Sabine wiped her hands on the sink towel. She was not about to let Nellie know she was interested in her stepbrother; however, she didn't mind being mysterious. "Could be!" she replied.

By eight o'clock, everyone was seated comfortably in the living room. Rebecca was perched in her padded rocker, with Robinson sitting beside her in a straight-back chair. "Should we turn on a light?" she asked, glancing out the west window where the orange glow of the setting sun was being replaced in the sky by an exquisite amalgam of blues and purples. "It's getting dark."

In answer, Metcalf leaned over and switched on the floor lamp next to him. "Is that enough?"

"Perfect, thank you Doctor Bart." Rebecca folded her hands in her lap and gathered her thoughts together. "I suppose you're all wondering why I've asked you here this evening?"

Maggie glanced around at the little group of friends and family. Several heads were nodding in the affirmative. She wanted to speak, but bit her tongue.

"I certainly have been wondering," spoke up Hannah, from the other rocker. She was gliding gently back and forth. "But don't you worry, dear, whatever your news is, we all want the best for you. We're here to support you."

"Here, here!" added her husband.

"Thank you, Hannah. I knew I could count on my friends. But this isn't just about me, it's also about Wendell—and his legacy."

Wendell's legacy? Maggie wondered what that could possibly be. Was Robinson Crockett an artist who was going to paint a picture of Wendell?

"In fact, Wendell was working on his legacy before he … he passed." Tears came to the widow's eyes. She attempted to blink them away. "He and Robinson were working on a special project together. But perhaps I should let Rob tell you about it? I seem to be weepy this evening."

"Perfectly understandable," said Doctor Bart. "Take your time."

Robinson Crockett stood up. "Shall I?"

"Please," said Rebecca, daubing her eyes with a handkerchief.

Maggie didn't need to look closely to know the hanky Rebecca was clutching was one of Addie Russell's. "Never underestimate the power of a handkerchief" was one of Wendell's grandmother's favorite maxims (as told in a prior tale). The minister was glad Rebecca had the comfort of Wendell's ancestors at hand for this momentous occasion, whatever it was.

Robinson unconsciously ran his hand through his dark curls. "I approached Wendell about eight months ago with a proposal I thought he might be interested in," he began. The young man cleared his throat. "You see, I'm a solar farm developer. My special passion is helping people like Wendell and Rebecca—whose farms have been in the family for generations—keep their places going well into the future. Yesterday, Rebecca signed an agreement leasing to my company Wendell's western fields and woodlot for twenty-five years, with two, five-year renewal periods."

Sovereign, Maine was getting a solar farm? On Wendell Russell's fields and woodlot! Maggie was so surprised she almost fell out of her chair.

"What's thet? What's thet you said?" asked Leland, sitting bolt upright in his chair.

"We're going to have a solar farm here, Leland," Rebecca replied, buoyantly. "Just like Wendell wanted. The lease will provide enough money for Tad and I to live comfortably for ... well, for way past my lifetime!"

Leland rose to his feet, agitated. "Yer gonna have a solar farm? On Wendell's woodlot?"

"His fields and woodlot," clarified Robinson. "That's the plan."

"Yer gonna cut down all his trees?" the old woodchopper asked in horror.

"Not all of them," answered the developer. "We're going to leave about ten acres of woods around the Millett Rock. I understand that's a very popular picnic spot." The Millett Rock was on the Russell property.

"It's what Wendell wanted," Rebecca assured Leland.

"I don't believe it!" Leland stated baldly.

"Father!"

"I assure you it's true, Mr. Gorse," said Robinson, earnestly. "I'm sorry if you find this upsetting, but Wendell told me he was worried about his wife and young son and wanted to be sure they were provided for. Aren't you happy their future is secure?"

"Warn't never no need to worry 'bout Rebecca 'n Tad—we look out fer our friends here in Sovereign."

"I'm sure ..."

"And, no, I ain't heppy—I ain't heppy at-tall. In fact, I'm demmed unheppy! 'Twill be a cold day in hell afore I let you cut down Wendell's woodlot. Nossir! You ain't gonna cut Wendell's trees, not if I can help it!" With this ugly pronouncement, Leland stalked out of the room.

For a moment, there was an awful silence. Rebecca's face had blanched white. When the shed door slammed behind Leland, she burst into tears. Robinson dropped down into his chair, completely deflated.

"What just happened?" Duncan whispered to his wife.

"Hell froze over," Maggie whispered back.

"Father doesn't have a vehicle here," Trudy said quietly. "He rode with us."

Maggie glanced out the window, where in the gloaming she spied Leland stomping down the driveway, elbows flying. "I think he's walking home."

"It's five miles!" protested Nellie.

"The walk will be good for him," said Henry. "Give the old coot time to cool off."

"Don't worry, dear," Hannah reassured Rebecca. "Leland didn't mean what he said. You just took him by surprise. Things will be right as rain tomorrow, you'll see. I think a solar farm is a marvelous idea!"

Maggie saw Ryan and Trudy exchanging glances. She could read their unsaid words. Leland *had* meant what he'd said. He was adamantly opposed to the solar farm project!

Nick stood up. "I'll give him a ride home."

"You don't even own a vehicle," his father pointed out.

"Can I take your car?"

"How will Maggie and I get home?"

"Hannah and I will give you a lift," Henry offered. "Let the boy go after Leland. Maybe Nick can talk some sense into his thick skull."

"The keys are in the car," Duncan informed his son. Nick strode out of the great room.

"I'll go with Nick," said Sabine, standing up and retrieving her sweater from the back of the chair. Several pairs of eyes turned to the young minister, including

Maggie's. "What I mean is, I'll take them both in my car," she elucidated.

Maggie responded quickly, before anyone else could get their two cents in. "That sounds like the best idea. Nick might need some sympathy himself after dealing with Leland."

Hearing no objections, Sabine followed Nick out the door. She had seen Nick's shocked face when Robinson Crockett made his announcement and knew that the idea of cutting down Wendell's woodlot for a solar farm had horrified him as much as Leland.

That lovely pine cathedral! What would happen to that? Sabine wondered. Would the loss of the pine grove dampen Nick's enthusiasm for his spiritual calling?

Leland's outburst effectually brought an awkward conclusion to Rebecca's dinner party. There was no further discussion about the solar farm. Nobody asked Robinson any questions about the project, either.

"We need to get the kids home to bed," Ryan said, instead, trying to put a good face on their family's hasty departure.

Feeling badly for their hostess, Maggie pulled Rebecca aside. "I'm with Hannah," she said, with a hug. "I think a solar farm is a wonderful idea. It's not only good for the planet, it's great for you and Tad. Wendell would be proud of you for carrying on."

"Thank you," Rebecca replied gratefully. "I needed to hear that. Do you think Leland will come around?"

"Of course he will," Maggie reassured her friend. "Just give him some time."

But in her heart, Maggie had grave misgivings. She knew Leland well, and she suspected there might be trouble dawning on Sovereign horizon's.

Chapter 9

Stiff-Necked Duo

By the time Sabine exited the shed of the old Russell homestead, the evening dew had fallen. She pulled her sweater closer and peered around the yard in the gathering gloom for Nick. As she paused on the granite door stoop, she felt the soft air-kiss of a bat's wing on her cheek. Although not frightened of bats, Sabine instinctively pulled back.

"Nick?" she called softly. "Are you here?"

Seeing and hearing nothing of the bearded woodsman, Sabine walked out and looked down the driveway, where the dark roadway was clearly visible against the backdrop of the western sky. She spied Nick hiking rapidly up the road, chasing Leland on foot. His long legs quickly closed the gap between the two men. Sabine surmised that Nick, who was so used to walking everywhere, had forgotten to take his father's vehicle. Either that, or he had heard her offer to drive them both home. But if so, he wasn't waiting for her—he was pursuing Leland.

What should she do?

It took Sabine several minutes to retrieve her parked car and maneuver out to the end of the driveway. She braked to a stop and watched in the fading twilight as Nick overtook Leland up by the cemetery. The old woodchopper paused when Nick caught up with him. Leland angrily gesticulated something, to which remark Nick replied with equal passion. Leland then turned and headed west down the Cross Road. Nick, without even a glance over his shoulder to see if she was following, matched his friend's hot-tempered march toward Scotch Broom Acres.

They're two peas in a pod, Sabine thought, smiling to herself. Only one's a bit harder than the other!

Unbidden, however, a Biblical passage from Exodus popped into her head. "The Lord said to Moses, 'I have seen these people, how stiff-necked they are'."

Stiff-necked! That appellation perfectly described Leland Gorse. And from what Sabine had learned about Nick, she was afraid he, too, was possessed of the same characteristic. How else could Nick have fought off his Divine calling so long? Unfortunately, in the Bible, the future of those who persisted in remaining stiff-necked did not end well.

Aware that some of the others might be looking out the window, Sabine switched on her car's headlights and pulled out onto the Russell Hill Road. She motored slowly up the paved road toward the cemetery. By the time she reached the Cross Road intersection, Nick and Leland had disappeared down over the crest of the hill in the direction of Maggie's house and Scotch Broom Acres.

No, Nick certainly wasn't waiting for her! He could not have missed her headlights pulling out of Rebecca's place.

Feeling as though she needed to sort things out, Sabine drove the car straight ahead, past the Cross Road. She calculated that Leland and Nick could use some time to wear their anger out with their feet. Plus, she needed space to consider the best course of action for herself.

Sabine didn't know what to think about the proposed solar farm. The novel project was sprung on them so suddenly, it had taken everyone by surprise. While she believed Rebecca had the right to do what she liked with her property, Sabine also decried the destruction of Wendell's woodlot, particularly the pine grove, which meant so much to Nick and Leland. But she could certainly understand Rebecca wanting to provide for herself and Tad. And she believed Robinson Crockett when he had said he was motivated by a desire to help Rebecca keep the old Russell farm in the family. Sabine thought she had detected a sincerity in the man that matched his down-to-earth appearance and presentation.

What was the problem, then?

The problem was—her heart was telling her she should support Nick, regardless of the consequences!

Whoa! Was she in love with him?

Sabine's pulse quickened as she pictured the modern-day Thoreau. She enjoyed spending time with him, learning about nature through him. She found Nick's outlook on life refreshing. Altogether, his essential nature was attractive and compelling. His tall, muscular frame suggested strength and safety: "Come to me—I'll protect you." When Nick looked at her, Sabine felt as though he really *saw* her. His ardent brown eyes glowed with an intensity that made her want to lose herself in his being. He awakened in her a desire to meld with him, presaging a spectacular passion.

Suddenly, a white-tailed deer leaped out from the roadside into the glare of her car's headlights. Sabine instinctively swerved to the left; the deer kiltered to the right. A collision was avoided, but only by inches. The deer, unharmed, bolted off into the thicket. Heart pounding from the adrenaline rush, Sabine pulled over to the side of the road and parked. She realized she was shaking.

That was a close call!

If there had been an accident, she would have been at fault, Sabine admitted to herself. She had been daydreaming, thinking about Nick, barely watching the road. She knew that deer were active on the Russell Hill Road, especially at dusk. Normally, she would have been watching the roadside for their eyes, glowing green in the headlights. But her mind had unconsciously shifted from dispassionately considering the solar project to fantasizing about Nick.

Sabine rolled down her widow to let in some fresh air. The cool evening breeze carried to her ears the musical melody of the spring peepers. The tiny chorus frogs sounded like sleighbells in the distance. Listening to the peepers Sabine felt her pulse slow. She inhaled deeply, her equilibrium restored.

Sabine decided resolutely that she must shake off her romantic daydreaming. She had been down that road once before, and where had it taken her? Total disaster, that's where! She must consider the good of everyone involved, not just allow her passions to lead her into building castles in the air. From what she had learned about the nature of Sovereign residents over the past nine months, she suspected that the proposed solar farm was going to divide the town. As the current minister of the Sovereign Union Church, she could not take sides. Her job required her to remain level-headed, open-minded, and uncompromised. She must be able to help people in both camps!

True, Leland was not one of her parishioners, but Rebecca was. And Maggie had told Sabine that the job required her to be a pastor to the entire Sovereign community, not just to those who showed up at church.

"The church is the lynchpin of Sovereign," Maggie had said to Sabine, before she had accepted the interim ministry position. "It helps keep us together as a community. Everybody in town looks forward to our suppers and other fundraisers. Whether people come to church or not—and even to those who don't believe in God—the church still represents something special. I know several godless old-timers who were married here, and have never been back to church since. But each one of them would do anything to help keep the lights on. If you take this job, you'll need to be a pastor to everyone, whether they know it or not. That's how small church ministry works in Maine."

As Sabine sat in her car listening to the spring peepers, thinking things over, she wondered if she could faithfully fulfill the duties of her pastoral calling if she and Nick became romantically involved. From his words and actions this evening, she knew he was interested in pursuing a relationship with her. But a dark divide now loomed up between them, threatening to separate them before they had even connected.

After careful consideration, Sabine decided she would have faith. If she and Nick were meant to be together, they would work things out. Yes, she would have faith in him. In herself. And in the power of love.

With this new conviction, Sabine pulled back out onto the road. She motored up to Stephen Danforth's driveway and turned the car around. By the time she caught up to Nick and Leland on the Cross Road, they were half-way to Scotch Broom Acres.

As Sabine approached, the two men moved over to the far right, stopping beside the road. Nick shielded his eyes from her headlights to see who was coming. She slowed the vehicle to a stop and rolled down the passenger window. "Want a ride, fellas?" she asked, cheerily.

"Pretty dem good timing, Miss Sabine. I was gettin' tuckered out," admitted Leland, climbing into the front seat.

"Thanks," said Nick, opening the rear door and folding his large frame into the backseat behind Leland.

"I was havin' trouble keeping up with Walden," the old woodchopper continued. "Dem long-legged fella, ain't he?"

"He sure is," replied Sabine, with a light laugh.

Sabine sought Nick's face in the rearview mirror. She could see through his bushy beard that his lips were compressed. His jaw jutted out in stern determination. Their eyes met. A heightened sense of awareness passed between them. Sabine forced herself to look away from his impassioned gaze. She put the car in drive and moved slowly up the dirt road. "Help me keep a lookout for deer, please. I almost hit one a few minutes ago."

"Real hazards, ain't they?" Leland replied, assuming Sabine was speaking to him. "Almost as bad as them wild turkeys the state introduced back in the eighties. Ain't they multiplied! Them dem things clutter up the roadways and—worse—they can never figger out which way they wants to go."

"That's for sure! The only time I feel safe from turkeys running across the road is at night when they've gone up to roost. But then, that's when the deer come out to play."

The conversation between Sabine and Leland continued in the same light-hearted vein until they reached his family's farm five minutes later. Nothing was mentioned about the solar project. More worrisome to Sabine, however, was that Nick had not said a word, not even to inquire how she was after the near collision with the deer.

Sabine turned into the driveway at Scotch Broom Acres, tires crunching upon the loose gravel. She stopped in front of the attached ell of the pretty white farmhouse, where an outdoor light illuminated the granite stoop.

"Thank you, muchly," said Leland, popping open the door. A whiff of cow manure from the barn seeped into the vehicle.

"Anytime," said Sabine, watching as the elderly man, his limbs stiffening in the damp evening air, hobbled toward the shed.

Nick also exited the vehicle. But instead of taking the seat that Leland had vacated, as Sabine anticipated, he closed the car door and came around to the driver's side. She rolled down her window.

He rested his right palm against the upper doorframe and leaned down to speak to her. "I'm going to hang with Leland for a while."

Sabine was surprised and disappointed. She had been expecting to give him a ride, at least to Maggie's place. She was hoping they could talk over what had happened at Rebecca's. Although determined not to take sides in the dissension over the solar farm, she was anxious to know what Nick was thinking and feeling about the proposed project.

"Can I see you tomorrow?" he asked.

"Are you coming to church?"

Nick hesitated. "Not tomorrow. Can we meet up after?"

"I have office hours until three," she reminded him. "But let's meet on the trail like we did before. Only this time I'd like to come in from Maggie's end. Say, around three-thirty?"

"I'll be there." Nick pushed away from the car so she could turn the vehicle around.

Sabine slipped the engine into reverse, but kept her foot on the brake, loath to leave him. "How will you get home?"

"Walk. Like I always do."

"In the dark? The moon isn't even up yet!"

"It's a new moon, Sabine. There won't be any moonlight. Don't worry," he added, in a gentler tone of voice. "Ryan will lend me a flashlight. I'll be fine."

"Are you sure?"

He nodded. "Thanks for worrying about me."

"I care," she replied, simply.

"Yeah, me, too."

He waited and watched as she turned around in the dooryard, being careful not to hit the old John Deere tractor parked in front of the barn. When she was safely headed in the right direction, Nick waved, and headed into the house.

Despite his somewhat reassuring wave, Sabine was worried. Why was Nick staying with Leland? Wendell's best friend had obviously calmed down. Leland didn't seem to need emotional support now. Were the two men going to continue their conversation about the solar farm?

Or were they going to hatch plans to stop the project!

As Sabine drove back over the Cross Road on the way to her cabin, her instinct was to stop at Maggie's house and confer with her mentor. She noted as she approached the former schoolhouse that the indoor lights were on, signaling Maggie and Duncan had returned home from Rebecca's. She decided, however, that it was too soon to act on unfounded suspicions about Nick and Leland. Plus, she could be wrong about the residents of Sovereign. Maybe the townspeople would welcome Robinson Crockett's solar farm with open arms?

Sabine decided she would wait for the future to reveal itself. She calculated it wouldn't take long.

Chapter 10

Two Ministers Too Many

"Maybe I should go to church today?" Maggie suggested to her husband the next morning, while the two were at the sink washing up the breakfast dishes. "Just to make sure everything's alright."

"Everything?" questioned Duncan. He was drying the silverplate cutlery one piece at a time, as Maggie's grandmother had taught her and as she had instructed him. "Don't you mean you want to know what everyone thinks about the solar farm?"

"Smarty!" Maggie rinsed out a cup and placed it upside down onto the wooden dish drainer. "If Rebecca goes to church, which she usually does, I hardly think people will talk about it. Besides, all her friends will support the solar farm."

"I didn't get that impression last night. Leland didn't seem too happy about Wendell's trees being cut down."

"He'll come around—eventually."

"Do you really believe that?"

Maggie started to respond, but her husband uncharacteristically cut her off before she could reply. "Oh, I heard you reassure Rebecca that Leland will come around, but in your heart, you must know—heck, even I know!—that Leland will never get over the clear-cutting of his best friend's woodlot." Duncan tossed a dry spoon into the silverware drawer. The heavy silver spoon landed in its proper spot with a decided clang.

"Are you finished? Or ..."

"And what about Wendell's pine grove?" Duncan continued, as if Maggie hadn't spoken. "I happen to know those pine trees meant the world to Wendell. He's been thinning that grove for forty-five years, he said. Wendell took me down and showed me his pines two years ago. He was very proud of them."

Maggie squeezed out the sponge. She set the sponge on the sink edge and turned to face her husband. "Wendell was growing those pine trees to be cut," she pointed out. "He wanted the money from the sale of those trees to pay for Tad's education. Now they will. What's the big deal?"

"Tad is only nine! He doesn't need the money now. Besides, I hardly think Wendell would have clearcut his pine grove."

"Are we really going to argue about Rebecca's solar farm?"

"We're not arguing—we're discussing it," Duncan replied, heaving a fork into the drawer.

"You don't need to take your anger out on my grandmother's silverplate, Duncan."

"I'm not angry. Just—unsettled. I have difficulty picturing a solar farm on Wendell's woodlot. The fields, sure. But not the entire woodlot."

"It's not Wendell's woodlot anymore, is it?" asked Maggie, feeling her own ire rising. "Those three hundred acres belong to Rebecca now, and she can do whatever the heck she wants with them!"

"Of course."

"Besides," Maggie added, softening toward her husband, "Rebecca said Wendell wanted this solar farm project. Robinson was working with him on the project before he died. I think it's admirable of Rebecca to continue the solar farm as his legacy."

"But Wendell didn't sign any agreement with Robinson Crockett, did he? Don't you think this fellow could be taking advantage of Rebecca?"

The idea that the solar farm developer was taking advantage of their rather naive widowed friend had, in fact, occurred to Maggie during the night. But she was reluctant to admit it in the middle of an argument with her husband. "No, I don't—at least, I don't think he means to take advantage of her. Robinson seems very nice."

"Oh, he's friendly enough, I'll give him that," Duncan replied. He carefully draped the dish towel over the wooden dish rack. "But that doesn't mean he's honest."

Maggie was dismayed. "You don't think Rob would cheat Rebecca?"

"I don't know. I don't know enough about him or the project, yet."

Maggie thought a moment. If Duncan—calm, moderate Duncan—was worried about the proposed solar project, then there might be good reason to worry. "Maybe Ryan can review the solar agreement to make sure everything's copacetic?"

"I think it's probably too late for that. Rebecca has already signed the contract. But that brings up another suspicious point—why isn't Ryan involved? He does all the legal work for everyone in Sovereign. Yet Ryan was as surprised as the rest of us when Robinson Crockett made his announcement."

This fact was so obvious, Maggie was surprised she hadn't thought of it herself. Ryan MacDonald always did the legal work for Wendell and Rebecca. Why wasn't Ryan helping with the solar farm?

Duncan slid the silverware drawer shut. "I'm sorry I'm grumpy this morning," he said, contritely. "I didn't sleep very well. I laid awake thinking about Wendell's woodlot being cut down for this project."

Me, too, Maggie wanted to admit. But she didn't.

"But, back to where we started this conversation," he continued. "No, I don't think you should go to church this morning. You're not the minister now, Maggie; Sabine is. And if there's a problem in the congregation—or the greater Sovereign community—*she* should be the one to address it, not you."

"Ouch! Sounds like you want to mothball me."

"You mothballed yourself when you went on sabbatical and talked Sabine into taking your place." He reached for her hand. "I know it's difficult for you to let go, but you and I need to sit this one out, otherwise, Sovereign will have two ministers too many."

Maggie offered up a small sigh. "I hate it that you're so logical. But I love you for it at the same time."

Duncan kissed her forehead, then released her. "Didn't you say something about attacking your rhubarb patch today? I saw some seed heads in there when I emptied the compost last night."

"You did not! The seed heads can't be coming already—it's too soon."

"Then some alien-looking white thing is taking over your rhubarb."

"Arrgh! Climate change," Maggie expostulated. "We never used to have such hot weather in the spring. Well, I'm for Rebecca's solar farm 100%. We need to do everything we can to replace fossil fuels!"

"We can agree on that, anyway," Duncan said with a smile. "But you'd better get onto those seed heads, or your rhubarb won't last until the strawberries come in. And I know for a fact that your husband is looking forward to a fresh strawberry-rhubarb pie this summer."

By nine o'clock Maggie was knee-deep in her rhubarb patch chopping off the tall white seed heads that had dared to surface before their time. The early spring heat and rain had acted as a growth catalyst, maturing the rhubarb by several weeks. When Maggie saw the dozens of white seedheads sticking up, she kicked herself for becoming so preoccupied with Memorial Day that she had neglected her rhubarb.

Maggie's patch had come with her home, formerly a one-room schoolhouse where all the neighborhood children had learned their ABCs. (The nail holes for their little desks, although filled in, could still be seen in her kitchen floor.) The four-foot by twenty-foot, south-facing patch grew against a stone wall marking the boundary line between Maggie's and Henry Trow's properties. She guessed the rhubarb patch was at least a hundred years old and had likely been planted by a former teacher. Maggie, who loved rhubarb, blessed this unknown individual for giving her the springtime treat.

After Maggie disposed of the protruding seedheads, she pushed aside the dark-green leaves the size of elephant ears and groped around the base of the plants for upcoming buds. "Gotcha!" she exclaimed, grasping hold of a slippery, immature seedhead, which had been trying to pass itself off as an up-and-coming rhubarb stalk. She sliced across the pink neck of the false stalk containing the plump bud, releasing the rhubarb's sour essence. Her mouth puckered. Ah, fresh rhubarb!

Maggie tossed the tip into an open spot between plants. She always distributed the cut seedheads throughout her rhubarb patch, convinced (rightly or not, she didn't know) that the patch had expanded thanks to the grounded seeds. If left uncut, the seedheads flowered into gauzy white blooms, sapping the plant's energy. The advent of seedheads spelled the end of juicy rhubarb and the beginning of woody stalks. "And nobody likes woody rhubarb," she thought to herself, as she mercilessly sliced off another immature seedhead, arresting the plant's development. "Especially in pies!"

Maggie felt herself beginning to perspire. The temperature was in the low sixties when she had started in her rhubarb patch, but had risen ten degrees once the sun crested the tops of the softwoods in Henry's surrounding woodlot. The old fieldstone wall behind the patch soaked up the May sun, warming the micro environment around it. A solitary chipmunk, with whom Maggie was familiar, joined her as she worked. The chipmunk cheeped companionably as its tiny brown body darted in and out of the rock wall.

"Hello to you, Mr. Chippy," Maggie said. She gripped a thick rhubarb stem with both hands and yanked it up, separating the stalk from the rhizome base. She chopped off the leaf with her knife and placed the long stalk into her large garden trug. She picked up the leaf and tossed it into a pile. "Yes, I know, the bird feeders are empty. I'll get to them soon."

Maggie harvested several stalks from the one plant— performing a judicious thinning—and moved onto the next. She began to hum happily as she harvested rhubarb, thinking of all the delicious goodies she would bake that day. Some of the treats, such as rhubarb sauce and rhubarb bread, would be consumed now. Some would be enjoyed over the upcoming winter. In Maine, it was never too early to start stocking the freezer for winter, and rhubarb presented the first opportunity.

"I left you a pile of rhubarb leaves to compost," Maggie said to her husband, when she returned to their country kitchen.

Duncan glanced up from the table, where he was balancing the checkbook. "That's quite a haul you have there," he remarked. "Want me to help you process that?"

Maggie heaved her loaded garden trug of rhubarb stalks onto the counter. "No thanks. I'll do it myself, said the Little Red Hen."

"Wasn't she the chicken in the story who harvested and ground the wheat, cooked the bread, and—ate it all herself?"

"Yes, because nobody offered to help the poor thing. Miss Hastings told me once that 'The Little Red Hen' was one of her schoolkids' favorite songs."

Duncan folded the checkbook and stood up. "I'd like the record to show I offered to help, Ms. Hen." He fished the car keys out of the orange-colored Carnival glass candy dish strategically located atop the pine chiffonier next to the door.

"Offer noted—you can have all the rhubarb bread you want. Where are you going?"

"Down to Gilpin's to get the weekend paper. Need anything at the store?"

"No, thanks. I think I have everything I need for my bread and for dinner." Maggie started unloading the rhubarb into the sink. She suddenly recollected, however, that some of the Old Farts (of which self-identifying group Leland Gorse was one) might be at the general store, holding forth about the proposed solar farm. "Maybe ..." she began, then abruptly broke off.

"Maybe what?"

"Never mind." She faced the sink and turned the water faucet on full bore.

"Maybe I could find out if people are talking about the solar farm?" Duncan guessed.

"I can't hear you—I'm running water."

Her husband lightly clinked the key against the translucent orange dish.

"Don't chip my grandmother's dish!"

"You're a terrible liar, Maggie. If someone speaks to me about Rebecca's project, I'll listen. But I'm not probing for gossip." With this blunt pronouncement, Duncan departed for the Gilpin's General Store.

While Duncan was gone, Maggie chopped up three cups of rhubarb and mixed up a double batch of rhubarb bread. She popped the loaf pans into the oven and set the timer. As she was chopping up the balance of the stalks for rhubarb sauce, the shrill ringtone of their landline, which they maintained because of her position with the church, sounded. Maggie debated letting the phone ring, but reconsidered when she realized one of their friends could be calling to discuss Rebecca's surprise announcement last evening. She hastily rinsed off her hands, dried them on the dish towel, and picked up the phone.

Maggie was surprised to discover Nora, Duncan's daughter, on the other end. "Nora!" she exclaimed, glancing at the Regulator wall clock. Eleven-ten—or nine-ten in North Dakota. It was unusual for Nora to call so early. She hoped there wasn't anything wrong. "How are you, dear? Your father's gone to the store. He should be home soon, though."

"That's OK, Maggie. I can talk to you. Pops can call me another time. It's all good. I'm just checking in."

Maggie was relieved nothing was wrong with Nora. She was just being Nora. "Everything's fine, here, too. Your father's cholesterol is way too high, but I'm probably the culprit. I've got rhubarb bread in the oven now."

"Yum! I wish I was there to eat it. I love your rhubarb bread."

"I wish you were here, too. We miss you." Maggie wanted to suggest Nora come for a visit, but decided—with no little regret—that it wasn't her place to meddle in Duncan's relationship with his children. How would she feel if he meddled between her and Nellie? "How's work? Still telecommuting?"

"Oh, ya. Work's the same. Boring as ever. What's the latest news in Sovereign?"

Maggie thought a moment. "Leland says Miss Crump brings her chickens into the kitchen on cold nights."

Nora laughed. "That sounds just like her. She's such a funny old lady. Do you think Miss Crump will ever die?"

"Not until she gets the Boston Post cane. She's determined to outlive Bessie Patterson, at least that's what Bessie says—Bessie has Sovereign's Post cane now. Miss Crump's father had the cane, and apparently, she's hanging on just so she can get the cane back in the family."

"How old is Bessie Patterson?"

"One hundred and two—and still going strong. Miss Crump will have to wait a while longer for the Post cane, I'm afraid."

"Too funny! What else is going on in town?" Nora inquired. "What are the Old Farts at Gilpin's talking about these days? Anyone win the Power Ball?"

When Nora mentioned the Old Farts, Maggie instantly thought of the solar farm. But Nora couldn't have heard about the proposed project already, could she? Nick didn't even own a cell phone, and if he did, he was unlikely to call his sister. "We certainly didn't win the Power Ball," she answered. "And the only other news I know is that somebody dumped some old tires next to the historical society."

"Haha. Maybe they thought tires were collectable. That's all the gossip?"

Maggie wondered if she should tell Nora about Rebecca's solar farm, but decided it was better not to mention it. Duncan was obviously bothered by the project and she didn't want to do or say anything until she and he had worked out their differences. "That's the latest Sovereign scoop, unless your father finds out something interesting at the store. Do you have Memorial Day off?"

"Yep. A friend and I are going hiking tomorrow in Theodore Roosevelt National Park. You'd love the place.

The badlands are super colorful and there's lots of wildlife, like bison, bighorn sheep, and elk."

"Sounds like my kind of place. By friend, do you mean a special friend?" Maggie suggested.

"Nice try, Maggie, but no, just a girlfriend."

"Can't blame a grandma for looking out for more grandchildren! I'll only have two when Nellie's baby is born."

"You better get to work on Nick then," quipped Nora. "I can't believe you haven't got him hooked up with Sabine yet. You're slipping, Maggie."

"I'm trying, believe me! But your brother is a hard case."

"Tell me about it. Well, say 'hi' to Pops, for me. I'm heading to the laundromat now. Text me if he comes home with any juicy gossip."

"Will do. Be careful hiking, dear," said Maggie, but Nora had already ended the call.

Maggie shook her head. Millennials! She would never understand them.

Imagine Nora calling to find out the local Sovereign gossip! It was almost as though Duncan's daughter was fishing for something.

But what could Nora be fishing for?

And why?

Chapter 11

No More Killing Frost

Duncan returned not long after Maggie's phone conversation with Nora. He flopped the thick weekend edition of the *Bangor Daily News* onto the kitchen table. "No news down to the store," he reported, unbuttoning his flannel shirt.

Maggie, who was scooping out sugar for the rhubarb sauce, turned around and flourished the measuring cup at him. "Well, I have some news for you—Nora called."

"Nora! At this hour? Is everything OK?"

"Relax, dear. Nora just wanted to chat. You can call her later, she said. She's headed for the laundromat now."

"Figures she'd call while I was out," Duncan groused. "Why didn't she call me on my cell?"

"Not sure. Maybe she tried, but you were out of range." Maggie turned back to the sugar jar. "The store is in kind of a hollow."

"What did she have to say?"

"Not much. She and a girlfriend are going hiking tomorrow. Nora seemed more interested in the local Sovereign gossip than what was going on in her own life. Maybe she's missing us?"

"I doubt it," Duncan replied, flipping the newspaper open to the sports section. "She probably had an ulterior motive. I'll call her later. Ah! The Red Sox are playing the Milwaukee Brewers tomorrow," he added. "They'll probably lose that one."

Maggie dropped the measuring cup back into the jar and replaced the glass lid with a clink. "So, nothing from the Old Farts?" she prodded him, dusting the sugar off her hands.

Duncan laid down the paper. "Nope. Gray was the only one in the store while I was there. He said Leland didn't come in for his usual morning donut—I didn't ask, either, Gray offered that information up—and Maynard Nutter and John Woods were still at church. Gray must have thought I was looking for some of the other Old Farts to hang out with." Thirty-year-old Gray Gilpin ran the general store now that his grandfather Ralph Gilpin had retired. The store was a landmark in town and had been in the Gilpin family for several generations.

"John Woods went to church!" Maggie expostulated. "That's news. He almost never comes to church." Woods was the town of Sovereign's stoic First Selectman.

"Maybe he likes a pretty young minister better than a pretty mature minister?"

"Thanks a lot! But how do you know John was at church?"

"Because Gray *said* John and Ruth were at church, although how he would know that when he was at the store the whole time is a mystery to me."

"You forget that our accompanist is married to Gray. Courtney must have left right after the service without going to coffee hour." Maggie opened the oven and peeped at the rhubarb bread. "Good to see you consider yourself one of the Old Farts, now," she added, as retribution for his remark about "pretty young ministers."

"Hey, if being an Old Fart nets me free coffee and donuts every day, count me in! Mmm, your bread smells great."

"Donut, singular," she corrected him. "The first donut is free. After that, the Old Farts have to pay. And nobody can eat just one of Courtney's donuts."

"I knew there was a catch. " Duncan stood up to remove his shirt, draping the flannel across the back of his chair. "Thank goodness I have a wife who likes to cook."

"That's only because your wife likes to eat."

He leaned back against the chiffonier and folded his arms. "You know, I got the feeling Gray wanted me to ask him about the solar farm."

Maggie set the potholders on the counter. "What makes you say that?"

"Just something about the way he acted; some of the things he said."

"Maybe Gray was trying to feel you out about the solar project? Find out what you think about it—without sharing what else he's heard? Gray is a very prudent young man."

"That's possible."

"But if that's what Gray was doing, it doesn't bode well," she added. Maggie placed her white enamelware stock pot with the rhubarb and sugar water onto the stovetop and clicked on the gas burner.

"No?"

"No. It suggests—to me, anyway—that the town is beginning to take sides."

"Already? Rebecca and Robinson only told us about the solar farm last night!"

"Sixteen hours is plenty of time for word to get around this town." She moved to the sink and began scrubbing up three large Yukon Gold potatoes.

"Forget it—I probably imagined it. I've got solar farm on the brain this morning. How much longer on your rhubarb bread?"

"Five minutes. But the bread has to cool completely before it can be cut. The rhubarb chunks make the bread crumbly. Now where are you going?"

Duncan, who was half-way out the door, stopped in his tracks. "Up to the cemetery to water the geraniums."

"Again? I'm starting to think you and Frank Whitehouse have some sort of bromance going."

"Hey, I like the old fellow. He's probably not there, anyway. Are we expecting company for dinner?" Duncan asked, nodding at the three scrubbed potatoes, awaiting their turn in the oven.

"I was hoping Nick might stop by," Maggie admitted.

"After the debacle with Leland and the solar farm last night? Don't count on it!" And with this final comment, her husband headed for the cemetery.

As Duncan had predicted, and much to Maggie's disappointment, Nick did not show up for Sunday dinner. She was pleasantly surprised, however, when Sabine dropped in shortly after three o'clock. When the young minister knocked, Maggie was reading the *Bangor Daily News* at the kitchen table, while Duncan was napping on the back porch. Sabine had shed her Sunday finery and was now dressed in tan denim shorts and a purple cotton tee-shirt. Her hair was pulled back into a neat pony-tail.

Noting that her visitor was wearing hiking boots, Maggie's curiosity was raised, as well as her hopes. But she made no mention of Sabine's attire, nor did she mention Nick. "How was church today?" she asked instead, pushing the newspaper aside and indicating Sabine should take her customary seat at the table. "I hear John Woods was there."

Sabine was momentarily startled. "How did you know?"

"I have my sources," Maggie replied, smiling. She slid into her own chair.

"Yes, John and Ruth were both at church."

"Must have been a full house?"

"I'd hardly say that. The first four rows were almost empty," answered Sabine.

"That's par for the course. The back rows must have been pretty crowded, then?"

"Let's just say there was a lot of hymnal sharing happening up back."

Maggie laughed. "Would you like a piece of rhubarb bread? Freshly baked. I made it while you were enlightening the barbarians."

Sabine leaned forward and folded her hands on the cloth-covered table. "Maybe later, thanks. This is a professional call. I need some advice, Maggie."

Maggie, taking note of the young woman's change of tone, instantly adopted her pastoral demeanor. "How can I help?"

Sabine did not hold back. "I'm worried the town is heading toward a rupture over Rebecca's solar farm."

"Did anything happen at church?"

"Not at church, but at coffee hour. Mr. Trow made a point of congratulating Rebecca on the solar project, loudly, I might add. On hearing his congratulations, several people got up and walked out."

"Who?" demanded Maggie, angry that some of her parishioners had acted so boorishly toward the young widow.

"I'd rather not say."

"Are you sure they left because of the solar farm? They could have finished their coffee?"

Sabine shook her head. "Two of them had just sat down with coffee and cake. The third was at a different table. But that isn't the only thing. I overheard someone else tell

Rebecca she should—and I quote—'go back to Boston and take that Crockett fella with her.'"

"What?!" Maggie was shocked. This didn't sound like anyone she knew. Nobody in Sovereign would make such an ugly remark to Rebecca! Wendell's family was one of the town's original settlers. He himself had been beloved by everyone; the turnout for his funeral had been tremendous. No—no local who knew Rebecca or had known Wendell would have said such a thing. The person who issued that nasty remark must have been from Dixmont or Unity. "What did Rebecca do?"

"She put her head down on the table and burst into tears. Nellie got up immediately to comfort Rebecca, as well as several others …"

"Thank goodness!"

"… but I'm afraid the damage was done. We consoled Rebecca as best we could, but there really wasn't much any of us could say to take away the sting of that hurtful remark. Rebecca was heartbroken at being told to go back to Boston."

"I'm sure she was."

"She was very hurt to hear that she's not a fully-fledged member of the community. Or a welcome one."

Maggie heard the back screen door creak. Their voices must have woken Duncan from his nap. He stayed where he was, however, either on the back porch or in the living room, probably realizing the nature of Sabine's visit. "I can relate," said Maggie. "It hurt me when somebody once told me I was from Away."

"Seriously? But you're from Maine!"

"Yep. But not from Troy—that's where I was at the time, at the Troy General Store. And I was born in Winslow, only eighteen miles away from that store."

"People can be so thoughtless!"

"Thoughtless, and downright cruel, sometimes," Maggie agreed. "But I survived, and Rebecca will too. These things happen."

Sabine frowned. Maggie realized that her reassurance wasn't what the young pastor wanted to hear. But Sabine was new to the ministry, not an adept like Maggie. "People are mostly good," she explained. "Differences arise, true, but over time those differences dissipate. Hurt feelings, if dealt with properly, can often lead to a higher level of understanding and greater fellowship between the two parties."

"Hmm," Sabine replied, unconvinced.

"I wrote a sermon once about how special Sovereign is," Maggie continued. "I called it, 'A Frost Pocket of Goodness,' because the killing frost came just in time to quench all budding attempts at small-mindedness and mean-spiritedness. Evil doesn't exist in Sovereign, I said then, and I still believe it. I think it's because the early Sovereign settlers were forced to get along to survive. For the good of themselves—and others—they quashed their hate and greed, and their self-denial passed down through the generations. Love is Lord of All in Sovereign! Don't worry, Sabine, this too shall pass." Maggie, who had wound up to a poetic pitch during the recollection of her former sermon, now sat back in her chair, satisfied she had provided Sabine with the advice she needed.

Sabine, however, was not satisfied. "How long ago did you give that sermon?" she inquired.

Maggie found she could not remember the year she'd preached about Sovereign as a frost pocket of goodness. "I'd have to look it up. I can get you a copy if you'd like. I think it was one of my better pastoral messages."

"Was it last year?" Sabine persisted.

"No, it was probably 2010 or 2011."

"2010 or 2011! That was fifteen years ago. Things have changed since then, Maggie. And not for the better, either."

Maggie began to feel uncomfortable. Fifteen years! That *was* a long time ago. That was back when Twitter was still Twitter!

"Sovereign's not immune to the social changes that have occurred in America over the past decade," Sabine said earnestly. "Even here, I've noticed people have gravitated into two disparate groups. They watch different television programs; listen to different radio broadcasts; post on different social media platforms; and watch opposing YouTube channels. And what's the result? People in one group think the other group are … are brainless nitwits blindly following their political leaders like lemmings!"

"There's some truth to that," Maggie admitted.

"I love your metaphor, but I'm not sure you can still proclaim that Sovereign is a frost pocket of goodness. And while I'd like to wait for a killing frost to straighten things out, it's more in my nature to be proactive."

"Come to think of it, we don't get many killing frosts these days. Chalk another one up to climate change!"

Sabine stood up. "I'd better go. I'm running late. Thanks for taking the time to see me."

Maggie also rose up. "I'm sorry I couldn't be more help."

"It's good to have someone to talk to. I appreciate your point of view, but …" the young minister broke off.

"But you have to do what you think is right. As well you should!" Maggie moved to the counter and took a slicing knife down from the magnetic wall holder. "Let me cut you a piece of rhubarb bread before you go."

"Thanks. Could I have two pieces? I'm meeting up with someone on the trail. I'm going to leave my car here, if that's OK?"

Maggie's ears perked up. She ignored the last question about parking in the driveway, and went right to the heart of the matter. "Anyone we know?" she asked, hopefully. She sliced two large pieces from the loaf and wrapped the rhubarb bread in a white, flour-sack dish towel.

"Could be," Sabine replied with smile. "Could be!"

"Then, park where ever you like!"

Sabine exited with a laugh. Maggie waited for the outer door to close behind the young minister. "Don't even say it," she advised her husband, whom she knew had overheard most of their conversation. "I know, I blew that pastoral consultation."

Duncan came around the corner from the living room. "You get points for honesty."

"Maybe it *is* time for me to retire?" she mused. "I seem to be outdated and out-of-touch. On top of that, I'm just plain old!"

"You're not old." He put his arm around her shoulder and gave her a reassuring squeeze. "Maybe a little out-of-touch with the 'real world,' as they call it. We're not used to strife in Sovereign, especially between our friends. I suppose it had to come, sometime. Eventually, things will work themselves out and all our friends will be friends once again."

"How can you be so sure?"

"Because my wife said so—and far be it from me to say my wife is ever wrong."

Chapter 12

Nick's Calling

Sabine had only a short walk on the narrow trail from Maggie's house before connecting with the main Sovereign Woods trail. When she reached the juncture, she pulled her phone out of her back pocket and checked the time. Almost four o'clock. She had stayed longer with Maggie than she had planned. Sabine picked up her pace. She couldn't even text Nick she was running late because he didn't have a phone!

She turned a corner on the trail and spied the young woodsman pacing back and forth in a clearing near a mast oak tree in full verdure. "Nick!" Sabine called, waving. Thank goodness he hadn't given up on her.

She continued walking at her steady pace, but Nick strode rapidly toward her. He was unnaturally animated, Sabine thought, moving with a zeal that had been altogether missing from their parting the prior evening. Uneasiness stole over her. Was he pleased to see her again? Or was his ebullience due to some other cause?

"There you are! I knew you'd come," Nick declared.

"Sorry I'm late. I was visiting Maggie. Have you been waiting long?"

"Not a clue! Time means nothing to me, now."

Now? Sabine wondered. She attempted to shake off a heightened sense of foreboding. She unfolded the white dish towel and showed the two slices of rhubarb bread to Nick. "Look what Maggie packed for us—freshly baked this morning."

"Food? I'm not hungry! I've been waiting all night to talk to you."

Sabine didn't know whether to be pleased or dismayed by his response. She rewrapped the bread. "Should we sit? Or keep walking?"

"I can't sit." Nick clasped her free hand and pulled her along the trail northbound in the direction of the Millett Rock—and Wendell's pine grove. "Let's walk."

Even with her long legs, Sabine had all she could do to keep up with him. When Nick had first taken her hand, she felt the thrill of his touch. But as he propelled her forward, she realized that the feeling was not reciprocal. Whatever it was that was driving Nick, it was not infatuation with her. Her own amour faded.

She stumbled over a tree root. Nick instinctively pulled her up, stopping short. "Sorry! I'll slow down."

"Thanks. I need to catch my breath."

Sabine pushed some loose hair from her ponytail out of her eyes. She clutched her soft bundle, which she had managed to hang onto when she tripped. She hoped she hadn't squashed the rhubarb bread. She wanted to unwrap the bread again and check, but decided against it. In his present mood, such a prosaic act would surely net a derogatory comment from Nick, who was waiting for her to get herself together so they could continue. "There's not much birdsong today, is there?" she remarked, glancing around the quiet woods. "I wonder why?"

"Let God take care of the birds, Sabine," he replied impatiently. "They're not our worry. We have work to do."

"What kind of work?"

"We've got to save Wendell's pine stand—our forest cathedral. That's my calling! But I need your help."

His calling? Sabine was so surprised, this time she almost did drop the bread.

Nick, noting her preoccupation with the white bundle, relieved her of her burden. He set the wrapped rhubarb bread on a sawed-off tree stump next to the trail. He grasped both her hands and looked deeply into her eyes. "You must feel the same way I do? We've got to stop Robinson Crockett from cutting down Wendell's trees!"

Although Sabine had expected his opposition to the solar farm, she was startled by the violence of Nick's proclamation. His eyes blazed; his body was taut with passion, but not the passion she hoped for.

"God is calling me to save the trees! Don't you know it, Sabine? Can't you feel it? I'm a crude instrument, for sure," he said, with an unnatural, self-deprecating laugh, "but a willing and useful tool. You said God has a purpose for me and you were right!"

He had misunderstood her! Misunderstood the nature of the Divine call. She must correct his misunderstanding before it was too late. "A calling is a way to glorify God, not glorify ourselves, Nick."

"I *am* glorifying God, by protecting the woodland." He dropped her hands and gestured at the forest around them. "Can't you see it? Here's one small slice of the Garden of Eden. It's under threat from a snake, and I'm going to save it."

Sabine looked around, but barely registered the various trees. She saw only discord and disunity looming. "But Rebecca's trees aren't yours to save."

"You're wrong about that," he retorted, with a proud toss of his dark head. "Nobody can own the trees—they belong to all of us. Ask any member of the Penobscot, Passamoquoddy, and Mi'kmaq tribes—they'll tell you. We don't own the land; the land owns us. We have a responsibility to protect and defend it."

"Nick! Nick! I'm afraid you're letting your emotions run away with you. Please, please! Listen to me," she pleaded, taking him by the hand. "You're talking about picking a fight with your friends and neighbors."

"Robinson Crockett isn't my neighbor or my friend."

"Rebecca is your friend. What about her? What about little Tad? How will they feel if you turn against them? If you turn the town against them?"

Nick's eyebrows constricted as doubt flashed across his face. Sabine knew she had reached him, probably by mentioning Tad. Nick was very fond of the neighborhood children.

A moment later, however, he squared his shoulders resolutely. "I have to do what I think is right."

"Oh, that's what we tell ourselves when we want to justify doing something we know we shouldn't do!" Sabine was uncomfortably aware that she herself had said the very same thing to Maggie only half an hour ago. Somehow her avowal seemed different than his, though.

"I'm not trying to justify myself." Nick shook off her hand and thumped his chest with the flat of his fist. "I know in my heart that God is calling me to protect Wendell's trees! I thought you'd be on my side?"

"I can't take sides, Nick."

"Can't? Or won't?"

"I suppose it's the same thing. My job is to throw oil upon the troubled waters, not gasoline. You forget, I'm the minister of the Sovereign Union Church."

"All the more reason for you to take a stand, show people what's right!"

"Who am I to judge what's right or wrong in this case? I've only been in town a short while. Who are you to judge?" she accosted him, becoming heated. "My job is to help keep this community from breaking apart. To stop friends from hurting one another, perhaps irreparably. To do that I need to keep an open mind; try to understand both sides. I don't want to see Wendell's pine grove cut down any more than you do, Nick. But I can also see that the solar farm provides a lot of benefits, not just income for Rebecca and Tad, either, but in helping save the planet. I thought you were all for stopping climate change?"

"Trees are a natural carbon sink," he shot back. "Cut them down and the sink disappears. It's stupid to cut down trees for a solar farm."

"So, you're a NIMBY?" she challenged, hands on hips.

"No, because in this case my backyard—and the damn thing would be directly in my backyard—is not the right place for a solar farm. Can't you see that?"

Sabine felt frustrated. Nick seemed to have an answer for everything. "What does Leland think?"

"*He's* on my side. Leland knows Wendell would never have agreed to cut down his woodlot, let alone his pine stand. Leland thinks Crockett is pulling a fast one over on Rebecca. We talked it over last night and came up with a plan. I was going to share the plan with you today, but maybe that's not such a good idea."

This was exactly what Sabine had worried about. She had feared Nick and Leland would put their heads together and hatch a plot to stop the solar farm.

"So far it's working, too," he added.

And then it struck her what he and Leland must have done. Sabine was aghast. How could they have done such a thing?

"Was it part of your plan to have Stephen Danforth tell Rebecca to go back to Boston?" she accosted him.

He smirked. "I'll have to give Leland the credit for that one."

She was shocked by Nick's lack of compassion. "That hurt her! Rebecca was mortified. She started crying at coffee hour, in front of Tad and ... and everyone. It was awful! I thought Leland was Wendell's best friend? How could he have done such a cruel thing to Wendell's widow? Why didn't you stop Leland?"

"Because we're going to do whatever it takes to protect Wendell's trees, no matter the consequences. Leland and I decided last night that it's time to draw the sword, and throw away the scabbard."

"What are you talking about?"

"That's what Stonewall Jackson said in a speech to Virginia Military Institute cadets after the firing on Fort Sumter: 'It's time to draw the sword, and throw away the scabbard.'"

Nick's words filled Sabine with horror. "You can't mean you want to start a Civil War in Sovereign?"

"Not with guns. But there are other ways to fight. Ours is a glorious and righteous cause, Sabine. I'm surprised you can't see it?"

"Oh, I see it, alright! A 'glorious and righteous cause' is what Stonewall Jackson called defending the south's slaved-based economy. Whenever I hear men—and it is primarily men—use the word 'glory,' I know things are going to go badly for everyone else. Chasing after glory seems to give you men permission to kill one another or do other crazy things."

Nick inhaled sharply, as though Sabine had sucker-punched him. "You think I'm crazy?"

"No, I don't think you're crazy," she backtracked, carefully. "I think you're intoxicated by the idea of saving the pine grove. Please, don't do anything rash," she beseeched him. Sabine reached for Nick's hand again, but he pushed her away.

"I can't believe you're not on my side! I thought you'd be on my side? I thought you cared?"

"I do! I do care. But …"

"But you can't support me when I need you the most."

"I can't take sides," she finished, lamely.

"So much for those fancy words about my calling! Thanks a lot, Pastor Burbury." With that, Nick leaped over the stump upon which he had set the rhubarb bread, and disappeared into the thick woods.

****

After Nick absconded, Sabine retrieved her bundle of bread and sank down onto the sawed-off stump. She berated herself for losing her temper with him. So much for keeping her pastoral cool! But his Stonewall Jackson quote had pushed her over the edge.

Nick couldn't possibly be thinking straight, or he wouldn't have quoted a Confederate Civil War hero. Especially a general who was responsible for the deaths and maiming of thousands of Union troops, in order to protect a way of life that revolved around the enslavement of African Americans. Perhaps if she had not lost her temper, she might have been able to hear what else Nick had to say and come to understand him better. She did not question his motives—she knew he believed that stopping the solar farm was right—but she had little hope now of helping him realize that his and Leland's plan to wage war against Robinson and Rebecca, rather than working with them to find a compromise, would ultimately hurt him as much as them. She also wondered how many others would be hurt along the way.

As she sat and thought, Sabine unwrapped the rhubarb bread and broke off a crusty corner piece. She popped the piece in her mouth, unconsciously savoring its mix of sweet and tart flavors. She leisurely proceeded to eat the slice piece by piece.

She marveled that Nick was suddenly possessed with a sense of destiny. How much had her suggestion of a divine calling contributed to his new vision? The way he talked— his use of the words "righteous" and "glory" and his reference to Stonewall Jackson—reminded her of the war-like language found in the Old Testament, as well as many of the Psalms:

> "There are glad songs of victory in the tents of the righteous:
> 'The right hand of the LORD does valiantly;
> the right hand of the LORD is exalted;
> the right hand of the LORD does valiantly.'"

Sabine was afraid that, rather than turning away from God's electric fence, Nick had barreled through the wire, taking the fence with him. He was careening toward spiritual disaster. She must find a way to get through to him. She must help him!

A bluejay screeched nearby, awakening the young minister from her contemplation. Sabine spotted the corvid perched half-way up a pine tree. The jay screeched again, this time its cry was answered by a distant mate. She glanced down at the second piece of rhubarb bread resting on the white towel in her lap, aware that the jay was also eyeing the bread, hoping for a treat.

"Oh, what the heck," she said, aloud. "He's not coming back." And—rather than share Nick's slice with the greedy jay—Sabine proceeded to eat the bread herself.

Chapter 13

Tuesday at the Songbird Clinic

On Mondays, Maggie volunteered at the Songbird Medical Clinic so that her daughter could have a day off. Nellie usually employed the time in grocery shopping and running errands. Because Monday was Memorial Day, however, Maggie had offered to work Tuesday instead.

When she arrived at Metcalf and Nellie's house, formerly the home of Sovereign's music teacher Miss Hastings, Nellie had already departed. Maggie found her son-in-law in the kitchen, washing Jana's face, preparing his daughter for the school bus.

"I'll walk her out," Maggie offered, seeing that Doctor Bart appeared somewhat flustered.

"Thanks. I'm running behind this morning. I've got some paperwork to finish from last night."

"Did you have an emergency?"

"Not really. Just a cut that required a few stitches." Doctor Bart handed Jana her lunchbox, then bent over and kissed his daughter on the head. "See you after school, Sunshine."

"Bye, Daddy."

"Let's get a move on Pumpkin," said Maggie, taking the seven-year-old by the hand. "I think I hear the bus coming up the hill from Tad's house."

"Tad will make Mrs. Hopkins wait," Jana replied, unperturbed. "I need my jacket." She slipped away from her grandmother and pulled on a light-weight spring coat. "Now, I'm ready, Grammie."

Mrs. Hopkins halted the bus at the end of the Lawson's driveway, and tooted the horn. Despite Maggie's tugging, Jana walked deliberately down the long driveway. Not for the first time Maggie was struck by how much the child took after her careful father rather than her impetuous mother.

Freckle-faced Tad, who was sitting in the front seat behind Mrs. Hopkins, waved vigorously through the window at his friend. "There's Tad," said Jana, waving back. "I told you he'd make Mrs. Hopkins wait."

Maggie stayed and watched while her granddaughter crossed the road and took a seat next to Tad in the front row. She waved goodbye to the children as the bus driver pulled slowly ahead toward the Cross Road. Maggie wondered as she waved if when the bus reached Scotch Broom Acres, Jana would give up her seat to Hope MacDonald. Probably. Alice Rose would not want to sit with her younger sister, and Hope was Tad's favorite of his three neighborhood girlfriends. By sitting with Alice Rose, Jana would make all the neighborhood kids happy.

"I hope Nellie's baby is a boy!" thought Maggie, returning to the house. "We need to even up the sexes in this neighborhood."

Maggie entered the attached medical clinic via the front door, which she knew Metcalf would unlock for her. She inspected the waiting area, noting that room was clean, the furniture neatly arranged, and all the toys had been returned to the toybox. Seeing everything was ready for their first patient, Maggie sat down at the nineteenth century Georgian tooled leather-top desk (formerly Miss Hastings' father's) and studied the appointment book. Nellie had left plenty of open time in the schedule, she noted, since much of the clinic's daily business was often walk-ins.

The eight-thirty appointment was Nathan Gould, Jessica Gould's two-month-old baby, whom his mother brought in for his first round of immunizations. Although the incumbent U.S. Director of Health and Human Services had called into question the safety of vaccines, Doctor Bart—who was loved and trusted by the entire Sovereign community—was able to convince parents that vaccines were not only safe, but important and efficacious.

Once in the exam room, baby Nathan accepted his shots with relatively few tears, which his mother quickly kissed away. Maggie, who watched through the open door, thought Jessica felt the shots more than her infant son did. She chuckled to herself when Metcalf offered the Tootsie Pop jar to the young woman. "Take two, they're cheap," he encouraged Jessica, with his winsome smile. "You might need the second one when the other kids get home from school." Jessica and her husband Brad had four other children, in addition to Nathan.

After Maggie had admired the baby—cooing at him and getting him to smile—Jessica, with Nathan in her arms, exited the clinic. In the interlude before the next appointment, Maggie asked her prudent son-in-law what he thought about the proposed solar farm.

"I haven't given it much thought," Metcalf admitted, as he sanitized the countertop in the exam room. "In general, I support solar farms. We need to wean ourselves from fossil fuels, and regrettably, the demand for electricity is increasing exponentially due to the build out of data centers. Data centers are a blight on rural communities, too, draining our water, power, and other resources. But I'm not sure we can stop them."

"I read in the *Bangor Daily News* that there was a large data center being built at Loring Air Force Base," said Maggie. "That probably means jobs for the people of Limestone. But why do we need so many data centers?"

"Data centers are necessary to support the rapid expansion of AI—artificial intelligence, not artificial insemination," her son-in-law clarified.

"I don't live under a rock, Metcalf! I know AI doesn't mean breeding cows anymore."

Doctor Bart grinned and tossed the soiled paper towel into the trash. "Just making sure. Anyway, to answer your question, the high-performance computing infrastructure required for AI model training takes an enormous amount of electricity. Did you know, by 2030, data centers are estimated to consume 20% of the world's electricity?"

"No, I had no idea. That is a shocking statistic!"

"The proposed data center at Loring will utilize excess hydropower from New Brunswick, but most data centers rely on other types of electricity. The more alternative energy we source from wind and solar, the less we need to rely on climate-destroying fossil fuels. Crockett's solar farm has the additional advantage in that it would provide Rebecca and Tad with much-needed income."

"That's why I'm for it," said Maggie, firmly.

"I do have some reservations, though, and not just because we live across the road from the project, either."

"What are you worried about?"

Doctor Bart set the sanitizer bottle back on the shelf. "I don't mind if the Russell's hayfields are turned into solar production; they've been fallow for years. But I hate to see Wendell's woodlot cut down—or most of his woodlot, less the ten acres around the Millett Rock. Three hundred acres for a local solar farm seems like overkill to me. The state-owned solar arrays next to the highway in Augusta don't cover a quarter of that acreage."

"But there are quite a few sections of those solar arrays," Maggie pointed out. "There are some panels on the Route 3 connector, as well as the roundabout. I bet altogether they cover a lot more land than you think."

"That land wasn't useful to begin with, and very few trees were cut for that project because the roadsides were already cleared and mowed."

"Maybe three hundred acres is the amount of land Robinson Crockett needs for his company's solar farm to be profitable?" Maggie suggested.

"Perhaps." Doctor Bart tore the dirty white paper off the exam table, balled the paper up, and tossed it in the trash. "Or perhaps Crockett saw an opportunity and took advantage of it." He pulled down a clean section of barrier paper.

"You think he's taking advantage of Rebecca?" If Maggie's fair-minded son-in-law also thought the young widow was being hoodwinked, here was additional cause for concern.

"Like I said, I don't have enough information to make a fair assessment." Doctor Bart leaned back against the table and folded his arms across his chest. "We'll learn more about the project at the public hearing."

Maggie was surprised. "There's a public hearing scheduled?"

"Not yet, but I would think there would be one soon with a project this size."

Maggie fell silent, wondering whether she should share with her son-in-law that Duncan also had reservations. She decided not to say anything, however, not wanting to turn Metcalf against the project, which, despite her own unvoiced reservations, she still whole-heartedly supported.

"I'm going to get a cup of coffee," he said, straightening up. "Would you like a cup?"

"No thanks. I'll just take one of those donuts I saw on the kitchen counter."

"Nellie is always trying to fatten me up," he said, smiling.

"Better you than her. She's already gained—what, twenty pounds?—with this baby."

"Only eleven pounds. She's right on target. She's not due until early fall."

"How about 'targeting' me with the sex of my next grandbaby? A grandma likes to be prepared, and I know you know what the baby is."

"Nice try, Grammie. But Nellie would 'target' me if I told you."

"I'll just call Jane and ask her, then."

"When you call my mother, give her my regards. She's not speaking to me at the moment."

"Good grief! Why not?"

"Because I won't tell her our baby's sex, either."

At nine-thirty, Miss Crump arrived in the care of Doctor Bart's Aunt Hannah, who now drove the elderly lady to her appointments. Maggie, who spied the Trow's vehicle enter the dooryard, opened the front door and waited for the chicken-loving centenarian to hobble up the walkway. "Good morning, Miss Crump," Maggie called out cheerily.

Miss Crump stabbed the wooden stoop with her black-headed, rubber-tipped cane and hauled herself up. "You don't need to shout, Minister—I ain't deaf," she informed Maggie.

Maggie, who had known Miss Crump many years, had no compunction about teasing the centenarian. "How do you know *I'm* not hard of hearing?" she quizzed, stepping back so that the little hunched-back woman could maneuver inside. "I could be shouting for my own benefit."

"You ain't the one with the appointment, Missy." Miss Crump's small eyes darted around the empty waiting room. "Why ain't yer daughter here?"

Aunt Hannah, who was bringing up the rear, carrying Miss Crump's over-sized leather purse, winked at Maggie, as if to say: "We can see where we rate against the young people, can't we?"

"Nellie has the day off," Maggie answered.

"Tut, tut! 'Tain't Monday. Thet's why I never make my appointments on a Monday."

"My favorite patient!" Doctor Bart exclaimed, returning from the kitchen to greet Miss Crump. He set Maggie's donut on the reception desk. "How are you feeling today?"

"Favorite patient?" Miss Crump scoffed. "I bet you say thet to everybody!" Nevertheless, Maggie noticed Miss Crump looked pleased. She recollected that Nellie had once told her that the contrary old woman was one of their favorite patients. She was also one of the clinic's major benefactors, donating money from the proceeds of her gravel pit, which was a steady source of profit.

"I only say that to the centenarians. Come right in, I'm ready for you!" Metcalf helped Miss Crump into the exam room and closed the door behind the two of them.

Aunt Hannah, who was in her eighties, sank into one of the two padded rockers, holding Miss Crump's bag in her lap. "I swear, she's getting worse every day. Helen treats me like it's a favor for me to drive her around. But I know she doesn't mean it, so I try not to let it bother me." Hannah began to rock back and forth.

Maggie returned to her seat at the desk. She pointed at Miss Crump's leather purse. "At least she didn't insist on bringing a chicken as payment, this time."

"No, she wants to give Doctor Bart a check today. A big one, I think. That gravel pit she owns really pays off."

"Miss Crump—and you and Henry—are keeping this place going. Nellie says regular donations are down because of the inflation. Groceries are so expensive! People can only stretch their money so far." Before Doctor Bart and Nellie opened the free Songbird Clinic, many of the locals went without medical care because they couldn't afford to go to a doctor.

"Thank goodness for this clinic! I'm afraid some people who are on Medicaid now might lose their coverage. Henry and I were talking about the cuts to Medicaid just the other night. You'd think in a country this wealthy that health insurance would be a right, not a privilege."

"Unfortunately, the privileged don't want to share their wealth, especially with those they think don't want to work."

The two mature women fell silent. Maggie wondered whether she should bring up what had happened to Rebecca at church, since she knew that Hannah and Henry were involved in the drama that played out during coffee hour. Then she remembered that Sabine had spoken to her in confidence about the unfortunate incident, and her lips were sealed.

Hannah Trow, however, was not under a veil of silence. "Have you seen Rebecca?" she asked.

"Not since Saturday night." Maggie had desperately wanted to visit Rebecca Sunday, but Duncan had convinced her to wait until Sabine had first called on the widow. He reminded her that, currently, she was not Rebecca's pastor.

"I'm sorry you weren't at church, Maggie. There was an awful row about the solar farm, and we missed your calming presence. But Nellie stepped up to take your place. Sabine was very comforting, too."

"What happened?" Maggie asked, interested to hear Hannah's take on the incident.

"During coffee hour Henry took Rebecca aside and congratulated her on the project. We're both so please for her and Tad to have that financial security, you know. But I'm afraid Henry spoke rather loudly and when he mentioned the solar farm, several rude people got up and stalked out. Henry called them something he shouldn't have—'idiots' and 'deadbeats,' I think—you know how hot-tempered Henry can be! Well, then Stephen Danforth got up and ..."

"Not Stephen Danforth!"

Hannah nodded. "... and told Rebecca she should go back to Boston and take Robinson Crockett with her. It was an awful moment. Poor Rebecca!"

"How horrible! That doesn't sound like Stephen at all. I've known him for years and Stephen is one of the most soft-hearted men I know."

"Well, I'm afraid he wasn't on Sunday. This solar farm is making people say and do all sorts of crazy things! Rebecca started crying, and that's when Nellie gave her a hug and told her to never mind what Stephen had said, that all her friends loved her and wouldn't dream of letting her move away."

"Good for Nellie!"

In reliving the incident, Hannah had once again become angered. She stopped rocking and leaned forward in the wooden chair. "Do you know what I did? When I got home from church I called up Nadine Danforth and gave her a piece of my mind! The nerve of her husband saying something like that, hurting a young widow like Rebecca. It was a mean, ugly thing to say, and I told her so. Before I finished my piece, Nadine hung up on me. But I don't care, even if we have been friends since kindergarten!"

Friends since kindergarten? And now Hannah and Nadine were no longer on speaking terms! This was a sad turn of events!

Maggie and Hannah had been so deep in their conversation, that Miss Crump exited the exam room before they noticed her. "More fools, you two, thinking Stephen Danforth was the culprit," she pronounced, hobbling forward.

Startled, Maggie swiveled the desk chair around to face Miss Crump. The elderly lady's thin nostrils were flared; her eyes ablaze with anger.

"'Twas thet damn Leland Gorse as put Danforth up to sayin' them nasty things to the widow," Miss Crump declared, the white bun on her head bobbing with certitude.

"Now, Helen, you don't know that," pleaded Hannah.

"Don't I? I have my sources, Hannah Trow. I know what's what in this town, almost as much as the minister here does."

"Miss Crump, I don't know ..." began Maggie.

"Don't 'Miss Crump' me, Maggie Faulkner. I know you and Leland are thick as thieves."

"You don't think I had anything to do with it?" Maggie asked, horrified. "Rebecca is one of my dearest friends!"

"Maybe not. But now thet you know what thet damned skunk has done, what are you going to do about it?"

Maggie was both shocked and confused. Could Leland have put Stephen Danforth up to telling Rebecca to go back to Boston? His best friend's widow! If so, what should she do? What *could* she do?

"I see how 'tis," Miss Crump continued, mercilessly. "Still takin' Leland's side, are you? Well, I'll tell you what I aim to do. I'm going to call the state department of environment protection and tell them about his illegal brook crossing! Leland ain't got no permit and he ain't got no bridge, neither, not according to the boys as run the gravel trucks. He's breaking the law, and I aim to put a stop to it, and to him. Leland's wood cuttin' days are over! Let's go, Hannah." With that Miss Crump stumped toward the door.

"What about your check for the clinic, Helen?" asked Hannah, rising from the chair, clutching the elderly lady's purse to her ample bosom.

"I kin mail it to Doctor Bart. I got to get home and make thet phone call to the state."

Maggie got up to open the door for Miss Crump. After the two ladies departed, she returned to the desk and sank into her chair.

The pastoral message she had recounted to Sabine yesterday today seemed facile and superficial. A killing frost would no longer be enough to save Sovereign, she realized, sadly. The proposed solar farm was much more divisive than she had expected, revealing fault lines in the community that had been simmering beneath the surface. Sabine had seen the fault lines, but she had been blind to the social changes that had occurred over the past five or ten years. Rather than a killing frost, it was now going to take another "Year Without a Summer," such as the townspeople tragically suffered in 1816, to bring Sovereign residents to their knees!

Chapter 14

Robinson Crockett

By 3 p.m. Thursday afternoon, when Sabine's church office hours ended, nobody had shown up to talk or seek pastoral counseling. She had utilized the period of quietude to work on her sermon for Sunday. But she was disappointed. Sabine had expected, given the division over the solar farm currently fermenting in Sovereign, that she would have received two or three agitated visitors at least. (Sabine had discovered that her usual drop-in rate was one.) She had hoped—rather naively, she now realized—that by listening to and validating one person at a time she could find a way to weave the town back together before the rupture was irreparable. Her plan wouldn't work, however, if nobody showed up to talk. She would have to go to them.

Sabine suspected that beneath the solar farm dispute lay an ocean of unrelieved pain. Some of the pain was likely caused by social and economic issues beyond her control. But some, she believed, stemmed from the recent death of Wendell Russell. His family, his friends, and the greater community of Sovereign, had not fully grieved their loss, and this, as a pastoral counselor, Sabine could assist with.

While Wendell had never been a mover and shaker in town—he never ran for selectman or representative to the state legislature—he had represented something more important: a touchstone of Sovereign's humanity. Sabine had learned more about Wendell since his death, than she had garnered from him while he was alive. He had been kind, thoughtful, and possessed of a wry sense of humor. Wendell never had a mean word for anyone, she had been told many times; and he would give the shirt off his back to help a stranger. In Sabine's eyes, Wendell represented the true Christian example of brotherly love. Without him, the townspeople were not only grieving their loss, but also groping for his replacement. Sabine's job, as she saw it, was to help each individual realize that he or she could take Wendell's place. Rather than seeking a role model outside themselves, Sabine hoped to encourage each member of her flock to become the decent human being that Wendell had exemplified. It was a tall order to bring brotherly love back to a broken community, she knew. But it was not impossible. Indeed, despite Wendell's death, the true Christian hallmarks of love and forgiveness were still very much alive and well at the old Russell homestead.

After the fiasco at church the prior Sunday, Sabine had gone Tuesday afternoon to see Rebecca. She found the young widow disconsolate and confused. But rather than blame Stephen Danforth for his hurtful words to her, Rebecca excused her friend and neighbor. "Stephen must be going through a difficult time. He didn't know what he was saying," she assured Sabine. "Stephen made the crib Tad used when he was a baby, you know. And Nadine sewed him the most beautiful baby quilt. I hope they aren't having money trouble!"

Sabine, knowing that Leland had instigated Stephen Danforth's heartless comment to Rebecca, bit her tongue. How much more hurt would Rebecca feel if she knew that Leland Gorse, her late husband's best friend, had been behind the nasty remark? Would she be able to forgive Leland's betrayal of their friendship?

Sabine felt, rather than heard, someone enter the church as she was meditating upon the sad rift caused by the proposed solar farm. She had learned to recognize the exchange of air that occurred when the heavy wooden door was pulled open and then gradually shut with the door-closer. She did not rise from her desk, however. Maggie had told her that sometimes individuals came to the church to offer solitary prayer or to rest in the pews and contemplate, with no desire for further company other than the Divine. She waited to see whether the visitor was for her or for God.

She didn't have long to wait. A moment later Robinson Crockett poked his dark head around the corner. "Mind if I come in?" he asked, stepping inside the small, book-lined office before Sabine could reply.

"Please do," she replied, attempting to hide her surprise at seeing the out-of-town developer at the local church. She stood up. "I was just about to close up shop for the day, but I don't have any other plans. In fact, I was just thinking about you."

Robinson Crockett, who had removed his baseball cap upon entering, nervously turned the hat around in a two-handed clutch. "Nothing bad, I hope?"

Sabine paused, noting his uneasiness. How should she proceed? If he had come to her for help, shouldn't she at least find out what he wanted before quizzing him about the solar farm?

"Nothing important," she said, sweeping the skirt of her full dress behind her and reclaiming her chair. "How can I help you, Mr. Crockett?"

"Well, you can start by calling me 'Rob.' Mr. Crockett makes me sound like Davy Crockett's grandfather. No relation to the frontiersman, in case you were going to ask."

"That was my next question. I bet you get asked that a lot?"

"Too much. But at least I never have to spell my last name."

Sabine chuckled. "That's a help. I always have to spell both my names, especially my first name." She gestured toward the empty chair situated in front of her desk. "Have a seat, Rob."

He flashed a crooked grin and gingerly appropriated the velvet-lined antique chair. Sabine found his grin charming. Robinson Crockett's dark curls tumbled over his ears, signaling he needed a haircut. No wife or girlfriend to attend to it, probably. He wasn't wearing a wedding ring so she assumed he wasn't married. As she studied the developer, she saw the humor fade from his eyes. Sabine realized he was wondering where to begin. She waited for him to speak, having learned to give her visitors time. Very few who sought advice or aid were able to dive right in.

"I'm afraid our solar farm project has gotten off to a rocky start," he said, finally. "I've been talking it over with Rebecca and, uh, a friend, and my friend suggested you might be able to help us."

"Me? What can I do?"

"Help the townspeople come to see that a solar farm in Sovereign is a positive, forward-looking endeavor."

"That's your job, isn't it? To 'sell' your project? That really isn't the job of the local minister."

"Yes, but you talk to a lot of people, don't you? Maybe you could put in a good word for us? I know Rebecca is your friend."

"Mr. Crockett—Rob—I'm uncomfortable with the direction this conversation is taking," said Sabine. She leaned back in her chair, reflexively putting distance between them. "It sounds as though you want my help winning over the locals to your solar farm. Is that correct?"

"Well, yes," he admitted. "I'll be honest with you, Miss Burbury ..."

"Sabine, please."

"I'll be honest with you, Sabine. I've got quite a bit of money tied up in this project, most of it borrowed. Because of the impending tariffs on Chinese-made goods, I've already purchased everything for the solar farm: panels, racking and mounting systems, cables and wiring, inverters, charge controllers, monitoring system, switches, meters ... everything."

Sabine was appalled. "You bought all that without knowing for sure you'd be able to build a three-hundred-acre solar farm?"

Robinson leaned forward, elbows on the knees of his work jeans, hat in hand. "Wendell and I had agreed to most of the particulars before he died," he stated earnestly. "Rebecca had given her consent, too, so—given the threat of huge tariffs on anything manufactured in China—I went ahead and ordered my equipment. The balance of the system is now sitting in containers at the Conley Container Terminal in Boston, and the demurrage and storage fees are killing me. I have loggers and an excavation crew on standby. I can break ground tomorrow, and would, except that Rebecca has asked me to wait. She's upset that some of her friends are opposed to our project. That's why we need your help."

Despite her determination to remain calm and open-minded, Sabine felt her exasperation growing. "People are opposed to the project because the idea of a solar farm in their back yard was sprung so suddenly! You haven't even been to the planning board or held a public hearing yet, as far as I know. When are you going to do that?"

Robinson shook his head and unconsciously resumed turning his cap. "None of that is necessary in Sovereign. Several months ago, I went to see John Woods—the First Selectmen—and he told me that Sovereign doesn't even have a comprehensive plan or a zoning ordinance, let alone an ordinance covering solar farms. As far as he was concerned, I could build the solar farm wherever I pleased—no permit required—once I had a legal contract with the landowner."

This was news to Sabine! Even in Alaska there were zoning requirements and comprehensive plans. "Is that why you chose Sovereign for your site? Because the town was easy picking?"

"No, no. I had no knowledge of the regulations, or lack thereof, when I selected Sovereign. A mutual friend—the one I mentioned I'd spoken with earlier—suggested the town as a likely place and the Russells as a good candidate for the solar farm."

"You mean, you targeted Wendell and Rebecca?"

"Like I said, a friend who knows the Russells told me they owned a lot of land and that they might need some additional income, so I approached Wendell over the winter." The developer pulled at a loose thread in his plaid flannel shirt. "Whether you believe it or not, I was trying to help them," he declared.

"Who is this mutual friend? Is he somebody we all know?"

There was a moment's hesitation before Robinson replied to her question. "My friend asked me not to say."

"I see," said Sabine. But she didn't see at all. Who was this person who had suggested Wendell and Rebecca's property for a solar farm? It couldn't be someone from town, because whoever he was, he was obviously unfamiliar with the conservative make-up of the town's population. Both Robinson and his friend were completely clueless about how negatively a solar farm would be received in Sovereign. "I don't think I can help you," she said, finally. "But I won't oppose the solar farm, either. I can't take sides. I'm sorry, Rob, but that's the best I can do."

Robinson Crockett stood up to leave, disappointment clearly showing on his face. "OK, thanks. I guess that's all I have a right to expect. I appreciate your time." He held out his hand.

Sabine, feeling she had short-changed her caller, came around the desk to accept the handshake on a more personal level. His hand was rough to the touch, she noted. They were the hands of a man who worked for a living, not the hands of a smooth-talking city developer.

"You do believe that I wanted to help Rebecca?" he inquired anxiously. Robinson Crockett examined her face, searching for a spark of compassion, gripping her hand with both of his.

Sabine found she did believe him. "I do. I think you are concerned with Rebecca and Tad's welfare."

"Thanks. That means a lot."

As Rob's eyes met hers, Sabine read in his gaze the apprehension of a troubled soul. This solar farm project was indeed weighing upon him, she realized. Sabine decided that, despite his fiscal imprudence, the developer had a good heart. She rewarded him with an encouraging smile.

Unfortunately, Nick, whom Sabine hadn't seen since their argument in the woods, chose this exact moment to burst into her office. She had not closed her door, because Robinson Crockett's was not a pastoral visit. Nor had she noticed the air exchange from the front door of the church. As a result, when Nick entered the office with his usual alacrity, he discovered her holding hands with Rob, gazing into the handsome developer's eyes.

"What the heck!" Nick exclaimed, stupefied.

Sabine jerked away from Rob, nearly as startled as Nick. Her sudden movement to reclaim her hand, however, only made her appear guilty.

Nick turned on his heel and departed. Before she could call him back, he had exited the church as silently as he had come.

Chapter 15

Garden Divisions

On Saturday evening Maggie received an unexpected phone call from her daughter. "Jana just vomited her supper," said Nellie, in a matter-of-fact voice.

"Oh, dear God in heaven! Is she OK?"

"She's fine. Metcalf thinks she ate too many sweets at Aunt Hannah's."

This reply exasperated Maggie. "Why can't you talk like ordinary mothers, Nellie, and just say she tossed her cookies or puked? 'Vomited' sounds so clinical and Black Plague-ish. You had me worried."

"Because I'm married to a doctor, Mom, which, if I may remind you, is what you always wanted for me."

"OK, I'll give you that one."

"I'm calling with a child opportunity. Since you don't go to church anymore ..."

"Not because I don't want to," Maggie interrupted.

"I know, I know. You don't attend out of some sort of pastoral courtesy. Anyway, can you take Jana for a few hours tomorrow so I can go to church? If Jana *is* coming down with something, I don't want her to infect the other children."

"But it's OK to infect her elderly grandmother?"

"You're not elderly, and Metcalf says you're in perfect health, now. Besides, he doesn't think Jana has anything contagious. But if she's worse tomorrow morning, of course we'll keep her home."

"Say no more. You know we'd love to have Jana. Have her bring her trowel. I'm working in my gardens, tomorrow."

"Sounds fun—not! See you then."

Nellie and Doctor Bart dropped Jana off around eight-thirty Sunday morning. Maggie was already out back digging in her gardens when they arrived. "Hi, Pumpkin," she greeted the seven-year-old, dropping the long-handled spade to scooch down and give her granddaughter a hug.

"Grampa is coming outside, too," Jana informed her grandmother. "He says if I dig some worms, he'll take me and Tad fishing." The little girl was dressed in yellow-green pants, pink rubber boots, and a matching pink sweater.

Maggie pushed a soft curl out of Jana's bright blue eyes. "What about Hope and Alice Rose? Don't you want to invite them to go fishing, too?"

Jana took a few seconds to think. "Hope can come, but I don't want Alice. She's too bossy."

Maggie bit her lip, trying not to laugh out loud. Truer words were never spoken! "Alice is older than the rest of you. Maybe she thinks she should be the boss?"

The little girl frowned, her lower lip curling. "Well, I don't like it."

"I don't like it, either, when somebody bosses me around. But I try to be nice to them anyway. Sometimes when people are bossy or mean they just aren't feeling well."

"Like Miss Crump?"

"Like Miss Crump," Maggie repeated, surprised—and pleased—that the child had followed her explanation into the real world. She heard the screen door on the porch clap shut and looked up to see Duncan striding across the back lawn.

"This is for your worms," he said to Jana, bending down and handing her a clean aluminum can. He had taken care to file down the sharp edges.

"Thank you, Grampa," the young girl replied, taking the can and pulling away from Maggie's clasp. "How many worms do I need?"

"Oh, ten or twelve, at least."

"OK. But we're not taking Alice fishing with us this time," she clarified, seriously. "Just Tad and Hope."

"I see," Duncan replied, holding back a smile. "Then eight or nine worms should be enough."

"Can we go to the Toad Stools today, too?"

"You bet. I feel a good story coming on."

"That's good, Grampa. Hope and Tad really like stories. I do, too." Jana looked around the sizeable backyard. "Where should I dig?"

"How about that big black hole your grandmother left over there?" Duncan pointed to where Maggie had dug up several opportunistic burdocks that were crowding her young fruit trees, leaving behind pockets of loose soil. "That looks like a good spot."

"OK, Grampa." Jana picked up her little trowel and walked to the hole. She carefully set the tin can down on the grass and began to dig in the dirt, searching for worms.

"So, we're not inviting Alice this time?" Duncan said softly to his wife. "That's something new."

Maggie moved over to her rhubarb patch. "Do you blame her? I wouldn't invite Alice to go fishing either. She'd scare the fish. Hand me that shovel, please. I have some interlopers here I need to dispose of."

Duncan picked up the spade and passed the shovel to his wife. "I must admit, Alice is not my favorite neighborhood child."

"She can't help it, poor thing! Alice inherited too many of her grandfather's genes."

"Leland's quirky character traits I find funny and endearing. But somehow, in Alice, those same characteristics seem off-putting and obnoxious. Now, what are you doing?" Duncan asked, as Maggie thrust the shovel into the middle of the rhubarb patch.

"Weeding the blue globe thistle out of my rhubarb." She stomped on the edge of the spade and, with a practiced movement, bent over and pulled the thistle out of the ground. She tossed the plant over the stone wall, into the tall meadowgrass.

"I thought you planted that thistle? You told me it was ornamental."

"I did plant it—over there." Maggie pointed to her herb garden, which free-spirited patch of herbs and flowers abutted the rhubarb patch at the north-west corner of the stone wall. "It needs to stay where it belongs."

"That's asking a lot of a wild plant, isn't it? Not to propagate itself where it can?"

Maggie dug up another clump of the invasive blue globe thistle. This clump also followed the first over the rock wall. "I don't care. If the thistle can't stay on its own side, it's out."

"What about that other plant in there? That's not rhubarb. Why aren't you digging that up?" Even after eight years of marriage Duncan was still learning his wife's gardening customs, which he knew she had absorbed from her grandmother.

"That's horsemint. That's OK where it is. Mint and rhubarb are companion plants. At least, I think they are. I always used to see horsemint growing with the rhubarb at the old homesteads in Winslow and Norway, so I assumed that's what the old-timers thought was best."

Duncan fingered the square hairy stem of one of the horsemints, releasing its sweet bouquet. "Maybe that's what the mint thought was best and the old-timers were too busy to weed?" he suggested.

"Probably," Maggie agreed, laughing.

"You know, your garden divisions remind me of this debate over the solar farm. Those who are opposed to the project won't even listen to an argument from the other side. They just want to toss the entire project over the stone wall and have done with it. I wonder what it would take to get people in this town to listen—really listen—to one another? Hear what their friends and neighbors on the other side have to say?"

Duncan's rhetorical questions were commonplace in their married life and so Maggie knew he wasn't expecting her to answer. Still, she found the question unsettling. She had not yet told her husband what Miss Crump had divulged about Leland, that he had prompted Stephen Danforth to say the cruel words to Rebecca. She knew that Duncan was fond of the old woodchopper and she disliked the thought of sowing enmity between the two men. But, if Leland really was behind the incident, Duncan needed to know the truth, and he should hear it from her. "Miss Crump said something odd the other day at the clinic," she apprised her husband, inserting the tip of her spade under another blue globe thistle.

"Miss Crump always says odd things. She and Leland crack me up. Talk about characters right out of a novel!"

"Strange you should mention Leland again. What she said was about him."

Duncan raised his eyebrows. "And …? Let's have it, Maggie. What haven't you told me?"

Maggie stomped on the shovel. "Miss Crump said Leland put Stephen Danforth up to telling Rebecca to go back to Boston."

"Now, why would Leland do a hurtful thing like that?"

"Because Leland is hurt himself—angry that his best friend up and died on him—and he doesn't want to see Wendell's woodlot cut down for the solar farm."

Duncan bent down and grasped the uprooted clump of thistle. He tossed the clump over the wall.

Maggie, resting her foot on the shovel, tried to gauge her husband's reaction; however, the expression on his face was inscrutable. "Aren't you going to say anything?"

"I can hardly credit that Miss Crump's assertion is true," Duncan replied, finally. "Leland is a decent man. Oh, he has his faults—we all do. But he was Wendell's best friend. I can't believe he would stoop to such a low level."

"I couldn't believe it, either, when Miss Crump first told us."

"Us?"

"Hannah was there, too. Miss Crump was speaking to both of us."

"Well, if Hannah knows, then Henry knows now, too. That certainly won't raise Henry's opinion of Leland any."

"Unfortunately not. What should I do?"

There was another long pause while Duncan considered her question. Maggie, impatient as usual, prodded him. "Should I go see him?"

"Henry?"

"Of course not! You know I'm referring to Leland. Should I go see Leland?"

"Maggie, if you can't trust Sabine to shepherd your flock," Duncan said, soberly, "you shouldn't have taken a sabbatical."

"But Sabine doesn't know Leland like I know Leland!"

"I think she has a pretty good idea of his character. It's not hard to fathom."

"Well, maybe so. But she doesn't know it was Leland who put Stephen Danforth up to that nasty remark."

"We don't know that for certain, either. As far as I can tell, it's hearsay. How does Miss Crump know what Leland did—or did not—do?"

"Miss Crump said one of her gravel truck drivers told her. Stephen still drives occasionally for Waterhouse Trucking. Maybe he was feeling badly about what he said to Rebecca and confessed to a coworker?"

"I hope so, because it was a mean remark."

"So, you don't think I should try to shame Leland into confessing and apologizing to Rebecca?"

"No, I don't. It's been my experience that when people know they've done something wrong, they already feel ashamed. Pointing their transgression out to them generally doesn't help matters any. In addition, I know you, Maggie, and you'll take the opportunity to try and persuade Leland to get on board with this solar farm. And while you and I can respectfully agree to disagree ..."

"We disagree about the solar farm?"

"You know we do. Anyway, while you and I can respectfully disagree, I'm not sure Leland will be able to. I'd hate to see you lose a dear friend over the solar farm, which might never even be built. Good friends are hard to come by at our age."

Duncan's remarks left Maggie feeling deflated and disappointed. He was always so reasonable! "Do you expect me to do nothing, then?"

"No, I think you should work on your book—you know, the book that you're taking this sabbatical to write? And have some fun with your husband and granddaughter. Let Sabine take care of the heavy lifting."

Jana, who had walked slowly up behind her grandparents while they were speaking, now tugged on Duncan's arm. "Grampa, I've got five worms already!" She held out the can of crawling worms so he could see them.

"That's great, Sweetie! But you need to put some dirt in the can so the worms will live until we get to the fishing hole."

"Can we go fishing today?"

"Sure, if it's OK with your Mom and Dad. We can go after dinner. Is that OK with you, Grammie?" Duncan asked, turning back to Maggie.

"Only if you promise to bring me back some brook trout."

"We will, Grammie," the little girl assured her.

Duncan gave Jana an affectionate pat on the head. "Would you like to ask Tad and Hope to go with us this afternoon?"

She nodded. "Yes, please."

"I'll call their mothers," Maggie said to her husband. "Unless you think I'm overstepping my bounds?" she added, facetiously.

"Not in this case. I think it's a grandmotherly thing to do."

"Gee, thanks."

Jana spoke up suddenly. "Grammie, Alice says Tad doesn't pee sitting down. She's not telling the truth, is she?"

The little girl's question startled both adults. Maggie's eyes widened. Good Heavens! How should she reply? She looked helplessly at her husband for an answer.

"Don't look at me," he said, holding up his hands.

"But you had a boy and a girl—I only had a girl."

Confused, Jana turned from one adult to the other, trying to follow the gist of their conversation.

"Um, Alice wasn't lying this time, Pumpkin," Maggie answered, finally. "Boys can pee sitting down *and* standing up."

"Why can't I pee standing up?"

Maggie opted for the easy way out. "Why don't you ask your Daddy that question? He's a doctor. He'll explain everything to you."

"OK, Grammie." Jana walked away, singing to her worms.

"Phew, good save there," Duncan declared.

"Thank you. I certainly hope Nellie and Metcalf have a boy! Jana needs a brother."

"That would help. What did you tell your daughter when she asked you that question?"

"I've no idea. Do you remember what you said to Nora?"

"I don't think I told her anything. I think Nora figured it out on her own. She had an older brother, remember?"

Maggie retrieved her shovel. "Speaking of Nora, did you ever connect with her? You never said."

"I didn't mention our conversation because Nora didn't have much to say, except what you already knew. She described her trip to Theodore Roosevelt National Park, and asked after the Old Farts."

The Old Farts again! Maggie was surprised. Nora was definitely fishing for something.

She began to suspect that in some way, somehow, Nora was connected to Rebecca's solar farm.

But how could that be possible?

Chapter 16

The Old Nutt Place

After Nick had burst into Sabine's office—and then fled—the young minister ushered Robinson Crockett out as graciously as she could, under the awkward circumstances. The developer shook hands with her once again, warmly thanking Sabine for her time. After Rob departed, she rushed to her office window to try and catch a glimpse of Nick. But he had moved so fast he had already disappeared down into the Sovereign Woods.

Sabine sank into Maggie's overstuffed armchair by the window to contemplate the situation. Why had Nick sought her out? Surely, he wasn't going to try again to convince her to help him stop the solar farm? No, she had made herself abundantly clear—she would not take sides. Nick had received that message, she was sure.

Had Nick wanted to apologize?

Given his boorish behavior at their last meeting, she thought he probably had felt ashamed of himself. Sabine was ready to forgive him, although perhaps not quite ready to forget.

She glanced unseeing out the window. Could she catch up with him in the Sovereign Woods? If Nick wanted to apologize, she was ready to give him the opportunity. But running after him? Was that necessary?

She searched her heart and admitted to herself she was also anxious to assure Nick that what he had interrupted wasn't a romantic interlude between herself and Rob. Nor was their hand-holding an assurance on her part that she would help the developer with his project.

But no, she would not chase after Nick. She would look desperate—and ridiculous—streaming down the trail in her floral silk print dress and black flats, calling his name. Still, Sabine knew how stiff-necked Nick was. He would not make another attempt to visit her, she knew. If she wanted to see him again—and she did—she would have to go to him.

Sabine arose and returned to her desk. She studied her calendar. The next five days were crammed full, with the church service and office hours on Sunday, regular church activities on Friday and Tuesday, and pastoral calls Monday and Tuesday. But she would find time to hunt Nick down and speak with him. He was a hard man to catch, so she would corner him at his house. Sabine knew where he lived—Maggie had pointed out Nick's restored post-and-beam home last year—and she thought she could find her way out there again.

The following Wednesday, nearly a week after Nick's awkward entrance into her office, Sabine rose at sunup and dressed for hiking. Because the June morning was cool and damp, she slipped a yellow LL Bean fleece pullover over her cotton tee and off-white jeans. She drove to the church and parked. The sun was just cresting the tall pines to the east of the church when she arrived. Sabine checked her phone. Five-thirty. She was confident she would find the woodsman at home at this early hour.

Sabine hiked steadily along the main trail, pausing momentarily at the bridge to watch the mist rising wraith-like from the black water. She passed the side trails to the

Millett Rock and the Russell's house, and fifteen minutes later found herself at the turnoff to the narrow trail that led to Nick's house, formerly the abandoned Nutt place.

Maggie had given her a history of the property last year. Jacob Nutt, Maggie had said, had been one of the first settlers in Sovereign. He built a log cabin next to Black Brook in Waldo Patent territory not yet surveyed. After other settlers had followed him to Sovereign, they cut an ox cart path through the woods to Thorndike, the nearest settlement. Once the ox cart road was cleared, Nutt built himself and his family a post-and-beam house. Unfortunately, when the well-to-do Lovejoy family arrived in Sovereign (whose property Henry Trow now owned) the location of the main thoroughfare shifted from the ox cart path to what became known as the Cross Road, to connect with the Lovejoy's farm. Jacob Nutt's wife died; his children left home and never returned; and the old ox cart path that nobody used anymore grew up to softwoods. When Jacob Nutt passed away (in his nineties), the house began to slowly deteriorate, until Nick had arrived to lease the property from Wendell nearly a decade ago. Since then, the woodsman had been bringing the old Nutt place back to its once and future glory. Eight years ago, with his father's financial help, Nick had purchased the homestead from Wendell.

Last year, when Sabine was out with Maggie, she had only seen the old Nutt place from a distance, and so she didn't know what to expect when she saw Nick's home up close. As she hiked down the narrow trail, which brought her to a pleasant, ordinary-looking rural Maine homestead, she was surprised and relieved by how normal the place appeared.

The old Nutt place, a story-and-a-half cedar shingle house, was a traditional center chimney cape. The house sported what appeared to be a new forest-green metal roof with matching green painted window trim. Old-fashioned lilac bushes, their purple blooms now spent, decorated the south-facing front of the natural-colored, rain-washed main house. The attached ell was set back from the main house by a window's width, just enough for the late afternoon western sunlight to gain entrance. The window frame and grills had recently been painted green, but the glass in the windows was wavy. Nick had obviously repaired the wood in the windows, but had kept the original cylinder glass, maintaining the home's antique character.

Nick must had started a vegetable garden immediately upon his return from his travels, because Sabine spied—already showing through the ground in the fenced-in area—peas, beans, cabbage, broccoli, beets, and Swiss chard. Various herbs and perennials were tucked in next to both sides of the flat stone walkway leading up to the original, unpainted front door. In front of the ell was a cold frame, propped open several inches, in which Sabine spied tender mixed lettuce greens. She had often wondered what Nick ate, suspecting, after seeing him decline to eat pork at Rebecca's dinner party, that he was a vegetarian. And now she knew. Nick ate what he grew himself, supplementing his diet with wild mushrooms, those he didn't sell, anyway. Maggie's daughter Nellie, Nick's stepsister, had told Sabine that Nick also traded mushrooms for eggs, milk, cheese, and butter from Scotch Broom Acres.

Various fruit trees of different ages and sizes, as well as raspberry, blackberry, and blueberry bushes, were judiciously situated around the front yard. Nick had strung a clothesline between two ancient apple trees, upon which were neatly hung men's shirts, pants, boxers, and wool socks. Sabine was amazed that, for a bachelor's homestead, Nick's place was remarkably neat, clean, and well-ordered.

Having paused several minutes on her approach to take everything in, Sabine now registered the pleasing scent of

166

woodsmoke. She looked up and spied wispy gray smoke swirling up from the brick chimney. Nick was at home!

As she moved up the stone walk, Sabine trod over the low-growing creeping thyme around the rocks, releasing a peppery scent. When she reached the granite slab that served as the door stoop, she noticed the black cast-iron bell hanging from a decorative frame. The bell was mounted on the wall to the right of the heavy door. She stepped upon the stoop, grasped the string dangling from the clapper, and rang the bell several times. The bell's tone was soft and dulcet.

While waiting for Nick to answer the door, Sabine turned and surveyed the homestead from the front stoop. An appealing prospect spread out before her. She could see why Nick loved the place, and felt that she, too, could easily come to love it. Although cut from the Sovereign wilderness, the home appeared embraced and protected by the woods, not threatened by the encroaching forest. The morning sun slanted in through the trees, highlighting a delightful collection of objects: a hollowed-out stone bird bath; one lilac bush; an old hoe, leaning up against a cedar fence post; and the crescent moon-shaped window in the east side of the outhouse.

Nick not having answered the door, Sabine rang the bell again. This time she noticed a small, hand-carved sign hanging to the right of the bell: *"If I don't answer, make yourself at home. I'll be back."*

Sabine chuckled when she read the weathered sign. A visitor last winter would have had to wait many months for Nick to return home!

Bolstered by the sign's invitation, she lifted the iron doorlatch and stepped inside. Sabine kept the door open behind her so she could see where she was going in the dark entryway. The door had no window lights, an oversight on the builder Nutt's part, Sabine thought.

She had entered a small foyer, containing a single straight-back chair with a rush seat, a pair of tall Muck boots nestled next to the chair, a blue and red braided rug, and a Shaker-style wall coat rack which held a small collection of men's exterior clothing. From the foyer, Sabine had the choice of going to the left or to the right. Seeing that the door to the left was open, she closed the front door behind her and moved into that room, which she discovered was Nick's kitchen.

The room was very warm, perhaps seventy-five degrees. There was—or had been—a fire going in the nickel-plated cast-iron wood cook stove situated to the right of the door, likely the source of the woodsmoke. A zinc tea kettle perched like a setting hen upon the back of the stove. The striped café-style curtains were open, allowing shards of daylight to stream into the country kitchen. Sabine recognized the curtain material from some pillows at Maggie's house and surmised that Nick's stepmother had sewed his pretty window treatments.

The floor was fashioned from wide pine boards, newly-sanded and stained a chestnut color. The eight-by-eight ceiling beams were exposed, revealing Jacob Nutt's crude axe handiwork. About a dozen bunches of last year's herbs hung from the oiled beams, diffusing a faintly sweet scent throughout the room. The walls were covered by what appeared to be horse-hair plaster—probably original, Sabine guessed—but freshly-painted white.

A rectangular oak table rested up against the short wall in front of the furthest of the two south windows. A grouping of yellow beeswax candles of different heights decorated the center of the table, as well as a pint jar of Wendell's golden honey. Three straight-back chairs were parked at each of the three open sides of the table, like guests waiting to be served. The chairs reminded Sabine of Thoreau's oft-quoted passage from *Walden*: "I had three chairs in my house; one for solitude, two for friendship, three for society."

An oak rocker was situated between the door to the foyer and the wood cookstove, with an oil lamp perched on a shelf next to the rocker. Several books also lay upon the shelf. Sabine picked up one and read the title. The book was a biography of Stonewall Jackson.

So that's why Nick had quoted Stonewall Jackson! He had been reading a biography of the Civil War Confederate general. She opened the cover and spied his father's name scribbled on the flyleaf. Under the Jackson biography Sabine discovered—much to her astonishment—a nineteenth century copy of *The New England Primer* and *The Eclectic First Reader for Young Children with Pictures*. Nick certainly had an eclectic taste in reading material!

Sabine set the books down and resumed her perusal of the kitchen, certain the room would yield other interesting clues about its owner. The cabinets, which spanned half of the west wall and all the north, appeared new, hand-made from white pine, and were stained to match the floor. The countertop was of glued wood, and was thick and waxed, like a homemade butcher's block. The counter held various mouse-proof tins, and two one-gallon square glass jars. One of the jars was filled with yellow, purple, and red kernels of Indian corn and the other with brown-and-white Jacob's cattle beans. Sabine spied a hand-crank corn and grain grinder attached to the west end of the counter. She had not realized, until seeing the grinder, that Nick was left-handed.

A slate sink was situated beneath the small north-facing window. Instead of water faucets, however, the immense sink was served by a cast-iron hand pump. Unable to restrain her curiosity, Sabine lifted the handle. The pump inhaled. She worked the handle up-and-down two or three times, the handle squeaking a short tune, and water soon came gushing out.

The old hand pump worked!

Of course, the pump works she berated herself. Nick's house was a real home, not a faux nineteenth century dwelling out of *Country Life*.

Beginning to feel like Goldilocks visiting the home of the absent Three Bears, Sabine called Nick's name again. Hearing nothing, except melodic birdsong audible through the thin glass windows, she wished she had not come. What if Nick had seen her approach and taken to the woods? What if he was hiding from her?

No, he might have been upset at finding her holding hands with Robinson Crockett, but she didn't think he would deliberately avoid her. Where *was* Nick?

Sabine tamped down her female curiosity (she wanted to peek into every cupboard and drawer), and opened the door leading into the attached ell. There, she discovered a woodshed, still half-full of firewood, various gardening implements, and hand tools. There was also a stack of recycled corrugated cardboard boxes of various sizes, probably for shipping Nick's mushrooms. Sabine also spied another door leading to what she assumed was the back yard. She hesitated. If she left now, he would never know she was there. But maybe he was just out back working? Perhaps he was cutting wood?

Unfortunately, Nick was nowhere to be seen when she stepped out onto the back deck. The backyard, which encompassed a small area about thirty feet away from a high-banked section of the brook, contained a firepit with a cast-iron tripod, and a wooden bench. A flat log bridge forded the brook, leading to a trail that disappeared into the woods. Nick wasn't home. He could be anywhere!

But where could he have gone at such an early hour?

Sabine closed the ell door and walked around the full length of the back side of the house. On the east side, she discovered a smaller deck between the windows, upon which perched a hand-woven willow rocker. The chair looked so appealing—and Sabine was tired—so she decided to sit and wait for him. Wouldn't Nick be surprised (like the Three Bears) when he returned home and found she had made herself comfortable (as his sign directed visitors to do) in his absence!

To her own surprise—and discomfort—Sabine soon heard someone whistling. The person was approaching the house via the narrow path leading from the main Sovereign Woods trail, the same path she had taken.

Had she ever heard Nick whistle? She didn't think so.

Sabine realized then that she was alone deep in the Sovereign Woods. Nervously, she twisted the willow rocker to the right so she could see who was coming. In two minutes, she perceived a youth—about twelve or thirteen—striding jauntily up the path toward the house. He was whistling and swinging a stick, chopping away at the underbrush growing beside the trail.

The boy, sensing her presence, glanced up. He spotted Sabine in the rocker and dropped the stick. "Hey-ho!" he exclaimed. He stood still, like a startled animal, unsure whether to run away or stand his ground.

"Hello!" Sabine called, raising her hand in a friendly greeting. She didn't stand up, however, afraid her height from the deck might further alarm the ungainly youth. "Don't worry—I'm a friend of Nick's."

The boy hesitated, studying her for a moment. Then, evidently deciding that the young minister was safe, he crossed over the un-mowed side lawn and approached Sabine. He examined her curiously.

"He ain't home yet?" the youth asked, placing a worn sneaker upon the lower of the three steps. He pushed a thatch of unkempt brassy-red hair out of his eyes, then leaned his elbow upon the knee of his patched jeans.

Sabine noted the holes in his gray cotton hoodie and saw that his hands were rough and chapped. "Yet?" she repeated. She pulled out her phone. "It's not even seven o'clock!"

The boy nodded. "Sometimes Walden don't git back 'til seven or eight. I come early to work on my readin'."

The youth did not go to school? This was Wednesday, and the young man—whoever he was—should be home getting ready for the school bus. Why was he out here in the middle of the woods? Didn't they have truant officers in Maine?

Sabine bestowed a charming smile upon him. "What's your name?"

"Gerald."

The boy pronounced his name with a hard "G"— "Garold." The name was unusual and old-fashioned. "Do you have a last name?" she asked, rocking back and forth in a companionable manner.

"Yep."

"Ah, you do have a last name, but you don't want to tell me?" A strong ray of sun poked through the branches of a pine tree to the southeast, forcing Sabine to shield her eyes to see him. She studied the youth.

"Nope," he replied, his eyes dropping from hers. He scuffed the bottom of his sneaker against the edge of the rough hemlock step.

"Very well. My name is Sabine. I'm a friend of Nick's. I came out to see him this morning, but according to you, I'm too early. I didn't know he was a vampire."

Startled, the youth looked back up. "Sartin, Walden ain't no vampire! He's out mushroomin'."

Mushrooming! Of course. Why hadn't she remembered? Nick had told her he often went mushrooming early in the morning. He needed to get the delicacies ready early for overnight shipping, he'd said. He also wanted to beat out any other mushroom hunters in the area.

"I forgot," Sabine said simply. "That was very stupid of me, Gerald."

"Aw, it ain't yore fault, ma'am," the youth declared. "Most folks don't know nuthin' 'bout mushrooms. Walden, he knows everythin'. He knows lots o' other stuff, too. He's wicked smart. He's larnin' me to read."

Ah, ha! The early readers on the bookshelf were for Gerald.

Sabine, spying a brown flash out of the corner of her eye, spotted a chipmunk scooting across the lawn. Gerald saw the chipmunk, too. He reached under the steps for a coffee can, removed the plastic lid, and rattled the can. "Come 'n get it, Scooter! She won't hurt you none."

The chipmunk paused, but—wary of Sabine—did not venture closer. Gerald reached inside the can and drew out a handful of sunflower seeds. He lowered his hand, palm open, and made a few chirping noises. The small brown creature darted up, grabbed a black seed, then retreated a few running steps. Gerald shook the can a second time, and the chipmunk repeated the process. Finally, the chipmunk came and stuffed itself until its cheeks were full. Then the tiny creature turned tail and scampered happily back the way it had come.

Gerald dusted off his palm against his pant leg. "That's Scooter," he informed Sabine, replacing the lid and returning the coffee can to its usual position under the steps. "Walden's got him 'n his sister trained. He's got chickadees as eat out of his hand, too. The chickadees don't let me feed 'em, but Scooter does, now," he added proudly.

Sabine was impressed, not only with Nick's abilities with the wild creatures, but also with the untamed youth. Gerald had natural intelligence, she realized, despite his poor grammar. "You said Nick is teaching you to read, Gerald. Why don't you go to school with the other boys and girls?"

Gerald appeared embarrassed. He hung his head. "I'm homeschooled, ma'am. My Pa says the regular school teaches bad stuff. He don't want me to larn nuthin' down there."

Sabine suspected that Gerald's father didn't want his son to learn anything at all, but she held her tongue. "Does your father give you lessons, then?"

"Nah, he works in the woods. Ma give me some books to study, but mostly I larn from Walden. I hep him with his mushroom business, too. He 'n me is sorta partners."

"You and Nick are partners? How do you mean?"

"I hep him clean the mushrooms 'n pack 'em up. It's a lotta work to git 'em ready to go. We put 'em in special packin' boxes 'n dry ice. See, we got regular orders from big city restaurants to fill. They give us labels to use, too. When the boxes is ready to go, I runs 'em over to Leland's place afore eleven, 'cause FedEx stops there every day for Trudy's butter 'n cheese orders. That's why I come early to study on my books."

Nick was not only teaching the boy to read; he was also providing the youth with some income! The extra money was likely much needed, she divined, given the state of Gerald's clothes and shoes.

"How long have you and Nick been partners?"

"Jest since he come back. I knows him afore that, course, but didn't help him none with the mushrooms."

"Well, then I'm holding you up from your studies," Sabine announced, rising. She descended the steps and, although she wanted to pat Gerald affectionately on the head, put her hand out instead to shake his rough paw. "Thanks for keeping me company, Gerald. It's been a real pleasure talking to you."

He shook her hand, shyly. "Thank you, ma'am. My last name's Danforth," he said. "Gerald Danforth."

"Any relation to Stephen?"

"He's my grandpa. Do you know my grandpa?"

"I've seen him a few times. My name is Sabine—I'm the minister of the church this year. Your grandfather comes to our church suppers with your grandmother Nadine."

He bobbed his head in acknowledgement of that fact. "Ain't ya gonna stay 'n wait for Walden?" he asked, looking up at her.

Sabine surveyed the youth in front of her, as well as the tidy homestead. "No, I think I've found out what I came for," she said, smiling. "Just tell Nick, when he gets home, that Sabine stopped by to say 'hello'."

"I surely will, ma'am," Gerald promised. He stuck his hands back in the pockets of his hoodie, and watched her walk away.

When Sabine reached the trail through the woods, she turned and waved at Gerald Danforth. The youth waved eagerly back.

Yes, she had certainly found out what had come to the old Nutt place for. She had learned a lot about Nick's character this morning!

Chapter 17

"A Subtle Magnetism in Nature"

Sabine strolled leisurely back along the Sovereign Woods trail toward the church, enjoying the deliciousness of the June morning. When she reached the bridge, she stopped and leaned over the wood railing. The mist had completely dissipated, leaving miniature sundogs sparkling on the water in its wake. Feeling warm, she removed her fleece and tied the yellow fuzzy round her waist.

She was gloriously happy. She had done the right thing by visiting Nick's home. She had plumbed his character, without even seeing him! Sabine laughed aloud, as she realized she had subconsciously imagined Nick's dwelling as a falling-down shack or hovel, simply because he marched to a different drummer and dwelt in the old "Nutt" place. Probably some of Henry David Thoreau's neighbors had harbored similar reservations about the nineteenth century naturalist and philosopher, she thought.

Although she didn't know for sure, Sabine believed, from some of the things Nick let slip, that his initial retreat into the woods a decade ago had been an attempt to escape from emotional and spiritual pain. It dawned on her then that Thoreau's escape into nature might also have been an attempt to escape from human suffering and pain. Thoreau's retreat to Walden had worked miracles for him. If only Nick's retreat to the woods could work out one one-hundredth as well!

Sabine was lost in a daze of admiration and tenderness for Nick, when she heard her name called aloud. She turned—there he was! Standing at the south end of the footbridge.

They moved at the same time, drawn toward each other by a magnetic force beyond their control. The distance between them evaporated. Sabine suddenly found herself in Nick's arms. Her own arms slid around his waist; her head nestled naturally into the hollow of his breastbone. She was home! She felt his heart thump in response to her own leaping pulse.

"I thought I'd lost you!" he cried, holding her tightly.

She turned her face up to his, her cheeks brushing against his wiry beard. Her eyes shone brightly with love. "No, no! Not unless you run away from me again."

"Never!" he proclaimed. Unable to resist the invitation of her open lips, Nick seized her kiss.

Sabine wound her arms around his neck, and swayed against him. Their bodies met and melded into one pulsating being.

She was the first to pull away. "Not here," she gasped. "Someone might see us."

He grinned through his beard. "Worried that someone might see you and think you're human, Pastor Burbury?" he teased.

"Not just human, but easy."

Nick laughed. "You're definitely not easy! But I get your concern. Come with me."

Taking her by the hand, he led Sabine across the bridge the way he had come, into the thick woods on the other side. She followed him eagerly, trusting Nick implicitly. Sabine wondered if he was taking her to a comfortable trysting spot where he could ravage her. If so, she thought she probably would let him. She didn't think she had the will to stop, now that he had awoken the passionate woman within.

They entered a small, moss-covered grove situated past a bend in the brook. The location shielded them from any prying eyes that might happen over the bridge or upon the trail. The grove was surrounded by towering oak trees, with an open seating area in the middle containing a curious collection of flat-top tree stumps. The stumps were of various widths—from eight to fourteen inches in diameter—their roots still firmly planted in the ground. The trees had obviously been intentionally cut to create the circular sitting area. Sabine, noting that the six woodland stools appeared to be waiting for someone, felt as though she had entered a children's storybook.

"Where are the Three Bears?" she asked, smiling broadly. Still holding Nick's hand, she turned to face him. "There are enough seats here for all three bears, plus Goldilocks and a friend or two!"

He pulled her closer, crushing her softness against his hard masculine frame. "You're my Goldilocks," he whispered, releasing her hair from the ponytail. He ran his hands through her dark golden locks. "And I'm a good friend of the bears." He cupped her face between his hands and inhaled just as she was exhaling, imbibing her spirit. He covered her mouth with his own, sharing his own essence with her. They sank to the mossy ground, limbs entwined.

Without warning, Nick abruptly rolled away from her. "Don't stop," she said, weakly, reaching out to pull him back to her.

He took her hand, stood up, and raised Sabine to her feet next to him. "Nope. I've been down this road before, playing the fool for desire, while my higher nature slumbers. Thoreau says that 'Chasity is the flowering of man.'"

Sabine laughed, and rolled her eyes in disdain. "Spoken like a man who had trouble getting women!"

"Thoreau also says that 'Man flows at once to God when the channel of purity is open.' You want me to flow to God, don't you?"

"Not unless God is willing to share."

"Come over here and have a seat, Temptress." Nick pulled Sabine forward and sat her down onto one of the larger stumps.

She leaned back, hands behind her, arching her back in a suggestive fashion. "Hello, big boy!"

"I hope you don't get pitch on those pants. They look pretty nice."

Sabine quickly hopped up, and brushed off the back of her off-white jeans.

"Kidding! The stumps are oak—not pine. You're safe." Nick parked himself onto the stump across from her. "And so am I, now."

Sabine resumed her seat. She made a playful face and crossed her legs at the ankle. "Well, since we're playing 'Quote the Transcendentalist,' I've got one for you. 'There is a subtle magnetism in Nature, which, if we unconsciously yield to it, will direct us aright.' I'm feeling that subtle magnetism, and I'm ready to yield to it!'"

Nick grinned. "It figures I'd end up in the woods with the only woman in the world who can up-quote me on Thoreau."

"I doubt that, but thank you for the vote of confidence in my literary abilities." Sabine, hands resting in her lap, examined the unoccupied stumps. "Did you make this interesting troll hangout?"

"Nope. Wendell found this spot and cut the trees down so Tad and the girls could have a place to safely play when they got tired of fishing. The kids call the stumps the Toad Stools. When they got bored, Wendell would sit them down and tell them stories about all the woodland creatures that live here. I never heard him tell the stories, but Jana says Wendell had special voices for each of his characters, including Tommy Toad."

"What a special man Wendell was! Such a great loss. I bet the kids really miss him, especially Tad, of course."

"My father brings the them fishing here now," Nick continued. "I will, too, now that I'm home. I really love these woods." His voice throbbed with feeling.

Sabine held her breath, knowing that the solar farm project was rising between them like the spectral mist from Black Brook.

"Don't worry—I'm not going there," he assured her, reading her thoughts. "But I do want to apologize for being such a jerk the other day."

"Apology accepted."

"Let's just agree to disagree about the solar farm, OK?"

"OK, it's a deal," Sabine promised. "If agreeing to disagree works for Maggie and your father; why shouldn't it work for us?"

Nick seemed surprised. "I thought they agreed on everything?"

"You thought wrong, then. Trust me, I know! I lived with Maggie and your Dad for six months."

"I'm sorry I stayed away from home so long. Just think of all that time we wasted!"

"You should be sorry! Maggie's been singing your praises since I first got back to Maine. I thought you'd never get home so I could meet you."

"I'm a little slow to figure things out, in case you haven't noticed."

"How did you ever end up in Sovereign in the first place?" Sabine asked, curious. "Maggie never said. Did you have friends in town?"

Nick peeled a piece of rotting bark off his tree stump and tossed the slab into the woods. "Now, that's a story! I'm not sure you'd believe me if I told you, though."

"Of course I'd believe you."

"Did you ever read Emily Dickinson's poem about the loaded gun?"

"I think so. Isn't that the poem where the gun is a metaphor for Emily?"

"That's the one." Nick rose to his feet, and struck a pose as he quoted Emily Dickinson's poem:

> "'My Life had stood – a loaded Gun –
> In Corners – till a Day
> The Owner passed – identified –
> And carried Me away –
>
> And now We roam in Sovereign Woods –
> And now We hunt the Doe –
> And every time I speak for Him –
> The Mountains straight reply –'"

Sabine clapped her hands. "Bravo! I don't remember that part about the Sovereign Woods, though. I think you made that up."

"Not a chance, and that's where my story gets really interesting." Nick resumed his seat.

"Do tell!"

"Well, I always fancied that line—'And now we roam in Sovereign Woods.' When Nora was attending Colby College, I came up to visit her and discovered there was a town named Sovereign nearby—with thousands of acres of unspoiled woods! As soon as I learned about the Sovereign Woods I hitchhiked over. I've been here ever since. At least, until last year when I went off to find myself. Turns out, there's no place like home!"

Sabine was amazed by his tale. "Sounds like you met your destiny here in Sovereign?"

"Maybe I have," he replied, with a suggestive grin.

She blushed slightly, understanding he was referring to her. "You know, I think Maggie is hoping we'll get together."

"Ya think? Maggie is a hopeless matchmaker. I'm just glad she decided to fix you up with me, instead of someone else, like…" Nick broke off.

"Robinson Crockett?" Sabine leaned over and put her hand on his left knee reasuringly. "There's nothing between him and me, Nick, and never could be."

"I know that now. But I did have a few rough nights." He rested his hand atop hers. "You know, it's actually more comfortable leaning up against these stumps." Nick slid down to the mossy ground and patted the soft earth beside him.

Sabine didn't hesitate. She moved over and seated herself next to him, leaning her head on his shoulder.

Nick threw and arm across her. "Better?"

"Much better!"

"To be completely honest with you, I wasn't very well-received when I first came to town," he continued.

"I find that hard to believe. Everyone in Sovereign is so nice!"

"They're nice to you, because you're nice. I was an ass when I first came to town, like a bear with my snout in a beehive. I had a lot of issues. Old stuff, you know. Still comes out now and again, unfortunately. Maggie has helped me a lot over the years. And I've got high hopes her pastoral replacement might be able to help me some, too."

Sabine squeezed his hand, but said nothing. Acknowledgement that one needed help was half the battle, she knew.

"The rest of the story is ironic, actually. I came to Sovereign in the first place because of Emily Dickinson's loaded gun poem, but instead of finding love, I found the wrong end of a shotgun."

"What?!"

"I was mushrooming on Henry Trow's land—he didn't like me much, then. He thought I dumped sulfuric acid onto his newborn Scottish Highland calf."

"You're joking! That doesn't sound like Henry."

Nick crossed his heart. "Scout's honor. Just before that Henry had posted his property and tried to warn me away, but I kept mushrooming there anyway, determined to show him that he didn't own the land. That's what I mean about being an ass. Anyway, one day he got his shotgun out and shot over my head, or tried to, anyway, to scare me away. Because I'm so tall, I ended up with some birdshot in my shoulder."

"Oh, good Lord!"

"Thank goodness for Doctor Bart's clinic! He and Nelly had just opened the place. Doc removed the birdshot, cleaned me up, and sent me home with some antibiotics."

"Are you OK now?" Sabine asked, anxiously. "Was there any permanent damage?"

"Only to my ego. And Henry's, too. Turns out the little calf wasn't burned by any acid I dumped on him."

"Of course not!"

"Doctor Bart figured out that the little fellow was struck by lightning. The calf's long hair was burned, scorching the hide badly. The burn was mean looking, so I understand Henry being upset. Doctor Bart took care of the calf, too."

"Poor little thing!"

"Poor Henry, too. He was pretty cut up when he found out what he'd done. He didn't even know his shot had hit me. Then to discover that the calf was struck by lightning, which had nothing to do with me! Well, he felt awful. The old guy's really a brick. He's been my friend ever since."

"What a remarkable story! I'm glad it had a happy ending. What happened to the lightning calf?"

"Henry sold the calf and its mother a few years ago. Lightning had gotten big by then, and I guess the bull charged Henry one day, so off to the slaughterhouse they went."

"Bummer!" Suddenly, it dawned on Sabine how much the nineteenth century Amherst poet had affected the lives of those she loved. "So, Maggie and your father wouldn't even be married if you hadn't come to Sovereign?"

"Nope. We Faulkners owe everything to Emily Dickinson."

"Better Emily than Henry David," Sabine quipped, with a cheeky grin.

"Hey, I thought you were into Thoreau's 'subtle magnetism in nature'?"

"Well, I am feeling that magnetism!" She tilted her head for another kiss. To her surprise, Nick, rather than kissing her, pulled his arm away.

"Look at those oyster mushrooms on that dead beech tree," he exclaimed, scrambling to his feet. "I knew the rain would flush them out." He pulled out his mushroom knife and stalked toward the tree, where a large family of white-fleshed, brown-capped mushrooms grew. "I've got a restaurant in Freeport that will pay big-time for these babies, if Gerald can get them over to Scotch Broom Acres before the pickup. Come help me, please. I left my creel with him."

Sabine rose to her feet, laughing. "Worsted by another female! I certainly can't compete with Mother Nature's charms. What do you need me to do?"

Chapter 18

Maggie's Mission

"Thank you for not waking me up last night when you came home," Maggie said to her husband, when he surfaced for breakfast the next morning. "Must have been a wild cribbage party with the boys."

Duncan poured himself a mug of coffee from the eight-cup percolator Maggie had left on the stove. "Given the ages of the card players, I think our profligate days are over, if they ever started." He touched the side of the stainless steel pot with his right hand. "This coffee's cold."

"Yep. That's what happens when you lounge in bed all morning." Maggie started to rise from the table. "Want me to perk you the small pot?"

"I think I'll survive lukewarm coffee." Duncan pulled up a chair at the table and joined his wife, who was perusing a book of baby names for their unborn grandchild.

"How much money did you lose?" she asked, without looking up.

Duncan selected a spoon from the Depression-era spoon holder and reached for the matching cut-glass sugar bowl. He shoveled some sugar into his coffee, and stirred. "What makes you think I lost?"

"Because you came in so quietly, like you had something to hide." Maggie closed the little book. "You know, all that sugar isn't good for you, Duncan."

"Why did you put the sugar on the table to tempt me, then?"

"Because I ran out of Wendell's honey. And I don't want to ask Rebecca if she has any left."

"Why not? I'm sure she still has honey. Wendell told me he extracted several hundred pounds last year. I can't image it's all sold."

"Because asking about the honey will remind Rebecca how much Wendell loved his bees—and now he's not here to take care of them."

Duncan reached for an orange from a wooden bowl of fruit setting in the middle of the table. "I understand your concern," he said, peeling the orange. "But why are you trying to protect Rebecca from her sorrow? She has a right to her grief. My personal belief is that we should give mourners the courtesy of choosing how they would like to grieve."

"Honestly, I almost wish sometimes that I hadn't married another minister! I think we'll have to agree to disagree on this one, too. Our pastoral styles are so very different."

"So I've noticed." Duncan devoured two orange sections. "By the way, I didn't lose money—I came home with fifteen dollars. I was the night's grand winner."

"You beat Henry at cribbage?" Maggie exclaimed.

He allowed himself a smile of satisfaction. "I did. I beat Henry at his own game."

"How did you manage that?"

"I've noticed over the past few years that Henry often wins by pegging extra points. Last night I thought I'd try his tactic, and it worked. Having the right cards helped, naturally."

"Naturally."

"The bottom line is I can now afford to take my non-working wife out for Sunday dinner," he said, popping two more orange sections in his mouth.

Maggie emitted a derisive snort. "With fifteen dollars! Did you hit your head and travel back to 1984? Fifteen dollars isn't enough to buy one dinner, let alone two. If you're lucky, it might cover the tip."

"Oh, I think I can add some of my retirement money to the pot. What do you say? Shall we go out to dinner on Sunday?"

Maggie rose up and kissed her husband on the forehead. "I think we can agree on that. It's a date."

She wrote their dinner date down on the wall calendar. Noticing that Nick's birthday was coming up, she recollected the piece of news she wanted to share with her husband. "I have a hunch that Nick and Sabine are seeing each other," she informed him, returning the pen to the chiffonier.

Duncan swiveled in his chair, throwing an arm over the back. "Oh? Did Nick say something to you?"

"No, he's too familiar with my penchant for matchmaking to even mention her name. But after you left, he dropped in and wanted to borrow the car."

"Borrow the car! That certainly suggests an important occasion, such as a date. Good thing Ryan picked me up last night so the car was available. Did Nick say where he was going?"

Maggie shook her head. "No, but he was gone long enough to take Sabine to the movies in Waterville." At her words, Duncan's face brightened. Neither of his two adult children were settled yet in life, and Maggie knew that this worrisome fact caused her husband many restless nights.

"I'd like to think my son was wise enough to court Sabine. But I'm not sure what it says about her perspicacity. Did he seem happy when he came home?"

"How should I know? I was already in bed! If I don't wait up for my husband, I'm certainly not going to wait up for my thirty-four-year-old stepson. Although I did hear the car door slam and note the time, because at first, I thought it was you."

"So, you were waiting up for me! Well, we'll have to wait and see if anything transpires between Nick and Sabine. Not a parent's favorite task—waiting. Maybe Sabine will let something slip?"

"Sabine is just as cagey as Nick," Maggie replied, patting down an errant lock of her husband's graying hair. "She never mentions him to me anymore. Yet before Nick came back from his trip, she wanted to know everything about him. Sometimes lack of information is just as revealing as too much information, I think."

"Good point." Duncan gathered his orange peels up into a tidy pile. "Did Nick mention anything about the solar farm when he came to get the car? It's funny we haven't seen much of him since Rebecca's dinner party, but maybe that adds more weight to your romance hypothesis."

"Not a peep. He was distracted, though, and fidgety, like he was running late. I chalked his fidgets up to Love, capital 'L'."

"You would, Maggie, because you're an incurable romantic. Me, I'd probably think he had indigestion. Probably Nick has forgotten all about the solar project."

"Maybe."

"I wish I could forget things that easily," Duncan continued, wistfully. "Oh, for the myopia of youth!"

Her stepson might have forgotten about the solar farm, but Maggie certainly had not. The fault lines in the community revealed by the proposed project had been worrying her for weeks. Yet every time she wanted to spring into action, Duncan had talked her out of it.

Thursday afternoon Maggie decided she would go see John Woods, Sovereign's First Selectman. While Duncan had dissuaded her from speaking about the project to Leland and Rebecca (urging her to leave that duty to Sabine), he had said nothing about not approaching town officials. After the lunch dishes were washed up, she told Duncan she was going shopping in Unity—which wasn't a lie, she did have some groceries she needed to pick up—and drove over to the Sovereign Town Office.

Maggie knew that John Woods, head of Sovereign's three-member Board of Selectmen, made himself available for complaints or compliments (and there were many more complaints than compliments) on Tuesdays and Thursdays. He could also be found at Gilpin's General Store with the other Old Farts around morning break time, enjoying Courtney's donuts and coffee. When she entered the old school, which had been repurposed as the town office, Maggie was greeted by the perky Town Clerk Betty Peabody. She exchanged a few pleasantries with Betty, then asked if could speak privately with Woods, whose blue Ford pickup she had noted was parked by the side door.

John Woods appeared as if by magic from around a partition wall. "I heard that. Come on into my office here," the lanky elderly selectman invited Maggie. He flipped on the light switch in the musty-smelling office set aside for private meetings, including requests for General Assistance, and lowered himself into a tattered desk chair. His 1960s-style metal desk was covered with manila folders, letters, catalogs, and town reports. "Push those files onto the floor. Betty will clean them up later."

Maggie carefully lifted a pile of stuffed manila folders from a black stacking chair in front of the desk, and set them on the floor. She seated herself in the old chair, the padded seat of which had been repaired with gray duct tape. "You need some new chairs."

"Tell you what—I'll buy two or three and add them to your tax bill," Woods replied. "Now … let me have it. What's this visit about?"

That was all the encouragement Maggie needed. "Have you heard about the proposed solar farm? The one on Wendell's land?"

"Oh, I've heard about that solar farm! Betty tells me we're getting more calls about the solar farm than the potholes, which is a nice change, I must say."

"It's worse than the potholes?"

"Yep, but nothing like that transmission line debacle last year. Not yet, anyway. I'm sorry about the friction the solar farm has caused, because I feel bad for Rebecca. And I like the young fellow who wants to build the thing." The First Selectman fiddled with a yellow pencil laying on his desk.

"You don't think Rob is taking advantage of Rebecca, then?"

Woods gave the minister a shrewd look. "So, that's what this is about? You think a wolf has got into your flock?"

"I'm not sure about the wolf, but the flock is certainly being divided up."

"You're barking up the wrong tree with Crockett, Maggie. Of course, I haven't seen Rebecca's contract, but I do believe he's a decent, honest fellow. She seems to trust him, anyway."

Maggie was relieved to hear the First Selectman's opinion of Robinson Crockett. For all his small-town affectations, she knew John Woods was an educated, sensible man. "That was my initial impression of him, too."

"So, what's the problem?"

"I'm worried about the division in town his solar farm is causing. Yet I feel so powerless to do anything! Now that I'm on sabbatical, Duncan doesn't want me to meddle. But you know how impossible that is for me, John."

"I've known you a long time, Maggie, and meddling is what you do best. No offense—I mean that as a compliment."

"Thank you. But a minister can't just stand by and see her flock torn apart!"

Woods tapped the pencil against the top of the metal desk. "Don't fly off the handle at me when I say this, but isn't it Sabine's job to worry about your flock while you're on sabbatical? She's the shepherdess now, right?"

"Not you, too," Maggie cried. "That's what Duncan says. And don't tell me I should be a good wife and listen to my husband, because that's what all husbands say."

"I wouldn't dare do that. But maybe you should be talking to my wife—who supports the solar farm, by the way—instead of sitting here wasting my time."

"Good for Ruth!"

"Ruth will tell you what you want to hear, too. Now, is there anything else I can do for you this afternoon? You'll probably learn more about the solar farm brouhaha at the special Town Meeting in July."

The First Selectman's words took Maggie by surprise. "There's going to be a special Town Meeting? What for?"

"Why, to consider the six-month moratorium against solar farms. I figured you knew all about it, what with your stepson being the driving force behind the moratorium."

"Nick? A moratorium? I'm completely clueless, John. What on earth are you talking about?"

"It ain't complicated, Maggie. Your boy there took a petition around town getting signatures for a special Town Meeting to consider a six-month mortarium against solar farms in Sovereign. He got nearly double the signatures he needed. Nick brought me the petition yesterday, along with the proposed moratorium, and we discussed it at our selectmen's meeting last night. We voted to schedule the special Town Meeting for Saturday, July 12th."

"But Nick doesn't even have electricity! He couldn't type up a petition, let alone put a moratorium together."

"There's a new thing called a library, Maggie," Woods said drily. "He probably went down to Unity Public Library and they helped him out. He had your car the night he was out gathering signatures—he came to our place, too, but Ruth quickly showed him the door—so I figured you knew all about it."

Maggie didn't know whether to be hurt or incensed that Nick had gone behind her back. He had borrowed their car, knowing full well she would think he was taking Sabine out on a date, and instead, drove around town collecting signatures on a petition to stop the solar farm! Nick was aware that she supported the solar farm, yet he didn't trust her enough to tell her the truth, trust that she would still loan him the vehicle if she knew his purpose. After all these years! And all they had been through together, not only as family, but also as friends. Maggie was so disappointed in Nick she wanted to cry. Yet she was also so mad at him she felt she could wring her stepson's neck. Then she thought of her husband.

Duncan! Oh, Lord. What would Duncan think?

He already had a low opinion of his son, which opinion Maggie had been attempting to improve over the past few years. But this chicanery on Nick's part would sink his father's opinion even lower. Why had she told Duncan she had a hunch Nick was on a date with Sabine? Why hadn't she kept her big mouth shut?

Was there any way she could intercede to make the looming nightmare less bad? She didn't think so. One thing was certain; she needed to tell Duncan what Nick had done before he heard about the special Town Meeting and Nick's solar farm moratorium from someone else.

Chapter 19

Reporter on the Scene

Duncan decided, after Maggie departed for the grocery store (and to see John Woods, of which visit he was unaware) that it was a good afternoon to wash windows. The pine pollen, the last and heaviest of the tree pollens, had finally dropped. And thanks to the recent rains, the fine dirt in the gravel of the unpaved Cross Road was not yet airborne. (Maggie called the fine brown dust stirred up by summer traffic "back road pollen.") It was a delightful June day, with the temperature in the mid-seventies and a light westerly breeze, a perfect day to wash the old schoolhouse windows.

Suzette, a ten-year-old feline, rubbed against Duncan's ankles. "At least we'll have a few weeks where we can see out the windows before back road pollen season arrives," he said, bending down and ruffling the cat's fur. Suzette placed her front paws against the edge of the kitchen windowsill and launched her fat body up. She yawned and stretched out along the sill, rolling onto her back so the sun could warm her belly. Duncan, who had begun gathering up paper towels and window cleaner, turned and spied the recumbent cat. "Don't mind me," he said, laughing. "I'll start outside."

Although the tall windows in the cobbled-together house were not original, they were still forty or fifty years old. Before they were married, Maggie, as a single mother, never had enough money to replace the wood-frame windows. Afterward, although she and Duncan had spoken about window replacements, the purchase of new vinyl windows had been postponed from day to day, year to year. While the heat loss through the old windows in winter was considerable, so was the heat produced by the home's two woodstoves. As long as wood remained their main source of heat, Duncan suspected he and Maggie wouldn't install energy-efficient double hung windows or the heat would drive them out of the house during the shoulder seasons. In winter, they always dressed in layers. "God created sheep so we could have sweaters," Maggie had once cheekily informed him.

The other major drawback to the old windows was that they were not modern tilt-wash. To wash the outside of the windows, he had to haul the heavy, eight-foot stepladder from the shed to the front yard, and attempt to find safe footing for the wooden ladder among the shrubs and perennials. In the annual battle of man versus ladder, the odds always seemed to favor the ladder. He had taken several tumbles off the ladder over the past few years, but fortunately had never yet broken any bones or crashed through a window.

Duncan was pleased, therefore, when his son appeared from around the back of the house. "Come hold this ladder for me, will you please, Nick?"

"Should you be up there, Dad? Why don't you let me wash that top window. I can reach that with a stepstool." Nevertheless, Nick obediently came over and steadied the paint-splattered stepladder for his father, who had one foot on the sixth step and one foot on the seventh.

"As you can see, I'm already up here. Just hold it please, but watch that peony. Maggie will kill us if we trample it."

Duncan sprayed glass cleaner between the white-painted wooden grills of the top three window panes, and rubbed them vigorously with a paper towel until the glass squeaked. "Don't I hate paint splatters! This window cleaner spreads the paint around and streaks the glass. Remind me to have a word with our house painter."

"Didn't you paint the window trim last year?"

"Yep, that's the guy I'm talking about." Duncan carefully stepped down a rung and proceeded to clean three more window panes. "Are you headed across the road to mushroom behind Henry's house?"

"No, I'm going up to Stephen Danforth's."

Duncan paused momentarily when he heard his son's reply. He recollected what Maggie had told him about Leland encouraging Stephen Danforth to tell Rebecca to go back to Boston and take Robinson Crockett with her. Could Nick have had anything to do with that unfortunate episode? He wasn't aware that Nick knew their truck-driving neighbor on the Russell Hill Road, let alone ever called on Stephen Danforth. Duncan attempted to repress his suspicions. Maggie was always telling him he was too hard on Nick and she probably was right. He resumed his squirting and scrubbing without commenting.

"I'm taking some books to Danforth's grandson Gerald," Nick continued. "I'm helping Gerald learn to read. The Unity Library sent away for some cool beginning-to-read books for him."

Duncan stopped his widow cleaning and looked down at his son. "Why, Nick, that's a wonderful thing to do! I'm proud of you."

"Thanks, Dad."

"Is Gerald that wild, red-headed ragamuffin I've seen in the woods and running up and down the road at all hours of the day?"

"That's Gerald. His father has some crazy idea that education is a bad thing, so he doesn't let Gerald go to school. Stephen and Nadine know I'm teaching him to read—they want Gerald to get an education—but they're only his grandparents, not his parents, so they don't have much say in the matter."

"I would think the truant officer would have some say."

"Gerald's homeschooled, at least, his mother tries to homeschool him. Not very successfully, I guess. The kid looks up to me, though, so it's easier for me to get him to hit the books."

"Do you like being a mentor?" Duncan asked, stepping down to wash the next three panes. "I've always found mentoring young people a rewarding experience."

"Yeah, I do. It's funny, last year, before I went away, Gerald used to bug me. He was always hanging around, asking me silly questions. Now, I look forward to seeing him every morning. I'm not sure which of us has changed the most during the past year—me or Gerald."

"Sounds like you both have altered—for the better. Does Maggie know what you're doing?"

"I haven't said anything to anyone yet. I don't want to get Gerald into trouble with his old man. You can tell her if you want to, though." Nick pointed to the lower left pane in the top window. "You missed a spot, right above the sash."

Duncan leaned back a few inches, looking for the spot. His eyes met his son's eyes in the glass. He smiled. "Wouldn't you like to tell Maggie yourself? She'll be proud of your foray into mentoring. You've come a long way from the young man who came to Sovereign and passed himself off as Walden Pond."

"I hope so. I'm a decade older, now. I'm almost thirty-five, you know."

"I see you have a birthday coming up. Maggie's marked 'Nick, 35' on the calendar in red."

"That's pretty old to figure stuff out, isn't it?"

"Old? Thirty-five! Why, you're just getting started, Nick. Look me up in forty years if you think thirty-five is old. No, you're what we in our generation call a late bloomer, which, according to Maggie, is par for the course for you Millennials." Duncan climbed down the few remaining steps of the ladder, carefully holding the spray bottle of window cleaner, the roll of paper towels tucked under his arm. "I can take it from here, son, thanks for your help."

Nick released the sides of the ladder and stepped carefully over the blousy white peony plant. "Are you sure?"

"Positive. I can reach the rest of the front windows with the stepstool."

"What about the tall windows on the west?"

"The ground is flat there; no perennials to trip me up. And while I'd like to have your company, I know you need to get those books up to Gerald. Sounds like he's got a lot of years to make up for. Come and have dinner with us Sunday, instead. You can tell Maggie what you're doing with Gerald."

"OK, Dad. I'll probably see you then." Nick weaved his way around the flower gardens that broke up the small front lawn. He lifted his hand and waved goodbye to his father.

"One o'clock," Duncan called after his departing son. As he watched Nick stride purposefully up the dirt road, Duncan mentally berated himself. What a poor father he was! He always thought the worst about Nick, rather than the best. Maggie was far more supportive of his son than he was.

He returned to his window washing, promising himself that he would worry about Nick less and praise him more. Only after Nick disappeared up the hill did Duncan remember he had forgotten to ask him what he thought about the proposed solar farm.

After Duncan finished the south-facing front windows utilizing the stepstool, he wrestled the eight-foot stepladder around to the west side of the house. He gathered up his window cleaning supplies and was up to the fifth step on the ladder when he heard a vehicle approaching slowly up the gravel road from the west. Duncan paused to see if the car turned into the dooryard or drove past. He knew the vehicle wasn't his wife, because Maggie always came down the hill from the Russell Hill Road. The western section of the Cross Road from the Ridge Road to their house was full of deep potholes, which had been worsened by the recent rains. In addition, a hundred yards from their home was a washboard section of road that required careful driving (although Maggie said her grandmother swore the only remedy for them was to drive fast across the peaks of the washboarding).

The vehicle, a white SUV, initially drove past the house. Duncan lifted his hand to wave at the driver (a courtesy observed on most back roads in Maine) and continued up the ladder. The driver of the vehicle, however, changed his mind, backed up, and pulled into their dirt driveway.

Duncan heard the SUV backing up. He hesitated—not having recognized the vehicle or the driver—but then good-naturedly clambered down the ladder to walk across the lawn and greet the unknown visitor. "Lost?" he asked as the young man climbed out of the SUV.

"Yes and no," the youth replied. "Am I still in Sovereign?"

"Yep. You can get there from here."

"Then I'm not lost." The visitor slammed the SUV door shut and stuck out his hand. "Jarod Palmer. I'm a reporter for the *Morning Sentinel*."

Duncan automatically shook the young man's hand. "What can I do for you, Jarod?"

"I'm writing an article about the proposed solar farm in Sovereign. I understand there's some controversy surrounding it?"

"Probably no more controversy than there would be in any other small town in Maine. What's your angle?"

"No angle. I'm just driving around town talking to different people. Asking residents their take on the solar farm. I understand it's going to be huge. Three hundred acres, isn't it?"

"I believe that is what's proposed," Duncan said, carefully. While he had some reservations about Robinson Crockett's solar project, he didn't want to hurt Rebecca's chances for much needed additional income. "Although I would hardly term that huge. The Tri-Corners solar project in Benton, Clinton, and Unity Township is over 900 acres."

"Tri-Corners is a horse of a different color, certainly. But compared to the Cianbro solar farm in Pittsfield, which is only 57 acres, the Russell solar farm project is big."

Duncan was somewhat taken aback. "I didn't know how big the Cianbro solar farm is. It looks larger than 57 acres."

"My point exactly. Did you know, the Cianbro solar farm has more than 40,000 panels? How do you think 240,000 panels will look driving up the Russell Hill Road?"

"You won't be able to see all the panels from the road," Duncan pointed out. He was beginning to be irritated at the reporter, who obviously was going to write about the proposed Sovereign solar farm with a negative slant.

"Sounds like you're in favor of the project?"

"I'm in favor of clean, renewable energy. You can quote me on that."

"Thanks, I will." The reporter pulled out a small notebook and pen, and scribbled a few words. He looked up. "What's your name?"

Duncan realized he hadn't introduced himself when the two men shook hands. "Duncan Faulkner."

The reporter glanced up. "Any relation to Nick?"

"Nick is my son. Why?"

"Nick's the one who called me up about this story. I understand he put together a moratorium against solar farms in Sovereign and collected enough signatures to force a special Town Meeting next month."

"My son forced a special Town Meeting? For a solar farm moratorium? Impossible! I was with him not fifteen minutes ago. You must be mistaken."

"Does your son live off-grid in a cabin in the Sovereign Woods?"

Duncan felt as though he had been kicked in the gut. His heart flopped unnaturally, as though that organ had turned over in his chest. He realized he was sweating profusely and that he suddenly felt faint. Who was this youth and why was he in their driveway?

The earth began to spin. Duncan collapsed to the ground.

Chapter 20

Wendell's Promise

Sabine decided it was time she had a heart-to-heart chat with Leland Gorse. She had now visited with Rebecca Russell several times since that sad morning at church when Stephen Danforth told Rebecca to go back to Boston and take the solar farm developer with her. But she had not yet confronted Leland about his role in putting Danforth up to that mean remark. Today, she would beard the aging lion in his den.

Sabine hoped to get the wily octogenarian not only to admit his role in the fracas during her visit, but also to learn his motivation. She suspected that, at his core, there was more going on for the old woodchopper than animosity toward the proposed solar farm. Certainly, until the project was announced, Leland felt nothing but fondness for Rebecca and young Tad. Now, he appeared to be going out of his way to make life difficult for them—in direct opposition to his deceased friend's wishes. She wasn't sure she would be able to get Leland to speak freely, but she was determined to try.

Sabine knew that on Thursdays Ryan MacDonald, Leland's son-in-law, volunteered with the Maine Volunteer Lawyers Project, so he would be away from the farm. She also thought if she waited until her usual office hours at the church were over, Leland's daughter Trudy would be home from her librarian job at the school. Wanting to speak with Leland privately, Sabine elected to skip her office hours on Thursday. She taped a note to her office door informing drop-in visitors that business called her away. She also left her cell number for anyone who needed to schedule a pastoral visit. Then she drove over to Scotch Broom Acres, the Gorse-MacDonald family farm.

When she arrived at the farm, Sabine was relieved to see that Leland's battered pickup was the only vehicle in the dooryard. Although his truck was parked in front of the white clapboarded house, she realized that didn't necessarily mean that the woodchopper was at home. Despite his advanced years, Leland still cut firewood for the family's use. He also sold firewood for pocket money. (Trudy and Ryan paid all the household and farm expenses, including taxes and insurance.) Leland could be out on the property with the team of oxen he used to twitch out logs in place of a tractor or bulldozer.

Sabine knocked on the outer shed door. No answer. She rapped again, harder this time. When still nobody replied, she opened the unlocked door and stuck her head inside the shed. She loudly called Leland's name and was debating whether to walk in and knock on the inner door, when she felt a tap on her back. Sabine whirled around. "Whoa! You startled me."

"Was in the barn, Minister," said Leland, with a grin. "I saw ya drive in. If you come to see Trudy, she ain't home yet."

"I'm not here to see Trudy," Sabine replied, with a smile.

"Ryan ain't home neither." Leland adjusted his battered cap, exposing a feather or two of-white hair. He scratched his head.

Sabine stepped down off the granite stoop so that she was at ground level with the old woodsman. "I'm here to see you."

"Me?" he asked, surprised. Leland's watery blue eyes met her brown ones. "I ain't done nuthin', 'cept I ain't been to church but once or twice since Trudy's Ma died."

On the drive over Sabine had considered how best to broach the subject of Leland's opposition to the solar farm. She suspected she would go further plumbing his emotional depths if she took a less direct approach and therefore had planned her opening shot with a good dollop of feminine charm. She patted his arm. "Don't worry, Leland, I'm not here to lecture you about not attending church," she assured him sweetly. "I want to talk with you about the Revere bell. The church bell has been repaired, but we need your help for the rededication celebration. Do you have a few minutes?"

Leland's ears perked up at the request for his help. "I guess I got time." He stepped up and pushed open the shed door, then moved aside so Sabine could enter. "Head on into the kitchen there and make yerself to home. I gotta take my boots off or Trudy'll have my hide."

Sabine entered the shed and walked across the worn wooden floor planks. She opened the door to the pretty country kitchen and stepped inside, waiting patiently in the large rectangular room while Leland removed his crud-encrusted barn boots. The traditional eat-in kitchen had a newish yellow-and-gray vinyl floor covering that was patterned after vintage linoleum. The kitchen was neat and clean. Various jars and tins on the counter were arranged by height, the contents of each legibly marked. A small cast-iron woodstove held a bouquet of freshly-cut wildflowers, arranged by youthful hands. Photos of Ryan and Trudy's two daughters, Alice Rose and Hope, were splashed across the refrigerator.

Leland shuffled into the room in his stockinged feet. Since the June afternoon was warm, he left the shed doors open behind him. One lone housefly followed him into the kitchen, as did a whiff of cow manure from the barn. "Have a seat," he said, gesturing toward the oval oak table next to the south window, around which five matching chairs were grouped. "Can I git you a drink o' water?"

"No, thanks. I'm fine." Sabine slid into the chair nearest the door.

Leland took the seat beside her and folded his gnarled hands upon the cotton placemat. "So, you got thet old bell repaired, didja?"

Sabine smoothed down the skirt of her dress. "We certainly did, thanks to the money we raised at our spring fundraiser. The Sovereign firefighters are going to rehang the bell in the steeple in early August."

"Thet so?"

"Somebody—I forgot who—is bringing over a crane to hang it with."

"Probably Amos Hunt," Leland stated, thrumming his fingers against the tabletop. "He bought one of them used cranes when he retired from the shipyard."

"Yes, I think it is Mr. Hunt," Sabine said, nodding.

"Hope he got them hydraulics fixed."

"Me, too!"

"Jest don't be offering rides on his rig to the bell tower," Leland advised, shooing away the pesky housefly.

Sabine laughed. "Crane rides are not on our itinerary for the day, but a good dose of history is. Did you know that one of Wendell's ancestors brought the Revere bell to Sovereign? Jonathan Russell hauled the bell on a wagon from Belfast with his ox team. I read that in one of the old town reports we have at the church."

"Seems factual. Warn't no other way to git thet bell here. She probably sailed from Boston to Belfast. Them packet ships sailed nearly every day back then."

"The bell did sail from Boston, I believe. The church celebration committee would like to recreate that event, not from Belfast, of course. We're going to truck the bell to the Sovereign train station, just to give us a fun starting point, although the train isn't running there yet, unfortunately. We wondered if you and your oxen could haul the bell from the station? We think it weighs about five hundred pounds."

Leland whistled. "Bringing up the bell the old-fashioned way. Won't the kids like thet! Ishmael 'n Isaac won't mind a bit, neither."

"I'm sorry, who?"

"Ishmael 'n Isaac—my oxes. Five hundred pounds is jest what they likes to haul, too."

"Perfect!"

"And 'tain't no distance from the train station to the church—'twould take less than an hour. Course we'll go by the old stagecoach road, not the main road. My boys don't travel too fast. Since I traded my hosses for oxes, even the Amish go zipping by us, nowadays."

Sabine laughed, picturing a neat Amish buggy pulled by a dark-colored standardbred horse trotting past Leland and his team of oxen. "Maybe your granddaughters and Tad and Jana could ride in the wagon with the bell?" she suggested. "That is, if the kids don't add too much extra weight."

Leland snorted. "Ishmael and Isaac won't even know them kids is in the wagon! They don't weigh much more 'n kitten apiece.

"We'll have to get their parents' consent, of course."

"Oh, they won't mind none. Leastways, Trudy won't. She trusts me with Alice Rose 'n Hope. I ain't so sure 'bout Rebecca, though," Leland added, as an afterthought.

"Rebecca? Oh, if Trudy trusts you with the kids, I'm sure Rebecca does, too."

"Oh, 'tain't cause she don't trust me. It's on account o' thet solar farm, you know."

Sabine caught her breath. Here was the opening she was looking for. "Because you and Nick are trying to shut the solar farm down?" she asked, carefully. "Why are you opposed to the project, if it's what Wendell wanted?"

"I ain't entirely opposed," Leland replied, testily. "I jest don't believe Wendell would have wanted to see *all* his trees cut down."

Leland's anger alerted Sabine that she had reached sensitive territory. "I'm sorry there's been a falling out between you and Rebecca," she sympathized. "She and Tad miss seeing you. Don't you miss them?"

"Course I miss 'em! I miss Wendell, too. He was my best friend." Leland angrily slapped his left hand against the tabletop. " Do ya know, he was fifteen years younger 'n me? He was nearly twenty years younger 'n Maynard Nutter, yet old Maynard is still kicking 'n Wendell is pushing up daisies. Jest don't seem fair Wendell went afore the two of us!" Two giant tears escaped the woodsman's watery eyes.

Moved, Sabine gathered up Leland's knobby hand between both of her own. His skin felt warm and dry to the touch. "If there's one thing I've learned, it's that life isn't fair," she responded, with feeling. "I don't like death much, either."

"You know what Wendell promised?" Leland continued. "He promised to live to be 110. Long 'nuff to meet his grandkids. Now, he ain't even gonna see Tad graduate from grade school."

Sabine gave Leland's hand an empathetic squeeze, but said nothing.

"When he promised thet, I said I'd live to be 120. Ain't thet a funny? I didn't mean it, but now I aim to live thet long, jest to spite the devil."

Somewhat startled, Sabine released the woodchopper's hand. "Do you think you'll be going to the hot spot when you die?"

Leland offered up a bitter laugh. "Course. And Wendell's in Heaven. He and I—we ain't never gonna see each other agin."

"Oh, I don't believe that! Well, I believe Wendell is in Heaven, certainly—he was such a kind, generous man—but I don't believe you're going to Hell, Leland. Why do you think you are?"

"Partly on account o' what I've done to Rebecca, and partly on account o' other things I'druther not mention. If my Pa was alive, he'd take me out to the woodshed 'n whup me fer shore."

"Because you encouraged Stephen Danforth to say what he did to Rebecca?"

"Yep. And now I don't dare look her in the face. She's like a younger sister to me 'n I know she's hurting, but still—I got to hurt her more. I feel like I fell off a sweet-smelling hay wagon into a pit o' liquid manure."

Although Leland's imagery was clear, Sabine was unable to follow his train of thought. "Why do you think you need to hurt Rebecca more? And why did you put Stephen Danforth up to saying that mean thing in the first place, if you feel such affection for her?"

"Cause I was mad at thet Robinson Crockett. And mad at Rebecca for sayin' Wendell wanted his woodlot cut fer the solar farm. I don't believe it! I know how much thet woodlot meant to Wendell."

"You don't think Rebecca lied!"

"Nope, thet Crockett fellow's pullin' the wool over her eyes. But she don't know no better," Leland allowed, with a sigh. "She's from Away."

Sabine pulled back. "I'm from Away. I suppose I don't know any better, either?"

"Aw, you was born in Banger, Minister. We don't hold it agin ya that yer Ma took ya to Alaska as a tot. You come back home now, didn't ya?"

"I'm not sure where home is, if you want to know the truth," she replied. "But I'm curious, Leland. Why did you and Wendell promise to live so long? It was a joke, right?"

"I was sort of funning, but Wendell warn't joking. He promised to live thet long so as he could take care o' Rebecca 'n Tad."

Sabine pondered the woodchopper's words. "Isn't that what Wendell was doing by agreeing to Robinson Crockett's solar farm? Ensuring that his wife and son would be taken care of if anything happened him?"

Leland scratched the white stubble on his chin. "I suppose 'twas."

"I'm beginning to wonder if Wendell hadn't been feeling unwell for a while, but didn't say anything because he didn't want to worry Rebecca?"

"Ayuh, I been thinkin' thet myself. He said at Christmastime he warn't interested in tappin' his maple trees this year. I shoulda known then somethin' warn't right."

"It's much easier to see these sorts of things in hindsight, Leland. It doesn't do any good to berate yourself now, though."

"It surely don't. He ain't comin' back."

"I know you're mad at Wendell for breaking his promise to live a long time, but doesn't Rebecca have more of a right to be mad at him than you do? After all, he promised to love and care for her at the altar?"

Leland heaved a heartfelt sigh. "Yep. Poor Rebecca. Poor little Tad! He's an awful good chap. A chip off the old block."

"Maybe you could go over and see them some afternoon when Tad's home from school?"

"Maybe I will. Tell you what, I'll go over to visit after the Town Meeting, if she still wants to see me."

"Why wouldn't Rebecca want to see you? She's as fond of you as you are of her."

"She might not be—not after Town Meeting."

Sabine was confused. "What meeting are you talking about? Didn't Sovereign already have its Town Meeting in March?"

"I means the special Town Meeting next month, the one where we're gonna vote on Walden's thingamagibbit."

Sabine felt a little stab of fear upon hearing Nick's former pseudonym. Now, what had Nick done? "What are you talking about?"

"The thingamagibbit sayin' we don't want no solar farms in Sovereign, leastways, not for six months. Walden done got up a petition 'n went round town gettin' signatures so as to bring it to a vote."

"You mean—a moratorium?"

"Yep. Thet's the word I was lookin' fer. Walden has wrote up a moratorium."

Sabine was dismayed by Leland's artless disclosure. She knew Nick opposed the solar farm, but it never occurred to her that he would shepherd a moratorium for the town to vote on. And a special Town Meeting had already been called!

Nick had done all this—and yet he had not mentioned one word about the solar farm moratorium to her!

Well, the truth was obvious. Nick didn't trust her.

Chapter 21

Duncan Delivered

Sabine departed Scotch Broom Acres not long after Leland's disclosure about the special Town Meeting and Nick's moratorium against solar farms. Rather than return to the church by the paved road, she decided to take the shortcut over the gravel Cross Road. By going this way, there was a slight possibility she might run into Nick mushrooming on Henry Trow's land. If she didn't see him, she would stop at Maggie's and walk in to Nick's homestead to speak with him. She wanted to believe that Leland had simply misunderstood what Nick had done, but no matter how hard she tried to convince herself that the elderly man was confused, she didn't believe it. No, Nick deliberately hadn't told her about his moratorium because he didn't trust her to remain neutral. And that fact hurt.

In addition, Sabine had not forgotten that during his visit to her office Robinson Crockett had informed her he had purchased all the equipment for the solar farm in advance. She knew the developer had financially extended himself and his company to do it, attempting to get ahead of the new tariffs being imposed on Chinese goods. And as far as she knew, all that material was still sitting in containers in Boston, racking up storage charges. If the town passed the six-month moratorium against solar farms, Robinson Crockett would not only likely go bankrupt, but also Rebecca would lose the income she needed to maintain herself and Tad. Was there no middle ground she could find between the two sides?

When she approached Maggie and Duncan's house, she was alarmed to see the Unity Ambulance parked in the driveway, red lights flashing. Sabine immediately pulled over to the side of the road near the ambulance, and jumped out of the vehicle. She rushed up to where two medical attendants were bending down over a body lying in the grass. It was Duncan!

"Oh, my God! Is he hurt? Did he have a heart attack?" Sabine queried, looking anxiously from one EMT to the other.

"Still breathing," announced one of the EMTs. "Are you family?" he asked Sabine, taking Duncan's wrist to check his pulse.

"I'm the family minister," she replied, with a professional brusqueness that belied her anxiety.

"Can you hear me, sir?" asked the second EMT.

Duncan opened his eyes. "What happened?" he asked groggily.

"We're trying to find that out. Just relax while we check you over."

Sabine was relieved that Duncan was conscious, but worried that he appeared confused. Was he having a stroke? She knelt on the hem of her dress, took his hand in her own, and squeezed it. He faintly squeezed back. She looked back up at the EMT. "Where's Maggie? His wife?"

"Not sure. Pulse is 135," the EMT responded. "I'll get the stretcher and alert Thayer that we're on the way." He headed toward the back of the open ambulance.

"There's nobody here but me," said a young man, hovering nearby. "Mr. Faulkner was washing windows, and I stopped to ask him a few questions about the solar farm."

"The solar farm!" Sabine exclaimed. She examined the stranger, whom she had not noticed upon driving up. "What for?"

"I'm writing an article for the *Morning Sentinel.* We were talking about his son Nick and …"

"Nick!"

"… and Mr. Faulkner sort of collapsed. I called 9-1-1 and then knocked on the door, but nobody else is home."

"We need to tell Maggie," Sabine declared. She pulled her phone out her dress pocket and dialing her friend and mentor. But Maggie didn't answer her cell, so she left a brief message advising her that Duncan had taken ill and that Unity Ambulance was going to deliver him to Thayer Hospital in Waterville.

Duncan, hearing Sabine's message to his wife, attempted to sit up. He groaned, however, and collapsed back down. "My head! No hospital," he said, through clenched lips. "I'm fine. Just need something to drink."

"We're going to hook you up to some IV saline solution, sir," the second EMT told Duncan. "You appear to be dehydrated."

"I've been washing windows. It was hot," Duncan acknowledged. "Sabine, tell them I don't need to go to the hospital."

Sabine looked at his pale white face. "I can't do that, Duncan. You need to let the EMTs do what they think is best. I couldn't live with myself if I sent them away and something happened to you. Think of Maggie, and you'll know we're doing the right thing by taking you to the hospital."

"I suppose so. Seems like a lot of trouble."

"No trouble at all, sir," said the first EMT, coming up with the collapsable stretcher. "We'll get you hooked up to the heart monitor in the ambulance. That way we can see what's going on and prepare the crew at Thayer."

"Looks like you don't need me anymore," the reporter interjected, edging toward his SUV. "Thanks for your help, Mr. Faulkner. Hope you feel better soon!"

Sabine rose up and quickly followed the reporter. "Not so fast!" She took the young man's arm and pulled him out of earshot as the EMTs lifted Duncan onto the stretcher. "You're not going to write anything about the solar farm for tomorrow's paper, are you?"

"Actually, I was. You see, I've been in Sovereign interviewing people all day."

"Well, whatever Duncan said to you—Mr. Faulkner, that is—forget it. He's obviously not himself."

"He was perfectly lucid during our conversation, I assure you."

"Let me try this another way," Sabine countered. "Do you want me to call your editor and tell him or her that you're taking advantage of an elderly man who collapsed while you were questioning him and was hauled to the hospital by an ambulance?"

The reporter's defiant stance crumbled. "Maybe the article can wait a few days. I'll give Mr. Faulkner a call next week."

"Do that, thank you."

The young man hopped into his white SUV and backed out of the driveway. Sabine joined the medics at the ambulance. "Can I ride with him to the hospital?" she asked, anxiously.

"There really isn't room," the first EMT replied without looking up. The two men loaded Duncan into the ambulance. "You can follow us to the hospital, though. That would be best."

Duncan struggled to sit up on his elbows. "Get my wallet from the chiffonier," he directed Sabine. "I'll need my Medicare card."

"Relax, Mr. Faulkner," encouraged the EMT. "We'll take care of everything."

"I'll bring your wallet, don't worry, Duncan," Sabine assured him.

"No siren, either," Duncan added, before dropping back down on the stretcher. "Don't want to scare the deer."

Sabine laughed, relieved to know Duncan was feeling well enough to joke.

The EMT chuckled. "We only use the siren in traffic, sir. Not much call for it in this neck of the woods."

Duncan was shortly closed inside the ambulance, attended by the first medic. The second EMT turned to Sabine. "We'll deliver Mr. Faulkner to Thayer safe and sound. See you there." Then he hopped into the driver's seat, backed the ambulance out of the driveway, and accelerated up the hill.

Sabine went into the house to look for Duncan's wallet. She found the creased leather wallet on the stenciled chiffonier and glanced around the kitchen, wondering what else she should do before heading to the hospital in Waterville. Should she bring an extra set of clothes for Duncan? No, he might not be staying, and anyway she could always come back for them.

Sabine exited the shed, leaving the door unlocked. Both shed doors—the inner and outer—only locked by a sliding bolt from the inside. She could lock the doors and exit through the back, however, Sabine knew that Maggie and Duncan almost never locked their doors, even when they went away. They trusted not only their neighbors, but also random strangers to Sovereign, and so far, their trust had been warranted.

The ambulance was already out of sight by the time Sabine left the house. She climbed into her vehicle and stuffed Duncan's wallet and her phone into her purse. She started the car and pulled into the driveway to turn around.

After she backed out onto the Cross Road, Sabine spied Nick loping down the hill toward the house. She stepped on the gas and drove up to him.

"What the heck is going on?" he asked, bending down to speak to her through the open window. "The ambulance just whizzed by me."

"Get in," Sabine enjoined. "I'll tell you everything on the way to the hospital." She reached over and picked up her purse, tossing the pocketbook into the back seat.

Nick strode around the front of the vehicle and folded himself into the passenger seat. "Was it Dad? Did he fall off the ladder?" he asked anxiously.

Sabine put the car in gear and took off up the hill in pursuit of the speeding ambulance. "No. Your father collapsed on the front lawn."

"Holy heck! What happened?"

"We don't know for sure. One of the EMTs said he thought your Dad was dehydrated. They hooked him up to a heart monitor in the ambulance, so we'll find out more when we get to the hospital. He seemed OK, just weak. He joked about not using the siren or it would scare the deer."

Nick shook his head in bewilderment. "I can't believe it! Dad seemed fine when I was with him only an hour ago."

Surprised, Sabine took her eyes off the road for a second to glance over at Nick. "You were with your father this afternoon?"

He nodded. "I held the ladder for Dad while he washed some of the front windows. There was nothing wrong with him, then. I offered to stay and help, but he said he could do the rest on his own. I bet it was that old wooden ladder! Dad shouldn't be hauling that heavy thing around at his age. He shouldn't be washing the high widows still, either."

As she listened to Nick vent about the wooden ladder, Sabine began to suspect that his agitation might have another cause. Had Nick told his father about the solar farm moratorium? Had Duncan been stewing over that when he collapsed? "What did you two talk about?"

"Not much. He wanted to know where I was headed and I told him I was taking some books up to Stephen Danforth's for Gerald. We talked about mentoring a bit, that was it."

She gripped the steering wheel with both hands. "Did you tell your father about your moratorium?" She heard Nick's sharp intake of breath.

"So, you know about that? No, I didn't tell him about the moratorium. I was going to, but Maggie wasn't there. I want to tell them both together."

Nick's lame excuse irritated Sabine. "When were you going to tell *me* about your moratorium? After the special Town Meeting was over? Did you think I wouldn't find out beforehand? Did you think your father wouldn't? Oh, Nick! What have you done?"

They reached the stop sign at the end of the road, and she automatically signaled a left turn. Sabine glanced both ways to ensure that the coast was clear, then pulled out onto the Russell Hill Road.

"I was going to tell you this afternoon, Sabine, honestly," he pleaded, "when your office hours were over. I was going to tell Dad and Maggie about the moratorium soon, too. Like I said, I was just waiting for the right time."

"Well, the reporter from the *Sentinel* wasn't waiting for the right time. He told your father about your moratorium after you left, I'm sure."

"Jarod Palmer was here already? Boy, he didn't let the grass grow under his feet!"

"You know him?"

"Yeah, we spoke on the phone."

Sabine shot Nick a dubious look.

"The Unity Library let me use their phone to call the newspaper," he clarified. "I asked for a reporter and was connected to Jarod. He seemed knowledgeable enough, so

I told him about the proposed solar farm—how huge it was compared to other solar farms in the area—and how we're planning to stop it. I mean, just look at that view!" Nick pointed down the hill at the Russell's western hayfields.

Sabine slowed the car, gazing at the view. The tall grass in the two unmown fields undulated in the breeze. The meadow seemed to flow down the hill, an ocean of green, until the grassland came to a stop lapping the eastern edge of Wendell's 300-acre woodlot.

"Now, picture 240,000 solar panels in place of the fields and trees," Nick continued. "Pretty hideous, right?"

"The view *is* beautiful," she admitted.

"So, you agree with me?" His eyes flashed triumphantly.

"Just because I think it's a beautiful view doesn't mean I'm going to oppose the solar farm. I said I'm not going to take sides, and I'm not." Sabine stepped on the gas. "Besides, with your father in the hospital, suddenly the solar farm doesn't seem so important."

A few seconds later they motored past the Russell homestead. Nobody was in sight. Sabine debated telling Nick that Leland was having second thoughts about his opposition to the solar farm. She realized, however, that what the old woodchopper had told her earlier had been revealed in confidence.

At the stop sign, she turned left onto Route 9. Traffic on the main road was steady, giving Sabine an excuse to focus on her driving. They drove in stilted silence for ten minutes, until she slowed down to cross the railroad tracks and navigate through downtown Unity. "I'm worried you're moving too fast, Nick," she said, finally. "People are getting hurt."

"What people?"

"Rebecca and Tad. And Robinson Crockett."

"I don't give a damn about Crockett—he's nothing to me."

"What about Rebecca and Tad? I know how fond you are of Tad. And I thought you liked Rebecca?"

"I do like Rebecca. And Tad is a champ. They'll be OK—the townspeople will take care of them. Who else am I hurting?"

"Your father?" she suggested.

"That's a low blow, Sabine! You don't know that the moratorium had anything to do with Dad's collapse."

"No, I don't. But I wonder how Duncan felt when he heard about the moratorium from the newspaper reporter? Especially after he had just seen you, Nick. And you never mentioned it!"

"He probably wasn't too happy with me," Duncan agreed, grudgingly. "Wouldn't be the first time."

Yes, but when will it be the last time? Sabine wanted to ask, but she didn't. Instead, she kept her mouth shut. Except for a few perfunctory remarks, they drove in silence the rest of the way to the hospital, each lost in his own thoughts.

To Sabine's relief, Maggie was already at the hospital when they arrived. Maggie met her and Nick in the waiting area at Thayer's Emergency Department. "How is he?" Sabine asked, holding out her arms to her friend.

"He's OK," Maggie assured them, brushing away a few tears.

Sabine hugged the other minister. "Thank goodness!"

"The ambulance heart monitor didn't show any sign of a heart attack. They're running some tests here, just to be sure. The doctor thinks Duncan was probably just dehydrated. He was out in the hot sun washing windows for several hours, and I guess he didn't bother to stop and get a drink."

"I was worried he fell off the ladder," said Nick. "Thank God it wasn't anything serious!"

Maggie made a face. "That damn ladder! When you get back to our house, haul that ladder out to the burn pile."

"Love to get rid of that thing! Can I see Dad, now?"

Maggie hesitated for the briefest of seconds. "Not now. They're still running some tests, I think. I'll go back in with him, but the room is pretty small. Why don't you two go home? You two don't need to waste the rest of your day here. They're not even going to keep him overnight for observation. We might be late, though. Would you mind feeding the cat?"

"Of course, whatever you need," said Sabine. "But don't you want us to wait here with you?"

"No, no. Duncan doesn't want to see anybody now. I guess he's tuckered out," Maggie added, awkwardly.

Nick took a step backward, as though struck by an unexpected blow. "He doesn't want to see anybody? You mean, me? He doesn't want to see me?"

Sabine registered the anguish in Nick's voice. We reap what we sow, she thought to herself. When would Nick learn?

"Your father doesn't mean anything. He's just tired, that's all," Maggie assured her stepson, somewhat unconvincingly. "Maybe you could call your sister? Oh, I forgot—you don't have a phone."

Sabine pulled her cell phone out of her purse. "Don't worry, we'll take care of everything," she told Maggie. "Text me if there's anything else you want us to do." She tugged on Nick's arm. "Let's go."

Nick turned and moved blindly toward the exit. "He doesn't want to see me!"

Sabine reached for his hand, but Nick shook her off. "You heard Maggie—your father didn't mean anything," she encouraged him. "He's just tired out."

"You don't know my father, Sabine. Dad doesn't get mad very often, but when he does—watch out!"

"Well, then, let's just be grateful he's healthy enough to *be* mad. He could have been like Wendell."

"What do you mean?"

"He could be dead. Now, you get a second chance to be honest with your father."

Nick shook his head sorrowfully. "I think I've used up all my second chances with Dad."

"Don't think like that, Nick. Think of Peter, and Jonah, and David."

"I don't know those guys."

"You would have if you hadn't stopped going to church when you were ten," Sabine gently chided him. "God gave Peter and Jonah and David a second chance. Some of them, He forgave a whole lot more often! And while you say I don't know your father, remember, I lived with Duncan and Maggie for more than six months. Forgiveness is a choice, Nick. Your father might be angry with you now, but if there's one thing I've learned about Duncan, it's that he always chooses to do what is right."

Chapter 22

A House Divided

Duncan was finally discharged from the Thayer Emergency Department at 10 p.m. Maggie drove straight home and was able to tuck her husband into bed by eleven o'clock. She went downstairs to check the landline for messages; pet the cat; and get herself something to eat. She also flipped on the outdoor light and reassured herself that Nick had disposed of the wooden ladder as requested. Then she went back upstairs and crawled into bed next to Duncan. She still had many questions she wanted to ask him, some of which she thought she knew the answers to; however, they would wait until the morrow.

When Maggie awoke the next morning, she was surprised to discover that Duncan was already up. She pulled on a cotton robe and padded down the narrow wooden stairs in her bare feet. Maggie found her husband, fully dressed, huddled over a cup of coffee at the kitchen table. He was staring out one of the windows he had washed the day before.

"You missed a spot," she joked, pouring a cup of lukewarm coffee.

"I missed a lot of spots," Duncan replied. He pushed his cup away from him and folded his hands on the table in a determined manner.

Maggie recognized the sign and knew that he was troubled. He had obviously been meditating on something while waiting for her to arise. "Want some scrambled eggs?" she asked brightly.

"Thanks. That would be nice."

She dumped the coffee grounds out of the basket and perked a fresh pot of coffee as she fixed them both scrambled eggs and homemade whole wheat toast. "Don't get used to this," she advised, setting the hot plate of food and a steaming cup of coffee in front of her husband. "This is to make up for yesterday, when I wasn't here."

Duncan caught her by the wrist. "You're always here," he said. His free hand lightly thumped his chest. "In my heart."

Maggie burst into tears and threw her arms around his neck. "Oh, I thought I'd lost you! When I listened to that message from Sabine, I went a little nutty. I'm surprised I didn't get a speeding ticket on the way to the hospital. I nearly pushed two pokey old ladies off the road in Unity Plantation when I passed them." She straightened up and wiped the tears from her eyes with a cloth napkin.

Duncan gently pulled her down into the chair next to him. "I think it's time we admitted we're the old people now."

"Not on your life! I'm not old, and neither are you, dear. According to the doctor, your heart is fine—you could live another twenty years. You were just dehydrated." She pointed to his plate. "Eat! Your eggs are getting cold."

Duncan obediently picked up his fork. "We've never spoken about getting old, Maggie, because we both feel so young, still. But I think it's time we had The Talk."

"The Talk? Oh, my God! We're not going to discuss death and dying, are we, Duncan?" Maggie rose up and retrieved her own breakfast, then reclaimed her seat.

"No, something even worse. Good eggs, by the way, thanks."

"What's worse than death and dying?"

"Getting there." He took a sip of hot coffee. "It's been my experience that dying is the easy part. The hard part is the debilitating journey along the way. I've noticed that not many of us humans are able to walk upstairs, brush our teeth, lie down in bed, and die peacefully in our sleep."

"My father did," Maggie remarked, biting into a piece of toast.

"Your father was a lucky man. How many other old people do you know who were reasonably healthy until they died in their sleep?"

When Maggie was unable to name a second individual, she finally admitted to the reality of the situation: they were getting old. Their bodies were wearing down. They needed to make some changes before being overcome with what would likely be future debilitations.

Over the course of the next hour, the two senior ministers discussed how they would prepare for their final years. Maggie fetched one of the yellow-lined pads that she utilized for her sermons and together they made a To-Do list. The old windows would be replaced by new, tilt-wash windows; the woodstoves would be supplemented by heat pumps and small electric radiators; and no new perennials or flower gardens would be planted. They would also make an appointment with Ryan to review their legal documents, as well as with Doctor Bart, to review their end of life choices. Finally, when the time was right, they would move their bedroom downstairs, into Nellie's old room.

"I really can't imagine why I haven't asked Nellie to clear her things out of that room," Maggie said, picking up the dirty dishes and placing them in the sink.

"I can. It's because you don't want to admit that your little girl has grown up and left home. I was the same way when Nora left for college. I didn't clean out her room until I sold the house and moved here."

"I suppose you're right," Maggie said, with a little sigh. "I'll add talking with Nellie about her stuff to my side of the list."

She scraped the egg scrids off the breakfast plates and filled the sink with hot soapy water. Now that their discussion about preparing to age in place was over—and Duncan's concerns had been addressed—she could tackle her own. Maggie had learned from the EMTs at the hospital that a reporter from the *Morning Sentinel* had been with Duncan when he blacked out. She suspected that the reporter had told her husband about Nick's moratorium against solar farms, and that this disquieting information had contributed to his collapse. Maggie felt she needed to know the truth about what had occurred, especially after Duncan had refused to see Nick at the hospital. When she had asked why, her husband had declined to give her an explanation. She hadn't pushed him further, then.

Fortunately, Duncan had left her an easy segue with their prior conversation. "Well, you'll be pleased to know we've already made some progress on our Elixir List." (Maggie had jocularly named their plan for aging in place their Elixir List, proclaiming the 'To-Do' list was a remedy for their final journey.) "The ladder you hate has already gone to the burn pile. Nick said he'd take care of it for me. I checked last night and the ladder is gone."

Duncan frowned at the mention of his son's name, but said nothing.

"Remind me to thank him next time he's here," she continued, rinsing off a plate and stacking it in the drainer. When Duncan still didn't respond, Maggie turned to face him. "Aren't you going to say anything?"

"What do you expect me to say?"

"How about, 'Good for Nick,' or 'He's a good son'?"

The frown on Duncan's face deepened, but he remained silent. His stubborn silence reminded Maggie of one of her mother's favorite admonitions: "When you have nothing nice to say, Margaret, say nothing at all." Duncan ascribed to that same philosophy. His silence was a bad sign, and almost certainly meant the reporter had told Duncan about the solar farm moratorium.

"Why didn't you want to see Nick at the hospital?" she persisted, unwilling to let the matter drop.

"I'm mad at him."

"I gathered that," she replied, drily. "What I want to know is why?"

He ignored her question. Instead, Duncan stood up and pushed in his chair. "I'm mad at my son and I don't want to talk about it. I need some time to think things over."

"Don't you think you'll feel better if you share what's troubling you?" she pleaded.

"No, I don't."

"Why not?"

"Because you always take Nick's side."

"I do not! Not always, anyway," Maggie amended, hastily.

"Almost always. I'm not sure if you stick up for Nick because you met him before you met me and you still have a soft spot for 'Walden Pond' or because ..."

"Remember, it was Nick who brought us together!"

"No," Duncan corrected her. "He brought you and my brother together. *I* brought us together."

Duncan was technically correct with that assertion, so Maggie decided not to argue the point.

"Or because that's just your MO," he continued, picking up where he left off. "You stick up for everyone, Maggie. And while I love you for that, sometimes I think people should be responsible for their own actions. If that means paying a high price, so be it."

Maggie was somewhat shaken by the seriousness of Duncan's tone. The words were harsh, too, especially as coming from her good-natured husband. "Pay a high price"? What was he referring to? Was he suggesting that he no longer wanted to have a relationship with his son?

"I'm going up and mow the cemetery before it gets hot," Duncan said, fishing in the dish on the chiffonier for the car keys.

Instantly, Maggie's thoughts were diverted to a new worry. "Do you think you should be pushing a lawnmower? On that hill?"

He gave her an incredulous look. "Weren't you the woman who just told me the doctor said my heart was fine?"

"Oh, go ahead—just be sure you have your phone with you."

Duncan patted his pocket. "Right here."

She waved him out of the kitchen with the dish towel. "Don't forget to check the geraniums," she called, as the door closed behind him.

Maggie finished cleaning up the kitchen and went back upstairs. While she was getting dressed, she plotted her next move. Should she speak with Nick? Try to find out if he knew why his father was mad at him? Or if he had anything to do with the newspaper reporter?

Or … should she call in the cavalry?

Maggie finally decided on the latter, and reached out to Duncan's daughter.

"I was just about to call you, Maggie," said Nora, when she answered her cell. "I've been worried about Pops since Sabine called yesterday. How's he doing? The hospital didn't admit him, did they?"

"No, he's home. He says he feels fine. In fact, your father has gone up to mow the cemetery."

"Seriously? Is he trying to tempt fate?"

"No, he's just stubborn. The doctor said there's nothing wrong with his heart. He was just dehydrated yesterday. Apparently, he was out washing windows several hours in the hot sun. You'll be glad to know your brother got rid of that heavy old wooden ladder, too."

"At least Nick did something right," Nora retorted.

Maggie was surprised by her stepdaughter's sarcastic comment. She knew that Nick and Nora weren't close, however, she wasn't aware that the brother and sister had had a falling out. "What are you talking about, Nora?"

"Oh, I heard about his solar farm moratorium. Nick has completely lost his mind this time!"

"That's a bit harsh. Your brother doesn't want to see Wendell's woodlot cut down and has a right to his opinion. He's concerned the solar farm is too large." Maggie realized after she spoke that she was once again defending Nick, even though she herself was in favor of the solar farm.

"He ought to be concerned for Rebecca! How is she going to pay the bills and put food on the table without the income from the solar farm?"

"I don't think her financial situation is as bad as that," Maggie reassured Nora. "Remember, we had that fundraiser for her and Wendell several years ago."

"I thought you were on Rebecca's side, Maggie?" Nora accused.

"I am on her side. I'm going to vote against Nick's moratorium."

"Are you going to speak at the Town Meeting?"

So, Nora knew about the special Town Meeting, too? Sabine must have told her everything, Maggie realized.

"I haven't made up my mind, yet. But I usually do, much to your father's dismay."

"Good for you! Thankfully Rebecca still has *some* local support."

"I'm not the only one who supports her. Henry and Hannah are voting against the moratorium. And Nellie and Metcalf, of course."

Maggie realized by Nora's attitude that she wasn't going to get any help from Duncan's daughter. In fact, Nora in her present mood would likely add fuel to the family fire.

"Nick never stops to think about anybody but himself," Nora continued, wrathfully. "Sometimes I think he deliberately looks for a boogeyman, just so he can swoop in and play the hero! I'm glad Pops is feeling well enough to mow the cemetery. Tell him I'll call him later. I've got to get back to work, now. I'm putting together a marketing campaign for a friend."

Maggie signed off, completely flummoxed. She had called Nora, hoping to enlist her aid in smoothing the troubled waters between Duncan and Nick. But instead, she had discovered that Nora was also mad at Nick!

Theirs was truly a house divided.

Chapter 23

The Special Town Meeting

The crush was already beginning to form Saturday morning July 12th by the time First Selectman John Woods arrived at the church banquet hall where Sovereign's Town Meetings were held. Nick's moratorium against solar farms had been the main topic of conversation in town over the prior three weeks, especially after the *Sentinel* published Jarod Palmer's hit piece detailing how large the project was going to be and how much of Wendell Russell's woodlot would be cut down. The article also implied that the fencing around the solar farm would prevent residents from accessing the Millett Rock, which was untrue.

While people would be prevented from walking into their favorite picnic spot from the Russell's house, nobody went that way anymore, anyway. Everyone now hiked to the Millett Rock from the church or from the trailhead near Maggie's house. Nevertheless, the thought of losing a perk they had always enjoyed had further inflamed many of the residents, especially those who were opposed to the solar project to begin with. Over the course of the past century that picnickers had enjoyed the Millett Rock, not one merrymaker had ever thought to offer the Russell family a tittle toward the real estate taxes paid on the property. The locals expected to freely enjoy the Millett Rock *in perpetuum*, much like they expected the leaves to fall in October or the hummingbirds to return in April.

John Woods maneuvered his way into the banquet hall where the church breakfasts and suppers were held, the only place in town large enough to hold public meetings. His forward progress was delayed by various townspeople who wanted a word with him (generally a word of complaint); however, Woods was practiced at keeping his words to a minimum, and so within ten minutes he had reached the banquet table up front that was reserved for the selectmen. Most of the other tables had been removed from the floor, and were stacked against the north wall.

The selectmen's table was situated to the left of the moderator's podium, facing two large groups of folding metal chairs, about fifty chairs in each block, with an aisle between the two groups. Dozens of attendees were clustered in and around the chairs like hens in a chicken house trying to decide whether it was time to roost. The two other selectmen, Bob Jessup and Gray Gilpin, had already preceded Woods to the selectmen's table. (Long-time Sovereign selectman Maynard Nutter had retired a few years ago, and Gray had been elected in Nutter's stead.)

"Quite a turnout," Woods remarked, sliding into the empty middle seat.

"That damn reporter got everybody riled up," replied Jessup, shifting uncomfortably in the metal chair.

"The article was obviously slanted in favor of the moratorium," agreed Gray, whose wife Courtney was minding the general store today. "Too bad about the mistake—if it was a mistake—about not being able to get to the Millett Rock. That won't help Rebecca's cause any."

"Nope." Woods suddenly noted that the podium where the moderator always stood was vacant. "Where's Jenny?" he asked, scanning the crowd. He then glanced over his shoulder at the large round analog clock on the wall above the closed server's window. "It's after ten. I don't want to be here all day." For the past forty-five years, dairy farmer Jenny Dalton had been elected moderator at all of Sovereign's Town Meetings.

"She's flown the coop," said Jessup. "Gone up north fishing."

"The devil she has!" exclaimed Woods. "She never trusts her cows to anybody else." Jenny was particular about her prize-winning Jerseys. "What's the true story?"

"I don't think she's run out on us, although she and Rebecca are good friends," answered Gray. "Jenny told me she had this trip planned for months, long before the moratorium came up."

"Why the heck didn't you mention that at our last meeting?"

"I didn't know then."

Woods, who was not just the First Selectman but also the elder of the three by decades, leaned back in his chair. He picked up a pencil from the table and began tapping it. "Well, then—you boys got any ideas who should moderate this mess?"

"Maggie?" Gray suggested, nodding toward the minister, who was seated in the second row of the left-hand section of chairs, directly behind Rebecca and Robinson Crockett.

"Nope. Maggie's got a dog in this fight," the First Selectman replied. "And her stepson has the other dog. Well, let's see what the rabble wants."

John Woods arose from his seat. He picked up the wooden moderator's gavel the Town Clerk had left on the table and rapped loudly to get the room's attention. "Settle down everyone! I'm calling this special Town Meeting to order. Now, our first order of business this morning is to elect a moderator."

"Where's Jenny?" yelled a rustic from the back of the room, where an unbroken row of chairs against the far wall was typically claimed by Old Farts and local characters. "We don't want nobody else."

"Jenny's gone fishing, so you're not going to get her."

"You look good with thet hammah, Woods," called another loudmouth from the crowd. "I nominate John Woods for moderator."

"Second!" responded a chorus of voices.

A loud burst of approval swept through the room, which in Sovereign was akin to a vote. Before he knew it Woods found himself elected moderator of the special Town Meeting.

John Woods gathered up some of the papers that Town Clerk Betty Peabody had left on the selectmen's table and moved to the podium, gavel in hand. "Settle back down," he encouraged the boisterous crowd, rapping the gavel sharply against the wooden podium. "You don't want to be here all day, do you? I sure as heck don't. Now, the only other order of business is this six-month solar farm moratorium. Be quiet while I read it to you."

Woods patted his shirt pocket for his reading glasses, realizing when he came up empty-handed that he had forgotten to bring them. He sighed, and held the two, eight-and-a-half by eleven sheets of white paper close to his face. The First Selectman began to read aloud, stumbling over some of the legalistic words that Nick had inserted in the borrowed moratorium language.

"We know what the damn thing says—you don't gotta read it," interrupted an agitated attendee.

One of Miss Crump's gravel truck drivers hopped up. "It says there ain't gonna be no solar farms built in town for at least six months. Ain't that right, Nick?"

"Hold on, now," Woods interjected, as Nick, who was sitting in the front row in the section of chairs across from Rebecca and the solar farm developer, stood up to respond to the truck driver's question. "I'm the moderator," the First Selectman reminded the crowd, "and any questions and comments will have to go through me." Nick sat back down, and Woods finished reading the moratorium language aloud. When he was done, he set the two pieces of paper down onto the podium. A dozen or more people began waving to get his attention, wanting to speak. Woods ignored them.

"For those of you who are inclined to sensible, Betty has put copies of this moratorium up back on the table there. She's also set out some flyers from the solar farm developer, this young fellow here, Robinson Crockett." Woods pointed out the developer, who rose up and waved briefly. "Now, we're going to discuss this moratorium like rational adults, not hooligans. And we're going to use Roberts Rules of Order, like usual. If you're not familiar with Roberts Rules, Betty has put copies of the rules back on the table, too."

At this last announcement, the perky Town Clerk looked up from her notetaking. She arose from the Selectmen's table and hurried to the podium, whispering something in the First Selectman's ear.

"Scratch that," Woods said. "Betty didn't bring copies of the rules today."

"I thought Jenny would be here," the Town Clerk added, ruefully. "She knows Roberts Rules of Order by heart."

The crowd hooted with laughter and derision. "We don't need rules, anyway!" "Rules are for libtards!"

Woods rapped on the podium again. "Simmer down. You elected me moderator, so we'll go by John's Rules of Order, today. The first rule is—you've got to be called on to speak, dammit, otherwise shut up."

Miss Crump, who was sitting on Rebecca's side of the room, wobbled to her feet. The centenarian was not a regular attendee at the annual Town Meeting; however, she had come today to support the young widow, a fellow chicken-lover. Although Miss Crump raised her blue-veined hand, because of her hunchback her wavering hand was barely visible in the crowded room.

Nevertheless, the First Selectman's eye had been roving the crowd, wondering who the dickens to call on first—and he spotted the hand. Woods pointed the gavel at the elderly lady. "Miss Crump. Go ahead—you have the floor."

The eccentric old woman pulled herself up to the front of the room with the use of her rubber-tipped cane in a slow, half-shuffling turtle walk. Maggie sprang up to help her, but Miss Crump shooed the minister off. "I don't need no help. I ain't on death's door yet," she said, tartly. She turned to face the crowd, clutching the knob-head of her black cane with both hands and leaning heavily against it. "What I got to say won't take long," she began, in a treble voice. "We don't need no moratoriums in Sovereign. We ain't Portland—we ain't even Banger. The widder Russell should be able to do what she damn well pleases with her property. That's all I got to say, except that anybody who thinks otherwise don't need to haul gravel from my pit no more. I'm talkin' to you, Daryl Foster," she added, singling out the truck driver who had spoken earlier.

"I didn't mean nothing by it," Foster hastily assured the elderly woman.

"I should hope not," Miss Crump retorted.

"That's blackmail," one of the firemen whispered loudly to a buddy. The two firemen were sitting behind Nick, in a show of support for his moratorium.

"So 'tis!" chortled Miss Crump in satisfaction.

"Oops," whispered the second fireman. "She heard you."

"I keep tellin' you people I *ain't deaf!* Maybe now ye'll believe me." With that, Miss Crump pulled herself back to her seat.

The room erupted with residents hopping up and waving, hoping to be called on to speak next. John Woods, who was attempting to moderate with an even hand, decided to give Nick the floor. "Let's hear why this young fellow thinks we need this moratorium," the First Selectman said, pointing the gavel at the woodsman, who was patiently holding up his hand. "It's his fault we're here today, anyway. The floor is all yours, Nick."

Nick, who was sitting in the front row, stood up and turned to face the meeting. As he gazed out over the swale of faces, he felt his palms and pits break out in sweat. The room swirled momentarily. But he soon sorted out the individuals in the crowd and realized that many were on his side. To help convince those who doubted the need for his moratorium, he had dressed carefully in clean khaki shorts and a dark blue tee-shirt. He had trimmed his beard, too, and pulled his thick black hair back into a neat ponytail.

Nick took a deep breath and cleared his throat. He was careful not to look at Rebecca, who was sitting serenely on the opposite side of the room. The clamor in the banquet hall settled into an expectant pause. "Thanks, Mr. Woods," he began, with a nod to the moderator. "First, I want you all to know I'm not opposed to alternative energy. I'm just opposed to this particular project. I think it's happening way too fast. We need more time to consider whether 300 acres is too big a solar farm for a small town like us. That's what the six-month moratorium is for—to give us time to put a solar farm ordinance in place that regulates things like size. My personal opinion is that 240,000 solar panels is too damn many. That many panels would necessitate cutting down most of Wendell's woodlot, including the stand of pine trees he tended for forty-five years, and which I happen to know personally that Wendell was extremely proud of."

"Two hundred and forty thousand is a freakin' lot of solar panels," a thirtyish woman called out in a strident voice. She was clutching a small child in her lap. "Them panels could give us radiation poisoning, too, ain't that right, Nick?"

Nick, understanding the rules—that all questions should go through the moderator—glanced over at John Woods behind the podium. "Go ahead, answer the question, son," the First Selectman directed him. "If you know the answer."

"Radiation poisoning isn't my main concern, Shelly," Nick said to the woman.

"Why not?" bawled someone from the back of the room.

"Because solar panels emit very low-level non-ionizing electromagnetic fields. There's not enough radiation to harm anyone, like there is with ionizing radiation from X-rays, which can cause radiation sickness."

"So, radiation from solar farms like the one Crockett is proposing isn't a problem," the First Selectman reiterated. "Good to hear. Thanks, Nick."

Askance, Shelly gripped her child closer to her chest. "You mean I can get sick from an X-ray? Demmed if I'll ever get one of them things agin!"

Nick, realizing his appeal to the voters was going off track, decided it was time to ratchet his emotional plea up a notch. "Most of you know me, and you know ..."

"We know ya, Walden!"

"You're the Mushroom Man!"

"... know how I came to Sovereign a decade ago," Nick continued, beginning to be annoyed by the many interruptions. At this rate, he would never work up to the proper poetic pitch. "What you don't know is why I stayed here. Well, I stayed because I fell in love with the Sovereign Woods. I bought a home in the woods, too, which I love as much as you love your homes. Wendell's stand of pine trees isn't much more than two thousand yards from my front door. It would be a big loss to me—and I think it would be a big loss to everyone in town—if Wendell's 300-acre woodlot was destroyed in one whack. Search your hearts and ask yourselves if that wouldn't be a BIG loss to the town?"

"But we'd net a BIG tax gain!" Henry Trow hollered. He and Nick were good friends, but Henry was irked by the youth's monomaniacal opposition to the solar farm. Without waiting for permission to speak, the crusty retired history professor stood up and addressed the meeting. "Those of us with woodlots don't pay much tax on 'em, thanks to the state's tree growth program. Wendell had his woodlot in tree growth, just like I do. But this solar farm developer, he'll pay personal property tax on his panels. LOTS of taxes! Isn't that right, Crockett?"

"Now, Henry, you know you need to wait until you're called on to talk," the First Selectman reproved him.

"Sorry, got ahead of myself, Chief."

"And Crockett can't speak until we vote him permission, since he isn't a resident. But I can answer your question. The town will get more in property taxes from Mrs. Russell when Wendell's woodlot is taken out of tree growth, but the solar farm itself is exempt from personal property tax. About five years ago the state passed a law exempting solar energy equipment from taxation to encourage economic growth and the transition to clean energy."

Henry appeared flummoxed. "Hell, I want a solar farm, then," he cried. "I've got over 500 acres!"

A murmuring swept through the audience with the speed and fluidity of a murmuration of starlings. No taxes on solar panels!

"But, like I say, Mrs. Russell will pay a lot more in real estate taxes once that property is removed from tree growth," Woods continued. "She'll have to pay a penalty, too." The First Selectman looked meaningfully at the young widow. "I hope you've factored that into the lease price, Rebecca."

Rebecca patted Robinson Crockett on the arm. "Rob is taking good care of me, I assure you, John. Wendell would be pleased."

"Good to hear." Woods turned back to Nick, who was still standing. "What else you got to say, son?"

"I think I'm done," said Nick, sulkily. He was sore at being interrupted and, after Henry's interruption, had lost his train of thought. The speech he had lovingly crafted and practiced in the woods while mushrooming had come out in fits and starts, about as efficacious as a sunken waterlily. "I just urge everyone to vote for this moratorium, that's all," he concluded, and abruptly sat down.

Sabine entered the hall as John Woods called upon Doctor Bart. She glanced around the full room, wondering where to sit, when she spied Duncan, occupying one of the chairs up back reserved for the Old Farts and town characters. He was hunched over, elbow on his knees with his chin resting on one hand. Duncan was by himself, five or six seats away from his nearest neighbor. Sabine hesitated, then stepped over and slid into the chair next to Duncan. "Why aren't you with your wife?" she asked, indicating Maggie, who was sitting behind Rebecca.

"Because I'm undecided about the moratorium," said Duncan, straightening up. "I think it's dividing the town as much as the solar farm is, if not more."

Sabine perused the residents in the two sections of seats in front of them, which were separated by the wide aisle. "It does sort of feel like walking into a wedding," she agreed. "Friends of the bride to the left; friends of the groom to the right. Only today the groom has more friends than the bride. Usually, it's the other way around."

"I'm not sure Nick's friends have helped him much."

"No?"

"Some of them are—shall we say—more colorful than astute."

"You mean, under-educated?"

"Or, as Maggie would say, a few sandwiches short of a picnic. Rebecca, on the other hand, has people like Henry and Hannah, Ryan and Trudy, and Nellie and Metcalf to help her make her case. And Miss Crump, too."

"Miss Crump spoke? I'm sorry I missed that! I had to do something for my aunt in Bangor this morning and had trouble getting away." Sabine wanted to ask Duncan whether Nick had spoken, and if so, how he had done. But Nick's father did not yet know that she and Nick were an item, and she wasn't prepared for twenty questions if Duncan became suspicious, especially since she wasn't sure where she stood with Nick at the present moment.

"Nick spoke, too," added Duncan, as though he had read the young minister's mind. "Although I think he probably hurt his case as much as he helped it. It wasn't his fault, really. He kept getting interrupted."

"That's too bad," replied Sabine, wanting to know every detail, but afraid to ask. "What about Leland?" she said instead. "How did he do?"

"Leland's not here."

"Get out! You're kidding me."

"I kid you not."

Sabine knew that Leland had been having second thoughts about opposing the solar farm; however, she didn't expect the octogenarian to completely wimp out on Nick. "Where is he?"

"Tending Jenny Dalton's cows, according to Ryan. Apparently, Jenny wanted to go fishing for a few days, and she asked Leland to stay at her place and take care of her herd."

That explanation sounded fishy, even to Sabine, who had been in town less than a year. "Does Jenny go away often?"

"Never, according to Trudy. She thinks her father didn't want to be here today and talked Jenny into helping him pull a disappearing act. Trudy says Leland is probably hiding out at Jenny's place and that Jenny hasn't really gone fishing."

Doctor Bart had now finished speaking, and made his way back to his seat on Rebecca's side of the room. John Woods ran his eye over the other side, wondering who to call upon next. Suddenly, in the back row of Nick's section, Stephen Danforth, young Gerald's grandfather, poked up like a bean seedling standing up out of the soil on a hot June day. He removed his summer ballcap with one swollen arthritic hand and held the other hand up to be called upon. Seventy-plus years of a hardscrabble life had stooped the old truck driver's shoulders; but he was still large enough to be seen over the seated crowd. Woods had been present at the May Breakfast when Danforth had told Rebecca to go back to Boston and take the solar farm developer with her. Knowing something of the man's true nature, the First Selectman had a hunch the truck driver wanted to atone for that unkind remark. Woods decided he would give him the opportunity. "Danforth, go ahead, you have the floor."

"I make a motion we table this here talk 'til our next Town Meeting," Stephen Danforth uttered, in his gravelly, cigarette-smoking voice.

"I'll second that," John Woods responded quickly.

There was a small commotion from the selectman's table. "You can't second it—you're the moderator," Bob Jessup hissed loudly. "And we don't have a Town Meeting scheduled until next March!"

"The people voted me moderator, Bob, and so we're going by John's Rules of Order today, remember? All in favor of tabling discussion on the solar farm moratorium until the annual Town Meeting say 'Aye!'"

The chorus of 'ayes' was so loud it nearly knocked John Woods over. "It's a vote," he declared, banging the gavel against the podium. "The solar farm moratorium has been tabled. Meeting adjourned."

Chapter 24

The Swarm

A few days after the special Town Meeting, Nick was sitting on his east-facing deck in the mid-morning sun. He was ruminating over his next move to stop the solar farm, when Sabine broke from the woods and came flying down the path to his house. She called his name and waved, obviously agitated.

Supposing something had happened to his father, Nick jumped off the deck and met Sabine half-way down the path, just beyond the stone walkway and creeping thyme. "What's wrong? Has something happened to Dad?"

"What? No, Wendell's bees have swarmed!" She bent over, clutching her knees, trying to catch her breath.

He threw up his hands. "Holy heck, Sabine! You just about gave me a heart attack."

Sabine stood back up, still a bit breathless. "Sorry, I didn't think of your father. I was just so excited because I was with Rebecca when it happened. You should have seen it, Nick! The swarm was exquisite! We were out back— Rebecca was showing me how well her vegetable garden was doing—when this strange, golden cloud floated down the field." As she spoke, Sabine attempted to simulate with her arms and hands the amorphous movement of the honeybees wafting down the hillside, midsummer sun shimmering on thousands of tiffany wings. Sabine's eyes sparkled. "Then the bees flew up into a spruce tree and formed a tight ball, just as though the tree limbs scooped them all up! The swarm surprised me, but Rebecca knew what was happening—she'd seen one before—and said she'd been worried Wendell's bees would swarm. Nobody's taking care of them now, you know."

"That's cool, Sabine. Swarms are very cool to see. But why did you run all the way out here to tell me that?"

"Because Rebecca needs your help!"

"My help?"

"Yes, you! You're the only beekeeper we know, Nick. Rebecca doesn't want to lose Wendell's bees. She says that, besides Tad, the bees are the only other living reminder of her husband she has." Sabine clasped his hand. "Won't you help Rebecca get them back?"

"I doubt the bees are all gone, Sabine. Probably half stayed with the hive. They just ran out of room, that's all. I'm surprised the bees didn't swarm sooner. Wendell would have split the hive this spring."

"You will help her, though, won't you?" she pleaded.

The love and trust emanating from Sabine's eyes made it impossible for Nick to refuse. He prevaricated, however, suspecting that it was Sabine who wanted his help with the swarm, more so than the widow. "Aw, Rebecca wouldn't want to see me at her place."

"You're wrong, Nick! She mentioned you right away— wondering if you would come up and catch the bees for her. I didn't even bring up your name. Honest! Rebecca doesn't hold a grudge. In fact, she hasn't even spoken to me about the special Town Meeting or your moratorium. Not once. She's still your friend."

"That's hard to believe." He rubbed his bearded chin in a thoughtful manner. "Especially after the meeting last

Saturday. I've been thinking about nothing else since then," Nick added, morosely.

Sabine wanted to chastise Nick for thinking only of himself, however, they needed his help, so she bit her tongue. "Will you come back with me?"

He shrugged. "Sure. If you think Rebecca really wants me?"

Sabine clapped her hands. "She does! We do. We've got to save those bees. I'll help you."

He smiled at her enthusiasm. "The bees might not be worth rescuing. Did you ever hear the old beekeeper saying? 'A swarm in May is worth a load of hay; a swarm in June is worth a silver spoon; a swarm in July isn't worth a fly.' This is July, after all."

"We're not just saving the swarm, we're saving a piece of Wendell," she reminded him.

"OK, then, I'm in. Did Wendell have a bee suit?"

"Yes, Rebecca is getting that out for you—we knew you wouldn't refuse—and his smoker and hive tools, too. She isn't sure the suit will fit you, though. Wendell had to stop wearing it."

"How come?"

"After they were married, she said he got too fat for it."

"I totally get that! Rebecca's a good cook."

"There's a veil you can use, if the suit's too small."

"The bee suit is for you, Sabine. I don't want to worry about you getting stung when I'm up a tree trying to capture a swarm."

"Oh, in that case, the suit will probably fit me just fine." Sabine and Wendell had been about the same height; however, the beekeeper had been a good fifty or sixty pounds heavier than her.

"Time is of the essence, though. Let's get a hustle on." Nick strode off down the path, Sabine scurrying after him. "Do you know how long the bees have been out of the hive?" he asked over his shoulder.

"Not really. We didn't see the bees leave the hive. Why? Is that important?"

"Yeah, a swarm usually moves twice. First, when the queen exits the hive with her swarm of attendants. They typically hang in a nearby tree while the scout bees go looking for a new home. That can take a day or two. The second move happens when the bees follow the scouts to their new digs."

They reached the intersection with the main Sovereign Woods trail. Nick stopped abruptly. "Which way did you come in?"

"From Maggie's. That's the quickest way from Rebecca's."

"Right." Nick paused. He had spoken to his stepmother at the special Town Meeting, and Maggie had seemed as friendly as ever; however, Nick had not talked with his father since the window-washing episode. Since his father had refused to see him at the hospital, as far as Nick was concerned, the rapprochement—if there was going to be one—would need to be initiated by Duncan.

Sabine noted his hesitation and immediately divined its cause. "They're not home," she informed him. "Duncan told me at church Sunday that he and Maggie were going sightseeing Down East today."

Reassured, Nick resumed his pace, striding down the trail toward Maggie's house. Because this trail was wider, Sabine was able to keep beside him, matching Nick's pace stride for stride. "I still don't get why it matters how long the bees have been out of the hive?" she asked.

"Just before bees swarm, Sabine, they pig out on honey. The only time a worker honeybee *can't* sting is when its abdomen is engorged with honey."

"Whoa! That's pretty useful information to know."

"If the swarm you and Rebecca saw was just leaving the hive, no worries! I can find the queen, move her into a new hive body and the rest of the bees will follow. I won't need a suit or a veil. But if Wendell's bees have been out a couple of days, watch out! They'll have consumed some of their honey and be able to sting—and probably be testy on top of that. I should have stopped to get a long-sleeved shirt," he added, with a rueful glance at his bare arms and legs. "And my jeans!"

Rebecca, who had been anxiously keeping an eye out for Sabine's return, threw open the shed door when they drove in the driveway. She met Nick on the lawn, hands outstretched. "I knew you would come, Nick! Thank you, thank you!" Her soft blue eyes filled with tears.

Although Nick had been friends with Rebecca for ten years, he suddenly felt bashful. Somehow their relationship seemed awkward without Wendell around. Plus, in his mind, the solar farm hung above them like the sword of Damocles. In fact, he had not visited at the old Russell homestead since the night of Rebecca's dinner party, when the solar farm project had been announced. Feeling sorry for the widow, however, he squeezed her hands reassuringly. "We can't let Wendell's bees fly the coop, now can we?"

"I just hope you don't get stung too badly trying to catch them," Rebecca worried.

"Me, too," he confessed.

The two women laughed. Nick, catching their enthusiasm, perked up. The ambience of the homestead reminded him of former congenial times with Wendell and Rebecca, and all of their mutual friends. Maybe those days weren't gone forever?

Nick surveyed the gear the Rebecca had spread out on the picnic table. "Smoker, hive tool, bee suit, gloves, and an extra veil. Great! We won't be taking any unnecessary risks."

"We?" questioned Rebecca, with a quick look at the young minister.

"I'm going to help," Sabine announced with no little pride.

"She's my ground woman," Nick explained. "I'll climb the tree and cut the branch the bees are on. Then I'll carefully lower the branch and bees down to Sabine."

"Oh, dear! That sounds dangerous on so many levels."

"Don't worry, I can climb trees almost as well as a black bear. I'll stay far enough away from the swarm so the bees won't even know I'm there. And Sabine will be safe in Wendell's bee suit. Do you have a small hand saw? I forgot to bring one."

"In Wendell's shop. I'll go get it." Rebecca hurried off.

"I need a large cardboard box, too," Nick called after the widow. He shook out the heavy white cotton bee suit and held the suit up to Sabine. "Your ensemble, milady."

As she took the suit, the attached veil flopped over so Sabine wasn't sure which way was front and which was back. "How do I get into this thing?" she asked, holding the suit up in front of herself.

Nick glanced up from sorting through Wendell's bee equipment. She looked so desirable with the suit pressed to her ample bosom, unfettered blonde locks tumbling over her shoulders, that he wanted to toss Sabine in the grass and ravage her right then and there. "If I stop to help you, we might not get around to rescuing the swarm," he warned suggestively.

Sabine batted her eyelashes at him. "We wouldn't want that, milord. Perhaps afterward … ?"

"It's a date! Zipper goes in front; veil in back," he instructed. "If you sit down on the bench, you should be able to pull the elastic legs over your sneakers. Just make sure you keep your socks up so your ankles aren't exposed. I don't think the bees are likely to sting, but if they've been out for a while, they might. Honeybees love to find the vulnerable spots, and I know from personal experience your ankles are mighty tempting."

"Thank you, sir." Sabine sat down on the picnic table bench and began pulling on the suit.

"Whatever happens, stay calm. Don't unzip your suit until I tell you to. You're protected while you keep the suit on. Got it?"

"I think so."

"And just zip the suit up to your waist for now," Nick added. "I'll help you with the rest when we get to the tree. I need to get something out of this deal."

She giggled at his inference. "By zipping me up?"

"I thought I might steal a kiss. But in the meantime, if you keep distracting me I'll never get this smoker going!"

Nick pawed through a metal toolbox containing some of Wendell's other bee equipment and located a bag of smoker fuel. He stuffed two handfuls of dried sumac blossoms into the stainless steel smoker and mixed in some short pieces of baling twine and a few dead oak leaves. Then, shielding the smoker from the light west breeze, he struck a wooden match. When the twine and leaves caught fire, Nick pumped hard on the bellows ten or twelve times until the sumac blossoms began to burn and the flames licked the rim of the smoker. He snapped the lid shut and continued to pump rhythmically until a full head of smoke poured out the spout. "One of the hardest parts of beekeeping is keeping your smoker going," he remarked, as the acrid smoke swirled around the picnic table before being carted off by the breeze. "We need the smoke to calm the bees."

Sabine coughed. "I think you've got enough smoke!"

Nick grinned at her. "You're not going to be a fair weather beekeeper, are you?"

"Not on your life!"

Rebecca returned carrying a hand saw and a good-sized cardboard box. "Will these work?"

Nick took the box and saw from her hands. "Just right, thanks." Into the box he loaded Wendell's helmet and tie-down veil, two sets of canvas and leather gloves, more smoker fuel, and a hooked-end stainless steel hive tool.

Sabine pulled the attached veil over her head and modeled the bee suit for Rebecca. "How do I look?"

"Too enchanting! I'm glad Trudy is watching the neighborhood kids today, otherwise Tad would be begging me to let him go with you."

"Can't start 'em too young beekeeping," Nick interjected, tossing the matches into the box. "I was about Tad's age when I started helping my neighbor with his hives. Mr. Tuell was a crusty old timer—Henry sort of reminds me of him—but he had a soft heart for kids and was an excellent beekeeper. I'll never forget my first taste of Mr. Tuell's comb honey, either! I didn't think life could get any better than that. I didn't know about sex then, of course."

Rebecca burst out laughing. "Would you believe? Wendell said the exact same thing to me not long after we were married!"

"Beekeepers don't agree on many things, but one thing we do agree on is that fresh honeycomb right out of the hive is just about the best thing going. Now, where's that swarm? I should have checked on that first to make sure the bees were still there."

"They're still there," Rebecca affirmed. "I looked when I went to the shop for Wendell's saw."

"I know where they are—follow me," said Sabine, eagerly. She headed for the garden, Nick following close behind with the handsaw, cardboard box, and smoker.

"Have fun, you two!" Rebecca called after them. "But be careful!"

In less than thirty minutes, the basketball-size swarm of bees was captured. Fortunately, the bees had been hanging from a limb only half-way up the thirty-foot spruce tree. Nick climbed up, cut the limb, and lowered the branch until he was able to shake the bees off into the cardboard box Sabine held up. Cascades of interconnected bees dropped with a whoosh into the box, buzzing and bouncing lightly against the bottom. After climbing back down the tree, Nick smoked the bees to calm them. Then he blew on the bees to separate the clumps, and, with gloved hand, gently pushed through the roiling mass of bees to assure himself that the queen was still there. She was! Nick loaded the box of bees and the bee equipment into the back of Sabine's car. "Don't take your suit off yet," he instructed her, as Sabine started to unzip. "Our job is only half done."

"Oh, I get it—we're taking the honeybees someplace else. Where are we going?"

"Over to your place. Don't worry, it's just temporary. We'll bring 'em back."

"Why aren't we taking the bees to your house, Nick?"

"Because I live on a wildlife corridor. Water is a draw for wildlife," he added, seeing the confused expression on Sabine's face. "Where I live next to the brook a bear would find the bees in no time flat. Wendell gave me a swarm once and it took less than a week for a black bear to destroy my hive. I learned an important beekeeping lesson the hard way—don't try to keep bees near a wildlife corridor, not without an electric fence, anyway."

While Nick and Sabine had been shaking the bees out of the tree, Rebecca rounded up some of Wendell's extra wooden ware, which she had set out on the picnic table. "I think I've got everything you need for a new hive," she said to Nick. "If not, there's more in the shed—and even more in the barn."

Nick gathered up ten frames with drawn comb, a bottom board, an inner and outer cover, and a deep bee box. After pawing around in Wendell's beekeeping toolbox, he located an extra entrance reducer. "Looks like we're all set. We'll bring the bees back in a week or so," he informed Rebecca. "I'm afraid if we don't move 'em more than two miles away now, the foragers will go back to their old hive."

"I wasn't worried," she assured him. "I remembered Wendell always moved his bees after splitting them."

By noon, Nick and Sabine had returned to Rebecca's to drop off the bee equipment. Before departing for the day, they checked on the original hive from which Wendell's bees had swarmed. Finding that the other half of the bees were hard at work putting up wildflower honey, Nick set two supers on top of the deep bee boxes. "The supers should hold the bees for a while," he said to Rebecca, when he and Sabine rejoined the widow at the picnic table. "I'll check the hive again when we bring the other bees back. Maybe Tad can help me then?"

"Tad would love that! I'll go right down to Swan's today and buy him a little bee suit. I can't thank you enough, Nick," Rebecca added, with heartfelt emotion. "I feel as though part of Wendell was saved today."

"Glad I was around to help," Nick replied, embarrassed.

"I wonder if Wendell is watching us from Heaven?" Sabine mused, unzipping the bee suit.

"I hope he is because I'm going to give you both a big hug!" Rebecca hugged Sabine and then threw her arms around the hefty woodsman's waist and gave him a fond squeeze.

Acceptance and love washed over Nick as he responded to the widow's embrace. He felt as though his world had righted after being off-kilter and on edge for the past three months. Beekeeping has a magical way of restoring harmony, he thought.

"How about some lunch?" Rebecca asked, pulling away. She brushed a tear from her eye. "I can make us a nice crabmeat salad?"

Sabine glanced at her phone. "I'm so sorry—I've got to run. Someone's coming in to see me at one o'clock."

"Nick?"

"Thanks, but I told Gerald I'd work with him on his reading this afternoon. He's probably back at my place waiting for me."

"Well, then, I'm giving you a rain check. How about when you bring the bees back?"

"Sounds good to me," said Nick, with a broad smile. "Although you don't need to do that, Rebecca. Not after the curtains."

"Curtains?" Sabine puzzled. "What curtains?"

"Rebecca sewed the curtains for my house. I never paid her for them."

"Don't be silly! Those curtains were a housewarming gift," Rebecca reminded Nick.

"I thought Maggie sewed your curtains, Nick?" Sabine asked.

The woodsman chuckled. "Maggie? She can't even sew on a button! My Dad does all the sewing in that house."

"But I've seen a pillow at her house made out of that exact same material," Sabine protested.

"I had some extra," Rebecca said, simply, "and Maggie wanted a little pillow when she was undergoing her breast cancer treatment. She's done so much for me and Wendell over the years, it was the least I could do."

It struck Sabine then that in Sovereign, Maine, one good deed always led to another. Pay it forward! That was why Rebecca had fallen in love with the place and its people, and why Sabine loved the town, too. Until the advent of the solar farm, Sovereign had been the epitome of the way Life *should* be lived in rural America. Today had been a big step toward reclaiming that harmony, Sabine thought, thanks to the swarm of honeybees.

Maybe—from Heaven—Wendell was doing more than just watching?

Chapter 25

Nora Arrives

"More iced tea, Ryan?" asked Maggie, hovering next to the kitchen table, pitcher in hand. The attorney had stopped by to review with the two ministers their legal documents (wills, living wills, durable powers-of-attorney, and DNRs), one of the To Do items on Maggie and Duncan's Elixir List.

"No thanks. I've got to get going," the forty-something farmer-lawyer replied, gathering up the documents. "I told Trudy I'd work on fencing the east hayfield this afternoon. I'll make the changes we talked about and get back to you soon."

"You're fencing the east hayfield?" Maggie wondered. "What about second cut?" She had been born and raised on a small Jersey farm similar to Ryan and Trudy's and understood the significance of fencing in a hayfield.

"We'll have to sacrifice second cut in that field, assuming we even get a second cut this year. Because of the drought, we need more pasturage for the girls. Our milk production has dropped a couple hundredweight a week. That's more than ten percent."

"Ouch!" replied Maggie, with feeling. "How many cows are you milking?"

"Forty, at the moment."

"Young stock?"

"We have about the same number. Leland says we've only got enough decent pasture for half our herd. We're either going to have to supplement with hay—an anathema in Maine in summer, I know," Ryan conceded, as Maggie started to protest, "or move the young stock off farm, or fence in the east hayfield."

"If you sacrifice the second cut on that field, does that mean you'll have to buy hay this winter?" asked Duncan. A city boy, he was still learning the rural lifestyle into which he had married.

"Not if I know Trudy," Maggie declared, setting the iced tea pitcher on the counter. "I bet they still had three-quarters of their hay in the barn at Groundhog's Day."

The attorney nodded, understanding the minister's allusion. "A bit more than that, actually."

Duncan was baffled. "I don't get it."

"There's an old New England saying that all good farmers follow," Maggie explained. "'Half your wood and half your hay, you should have on Candlemas Day'."

"Candlemas Day, the day the baby Jesus was presented in the Temple. Is that the half-way point of winter?" asked Duncan.

"Good guess! Only Candlemas Day has been coopted by Groundhogs Day; a poor substitute, in my opinion. Any farmer without half his wood and half his feed in early February could face lean times if there was a hard spring. Not that we get many late April snowstorms nowadays. Ryan and Trudy came into the spring with extra hay in the barn. First cut this year probably gave them enough for winter."

"Just about." Ryan rose from the table and hefted his leather briefcase under his arm. "My wife remembers some hard years during her childhood, though, so we always try to put up more hay than we need. Prudence pays off in a drought year like this."

"And prudence also gives you the opportunity to make a killing when hay is short in the spring."

The lawyer smiled at Maggie. "We've been known to sell a few bales in March and April, though we try not to gouge our neighbors."

"Sounds like a sensible policy," Duncan commented, rising and pushing in his chair. "That's just what I would expect of you and Trudy, although not, perhaps, of your father-in-law."

"Trudy runs Scotch Broom Acres now," Maggie reminded her husband. "There's a good reason for that."

"In fairness to my father-in-law," Ryan interjected, "Leland would rather play with his grandkids than study the account books or breeding records these days."

"Entirely understandable. How about I help you with the fencing detail? I have the rest of the afternoon free. Unless my wife objects?" Duncan glanced at Maggie, seeking confirmation.

"Shoo! I'm airing bedding this afternoon. You'll only be underfoot here. Just don't dig any post holes!"

"We have the tractor for that," Ryan reassured Maggie. "An extra pair of hands keeping the wire from tangling would be most welcome. The neighborhood kids are at our house this afternoon, which means Trudy will be busy monitoring Alice Rose. Regrettably, our eldest is not her best self when Tad's around. She's gets miffed because Hope idolizes Tad."

"She'll get over that in a year or two," Maggie suggested. "Once Alice discovers boys her own age."

"God forbid! Let's not rush that."

Duncan chuckled and picked up his Red Sox baseball cap. "I'll get my work gloves. Meet you out at the truck, Ryan."

"Be right there." The attorney rested his thick briefcase atop the back of the wooden chair. "There's one other thing I want to speak with you about, Maggie," he said, after the door closed behind her husband.

Sensing an impending dilemma, Maggie instantly reverted to her ministerial demeanor. "How can I help?"

"I looked over Rebecca's contract with Robinson Crockett, and it's more than fair. I reviewed several other land-lease contracts for solar farms before making that assessment, too." The attorney stopped short, bestowing a meaningful look upon Maggie.

"I admit, that's a relief to hear," she confessed. "Duncan and I have both lost some sleep worrying about that. But should you be sharing this information with me, Ryan?"

"I assure you I have Rebecca's permission. At the special Town Meeting, Rebecca became aware that some of her friends were worried Rob was taking advantage of her. She asked me to review her contract and offer my honest opinion, which I did. I suspect now that Wendell was embarrassed by how big their windfall would be and that's why he never asked for my legal advice."

"That sounds like Wendell," Maggie agreed.

"After I assured Rebecca that Crockett's contract was propitious, she allowed as though it might be useful for that information to get around town."

Maggie burst out laughing. "So, Rebecca told you to tell me?"

"Let's just say we both agreed you might be the best person to casually disseminate my legal opinion."

"I'll get on it right away. Our final Revere Bell Rededication meeting is tomorrow afternoon. I was going to skip the meeting, but now I've got a reason to go. You can bet that by tomorrow night the entire town will know you think Rebecca's contract is fair."

"More than fair. Propitious!" Ryan hefted his briefcase back under his arm.

"I can't use that word, Ryan. The ladies will think the contract is full of holes or it stinks. I'll say bounteous instead. People around here understand bounty." Maggie walked the attorney out into the shed. "But does it matter now what people think since Nick's moratorium has been tabled until next spring?" She swung open the outer door. "Rob can just go ahead and build the solar farm, can't he?"

"Legally, yes. Crockett can break ground anytime; however, Rebecca has asked him to hold off a few more weeks so they can propitiate people. Sorry, couldn't resist," Ryan added, with a grin. "Frankly, until the special Town Meeting, Rebecca had no idea so many of her friends and neighbors were opposed to the solar farm. My personal opinion is that if she hadn't signed the contract, Rebecca would back out of the solar farm deal. Now, however, she feels under obligation to Crockett, to say nothing about Wendell's memory." The attorney stepped down onto the granite doorstep.

"Poor Rebecca! No matter what she does, people are going to be unhappy with her. I'll do the best I can with those who will listen to me, Ryan. Maybe I'll even screw up enough courage to bell the cat?"

"Which two-legged feline might that be?"

"Nick. I fully expect him to camp out in one of Wendell's white pines at the first sound of a feller buncher in the woods."

"Good luck getting Nick down from a tree! By the way—speaking of bells—Leland has Ishmael and Isaac all gussied up for Saturday's delivery of the church bell. The kids are excited, too, about riding along in the wagon with the bell to the rededication celebration. See you then!"

Maggie spent the rest of the afternoon hauling quilts and blankets out to the clothesline for airing out, a task she enjoyed because it reminded her of her grandmother. A half century earlier when she lived with Gram, airing the bedding was a regular summertime chore. Back then, she and Gram had also carted out featherbeds for airing, draping the heavy, down-filled featherbeds over the cedar railing. (The fancy Bates Mills bedspreads, only used for special company, would be washed and line-dried on a different day.)

While Duncan was helping Ryan with the fencing, Maggie also took the opportunity to deep-clean Nellie's old bedroom. Her daughter had boxed up and removed what few personal effects she wanted to keep, and the rest Maggie had donated to Goodwill.

Around four o'clock, just as she was putting the vacuum cleaner away, Maggie thought she heard a faint "hallooing." She closed the broom closet door and was about to look out the window, when, suddenly, her stepdaughter popped into the kitchen.

"Surprise!" Nora dropped her purse onto the chiffonier and rushed to give Maggie a hug. She was a tall, willowy woman in her early thirties, about the same age as Nellie.

"Nora! What on earth ...?" Maggie expostulated, as she returned the embrace.

"I'm here to see Pops." Nora sprung away and peered around the corner into the living room. "Not that I don't want to see you, Maggie, but I've been worried about Pops since his little fainting episode."

"Your father is perfectly healthy, Nora, like I told you on the phone. But he'll be thrilled to see you, of course. He's helping Ryan with some fencing. He should be home soon." Maggie ushered her stepdaughter into a chair. "Let me get you some iced tea and cookies."

"Just the tea, thanks. I ate on the plane."

"Ugh! Airplane food." Maggie retrieved the iced tea pitcher from the refrigerator and poured Nora a glass. "Why didn't you tell us you were coming?"

"I wanted to surprise you—you know how I am."

Maggie did, indeed, know Nora's impetuous nature. In many ways, she and Nick were very similar. Except for their dark locks, Duncan's children must have taken after their mother, she suspected. "You could have called us from the airport. That would have surprised us and saved you an Uber fare from Bangor."

"I flew into Logan." Nora took a sip of tea. "Mmm! I love your herbal tea, Maggie, thanks."

"Logan! How did you get here from Boston?"

"Rental car. No worries. My friend paid me for the marketing flyers I created for him. You remember, the project I was working on when we last spoke?"

"Oh, yes, you said you were working on a marketing campaign for a friend. Well, your timing is perfect. I just finished cleaning Nellie's room. It's all ready for you, or will be once I get the bedding off the clothesline."

"Oh, I can't put Sabine out again! I'm staying at an Airbnb in Unity."

Maggie poured herself a tall glass of iced tea "I hope you can get your money back, Nora. Sabine isn't staying with us anymore. She's been renting Mike Hobart's cabin since she took the interim job at the church. Nellie's bedroom is our guest room, now. And you are our first guest!" She sat down at the table across from her stepdaughter and smiled brightly at Nora.

"I already checked in, Maggie," Nora replied, a stubborn expression on her face. "I dropped my bags off on the way here."

Warning bells began to ring in Maggie's head. She recollected Nora often had ulterior motives for everything she did. What was the real reason she was here?

The minister took a sip of tea and returned the frosty glass to the tabletop. "I thought you told me your friend was a woman? Just now you said 'him'? I don't let many 'hims' slip by me, Nora."

Nora blinked. Maggie could almost see the wheels turning in the young woman's head as her stepdaughter plotted her next move.

"The friend I went hiking with over Memorial Day was a woman," Nora clarified, carefully. "The friend I'm helping with the marketing campaign is a man, yes. He's just another friend."

And then there flashed into Maggie's mind the face of a man she had seen this spring on Nora's Instagram feed, but had not seen there since. A man with a craggy, good-natured face and a crooked smile. Robinson Crockett!

As it happened, the solar farm developer had let drop at the special Town Meeting, when he and Maggie were chatting, that he was staying at an Airbnb in Unity. Was Nora's "friend" Robinson Crockett?

Of course he was! Everything now made sense. How the developer had known that Wendell Russell owned a large quantity of land. How he knew that Wendell and Rebecca might need extra income to keep the farm for Tad. Why Nora was so concerned about the news in Sovereign every time she phoned. Why she was upset with Nick, after her brother successfully initiated the special Town Meeting to consider the solar farm moratorium. All the pieces suddenly fell into place.

Maggie pushed her iced tea aside and folded her arms upon the table. "OK, Nora, out with it," she demanded. "Your flimflam might work with your father, but it won't work with me. Tell me everything there is to tell about you and Robinson Crockett."

Chapter 26

A Pastoral Visit

Thursday afternoon, as Sabine was considering whether to wrap up her office hours early (the July afternoon was warm and she had yet to receive a caller), she felt the curious exchange of air that occurred when the front door of the church was opened. The venerable church inhaled a deep breath, before steadily breathing out as the arm of the door closer pulled the heavy door shut behind the visitor.

Well, that answers that question, Sabine thought, waiting to see if the caller was for her or was a communicant for the Divine.

A few moments later, there was a knock on the wood doorframe (her office door was open) and Duncan stepped into the small room. Sabine leapt to her feet. "Duncan! How nice to see you."

"Am I disturbing you?"

"Only from a nap." She shoved to one side of her desk a pile of beekeeping magazines she had been leafing through. "Come in. Is Maggie with you?"

"Not today. This is a private matter."

Duncan's was tone disconcerting. In addition, his normal easygoing manner seemed constrained. At seminary, Sabine had been taught to read faces and body language and she now perceived that her friend was in despair.

"I've been wrestling with some demons, lately, and I thought you could help," he continued. "Do you have a few minutes?"

"Of course, that's what I'm here for. But to be honest, Duncan, you're my first pastoral visit with another minister."

"Retired minister," Duncan corrected, with a faint smile. "May I?" He indicated the nearest of the two gothic-looking mahogany chairs.

"Please do." Sabine came out from behind her desk and closed the office door so they wouldn't be interrupted. On the return trip to her desk, she pulled the window up eight or ten inches, letting in some fresh air. With the door shut, the cramped office quickly became stuffy. "The fact that you're retired is only moderately reassuring," she said, resuming her seat.

"Don't worry. You'll soon discover that clergy are some of your best customers."

Sabine laughed, her nervousness dissipated by his remark. "Thanks for the heads up." She folded her hands upon her desk. "I can see something's bothering you. What's up?"

He sighed and sank back against the burgundy seat cushion. "Don't ever have children, Sabine. They will only break your heart."

Hearing this prelude, Sabine's intuition went into overdrive. Was Duncan about to launch into a denunciation of Nick and his opposition to the solar farm? If so, she needed to prevent her friend from saying anything the two of them might later regret. "Stop, please. Before you go any further, you should know—I'm in love with your son." Duncan appeared bewildered by her disclosure, but not surprised.

"Thank you for your honesty, Sabine," he said. "Maggie suspected as much, but I had my doubts, mostly because I thought you could do better. Might I ask if Nick returns your affection?"

"I think he does. Actually, I know he does," Sabine answered, truthfully. She and Nick had been together twice since their beekeeping adventure.

"I see. Well, then, my confession this afternoon—such as it is—might make your relationship with Nick awkward, and I certainly wouldn't want that." He stood up to depart, a melancholy expression on his face.

Sabine remained seated, taking a few seconds to consider the situation. She disliked allowing Duncan leave when he was distressed. Could she hear him out with an open heart and mind, and still remain true to Nick? She thought she could. "I can't bear to see you like this, Duncan. If there's anything I can do to help, please let me. Don't worry about my relationship with Nick," she urged him. "I think I can handle it. Just don't tell me anything you wouldn't want him to know in a year or two. I can promise to keep this pastoral visit confidential for that long."

Duncan sank back down. "Your candor is very refreshing. I'd be proud to have you as a daughter, Sabine, if that comes to pass. You and Maggie—and many others in Sovereign, apparently—see something in Nick that I don't discern. To my eyes, my son lacks maturity and right feeling. He puts his own needs and wants before the needs and wants of others. And he rushes headlong into things— the solar farm moratorium, for example—without deliberation, as though he's on a mission to save the world."

Sabine, who understood only too well that Nick felt his spiritual calling *was* to save Wendell's pine grove, said nothing.

"And then there's Nora."

"Nora?" Mention of Duncan's daughter surprised the fledgling pastor. She had not expected Duncan to pivot so quickly away from Nick and his foibles. "Have you heard from her recently? I hope nothing's wrong?"

"Everything seems wrong these days. Nora is here in town. Let me amend that—she's not in Sovereign, she's in Unity, with Robinson Crockett. They're engaged to be married, as it turns out."

"Nora and Rob? Engaged!"

"Yes. They've been engaged the whole time that Rob has been among us. But did he say anything to me and Maggie about their relationship? Or to Wendell and Rebecca? Not one word! Did Nora? No. Selfish, self-centered, and unfeeling, the two of them."

In a flash, Sabine recollected her meeting in the spring with Robinson Crockett. The solar farm developer had told her in this very room that he had approached Wendell and Rebecca on the advice of a friend. Now she knew that friend was Nora. "It all makes sense, now," she mused.

A hint of accusation gleamed in Duncan's eye. "Don't tell me you knew about Nora and Rob?"

"No, no. I only knew that someone with a local connection pointed Rob in Wendell and Rebecca's direction. I wondered who it could be at the time, and now it makes perfect sense that it was Nora. She was familiar enough with the Russells to know of their struggling financial situation, but not familiar enough with Sovereign to realize that a solar farm would be met with serious opposition."

"Opposition galvanized by her own brother! I'm so ashamed of my children I can hardly bear it," Duncan replied in anguish. "Look at all the trouble they've caused! The town divided; all because of them. Leland separated from his dear friend Rebecca; Hannah Trow and Nadine Danforth are no longer speaking to one another; and other lifelong friends have turned against each other. I've gone wrong somewhere in raising Nick and Nora, and for the life of me I can't figure out where. They didn't get their duplicity from their mother, that's for sure. I must have done something terribly wrong."

As he admitted his failure, Duncan's eyes sought out Sabine's. She read in them his agony of spirit. "The division in Sovereign would have erupted sooner or later, Duncan," she assured him. "I noticed the underlying tension in town not long after I arrived last fall. It's a symptom of the times, unfortunately, and probably easier for me to see because I didn't have any preconceived notion about Sovereign. Maybe the town was once a 'frost pocket of goodness,' as Maggie preached years ago, or maybe that's how she chooses to see this place?"

"Maggie does prefer to view the world through rose-colored glasses, but she's not naive. And I hear what you say about dissension. Certainly, we're in a period of grave national discord, and Maine is not immune; however, do you really believe the current strife in Sovereign would have occurred had it not been for the maneuvering of my children in this solar farm affair?"

Sabine pondered his question. "Well, there was a lot of dissent over that massive transmission line project last year?"

"And we weathered that controversy without friend turning against friend. No, Sabine, I appreciate your attempt to let me off the hook, but as Mr. Bennett remarked to his daughter Elizabeth in *Pride and Prejudice*: 'Let me once in my life feel how much I have been to blame.' Except that in my case, the feeling will not pass away soon enough."

Sabine suddenly felt moved to drop her pastoral counseling posture and speak as herself. "I don't think you understand how difficult it is to be a TO, Duncan—a Theological Offspring—as we call ourselves. Nellie and I have talked about being TOs, and we both agree that it's a lot harder than anyone would think. In my opinion, that explains a lot of Nick and Nora's behavior."

Duncan leaned forward with indignation. "What! Growing up in a comfortable home with plenty of food on the table? With two parents who love and cherish you? Should I have starved and beaten my kids?"

"Of course not. But you don't realize the psychological effect of being raised by a parent who is perfect, and …"

"Nobody's perfect, Sabine, certainly not me," he interrupted.

"Almost perfect," she amended. "When we TOs compare ourselves to our pastoral parents, we come up short. We know we can't live up to them—we can't ever be as good as they are, no matter how long we live—so we go in the opposite direction. It's dumb, I know, but it's human."

"But you had *two* parents who were pastors—my kids only had one—and look how well you turned out!"

Sabine gave a bitter laugh. "I assure you, Duncan, I wasn't always the woman you see today."

"I find that hard to believe. You're the most level-headed, mature young woman I know, Sabine."

"You should have known me eight or nine years ago, then. Both my parents wanted to disown me."

"I can't believe that!"

"It's true. You know I took a year off between high school and college, but what you don't know is that during that year I ran off with the drummer in a heavy metal band, a man who was old enough to be my father. My parents freaked out, which is probably what I was hoping for. I always seemed to come last with them. Mom, especially, was always too busy with church or making pastoral calls or visiting her parishioners at the hospital to pay much attention to me. Dad was occupied with his own church and his second family in Florida. But let me tell you, a

Harley-riding, coke-snorting, older man with lots of tattoos and nose rings gets their attention pretty quick!"

"I don't know what to say, Sabine. I'm shocked, as your parents much have been. What happened?"

"What happened? I married him. Oh, don't worry, I divorced the drummer six months later. I'm not a complete idiot. I was lucky enough to have a friend—the base guitarist's girlfriend—who steered steer me in the right direction. She was a junkie, too. She said it was too late for her, but it wasn't too late for me."

"Thank God!"

"Yes, thank God and Michelle. But no thanks to my pastor parents, who literally inferred I was crazy and were ready to commit me to a mental institution. I tried to explain to Mom how hard it was to live up to her, and much like you, she just couldn't understand where I was coming from."

"Dare I ask what happened to your friend Michelle?"

"She OD'd on fentanyl in 2018."

"I'm sorry to hear that."

"Me, too. There, but by the grace of God go I." Sabine, becoming aware that her entire body was tensed up, relaxed back in her chair. "I didn't mean to tell you that whole drama, Duncan, but when you were speaking of your despair over your children, I felt you needed to know my truth. And, unfortunately, I just realized while pointing this out to you, that I've been guilty of contributing to Nick's TO complex, too."

"You? How could you?"

"Nick and I have talked about you many times—don't worry, I'm not going to break his confidence. In some of those conversations I've described you in very exemplary terms. I remember once I said something like, 'One thing I know about your father is that he always does what's right'."

"I do try and do the right thing," Duncan acknowledged. "Is that so bad?"

"No, but holding you up as a model of perfection to Nick only added insult to his injury. Nobody knows that better than me, either, because my whole life I've been compared to my mother. But whenever I held the mirror up to see for myself—as all young people do—I'd see someone who fell short, very short. You're a good man, Duncan, and I admire you very much. But it's probably not helpful for Nick that his girlfriend thinks his father is perfect."

"Almost perfect," Duncan countered, with a smile. "And I'm pretty sure Maggie would dispute that."

"No offense, but I don't want Nick to be like you. I had a New Testament professor my first year at Iliff who was a former Catholic nun. She didn't wear a habit or anything, but she did wear a wedding ring. Not being familiar with Catholicism at the time—and being plagued by my ex-husband, who wanted to get back together—I went to see Dr. O'Brien and asked her for marital advice. Imagine my surprise when I discovered she was married to Jesus."

Duncan laughed aloud. "Not much help there! She was married to the one perfect man."

"Exactly. I'm not looking for a perfect man. I love Nick as he is, warts and all."

"Oh, Sabine! I can't tell you how much you've helped me. Your personal story is very illuminating, and your understanding of the challenges facing Nick and Nora as preacher's kids—PK's as we called them in our day—is insightful. Does Maggie know about your Harley-riding drummer?"

"Given how close she and my mother have been since their days at seminary, I'd be surprised if she didn't know, but Maggie and I have never spoken about him."

"She never mentioned this particular episode in your life to me, although that doesn't surprise me. Maggie is very good as disseminating information; however, she's even better at keeping a confidence. I'm still perplexed, though. You're an extremely confident, self-assured young woman, Sabine. How did this wonderful transformation from defiant groupie to ordained minister come about?"

"It didn't happen overnight, let me tell you! I had heard God's Call as a teenager, but fell away from listening during my wild year. In college, I unstopped my ears again. Hearing a renewal of the Call, I elected not to fight it—I have another friend to thank for that. I followed the Call to seminary. At Iliff, somewhere between doing exegeses on the Gospel of Mark and the Gospel of John, I realized that I had to be myself and stop trying to be my mother. That was a challenge, because I desperately longed for her approval. But the funny thing was, on the way to becoming me I earned her approval. Iliff helped make that happen, too. Mom took a sabbatical during my second year there and came to visit me. Naturally, I showed her around, introducing her to my friends and my favorite professors, including Dr. O'Brien, by the way. For the first time in my life—in our lives—Mom was regarded simply as the mother of Sabine. Nobody at Iliff knew who she was or that she pastored a large church in Fairbanks. You know the old saying: 'Jesus doesn't want us to be Jesus; He wants us to be ourselves?' Well, the same is true for parents, I discovered. Trust me, Duncan, there will come a time when Nick—and Nora—learn that all they have to do to win your approval is be themselves."

As she was concluding her narration, Sabine espied an expression of dismay on Duncan's face. "What's the matter? Did I say something wrong?"

"On the contrary—you said something only too right. It just dawned on me that Nick came to Sovereign a decade ago to start a new life, a life separate from me. And what did I do? I followed him here! Not only that, I stayed and made my home in Sovereign. I foiled my son in his bold attempt to become his own man! No wonder Nick took off last year to go looking for himself. He had to get away from me. What have I done?" he beseeched her.

Sabine didn't hesitate. "You've done what anyone would do—you fell in love with an amazing woman and created a wonderful life here in Sovereign with her."

The harsh cry of a blue jay interrupted their conversation. Distracted by the loud screech, Duncan peered out the open window and spied the corvid picking over seeds in a swinging birdfeeder. "That's a new addition," he remarked. The bluejay hopped around on the white-painted feeder, which was shaped like a hanging porch swing.

"Nick built it for me."

"So, I surmised. He made Maggie a birdhouse exactly like this little white church. She loves it and the swallows do, too. I putter around the house trying to fix things, but the truth is I'm not very handy. Nick inherited his ability to work with his hands from his grandfather, not me."

"Your father? Or his mother's?" Sabine asked, curious.

"Mine. My father was a brick-layer in New York City. He came from a long line of Scottish brick-layers, the branch of the family that parted ways with the falconers. Our ancient ancestors were once falconers to the King, or so they say."

"Faulkner—Falconer! Of course."

"My father was very proud of his work," Duncan continued. "Rightly so. He did beautiful brickwork. Many of his houses stand just as true today as the day he finished them. But he told me once the proudest day of his life was the day I graduated seminary. I was the first ordained clergy in our family. He died just before Nick was born, unfortunately. He and Nick would have loved each other. Nick inherited Father's passion for life, too."

Duncan fell silent, his eyes seeing beyond the present, into the past, as well as to a possible future. Sabine, understanding the importance of reflection, maintained a respectful silence, a Quaker timeout, as Maggie called it, an opportunity for the Divine to work upon a caller's heart.

He straightened up with a sigh. "So, now what?"

"Well, if you want my professional advice ...?"

"I do."

"I think you need to have the conversation we've had this afternoon with Nick, especially the part about your father. You're obviously proud of your father—I hear it in your voice and see it in your eyes—yet you told me that he was just as proud of you. Isn't that what every son wants to hear?"

"That's what I wanted to hear as a young man, certainly."

"Well, then—is Nick so very different from you?"

As Duncan was contemplating her query, Sabine rose gracefully from her chair. She smoothed a wrinkle from her summer linen dress and bestowed a winsome smile upon the former Presbyterian minister. "Now, if you'll excuse me, Duncan, I need to go change. I have a date with your son."

Chapter 27

Nora and Rob

The following morning, around ten-o'clock, Nick was organizing the shipping boxes and packaging material in his shed, when Gerald burst in through the back door. "You got visitors comin', Walden," the youth announced. "I seen 'em from the woods."

Nick stood up and regarded his sweaty young partner, who had obviously been running hard to bring him back this news. "Thanks for the heads up, Gerald, but you better get a hustle on or you'll miss FedEx."

"I done delivered the packages to Leland's already," Gerald replied, scornfully. "I ain't stupid—I knows my duties. I seen 'em on the trail on the way back."

Nick was incredulous. "You didn't get over to Scotch Broom Acres already, did you?"

"I shore did."

"It's four miles, round trip! Did you fly there?" Nick joked.

"Nope. I cut through the swamp."

The woodsman was taken aback. "The swamp! That's dangerous business, Gerald. Even I don't venture very far into the swamp. You could get lost in there and nobody

279

would ever find you except the coyotes. Your grandparents would kill me if you got lost there."

"Aw, ain't much water in the swamp nowadays, on account o' the drought. I followed the deer trail, too, jest like you larned me."

"I don't care if you follow bread crumbs. Promise me you won't take that shortcut anymore, OK?"

"Oh, alright, boss."

Nick relaxed, and ruffled the boy's mop-headed red curls. "Now, tell me about my visitors?"

"Looks like that solar farm guy, 'n he's got a girl with him."

"Sabine?" Nick asked, hopefully. He no longer had any qualms about the young minister spending time with other men. It was just part of her job.

"Nope. 'Tis yore sister."

Nick snorted. "Fat chance! She's in North Dakota." He opened the connecting door to the kitchen and shooed the youth in front of him. "But let's go see who's coming."

Together, they peered out one of the south-facing kitchen windows, Nick viewing through the top of the double-hung window and Gerald, standing in front of him, through the bottom. "I don't see anyone," Nick said. "Whoever you spotted went by, headed for a picnic to the Millett Rock."

Just as he turned away from the window Nick heard a high-pitched woman's voice. The sound was immediately followed up by deep masculine laughter. He looked again out over Gerald's head. A man and woman, indeed, were coming down the side trail to his house.

Gerald whistled. "Told ya, Walden! Sartin, 'tis yore sister."

Nick began to get irritated with the youngster. "How do you know what my sister looks like? You've never even met Nora, have you?"

"Yep. She give me twenty dollars once. I ain't likely to forget that!"

"Why the heck would my sister give you twenty dollars?"

"She said I was cute."

"OK, that's definitely Nora."

Nick was pleased that his sister had come back to Sovereign for a visit. But why was she consorting with the enemy? Was it possible Robinson Crockett was going to propose a compromise and Nora offered to show Crockett the way to his house? No, if anything like a compromise was in the works, Maggie would have told him.

Then it crossed his mind that Maggie—notorious matchmaker that she was—might be trying to hook Nora up with the solar farm developer. His stepmother would do anything, he knew, to get Nora home to Maine because it would make their father happy. But if that was Maggie's plan, she had made a big mistake. He would never accept Crockett as a brother-in-law, no matter what happened!

In another minute the two visitors were on the granite stoop, ringing the cast-iron bell. Nick warily swung open the ancient front door. "Hey Nora," he greeted her.

"That's all I get after a year and a half?" she cried. "Hey Nora! How about a hug, big brother?" She leapt up into the foyer and threw her arms around him.

Nick grudgingly accepted his sister's embrace. "What's this guy doing here?" he demanded, pushing away from her.

"Now, don't lose your temper, Nicky."

"Don't call me that. You know I hate that name."

"OK, don't lose your temper, Nicholas. Rob and I need your help with Pops. Can we come in?"

At that moment, Gerald sidled into the foyer from the kitchen, where he had been hovering just inside the door. "Hiya," he addressed Nora, before shyly hanging his head.

"Why, who's this nice-looking young man? This can't be Gerald Danforth?"

The youth perked up. "It surely is, ma'am."

"I hardly recognized you, Gerald. You've grown a foot!"

Emboldened by this pronouncement, Gerald offered the young woman a cheeky grin. "I seen you from the woods 'n knowed right away 'twas you. I come runnin' back to tell Walden."

Robinson Crockett, who had been standing on the stoop observing the exchange, now spoke up. "Who's Walden?"

"Oh, that's just what some people around here call my brother," Nora explained. "When Nick first came to town he used an assumed name—Walden Pond."

"Wish I'd thought of that," the solar farm developer remarked ruefully.

"Don't be ridiculous, Rob. You've got your reputation as a businessman to maintain. Nick doesn't care about stuff like that—he doesn't have to."

"Right you are, as usual."

Nick was confounded by the odd interplay between his sister and the developer. "Nora, what the devil's going on?"

He felt as though he was losing control of the situation, as he often did whenever he was with his sister. When they were very young, he had felt obliged to protect Nora, as the elder of the two. Once they reached middle school, however, the tables had turned and Nick's pretty and popular sister had been the one to fend off the students making malicious taunts about his size and hairiness. "Big Foot," they called him, until Nora came over and threatened to pound the bullies into the ground. He loved Nora, but she often embarrassed and bewildered him.

Nora's right hand flew up like that of a crossing guard. "Hold on a moment, Nick." She pivoted to Robinson Crockett. "Do you have a twenty? I didn't bring my purse."

"Twenty dollars? I think so." The developer pulled out his wallet and flipped it open. He perused the bills inside and located a twenty. "What for?"

"For Gerald, of course." She plucked the bill from her fiancée's hand.

"Why? What has the boy done?"

"He's turned into a handsome young man! That's what he's done." Nora handed the bill to Gerald. "Now, spend this on something fun," she instructed the youth.

"I surely will, ma'am!"

"Call me, Nora, Gerald. You're killing me with your 'ma'ams'. I feel older than Maggie!"

"Yes, ma' … Nora." Gerald stuffed the bill into his pants pocket. He bobbed his head in a goodbye salute, then darted back into the kitchen and out the shed door as quick as a chipmunk.

Nora turned back to her partner. "Isn't he adorable, Rob?"

"He seems like a nice kid, but I'm not sure he's worth twenty dollars."

Nick, overcome with frustration, forcibly took his sister by the arm. "Get in here." He steered her into the kitchen. "Now, tell me what you're up to. This obviously isn't a social visit. You're up to something, Nora, I can tell."

Robinson Crockett took a step up into the foyer. A loose board squeaked. "Should I come, too?"

"You can go to Jericho, for all I care," Nick retorted from the kitchen. He pushed his sister down into one of the ladderback chairs at the table. "Now, start talking."

"That's no way to treat your future brother-in-law," she scolded him. "Rob and I are engaged to be married."

"The Hell you are!"

The developer poked his head into the kitchen and looked around the room. "Cool place!"

"Get in here, Rob! I could use some support."

Crockett obliged by entering the room; however, rather than joining his fiancée at the kitchen table, he gravitated toward the slate sink. "Nifty pitcher pump you have here, Nick. Does she still work?"

"Oh, my God, Rob! You're no help at all."

"Yeah, it works," Nick replied, distracted by the developer's interest in the cast-iron pump assembly.

Crockett, a trained engineer, lovingly fingered the black-painted cylinder with his right hand, while his left played with the pump's handle. "How far can she pull?"

"Twenty-five feet from the static water level."

"That's what I figured. How often do you have to prime it?"

"Never, unless I go away. The pump holds the initial prime quite a while."

Robinson Crockett rewarded Nick with one of his crooked grins. "Remarkable piece of engineering, isn't it? Those old timers knew what they were doing. Does she have a leather cup gasket?"

From the table, Nora groaned. "Seriously?"

"I think the gasket is made of leather," said Nick, ignoring his sister. "Although I've never had to replace it." Beginning to warm up to the developer, he joined the other man at the sink.

"If you keep the leather wet you shouldn't have to replace it. The gasket should last a long time."

"Yeah, that's what I'm hoping."

"Do you mind if I try her out?"

"Be my guest."

The old pump inhaled as Robinson Crockett lifted the iron handle. He pushed down hard on the handle—nothing happened.

"You need a lot more elbow grease than that, Crockett," Nick commented.

The developer pumped again harder, several times, enjoying the feel of the resistance of the handle against his arm muscle. Soon, all three heard the gurgle of water rising up the shaft, into spout. A fountain of clear water poured out the downspout into the sink. Some of the water splashed onto the developer. "Awesome!" he exclaimed. He released the handle and patted his face dry with the tail of his cotton shirt. "I've always wanted one of these old pitcher pumps. Maybe when we build our own house someday, Nora, we can have one of these?"

"Right! Just what every woman wants. A hand pump in the kitchen—not! Next, you'll be suggesting I use one of those hand-crank wringer washing machines."

"That's what I use," Nick pointed out. "The wringer washer works fine for me."

"Does it?" replied Crockett, with interest. He leaned back against the wood countertop. "I've heard they eat socks. Do you lose many?"

"Not too many."

"You two are killing me," Nora proclaimed. "Like I'd ever trust my lace undies to those splinter-infested rollers!"

Nick laughed at the thought of his sister's delicate lingerie going through the wooden rollers of his wringer washer. "She's right," he said to developer.

"She usually is, isn't she?" Crockett straightened up and surveyed the rest of the kitchen.

"Unfortunately, yes. Care for a cup of tea, Crockett?" Nick asked, noticing that the other man was now admiring his cast-iron cookstove. "I'll fire up the Clarion for you."

"Geez, pretty hot day for that. Maybe another time." The engineer examined the nickel-plated, six-burner stove. "Fancy!" he declared, finally. "Great shelf placement and a good-sized water jacket. She's not original to the house, though, is she?"

"Nope, there was an old step stove in here when I bought the place. Unfortunately, that was too rusted out to save. I bought the Clarion from Bryant Stove in Thorndike, before they closed up shop."

"OK, get a room, you two, why don't you?" Nora mocked. "Come on, Rob! We came here to ask Nick to help us with Pops, remember?"

"Sorry," her fiancée apologized. "Got sidetracked. Mind if I have a seat, Nick?"

Nick flipped his hand toward the table. "Be my guest. Maybe then I'll find out what the heck is going on here."

Crockett looped his ballcap over the spindle of the chair next to Nora. He sat down, smiling broadly at his partner. "You never told me your brother had such a cool place."

"You never asked."

Nick appropriated the third chair. He threw his forearms on the oak table and leaned toward his sister. "OK, Nora, spill it—how did you meet this guy and why are you here?"

"It's not rocket science, Nick. Rob and I hooked up on Tinder."

"A dating app? You used a dating app!"

"Oh, grow up. You don't think I'm going to hang out in bars in North Dakota looking for men, do you? Tinder was much nicer."

"And safer for Nora, I might add," Crockett interjected, also leaning forward.

Nora patted her fiancée's arm. "Thank you, honey. Anyway, Rob was thinking about starting his own company—he's got all sorts of PE certifications—and so I suggested he develop a solar farm in Maine."

"*You're* behind all this heartache?" Nick demanded, incredulous. "My own sister?"

"I'm afraid I am," Nora admitted. Since arriving in Sovereign, she had learned only too well of the dissension the solar farm project had caused.

"What the heck were you thinking!"

"We're trying to save the planet," she said, simply.

"By cutting down Wendell's woodlot? Are you insane? Trees are a natural carbon sink."

"I told you," Rob said to Nora.

"Oh, please! Not what I need to hear now."

Crockett shrugged. He turned away from Nora and looked thoughtfully out the window at the woods beyond Nick's garden.

"Trees are renewable, Nick," Nora pleaded. "We'll plant some trees someplace else. Won't we, Rob?"

The developer took a few moments before replying. "Actually, I'm not sure how many of Wendell's trees we're going to need to cut down now. If the special Town Meeting hadn't ended so abruptly—and I'd had the opportunity to speak—you would have learned, Nick, that I've already downsized the project."

Nora was surprised. "You didn't tell me that. Rob! How come we're downsizing?"

"I had to sell some of the equipment to pay the demurrage and storage fees at the terminal. Fortunately, we made a healthy profit. Everything manufactured in China is more expensive now, because of the high tariffs."

"Aren't you glad now you listened to me?" Nora cried. "I told you to buy what you needed ahead of the tariffs, and once again, I was right!"

"You certainly were."

Nick, however, was not impressed. "If you made such a profit, Crockett, you should sell the rest of the equipment—lock, stock, and barrel. Then we can put this whole nightmare to bed!"

The developer plucked his ballcap from the back of his chair, and turned the cap in his hands. "I'm sorry, I can't do that, Nick. I have an obligation to Rebecca."

"She needs the money," Nora added. "For Tad."

"Sure, that's the reason."

Rob smiled at his fiancée. "Your brother knows we'll profit off the solar farm, too, Nora."

"Well, we have a right to make a profit!"

Nick felt his blood boil at the thought of Nora and Robinson Crockett profiting off the destruction of Wendell's prized pines. "How much are you downsizing?"

"One third, at the moment," Crockett replied.

"So, you're down to two hundred acres? Even if you used all the Russell's fields, you'd still take out half of Wendell's woodlot."

"Maybe so. But we could save the pine grove."

"It's called a stand, not a grove. A *stand* of pine."

"Rebecca calls it a grove," Nora pointed out.

"She can call it what she likes—Rebecca owns the trees."

Robinson Crockett stood up and flipped his ballcap onto his head. "You know what? I'd really like to see this stand of pine trees I've heard so much about. Got time to show me, Nick?"

Nora clutched at her lover's arm. "What about Pops? Nick is supposed to help us with Pops!"

Nick offered an embittered chuckle. "If that's the real reason for your visit, Nora, you've wasted your time. I'm in the doghouse with Dad, too." He stood up and pushed in his chair. "Let's go, Crockett. I'll show you the most beautiful sight you've ever seen. Sabine calls Wendell's pine stand a forest cathedral. I'll wager it's a sight you city boys don't see every day!"

The two men exited the house and soon were chatting away like old friends. Nora remained alone at the kitchen table, thinking. The house was suddenly very quiet. She heard a cricket chirp.

The meeting with her brother had not gone as she had planned, but she could cope. She was very good at pivoting. "At least they're getting along now," Nora adjudged aloud. "That's progress!"

Chapter 28

Bringing Up the Bell

"How do I look?" Maggie asked her husband Saturday morning. She pirouetted in the kitchen so that Duncan could appreciate the total effect of her dress: a bell-shaped skirt worn over two petticoats; a V-shaped bodice; leather ankle boots; and a double-ruffled linen cap. The celebration for the repaired Revere bell would begin in an hour and Maggie and Duncan were two of the four adult volunteers—dressed in period costumes—who would accompany Leland and his team of oxen bringing up the bell from the train station to the Sovereign Union Church.

Duncan glanced up from his newspaper. "The cap makes you look like Old Mother Hubbard, but other than that you look charming."

"Better Old Mother Hubbard than Mother Goose," Maggie quipped. Netting no response from him, she examined Duncan's face closely. "What's bothering you. dear? You haven't been yourself since Nora arrived." He winced slightly when she pronounced Nora's name, confirming Maggie's suspicion that her husband was still belaboring his perceived failure as a parent.

Duncan carefully refolded the weekend newspaper. "I went to see Sabine Thursday afternoon. She suggested I have a heart-to-heart with Nick. What do you think?"

Maggie took a moment for reflection. She was familiar with the passionate nature of her stepson, as well as the doggedness of her husband when he felt himself in the right, and foresaw plenty of opportunities for the heart-to-heart to go wrong; however, she disliked contradicting her fledgling pastor. Besides, who knew? Maybe Sabine, as an outsider, could prescribe for the disconnect between father and son better than she could?

"That's an excellent idea. It's been a long time since you two have talked, hasn't it?"

"We had the beginnings of a good conversation the day I washed the windows. Nick told me he was mentoring young Gerald Danforth while he was holding the ladder for me. He's teaching Gerald to read."

"Gerald? Stephen and Nadine's grandson? Good for Nick!"

"I was really impressed with him that afternoon, until the newspaper reporter let slip Nick went behind our backs with the solar farm moratorium."

"He didn't go behind our backs, Duncan. Nick just didn't tell me why he was borrowing the car that night."

"He didn't tell you because he thought you might object," Duncan noted.

"Well, had he told me I still would have let him use the car, but I probably would have given him an earful about the moratorium."

"Exactly. He went behind your back to get what he wanted, without a lecture. What I can't figure out—and I've been wrestling with since—is why Nick didn't tell me about the moratorium the afternoon we were talking? He had nothing to gain by keeping it a secret. Obviously, word about his moratorium was going to get around once the

Selectmen set a date for the special Town Meeting. Why not tell me himself?"

"The dreaded lecture?" Maggie suggested.

"Perhaps."

Maggie picked up her wallet and cell phone. "Can we finish this conversation later? We need to get a wiggle on or we'll be late. Stand up and let me take a look at you."

Duncan obliged, but without enthusiasm. He was wearing an antique black suit with long tails; long-sleeved white shirt, yellowed with age; and a celluloid collar.

"Put the hat on."

He retrieved from the chiffonier the rusty top hat Maggie had procured for him from the Fairfield Antiques Mall. Duncan settled the felt-lined hat upon his head and, catching some of his wife's spirit, struck a solemn pose.

"Oh, my! You look wicked shaap."

He turned around and examined his reflection in the oak-framed mirror. "I look like a very short Abraham Lincoln."

"Don't be silly. Lincoln wore a stovepipe top hat—that's a Wellington. Did you know that President Lincoln was seven feet tall when he wore his hat?"

"Thanks, but that makes me feel even shorter. Are you sure this outfit is appropriate, Maggie? I feel like I should be going to Ford's Theatre, rather than walking behind an ox cart."

"Of course it's appropriate! You might be shorter than Lincoln, but you're much handsomer, dear," she added, as a gratuity.

"Somehow, I don't find that reassuring. Every officer in the Confederacy was better looking than Lincoln, as well as every officer in the Union, excepting perhaps William Tecumsah Sherman."

"'Handsome is as handsome does.' Character is more important than appearance, as the country found out during the Civil War. Thank God Abraham Lincoln and

Ulyssis S. Grant were men of character! We sure could use a few good men like them, nowadays."

"That's a fact. I keep hoping character will come back in style," Duncan mused.

"Me, too." Maggie retrieved the car keys and tossed them to her husband. "Let's go. We're not just providing color for the celebration today; we have a very important job, too."

"What's that?"

"To keep three excited kids from falling off Leland's wagon. Woe to us—and possibly them—if we're late."

The drive to the train station was short, the decommissioned Sovereign depot being less than three miles from their house. Within ten minutes Duncan was turning into the dirt parking lot at the old station. He maneuvered into an empty space between the Scotch Broom Acres pickup and another vehicle. As he braked to a stop, a cloud of dust from the dry gravel parking lot floated in through the open car windows.

Maggie coughed and quickly rolled up her window. "Just what we needed, some back road pollen to give us proper nineteenth century veneer!"

Duncan switched off the engine and turned to face his wife, a serious expression on his face. "Am I really so unapproachable? Why don't my kids talk to me?"

"Oh, Duncan! Let it go and try and enjoy the celebration," Maggie advised, as she opened her car door. "The hanging of the church's Revere bell only happens once every 180 years. Oh, doesn't the station house look nice? The Brooks Preservation Society is doing an amazing job bringing this old place back to life."

The historic station house in Sovereign—the starting point for bringing up the bell—had been built in the latter half of the nineteenth century to facilitate the shipment of canned goods from the Sovereign Corn Shop to a larger market. The train also carried passengers for over a century, until train travel was replaced by the family automobile. Much like the local canning factory before it was resurrected by the Sovereign Ladies Auxiliary, the squat, hip-roofed depot had been allowed to sink into a state of disrepair. Recently, however, the train station had been purchased by the Brooks Preservation Society, a Waldo County 501(c)(3), which also owned the Belfast and Moosehead Lake Railroad. The B&MLRR currently ran an excursion train from Unity east to Thorndike, and the Preservation Society's long-term plan was to reopen the rail line between Thorndike and Sovereign to extend the distance of their excursions.

Over fifty people were already gathered at the station house by the time Maggie and Duncan arrived. Some were looking at the bell, and others were examining the recent repairs to the depot; however, most of the gawkers were clustered around Leland and his team of oxen. The garrulous old woodchopper was holding court in front of the train station, expounding upon the virtues of his yoke of oxen, Ishmael and Isaac. The team was hitched to a stout hay wagon from which the sides and front had been removed. Next to the team idled a flatbed semi with a Hiab crane. The restored bell rested upon a pallet atop the flatbed, a leather sling hooked to its crown through two of the bell's six canons. Seven-year-old Jana, standing up in the hay wagon with Hope and Tad, spied her grandparents approaching through the milling crowd and waved excitedly.

"Looking good, Pumpkin!" Maggie called, waving back. "I hope Leland gets the kids off the wagon before they put the bell on," she added in a lower voice to her husband.

"I think Leland has sense enough for that. One of them is his own granddaughter."

Maggie and Duncan gravitated to the flatbed to inspect the Revere bell, the crowd around the hay wagon making it difficult to approach Leland and youngsters. They were shortly joined by Ryan MacDonald and Doctor Bart.

"You have a lot of faith that your father-in-law won't accidentally squash your daughter," Maggie joked to Ryan.

"It's OK—I have an extra. Daughter number two is safe at the church with her mother, helping Rebecca with the flowers." The lawyer-farmer, who was dressed casually in a homemade Amish work shirt and pants purchased from Community Market in Unity, examined Duncan's formal attire. "Nice hat. You look like Abraham Lincoln, Faulkner."

"I told you, Maggie."

"Did I say something wrong?"

"No. Minor spousal dispute, which I lost. I just wish my eyes were at the top of the hat so I *felt* eight inches taller," Duncan grumbled.

"Why aren't you in costume, Metcalf?" Maggie asked her son-in-law. He was dressed in jeans, a summer cotton shirt, and LL Bean hiking boots. "You're walking with us, aren't you?"

"I am on child patrol, too; however, I'm also on call." Doctor Bart patted the two-way radio that was attached to his hip. He worked parttime at Unity Ambulance, the Sovereign Songbird Clinic not providing him and Nellie with enough income for their growing family.

"What happens if you get called out? How will you get to where you need to go?"

"We're only going to be an hour, Maggie. But if I get called out on the way to the church, Stephen Danforth said he'd give me a lift. He's going to follow us in his truck, just in case."

"You look tired, dear. I think you're overworking," Maggie worried. "You have too many irons in the fire."

"I'll survive," her son-in-law reassured her. "I seem to remember stories of you and my mother juggling several different jobs just to make ends meet when you were our age."

"That was different."

"Really? How so?"

"Because I wasn't a grandmother then!" The little group clustered around Maggie laughed.

Ryan leaned over and admired the bell. "I've never seen this thing up close. She certainly is a beauty!" He ran his hand over the pock-marked bronze of the nearly two century old Revere bell.

"Aunt Hannah says the bell has a beautiful mellow tone, too," said Doctor Bart. "The bell was still in use when she was young. She was always jealous because the boys got to pull the rope to ring the bell, but not the girls. Unfortunately, the bell cracked by the time Hannah was a teenager, and was never used again."

"Shame it's been silent all these years," Duncan remarked. "There's nothing like the sound of a church bell to cheer a person up or bring people together."

"Did you find the repair, Doc?" Ryan asked Metcalf, who had drifted around the back of the flatbed to examine the bell from the other side.

"Right here—it's easy to locate because of the new material. I hope the repair holds. Cracks in these old bronze bells are notoriously difficult to fix."

"I hope the repair holds—at least until I'm dead," Maggie declared. "It cost us a ton of money."

"Did you know that Paul Revere made three different size bells, not just church bells? His foundry also manufactured school bells and ship bells," Doctor Bart expounded. He gave the Sovereign church bell an affectionate pat. "These were the largest bells, though, weighing between 500 and 1,000 pounds each. I bet this one is about 500 pounds."

At that moment, the truck driver, a burly man in his mid-forties, separated from the crowd around Leland.

"Back up, folks!" he yelled. "We're gonna load 'er up now." He began shooing people away from the ox team and semi.

Maggie hurried over and lifted Jana off the wagon, while Ryan and Doctor Bart corralled the other two children. They led the youngsters up onto the raised platform of the train station where they could all safely watch the transfer of the bell from the truck to the wagon.

Once the audience was pushed back—except for Leland, who stood at the head of his unflappable team—the truck driver climbed into his cab and revved up the engine. He hopped back down and checked to ensure that the sling on the bell was securely fastened to the hook of the hydraulic crane. Using the crane's remote controls, he slowly—carefully—lifted the Revere bell from the pallet and placed the bell onto the center of the sturdy hay wagon.

"That good?" he called to Leland.

"Ayuh, she's solid!"

The driver continued to press the remote until the sling went slack, and then climbed onto the wagon and unhooked the sling from the bell's canons. Once the bell was free, he hopped down and clapped Leland on the shoulders. "She's all yours, Gorse! Want me to follow you to the church?"

"Thank ya, Ron, but Ishmael 'n Isaac will take it from here. We don't intend to lose 'er."

"Don't break any speed limits, haha." The truck driver secured the remote controls to his vehicle, climbed back into the cab, and took off.

In short order the children were hoisted back up onto the hay wagon. "You ready, Miss Minor?" Leland asked his granddaughter Hope, who was wearing a calico gown and matching sunbonnet. Rebecca had sewn the three children's costumes from a cute dairy farm patterned cotton calico material.

"Ready, Grampa!"

"Tad? Jana? All buckled up?"

Hope giggled and Tad broke into gales of laughter. "There aren't any seat belts to buckle, Mr. Gorse," Jana pointed out.

"There aren't no seats, neither," Tad pointed out, still laughing.

"So there ain't. Wal, you kids best sit down on yer bottoms afore you take a tumble. The startup might be jerky and we got some rough ground to cover today. We're takin' the old stagecoach road." In the nineteenth century the stagecoach road had been the main thoroughfare from Augusta to Bangor, however, after Route 9 was built, the road had been abandoned, and only recently rescued for the use of horses and off-road vehicles—and today, a team of oxen.

The three children obediently sat down upon the back of the wagon, feet swinging over the edge. Leland, after reassuring himself that his load was secure (at a pace of 2 miles per hour he knew the 500-pound bell wasn't going anywhere), joined the children up in the wagon. He seated himself in front of the bell on an overturned wooden crate.

Leland adjusted the leather reins in his arthritic hands. "Step up, Ishmael," he directed the older of the two oxen. He tapped the shoulder of the ox with his goad stick and the lead ox lunged forward in the harness, catching the weight of the bell on the wagon. As soon as Ishmael moved, Isaac sprang into action. The team shortly found its grove and settled into a steady trudge toward the Sovereign Union Church. The crowd, now that the excitement of the bell transfer was over, dispersed toward their vehicles, most heading for the promised refreshments at the church.

Maggie and Duncan fell into step behind the hay wagon, lagging back a bit to stay clear of the low cloud of dust loosened by thick hooves of the oxen. Ryan walked on the right side of the wagon next to the children and

Doctor Bart on the left. Leland gave Ishmael another tap. He began to whistle *She'll Be Comin' Round the Mountain.* Exhilarated by the festivities, the three children joined in singing and clapping their hands. Shortly, Ryan and Doctor Bart unleashed their baritones, and the venerable trees that lined the old coach road leaned in to listen to the odd musical parade.

The mid-morning early August sun shone, bright and warm, but not overly hot. A light breeze ruffled the lace on Maggie's cap. She adjusted her headgear and thoughtfully regarded the old hay wagon in front of them. "Four adults to look after three kids seems excessive, doesn't it?"

"It does seem over the top," agreed Duncan. "Especially as Alice Rose is at the church with her mother."

"What would their parents say if they could see how we used to ride atop the hay wagons when we were the same age as these kids?" Maggie wondered. "We didn't have any babysitters to catch us if we fell off, either—and those bales of hay were stacked ten or twelve high! I remember the whole load swaying from side to side going around the hayfield. You'd swear the load was going to tip over any minute, but it never did. Once I slipped off from the top of the hay stack and my mother, who was driving the truck, didn't even stop to see if I was OK. I had to pick myself up, dust myself off, and run to catch up to the wagon."

"Their parents would probably think your parents were unfit. I had a similar experience, albeit that of a city boy rather than a country girl. I used to ride the bus into the city by myself when I was ten."

"What on earth for?"

"To buy comic books. Imagine any parent letting a child do that nowadays?"

"Not likely! You'd be arrested for child neglect."

"There weren't any druggies on the buses back then, although there were a few old drunks, I remember."

The little group had covered nearly half the distance to the church, when the siren on Doctor Bart's two-way radio went off, followed by the screech of an emergency call: "*10-52, North Troy Road, Sovereign.*"

"Stop, Ishmael," Leland commanded, bringing the team to a halt.

"That's it for me," said Metcalf. He signaled to Stephen Danforth, who had been creeping along in his pickup behind the strange ensemble.

Maggie hurried up to the wagon. "What is it?" she asked her son-in-law.

"Motor vehicle accident with an ambulance call out. Someone's been hurt. Gotta go—see you later!" Doctor Bart hopped into the slowed pickup and slammed the door shut. Danforth swung the truck around in the road and went roaring back the way they had come, kicking up a cloud of dust.

"Did you hear where it was Ryan?" Maggie asked, waving away the dust.

"North Troy Road, somewhere."

"I hope it's nobody we know!"

"What's the matter Grammie? Did somebody get hurt?"

"We don't know, Pumpkin, but if they have, your Daddy will fix them up." Realizing that some of the effervescence of the morning excursion had dissipated with the emergency call, Maggie suggested another song. "Who knows a good one?" she asked.

"*Old MacDonald's Farm*!" yelled Tad, proceeding to warble out the first line of the song, "Old MacDonald had a farm ..."

"Step up, Ishmael," Leland instructed, tapping the ox's shoulder with the goad stick.

"*My* personal favorite," said Ryan MacDonald. He hopped onto the back of the wagon with the kids and started swinging his long legs. The lawyer joined in on the second line: "And on this farm, he had a pig …"

"E-I-E-I-O!" they all seven sang together, including Leland. Ishmael pricked up his ears. The ox, warming to the tune, increased the team's pace.

"Onward to the church," Maggie cried. "We have a bell to hang!"

Chapter 29

"This Is All Your Fault!"

Meanwhile, back at the church's banquet hall, Sabine and Nellie were arranging platters of finger sandwiches for consumption after the rededication of the bell. Sabine had wisely tied a full apron over her cream-colored brocade bodice and ankle-length blue silk taffeta skirt. Nellie, who was now eight months pregnant, was dressed in her usual maternity jeans and an oversized print blouse.

"Didn't feel like wearing nineteenth century maternity clothes today?" Sabine asked her counterpart with a smile.

"I don't think there was such a thing. Pregnant women still wore corsets back then. Talk about painful!"

"Those poor women."

"Poor squeezed babies!" Nellie pulled some plastic wrap over a tray of ham salad sandwiches. "I notice you don't look much like a nineteenth century parson, either?"

"Nope, because they were all men."

Nellie laughed. "How quickly we forget! Well, I must say, that's a very fetching outfit you're wearing."

Sabine clasped the sides of her long skirt and effected a mock nineteenth century curtsy. "Thank you. I did bring a white robe to throw over this outfit for the ceremony."

"Dare I ask if you're wearing that outfit for someone special?" Nellie ventured.

"Could be!"

Nellie carried her wrapped tray to the walk-in cooler and returned with a cold bowl of egg salad mix. She set the bowl on the counter and unwrapped a new bag of finger rolls. "This is fun, Sabine. I'm glad we have a chance to spend some time together this morning."

"Me, too."

Nellie slid a spoonful of egg salad into one of the finger rolls. "This reminds me of when you and I cleaned up after Rebecca's dinner party."

"Whoa! That seems like a long time ago."

"Doesn't it? So much has happened in Sovereign since then." Both women fell silent, recollecting what had occurred in town since Robinson Crockett announced his plan to build a solar farm on Wendell's woodlot at Rebecca's dinner party Memorial weekend.

Nellie filled another sandwich and placed the finger roll on her tray. "Do you expect Nick today, then?"

Sabine stepped to the sink and rinsed off her hands. "Expect is too strong a word to use with your stepbrother, Nellie." She dried her hands on the sink towel. "He wouldn't promise me that he'd be here, although I know he'd like to see Tad ring the bell after it's hung. Unfortunately, Nick is still not speaking to his father. He wants Duncan to make the first move toward reconciliation."

Nellie shook her head in disgust. "Those two! They're just alike. Nick inherited his pig-headedness from Duncan, that's for sure."

This comparison of Nick to his father startled Sabine. "I never thought of Duncan as stubborn?"

"You don't know him well enough, then. Once Duncan makes up his mind to something—especially if he thinks he's in the right—watch out! And Nick is just the same.

Mom gets exasperated with both of them sometimes, I know." Nellie set her spoon in the bowl and turned to face her friend. "Please don't take this the wrong way, Sabine. But I need to know—do you love Nick? It's none of my business, of course, but Nick has had some bad breakups in the past and I'd hate to see him hurt again."

Sabine carefully draped the towel over the rack as she considered the question. She had confessed her love for Nick to him, as well as to his father. Was there any reason not to shout it to the rooftops? She thought not, although she could perceive that many things between them could still go wrong. "I don't intend to hurt your brother, Nellie," she replied, finally. "I do love him. But I can't guarantee that everything is going to work out for us. Since you know him so well, you know Nick can be his own worst enemy. I'll stand by him—and with him—as long as I can, but I can't stand by forever with a man who insists on shooting himself in the foot."

Nellie was relieved. "That's all anyone has a right to expect. I do hope everything works out for you two—I've always wanted a sister!" She gave the young minister an awkward hug.

"What about Nora?" Sabine laughingly asked, as she pulled away from the pregnant woman's embrace.

"Oops! Forgot about Nora. Side effect of blended families, I guess. But Nora is not usually around, and you and Nick are." Hearing voices from the banquet room, Nellie glanced over her shoulder through the open servers' window. "Looks like the multitude is gathering. Is the lemonade out?"

"Yes, Rebecca put the lemonade and water out before she and Trudy went to get the rest of the flower arrangements. The fruit and cheese trays are out, too."

"Perfect. Did you hide the cake?" Aunt Hannah had baked a cake in the shape of the Sovereign Union Church, with a black plastic bell hanging from the steeple.

"No worries! The cake is safely tucked away in the communion cupboard."

Nellie chuckled. "That's one place Leland and the kids would never think to look!"

Ten minutes later the pitch of voices in the outer room rose to an excited crescendo. Sabine glanced into the hall and saw that people had rushed to the front windows, pointing and smiling. Others were hastily heading for the exit. She untied her apron and placed it on the counter. "It appears our bell has arrived!"

Sabine quickly donned her robe, tying it with a gold cord. She and Nellie exited the banquet hall just as Leland and his ox team trudged into the church parking lot bringing up the bell. A loud chorus of cheers from the gathered crowd of a hundred or more welcomed the Revere bell back home. Nellie moved toward the wagon to greet her parents and the children, while Sabine pressed through the assembled mass greeting parishioners and other townspeople, but all the while looking for Nick. She failed to spot his handsome bearded face anywhere, however, and was disappointed that he was not there to share the rededication of the bell with her.

Leland halted his team next to Amos Hunt's large hydraulic crane. On hand to assist Hunt with the hanging of the bell were a half dozen volunteer firefighters. Four of the firefighters had already made their way up to the belfry, where they accidentally disturbed two nests of swallows from among the old hemlock joists and beams. Multiple agitated swallows now swooped and dove around the church. A local Bangor TV station had sent a crew down to cover the unusual event and one of the swallows dive-bombed the news crew. The unfazed reporter continued her interview with two ancient parishioners.

Once the wagon was discharged of its passengers—and the mass of spectators moved back to a safe location behind a roped-off area—Amos Hunt took charge. A former Bath Iron Works crane operator, he and one of the cranes had been retired at the same time, so he had brought the crane home with him. Sabine was surprised by how quickly and efficiently the older man worked. He soon had two of the bell's canons hooked to his crane and slowly hoisted up the bell, careful not to set it to swinging. Once the bell reached the height of the opening in the steeple, Hunt inched the bell closer to the church. Three of firefighters grasped the bottom of the bell as it came into the belfry, guiding the bell toward its original cast-iron headstock. Once lined up, the fourth fireman began reattaching the bell's six canons to the headstock. When the bell was securely reattached, the firemen disconnected the crane hooks, and Hunt swung the crane away from the church. The fire chief, one of the four men in the steeple, gave the bell a shove, and the Revere bell sounded a soft, melodious note. A cheer went up from the crowd below.

Leland cupped his hands together. "Send the rope back down, Bob!"

The fire chief lifted the heavy coil of hemp rope attached to the bell's headstock, and threaded the rope down through the gap to the entryway below. Sabine, seeing that the crowd was pushing ahead toward the church, realized that the rededication ceremony was progressing without her.

She rapidly made her way to the top of the church's wide steps and waved to get people's attention. Taking a deep breath, she entered into what she called pastoral mode. Sabine had planned to give a short history of the bell, however, reading the restlessness of the throng, she elected to skip that part of the program. "Let us gather together in the spirit of prayer," she called. A hush fell over the crowd.

"Dear Lord," Sabine prayed, "be with us today as we rededicate this bell to your good use. When we hear this bell ring, wherever we are—whether we are gathered here or at work in the field or at play—may the sound remind us that we are one community, gathered in love, to serve you and one another. Bless this bell as it calls us to worship Sunday mornings—whether we worship here in church or in a cathedral of pines or elsewhere. Bless this bell when in the future it announces the joyful union of a loving couple. And bless the bell also when it tolls for the loss of a beloved community member. May the sound of this bell always give us courage, hope, and good cheer—and faith in your love for us. Amen."

An "amen" in response murmured through the crowd. The sun shone bright. The swallows returned to their nest in the belfry.

"Now, Tad," Sabine called down to the boy, who had been alerted to his part in the ceremony. "Since your ancestor Jonathan Russell was the one who originally brought the bell to the church, c'mon up and ring her again!"

Tad didn't hesitate. He leaped up the painted wooden steps, into the church entryway, followed closely by Jana, Hope, and even Alice Rose. Sabine poked her head into the doorway watching as Tad swung himself onto the thick rope and kicked his legs. He rotated wildly, but the heavy bell failed to ring.

"Looks like you need a little help. Climb aboard, kids!" Sabine encouraged. "Help him out."

The two younger girls gleefully rushed headlong at the rope. Alice Rose, however, followed at a statelier pace. But as soon as her hand touched the rope, she recollected how much she enjoyed rope swinging at the pond. She hopped on, adding her more substantial weight to the swinging. Soon, the cast-iron headstock was tilting back and forth like a seesaw, tolling the bell. Most of those gathered had never heard the sound of the bell, which hadn't rung in nearly seventy years. A cheer arose from the crowd as the steady mellow tones of the bell reverberated throughout the valley.

Hannah Trow, who remembered the church bell from her childhood, was moved to tears. "I had forgotten how beautiful the old bell sounds! Doesn't it sound lovely, Henry?"

"Yep." The retired history professor gave his plump wife a fond squeeze. "Reminds me of Dicken's 'A Christmas Carol.' Peace on earth, goodwill toward men, and all that stuff and nonsense."

"That's not stuff and nonsense, Henry, that's Heaven!" declared Maggie. "I always wondered how this old bell would sound, and now I know. I'm glad I lived long enough to hear it."

"Me, too," added Duncan, taking his wife by the hand. His eye fell upon Sabine, who was the odd person out without a partner in the little group of adults who had gathered in the entryway with the children. He, too, had noticed that Nick had failed to show. "Nice job with the prayer, Sabine."

"Thanks. It wasn't exactly what I planned for the rededication ceremony, but I could see the natives were getting restless, so I hurried it along."

Maggie nodded in satisfaction. "Sometimes it's best to go with the flow—let the Spirit move us."

"How long are you going to let the kids ring the bell?" Hannah asked, worried that prolonged ringing might damage the bell's repair.

"They'll stop when their arms get tired," her husband pointed out. "Don't worry, the kids will be looking for your cake soon enough." They all laughed.

"Speaking of the cake," said Sabine. "I need to make a quick stop at the communion cupboard."

"You didn't!" Maggie declared, laughing.

"I did," Sabine replied, eyes dancing. "Meet you back in the banquet hall. Time for cake, kids!"

Half an hour later Nick entered the noisy banquet hall. He strode over to the children's table, where the four youngsters were finishing off large pieces of white-frosted chocolate cake. He was greeted with a hearty welcome. "I heard the bell, Tad," Nick said, resting his hand fondly on the boy's shoulder. "I'm sorry I'm late and missed seeing you ring it."

Tad beamed up at him in pleasure. "You heard the bell all the way down to your house, Nick?"

"I sure did. You rang it good and loud."

"Cool! I didn't think it would go that far."

"Me, either, honestly."

"We had to help him," Alice Rose interjected snidely. "Tad wasn't strong enough to ring the bell by himself."

"It's a heavy bell. I bet I'd have trouble ringing it by myself, too."

"I hurt my hands, Uncle Nick," said Jana. She lifted her chubby palms to show Nick her faint red rope burns.

"Me, too," said Hope.

"That's too bad. Maybe you should all wear gloves when you ring the bell on Sunday?"

Sabine, who was making the rounds of the tables chatting with some of the submarine churchgoers (those who only surface on Christmas and Easter), spied Nick with the children. She quickly threaded her way over to his side. Sabine joined the little group quietly, not wanting to interrupt the conversation; however, when Nick snaked his arm around her waist the girls giggled and Tad hooted with laughter.

"What's so funny?" Nick asked, feigning bewilderment, although his eyes were twinkling. "Can't I hug my girlfriend?"

"Kiss her!" Tad shouted.

Sabine put up a hand to stop Nick before he could plant a kiss on her lips. "Let me at least take off my robe," she demurred.

"Feeling guilty, Pastor Burbury?"

"Not in the least, Loverboy. I just want to show you my outfit—my very fetching outfit, according to your stepsister. But maybe not here." The kids broke into laughter again as Sabine took Nick by the hand and pulled him into the kitchen.

At that moment, Doctor Bart entered the banquet hall. He spied Nellie sitting at the table with Maggie and Duncan and their special friends. He headed toward the table, his face glum. He appeared tired and discouraged.

"I thought you'd never get ..." Nellie began, but broke off, realizing with a glance at her husband's face that something was the matter. "What's wrong?"

Metcalf dropped down into the empty folding chair beside his wife. "It's Miss Crump."

"Miss Crump! Did she fall again?"

"No, I'm sorry to say she's dead." Doctor Bart put his elbows on the table, and covered his face with his hands.

"Oh, my God!" Maggie declared. "Poor Miss Crump. Tell us what happened, Metcalf!"

Doctor Bart straightened up. "She tried to drive herself to the church and went off the road. She was dead by the time I arrived at the scene."

Aunt Hannah emitted a heart-rending shriek.

"There was nothing I could do, Aunt Hannah. I'm sorry."

"But Helen told me she had another ride!" Hannah cried. Then the kindly octogenarian burst into tears.

Confused, Maggie turned to Henry. "Don't you always drive Miss Crump everywhere? Why didn't she ride with you and Hannah today?"

Henry put his arm around his wife's shoulders. "Because Hannah accidentally let slip that I was hedging off toward Nick's way of thinking. He's right about Wendell's pines—that fine old stand shouldn't be cut down! Not for a damn solar farm, anyway." Regrettably,

Henry had forgotten that Rebecca Russell was sitting at the table with them.

"This is horrible!" Rebecca pronounced, jumping up, overwrought. "It's all my fault. I should never have agreed to that solar farm!" She burst into tears and hurried off toward the bathroom.

A stunned silence ensued. "I'll go after her," said Maggie, finally. She glanced at her husband, and added, as if to excuse herself, "Sabine seems to have disappeared."

Duncan nodded. "Do that. We'll keep an eye on Tad."

Hannah fumbled in her purse for her handkerchief. She daubed her eyes. Doctor Bart reached over and took his great-aunt's right hand within his own. "I'm sorry, Aunt Hannah. I know how fond you were of Miss Crump. Nellie and I are going to miss her, too." He looked at his wife. Both knew that their medical clinic's survival depended upon the largess of their oldest benefactor and her gravel pit. "Thank God she didn't suffer! Her neck was broken— she died instantly. I know it's not much consolation, but it's something."

Despite Duncan's assurance to Maggie about keeping an eye on Tad, none of the adults noticed that the children's table—which was next to their own—had ominously fallen silent. The youngsters had overheard Doctor Bart's sad announcement, as well as the adult conversation that followed. A giant tear rolled down Hope's smooth little face. Tad blinked hard, attempting not to cry.

"I liked Miss Crump," Jana said, softly. "She was good to her chickens."

"She gave me a pink button once," said Hope. "From one of her sweaters. Miss Crump said it was special. I still have it." The little girl started to whimper.

"Don't be a crybaby, Hope," Alice Rose ordered her younger sister.

"I'm not a crybaby! I'm sad."

Alice Rose turned to Tad. "This is all your fault! If you hadn't been born, Miss Crump would still be alive."

"That's very mean, Alice Rose," Jana said, glaring at the older girl.

"Maybe, but it's the truth. Grampa says Mrs. Russell needs the money from the solar farm to take care of Tad. And if everyone wasn't fighting over that stupid solar farm, Miss Crump wouldn't have tried to drive herself here and gotten killed."

There was a twisted logic to Alice Rose's reasoning, but twisted as it was, nine-year-old Tad had followed it. And he knew what he needed to do.

Chapter 30

The Fugitives

Hurt burns hot in the breast of a child—but not for long. Children under the age of ten are constitutionally incapable of prolonging their grievances for more than a few hours. Had Tad experienced injustice or persecution (or perceived injustice or persecution) on Saturday at the rededication of the bell he would not have planned to run away on Monday—he would have left that afternoon. Tad was wounded by Alice Rose's unkind remark, but if hurt was all he felt Tad would have forgotten it by bedtime. Tad's decision to fly the nest originated rather from a heroic impulse—he wanted to relieve his mother of the burden of himself. Without himself to support, his mother would not need to build the solar farm; therefore, everyone in Sovereign would be friends again.

Thus, motivated as he was by a waxing desire to become a hero like fictional adventurers Tom Sawyer and Jim Hawkins, Tad took time to plot. Saturday night he lay awake in his little bed under the eaves of the old Russell homestead thinking about running away. A few fat tears escaped his eyelids as Tad pictured how sad his mother would be when she read the note he would leave behind, yet he managed to convince himself that his mother would be better off without him. He would leave her a note explaining everything; fill his backpack with supplies; and disappear into the Sovereign Woods never to be seen again—or at least not for a few years. He would live in the woods, eating mushrooms and berries like Nick, until he was grown up, and then he would return home to claim his heritage. His mother would fall on his neck weeping, crying that she knew he would return someday—and thanking him for his great sacrifice. Tad's one stumbling block, however, was that he didn't want to run away alone.

As he lay in bed listening to the mice scampering in the walls, Tad thought about asking Hope to run away with him. Hope was his favorite of the little group of neighborhood friends. He could imagine the two of them fishing in the brook (which reminded him he needed to pack fishing line, hooks, and matches) and building a cabin (and pack Papa's hatchet). But then Tad worried that if Hope declined to go with him, naturally preferring the comforts of her family and home at Scotch Broom Acres, he might lose his courage.

Tad lay awake pondering the situation, only occasionally distracted by the mice nibbling on the horsehair plaster. He finally concluded that he would tell Hope of his plan to fly, but not specifically invite her to go along. If she offered to accompany him on her own, well, that was a different story. They would run away together. Tad felt very heroic as he came to this conclusion, so much so that he banged his fist against the wall—and noted with satisfaction that the mice fell silent.

On Sunday morning, Rebecca elected not to go to church. Unbeknownst to Tad, his mother was feeling hurt and confused about whether she should proceed with the solar farm. Rebecca, like her son, had spent a portion of the night lying awake. She decided she didn't want to see or talk with anyone until she had made up her mind what to do. This almost derailed Tad's plan to take Hope into his confidence at church, until Rebecca remembered the religious edification of her son. "I think you should still go to Sunday school, Tad," she said to him that morning. "And church if you want to. Mr. Faulkner and Sabine would miss you."

Tad was relieved. "Oh, yes, Mama. I told Hope I would be there today."

Rebecca drove him down to the church and dropped Tad off in time for Sunday school. "Doctor Bart said he'd give you a ride home. Make sure you leave when Jana leaves—don't make Doctor Bart wait."

During the short break between Sunday school and church, Tad was able to pull Hope aside by herself. "I'm running away," he whispered to his friend. Although he and Hope were the same age, she was taller and Tad had to stand on tiptoe to speak directly into her ear.

"Running away!" Hope repeated, aloud.

"Shhh! I don't want nobody else to know."

Hope's eyes opened wide as the significance of her friend's words dawned upon her. "Why?" she whispered back.

"So Mama doesn't have to build the solar farm."

Hope nodded in empathetic understanding. She had heard the mean remark her sister had made to Tad on Saturday and was able to follow the twisted logic to the same conclusion. Without Tad to support, Mrs. Russell would not need to build the solar farm. "When are you going?"

"Tomorrow. Don't tell anyone."

Hope looked solemn, but Tad failed to notice she did not actually promise *not* to share his news. Unfortunately, she did not offer to accompany him, either. But when he climbed into the backseat of Doctor Bart's car after church, Jana gave him what all youngsters recognize as THE LOOK. Tad raised an eyebrow, but before he could ask her about THE LOOK, the seven-year-old shook her head. "Daddy, can Tad come to our house? I want to show him my new kittens," Jana said, instead.

"Sure, Sunshine. I can give Tad a ride home afterward."

"He can walk home from our house, Daddy. Mommy lets us walk all the time, if we take your path through the field."

"OK, I'll just call Mrs. Russell and let her know Tad is coming to our house first."

"Thanks, Daddy."

While Tad was in the shed admiring her new kittens, Jana informed her friend that she and Hope had talked Tad's case over and decided they couldn't let him run away alone—they would both go with him. This was a situation which Tad had not planned upon. He and Hope were both nine, but Jana was two years younger. Wouldn't Jana be a drag on him and Hope?

"Are you sure you want to come?" Tad asked the younger girl. He leaned into the cardboard box in which the kittens were nesting with their mother and patted the soft downy fur of one of the little ones. The blind kitten wriggled and mewled pathetically, searching for a nipple. "Who's going to take care of your kittens if you run away?"

"Their Mama," Jana replied, with the wisdom of a child who has experienced the birth of two or three litters of kittens.

Tad thought he spied a silver lining. "Can we bring one with us?" he asked hopefully.

"No, they're too young to leave Misty." Jana affectionately scratched under the neck of her Siamese cat. Misty began to purr.

Tad suddenly wondered if he was too young to leave his mother, but heroically brushed away the childish concern. He wasn't running away alone. Now there would be three of them, and Jana *was* very smart. He felt much braver. "Bring your backpack tomorrow when you come to our house," he instructed his young co-conspirator.

(Monday was Rebecca Russell's day to watch the neighborhood kids.) "And some food."

Jana nodded. "I'll tell Aunt Hannah we want to have a picnic in the field. She'll pack us some sandwiches to take."

Tad perked up even more. Jana was proving a very valuable addition. "And some cookies?"

"Oh, we always have lots of cookies at our house." Aunt Hannah still cooked for Doctor Bart and his family three days a week.

Monday morning the three youngsters stuffed their school backpacks with a variety of items each thought he or she would need when running away. Favorite books, flashlights, dolls, blankets, pillows, stuffies, jackknives, clothes, Aunt Hannah's sandwiches and cookies, juice boxes, candy, and more were included in the necessary gear. Surprisingly, Ryan MacDonald was the only parent who noted the bulging packs and extra blankets. "You kids planning on running away?" he joked, as—after picking up Jana—he drove Hope and Jana down to the old Russell homestead.

The two girls exchanged shocked glances. How had Hope's father discovered their plan? They hadn't even told Alice Rose! (Fortunately, Hope's older sister was off to a school chum's birthday party today.)

"Or maybe you're building a fort?" the lawyer-farmer continued, glancing in the rearview mirror at the two silent girls.

Hope looked down. She could not lie to her father.

"We're going on a picnic, Mr. MacDonald," Jana answered. "Aunt Hannah made us lots of sandwiches."

Hope's little head shot back up. "That's why I brought my blankie," she added, relieved to be able to stymie her father, yet not bold-face lie to him.

"Good thinking! You wouldn't want ants to get your lunch."

Hope giggled nervously. Jana smiled.

Tad met his friends at the door to the shed. "Leave your pack here," he directed Jana. "Not you, Hope. Come with me."

The younger girl dropped her heavy pack. Tad then led Hope and Jana down the winding black iron staircase into the old hen pen, where his backpack and other gear were already stashed. "Put your pack and blanket here with mine, Hope. You didn't leave a note, did you?" Tad anxiously inquired of both girls.

"No," said Jana.

"You said not to," Hope pointed out.

"Well, girls don't always do what I say," Tad excused himself. "I left a note for Mama on her pillow, but she won't find it 'til she goes to bed."

"Why do you get to leave a note and we don't?" Hope asked.

"Cause I'm the reason we're running away. That way, my Mama will explain everything to your Mamas, and then they'll understand."

"I don't like lying," said Jana. "Grampa said in Sunday school lying is one of the Ten Commandments God gave to Moses." She had paid attention during Duncan's weekly lessons.

"So is, 'Honor your father and mother,'" Hope rejoined. "That comes first, too, before the lying commandment. And that's what Tad is trying to do by running away—honor his mother." Hope had also paid attention to Duncan's lessons.

Jana wrinkled her brow. The most logical of the three children, she attempted to weigh in her head the nineth commandment against the fifth. "Maybe it's OK to break one commandment to keep another? If the other one comes first."

Tad offered a heartfelt sigh. "I hope so, 'cause I got to lie to Mama now."

The three young people made their way back up the circular stairway and entered the kitchen, where Rebecca was sitting disconsolately at the table over a cold cup of coffee. She looked up when the three entered and feigned a smile. "Hi, Hope! Hello, Jana!"

"Hello Mrs. Russell."

Rebecca bestowed a fond glance upon her son. "How are you planning on entertaining your friends today, Tad?"

Tad shuffled his feet. "We're going on a picnic in the field across the road."

"A picnic! That sounds like fun. What would you like me to pack for your lunch?"

Jana clasped the handle of her backpack with both hands and lifted the heavy pack to show Tad's mother. "Aunt Hannah already packed us a picnic lunch."

Rebecca's blue eyes filled with tears, as she assumed that Hannah Trow was attempting to assuage for her husband's remark that Wendell's pine grove should not be cut for the solar farm. "That's so thoughtful of Hannah! I'll have to give her a call."

Jana crossed her fingers behind her back. "Not right away, Mrs. Russell. Aunt Hannah said she was going to Bangor today," she lied.

"Oh, OK. Well, I'll come out in an hour or so and see if you need anything."

Hope put her hand on Tad's arm to prevent him from speaking. "We want to do everything ourselves," she said, relieved to discover it was easier to lie to Tad's mother than to her father.

Rebecca chuckled. "Well, I know when I'm not wanted! Have fun, kids. Let me know if you need anything."

"We will, Mama. Goodbye." Tad rushed at his mother and gave her a big hug.

Rebecca, accepting Tad's embrace as an attempt to cheer her up, gave him an affectionate hug in return. She dropped a kiss on the top his head. "Be good, now, you three," she advised.

All three children instantly put their hands behind their backs and crossed their fingers. "We will," they promised in unison.

Ten minutes later, packs on their backs and trailing blankets and other accoutrements, Tad, Hope, and Jana crossed the road and set off down the hill through the field. Their progress was necessarily slow, since their packs were heavy and the hayfield had not yet been mowed, even though it was August. A bobolink shot up out of the tall grass in front of Tad and flew twenty feet off, trying to draw the children away from her nest in the grass.

"Oh, that scared me!" Hope exclaimed.

"Me, too," Tad admitted.

"It's just a bobolink," said Jana, unfazed. Her father often took her birding. In fact, the seven-year-old already had her own Life List started.

In half an hour the children had located the overgrown woods road leading down to the Millett Rock. Tad, who had appointed himself captain of his runaway crew, led the way down the road followed single file by the girls. Families of balsam firs were growing up in the middle of the road and Tad had to weave around the saplings and other puckerbrush. In some places they were forced to climb over or crawl under dead trees that had toppled into the old road. Once Jana got her backpack stuck on a stiff dead pine limb. Tad unhooked her pack, and pushed Jana and the pack under the blowdown.

An hour after the children had left the house, Hope begged Tad to stop. "I'm thirsty," she said. "It's hot!"

The August sun was warm. The sky was blue and crystal clear, so sharp, in fact, that had Tad climbed one of the tall wolf pines back at the edge of the field he might have been able to see the ocean, twenty-five miles to the eastward. While in the field, a light breeze had tousled the timothy and other tall grasses, but the cooling breeze had petered out in the woods.

"OK, we can rest," said Tad. "But not too long."

Hope rummaged through her pack and brought out two juice boxes. "It's all I could find." She offered the boxes to Tad and Jana.

"I'm not thirsty," said Tad, stoically.

"Let's all share one," Jana suggested, "and save the other box for later."

The three slid out of their heavy packs and sat down. Hope passed the juice box around. Soon, out came a bag of Aunt Hannah's chocolate chip cookies. When the runaways were done refreshing themselves, Hope packed the empty box back in her pack and Jana stowed away the used baggie. They donned their packs, picked up their blankets, and resumed walking.

By ten o'clock the three stumbled onto the main Sovereign Woods trail. Up the trail to the right—northward—was the bridge that led to the church; to the south was Jana's grandparent's house and the turnoff to Nick's place. The trail across from where they had come out led to the Millett Rock.

"Which way should we go?" asked Hope, taking stock of the multiple possibilities. She had only ever been that far in the woods with adults and had never paid the slightest attention to how they got to where they were going.

"Let's go to the Millett Rock," said Jana, who recognized the trail to the picnic spot, where she had often been with her grandparents.

"No, that's too easy," replied Tad. "They'll look for us there."

"The Toad Stools?" Jana suggested next. The sawed-off tree stumps near the brook crossing at the bridge were one of her favorite play spots. But then she thought a moment, and sighed. "No, my Grampa will look for us there."

"I'll figure it out—don't worry," boasted Tad, somewhat prematurely, as he had just come to the realization that there was a major deficiency in his plan. When he had thought about running away, he had simply planned to go into the woods and hide. He had not thought about *where* to hide. Now, he put on his thinking cap.

A bluejay called out a warning, followed shortly by the sound of whistling coming up the trail from the south. As the whistler approached, the jay fluttered off, squawking. The three runaways exchanged worried looks. Were they going to be discovered already?

Gerald Danforth strolled around a corner of the trail, coming from Nick's house. He spied the three youngsters and stopped—mid-whistle—surprised to see them. "Hey-ho! What's goin' on?"

"Oh, it's only Gerald," a relieved Hope informed her co-conspirators. She recognized the youth, who regularly ran mushrooms over to their farm. Hope smiled and waved at the newcomer. "Hello, Gerald!"

The youth approached the runaways, bobbing his head at Hope and casting a wary eye over the two unknowns. "Hiya, Hope. Whatcha doin' out here?"

"We're running away."

Tad glared at Hope. "Why did you tell him that? Now, we're in for it!"

"Don't worry, Gerald won't tell anyone he saw us, will you, Gerald? He's my friend."

Gerald scratched his head, unsure whether he should give Hope the required promise. "Why're you runnin'?"

"So his mother doesn't have to build the solar farm," the girl explained.

The youth examined Tad from the top of his short head down to his sneakers. "So, yore Ma's the one who wants to cut down Wendell's woodlot? Walden says that's a sin."

"That is not a sin!" Tad declared hotly. He had paid attention in Sunday school, too, and had never heard Mr. Faulkner say cutting trees was a sin. If it was, there were a lot of people in the Maine woods who were sinning, especially Hope's grandfather.

Hope moved close to Gerald and put her hand to his ear. "That's his father," she whispered. "Wendell was his father."

"Oh? Wal, sartin ain't no sin, then," Gerald allowed. "You got a right to cut down yore own trees, if you want."

"Thank you. But I'm running away so Mama doesn't have to cut down the trees."

Gerald looked perplexed. He had not heard Alice Rose's mean remark to Tad, nor could he have followed the logic that motivated the runaways if he had. "Where ya headed?"

"We don't know, Mr. Gerald," said Jana, who had been standing by quietly until now. "Where should we go?"

"Wal, I don't rightly know. I ain't never runned away." This from the youth who ran wild through the Sovereign Woods and only rarely was to be found at his parent's home in Thorndike.

Tad, anxious to make a good impression on the older boy, spoke up. "We've got sandwiches and blankets, and I brought fishline and hooks. And my Papa's hatchet. We need a place where Mama can't find us."

Gerald was impressed with Tad's preparedness. He thought a moment. "I know somewheres, but if they find ya, you gotta promise to say I had nuthin' to do with it. Walden would fire my arse, fore shore."

"We won't tell anyone," Hope assured the youth. "We don't want you to get fired from your mushroom job."

"Well, then, foller me." Gerald turned on his heel and trod back a few steps the way he had come. He glanced over his shoulder at the three runaways, still standing in place. "Be quick about it! Afore Walden leaves the house. You don't want him to see ya, do you?"

"No!" the youngsters exclaimed. They all loved and admired Nick, but they knew that—as fun as the woodsman was—if he discovered that they were running away he would take them home to their parents. The runaways quickly retrieved their backpacks and blankets, and hurried after Gerald.

Gerald led them to where the deer trail he often used to cut through the swamp intersected with the Sovereign Woods trail. Despite Nick's edict to him, the youth still utilized the swamp trail when running the packed mushrooms over to Scotch Broom Acres for the FedEx pickup. Gerald held aside the low-hanging branches of a flaming-red swamp maple, and pointed out to the three kids the meandering wildlife trail. "Jest foller this trail 'til you come to the big rock by the brook. The water ain't deep there now, on account o' the drought, but I caught a brookie there t'other day. If I was runnin' away, that's where I'd set up shop."

"Won't the fishermen find us there?" worried Tad.

"Nah, ain't nobody knows this trail is here but me 'n the deer. Them fishermen all fish up by the bridge. They's afeared o' gettin' lost in the swamp. You ain't afeard, are ya?"

Tad swallowed hard. "No."

"I am," Hope admitted. "I don't want to be lost. Not forever."

"Aw, you'll be OK, Hope, so long's you stay on the deer trail. You got flashlights?" Gerald inquired.

The three children nodded. They had been camping in their backyards before and knew how dark it was at night. Jana, in addition to her flashlight, had even thought to pack extra batteries.

"Smart crew. Gets mighty dark in the swamp at night." Gerald considered telling them a story or two about minnawickies or about the mysterious flickering lights of the swamp spirits, but looking at their solemn little faces, decided against it. "I'll likely see ya tomorrow, if we git 'shrooms to mail out."

Tad found this casual pronouncement greatly reassuring. "Thanks, Gerald." He wiped off his sweaty palm and held his hand out for the older boy to shake.

Somewhat amused, Gerald shook the proffered paw. "Ain't no trouble at-tall."

"You're a good friend, Gerald," declared Hope.

"Aw, I ain't that good, Hope. I cain't even multiply yet. But Walden is larnin' me how. See ya tomorrow!"

Gerald resumed whistling and headed back up the Sovereign Woods trail. When his whistling faded away, Tad began picking his way through the thousand-acre swamp that diverted Black Brook into multiple meandering streams, some of which were dry because of the drought. Hope and Jana followed at his heels. A bluebird flying overhead with a worm dangling from its mouth, spied the strange little group, and dropped the worm.

Practiced woodsmen can pick out a deer trail with barely a glance at the ground; however, the three youngsters had never been in the wilds of Maine unaccompanied by an adult. To Tad's neophyte eyes, there were deer trails everywhere. There was a trail that weaved around several bunched-up hummocks of grass; one that went through a humungous swath of cattails; another path that hopscotched over bleached driftwood; and a trail that Tad was sure went straight through the smelly black muck in front of a dead cedar tree. He pushed forward, the two girls trudging behind him, carrying blankets draped over their backpacks and shoulders. They stepped carefully to keep from slipping into a wet hole. The red of the red-winged blackbirds flashed as the birds darted from cattail to cattail. Swamp sparrows trilled. Butterflies of all colors fluttered dizzily. The sun rose higher in sky. Soon, they were lost.

Chapter 31

"What Have I Done?"

After the children departed, Rebecca rose from the table and perked herself a fresh pot of coffee. She took the hot cup into the great room and peered out one of the west-facing living room windows, looking for the children. But Tad and the girls had already disappeared down over the hill. Rebecca idly noted the height of the tall grass in the field and proliferation of Queen Anne's Lace, and imagined with amusement how like explorers they must feel searching for the perfect picnic spot.

Oh, to be young again! She would be free from her inner wrestling over the solar farm, then.

Rebecca returned to her seat at the table, where she continued her ruminations. Should she ask Robinson Crockett if she could break their contract? She needed the money from the land lease, true. But many single parents worked out and she was still young enough to get a full-time job, although employment in or near Sovereign was scarce. Perhaps she could work as a clerk at Gilpin's General Store?

But then she wondered whether breaking the contract was fair to Rob. Because of her waffling, Rob had already been forced to sell some of his equipment to pay his port storage fees. Could he sell the balance of the panels and other equipment and not lose money? But if their solar project never got off the ground, wouldn't that negatively affect the reputation of Rob's company? Who would want to do business with him, then?

Yet … even her dear friend Henry Trow was beginning to think she was doing wrong cutting down Wendell's pine grove! Was she making a mistake? Nick—as well as many others in Sovereign—certainly thought so.

It was so hard to know what was the right thing to do! Wendell had given his blessing to the solar farm, and in fact had all but signed the contract before he died. But Wendell wasn't here to experience the angst and turmoil the proposed solar farm was causing. Friend had turned against friend in Sovereign. And it was all her fault.

At noon, Rebecca fixed herself a tuna fish sandwich. She wondered what Hannah had prepared for the children to eat. The older lady was known as an exceptional cook, so no doubt the picnic was very nice. She picked up her cell phone to call and thank Hannah, but then remembered Jana had said Henry's wife had gone to Bangor for the day. She set the phone back down and made a mental note to call Hannah later.

After lunch, Rebecca unrolled a colorful bolt of material onto the dining room table. The material was for curtains she was sewing for the windows in the church's banquet hall. The church board had recently given Rebecca this large commission, probably because they knew how snug her finances were. Nevertheless, Rebecca was grateful for the addition to her income, which enabled her and Tad to live upon the modest annuity Wendell had set up for them from his naval pension, without dipping into savings.

As Rebecca was cutting out one pair of curtains, she spied the mailman stopping at her box. Knowing she couldn't count on Tad to remember to fetch the mail when he came in, she laid her scissors on the table, and walked down the long driveway to the mailbox. Rebecca retrieved several letters from the box, discouraged to see that several were bills.

She put the letters in her apron pocket, then hesitated. Rather than return to the house she walked across the warm tarred road. Rebecca stared down over the hayfield looking for the children's encampment, but she couldn't see their picnic spot anywhere. She put her hand to her ear listening for childish laughter on the breeze, but heard only the garrulous warbling of a noisy flock of starlings in a nearby maple tree.

"Do you have to be so loud?" Rebecca questioned the starlings. The black birds ignored her and continued to chatter over one another's voices.

Viewing the field from the roadside, Rebecca could see where Tad and the girls had tramped in through the tall grass. She thought she would just follow their trail and go down and see if they needed anything. Then Rebecca recollected Hope's remark: "We want to do everything ourselves." No, she wouldn't intrude upon their fun. She had sworn she wasn't going to be a helicopter mother, and she wouldn't begin now. Besides, Alice Rose, the perpetual troublemaker, wasn't with the three younger children today. Let the kids enjoy their day by themselves without Alice. Rebecca returned to the house and resumed her sewing.

Shortly after two o'clock Sabine dropped in. Rebecca, grateful for the pastoral visit (and completely forgetting her earlier determination to figure things out herself), spent the next hour and a half unburdening herself to the young minister. She came to no firm decision about the solar farm during the visit, but felt better just talking over her problem with Sabine.

"Would you like another glass of lemonade?" Rebecca asked, as the minister made signs to leave.

"No, thanks. I've got to get going."

"Hot date?"

Sabine stood up, laughing. "I think we'll be hot. Nick is coming over to my place and we're going to split firewood."

"How about some cookies for extra energy, then? I've got plenty on hand because Hannah packed the children a picnic lunch today."

"Cookies would be awesome, thanks. Where did the kids go for their picnic? Out back?"

"No, in the field across the road." Rebecca retrieved four thick molasses cookies from the cookie jar and wrapped them in a cloth napkin. "These are Grammie Addie's recipe, Wendell's grandmother, you know."

"They look delicious!"

"They are good. I use her cookbook, and … oh, my goodness!" In moving back to the table to show Sabine the antique cookbook, Rebecca noted the time on the white Sessions wall clock. "I had no idea it was almost four o'clock! Ryan will be here any minute, and the kids aren't back in yet."

Sabine chuckled. "Those lollygaggers! Want me to go hunt them down?" She took a bite out of one of the soft molasses cookies. "Mmm. These are excellent."

"Would you mind? They went into the field across from the mailbox. You can follow their trail through the tall grass."

Fifteen minutes later, Sabine returned to the house alone. She was hot, out of breath, and slightly worried. "I couldn't find the kids anywhere. Are you sure they're not out back? I yelled loudly, too."

"Oh, dear! No, they must have walked Jana home. Tad and Hope do that sometimes. Doctor Bart mows a path between our houses. I'll just give the clinic a call."

Since it was Monday, Maggie was working the front desk at the Songbird Medical Clinic and answered

Rebecca's call. "The kids? No, I haven't heard a peep out of them all day. I thought they were down with you?"

"They were, but they had a picnic in the field and haven't come back into the house. They're probably walking Jana home. When you see them, send Tad and Hope down right away because Ryan will be here any minute." Rebecca was about to hang up, but remembered she wanted to thank Hannah for packing the picnic lunch for the children. "By the way, is Hannah back from Bangor yet?"

"Hannah didn't go to Bangor today. She was here until three. Then she went home to fix Henry's supper."

Rebecca, who had not been worried about the children until that moment, now felt a stab of anxiety in her bowels. "That's strange. I distinctly remember Jana telling me Hannah was going to Bangor."

"Not today. Are you feeling OK, Rebecca? You sound funny."

Rebecca sank back in her chair. "I don't honestly know, Maggie. Oh, dear! I think I may have lost the children!"

"What?!"

"They went for a picnic across the road, but Sabine just went to look for them and couldn't find them."

"Stay put, Rebecca," Maggie ordered. "Nellie's not home yet, but Metcalf and I will be right down."

Within fifteen minutes, Maggie, Duncan (who had come to pick her up), Doctor Bart, and Ryan (who had come to pick up Hope and Jana) had converged at the old Russell homestead, joining Rebecca and Sabine. While Rebecca was talking to Maggie, Sabine had gone out and searched the backyard and the path up to Nellie and Doctor Bart's house. She had failed to find the kids. It was a puzzle where the young people had disappeared to.

"Ten to one they've run away," Maggie declared. She had run away when she was young, and still remembered—with pleasure—how liberating the experience felt.

(Unfortunately—or perhaps fortunately—her father had tracked her down and discovered Maggie's hideout in the woods before nightfall.)

"Why would they run away?" Duncan asked, somewhat amused by his wife's suggestion. "I never saw happier children in my life."

Ryan slapped his thigh. "By, God—I bet they have run away! I thought it was strange Hope and Jana had their backpacks stuffed to the gills this morning, but now it makes sense. They had blankets, too."

"No, no. Only Jana had a backpack," Rebecca corrected the lawyer. "I remember quite well. When they came into the kitchen, only Jana had a pack. And Tad's pack is right here." Rebecca rose from the table and went into the shed. She soon returned emptyhanded, musing, "He must have left it up in his room. I'll go check."

In a few minutes the adults in the kitchen heard a shriek from the floor above, and then a heart-felt sob. A near hysterical Rebecca flew back down the stairs, waving Tad's note, which she had found on her pillow. "Heavens, they *have* run away! Oh, dear! Oh, dear!" She sank into a chair and burst into tears.

Maggie patted Rebecca on the shoulder, attempting to console her. "Don't worry, all children run away, at some point. They'll be fine—we'll find them."

"I never ran away," said Duncan. Maggie frowned and shook her head at her husband.

Doctor Bart retrieved Tad's note from where Rebecca had dropped it on the table. He read the note aloud: *"Mama, I am runing away so you don't got to build the solar farm + everybody will be freinds again. Hope + Jana have runned away with me. Tell their Mamas. Love, Tad."*

A shocked silence ensued. Metcalf laid the note back down. "How long have they been gone?" he asked Rebecca.

She straightened up and wiping her wet eyes with a napkin. "Since about eight-thirty."

"You haven't seen them since?"

"No, I went out at noon, but they said they wanted to do everything by themselves. I … I let them. Oooh!" Rebecca put her face in her hands and resumed weeping.

"Which way did they go?" Ryan demanded, rising up. "We need to go after them before it gets dark."

"Across the road, through the field," Sabine replied. "I followed their trail, but didn't find them. I assumed at the time they had come back here."

"They must have gone into the woods. Let's go!" Ryan headed for the door.

Doctor Bart put out his arm, stopping the attorney. "Wait a minute, Ryan—let's think this thing through. We've got several hours before the sun goes down. Better to have a plan than go off half-cocked and get ourselves lost as well as the kids."

Ryan grudgingly returned to his seat. "What do you suggest, Doc?"

"Nick. We need Nick. He knows the Sovereign Woods better than anyone. If anybody can find our children, Nick can."

Sabine leaped up. "Whoa! I totally forgot. I was supposed to meet Nick at the church half an hour ago. We have a date—I hope he's still there!"

"Oh, he'll still be there," Maggie predicted.

Doctor Bart was relieved. "That's perfect. He's a hard man to find otherwise. Why don't you go down and tell Nick we need his help, Sabine? The rest of us will follow in a few minutes. I need to call Nellie, first."

"Oh, God," Ryan groaned. "This will kill Trudy! Should we tell Leland?"

"Yes. We might need his help, too. Leland is almost as familiar with the woods as Nick is. We might as well use the banquet hall as our headquarters of operation," Doctor Bart continued. "Could be a long night."

"I'm on it," said Sabine. She raced out to her car, started the vehicle up, and barreled off down the road.

To Sabine's relief, she found Nick still waiting for her in her office, sitting in her desk chair. "Thank God you're here!"

Nick stood up and grinned. "Somebody's glad to see me. I was beginning to think ministers didn't care about a man's time."

Sabine strode to his side and clasped his arm. "We need your help, Nick! Tad, Hope, and Jana have run away."

"What?! You're joking, right, Sabine? Why would they run away?"

"Because of the solar farm! Tad left a note. He said if he ran away, his mother wouldn't need to build the solar farm and everyone would be friends again. We think they've gone into the Sovereign Woods."

A look of abject horror came over Nick's face. "They ran away? Into two thousand acres of woods and swamp? Because the town is fighting over the solar farm!"

Sabine nodded. "That's what the note said, yes."

Nick dropped down into the chair and slumped back. "Oh, my God! This is all my fault," he cried. "If I hadn't fought to stop the solar farm, the town wouldn't have become divided—and Tad and the girls wouldn't have run away! What have I done?"

Hearing these self-pitying lamentations, Sabine—without hesitation—flattened her right hand and struck Nick broadly across the face. "Stop it! Stop feeling sorry for yourself. This isn't about you It's about the kids!"

Astonished, Nick touched his fingertips to his flaming cheek, but remained silent. He looked at Sabine as though seeing her for the first time.

"Get a grip," she continued. "We need your help. There's nobody who knows the Sovereign Woods like you do, Nick. The others will be here any minute. You've got to get it together so you can tell us all what to do!"

Sabine could see that her slap had been efficacious. Nick looked humbled. Embarrassed to witness the collapsing of his ego, she looked away from him, glancing instead out the window, where a chickadee was clinging to the hanging feeder. The tiny bird attempted to peck open a black oil sunflower seed. Unsuccessful after several tries, the chickadee flew off with the seed clamped in its black beak.

The sound of the desk chair scraping the wooden floor brought her gaze around again. Nick was now a changed man. He had straightened up and was sitting forward in the chair, his left forefinger absently tapping the desktop. His brown eyes were set and determined. A furrowed brow informed Sabine he was thinking—hard.

This! This was the man she had fallen in love with!

"What should we do?" she beseeched him, as though asking the question for the first time.

"How long have they been gone?" Nick demanded.

"About eight hours, we think."

"Did you find their trail?"

"I tracked them through the field across from Rebecca's house, but that's as far as I went. They must have gone into the woods from there, following the old woods road, the one you took me on."

Nick stood up and pushed in the chair. He gave a thoughtful tug to his beard. "Well, they've got a good head start on us, but we have one important factor in our favor."

"What's that?" she asked eagerly.

"Longer legs," said Nick, He grinned.

Sabine burst out laughing. "Oh, you! That's too funny."

He pulled her close to his chest, dropping a kiss on Sabine's forehead. "'I live for your laughter, and love ever after, across a sea of longing'," he quoted. "Thank you for knocking me from the pity pot, darling. Now, where's my crew? We need to get started." Nick released the young minister.

"Open your eyes—your crew has arrived," said Maggie, entering the office, with Duncan following close behind her.

"Thank God you're still here, son," Duncan exclaimed. He stepped up to Nick and took him warmly by the hand. "There's no one so good as you in the Maine woods, Nick. I know if anyone can find the children, you can!"

Nick threw an arm around his father's shoulders and gave Duncan a reassuring hug. "Don't worry, Dad. I'll bring Jana and her friends back safe and sound. They can run—but they can't hide."

Chapter 32

"Now the Day Is Over"

Nick immediately set up a command center in the church's banquet hall and began assigning tasks. Sabine was to contact the Sovereign Fire Department and ask for volunteers and extra two-way radios and flashlights. Henry was to alert the Waldo County Sheriff's Department as well as the Maine Warden Service. The mothers of the missing children—Rebecca, Nellie, and Trudy—were to prepare sandwiches and beverages for the search party under the steadying oversight of Hannah and Henry Trow.

"Thanks, Nick," said the very pregnant Nellie in relief. "I need something to keep my mind occupied."

"Idle hands are the devil's workshop," Maggie commented.

"I agree," added Trudy. "When Alice Rose gets back from her birthday party, we'll keep her busy here with us. We don't need any more lost children."

Nick thoughtfully regarded the school librarian. "Do you have access to the school's text alert system? If so, maybe you can also send out a text giving parents a heads-up? Just in case somebody spots the kids."

"Good idea! I'll need to get the principal's permission, but that's no problem," said Trudy.

"What about us?" Maggie asked. "You're not going to bench me and Duncan are you?"

"Nope. When the flashlights and radios get here, Maggie, you and Duncan with some of the firemen follow the kids' trail from Rebecca's house. Inform the command center if you find any evidence they deviated from the old woods road—you're familiar with that, I know. If not, when you reach the main trail, check in again and then stay put. I want all the search parties to converge at the turnoff to the Millett Rock."

Leland, who had been uncharacteristically quiet during the delegation of responsibilities, now spoke up. "What about me? I ain't gonna jest sit here twiddlin' my thumbs while my granddaughter's gone missin'!"

"No, I want you and Ryan and some of the other volunteers to go into the Sovereign Woods from the Cross Road. Start at Maggie's house, Leland. Keep a sharp eye out to see if the kids hooked off the main trail. They're not Wabanakis—they'll have left clues."

"Ayuh, I can do thet. You know, I reckon them kids must be powerful hungry by now."

"I hardly think that can be," Hannah interjected. "They had plenty of food. I packed them six ham and cheese sandwiches, half a dozen stuffed eggs, cheese sticks, carrots and celery, apples, potato chips, plenty of snickerdoodles and hermits, and six Needhams."

"Oh, my!" Rebecca exclaimed. "That's quite a feast for three young children. By the way, Hannah, Tad loves your snickerdoodles."

"I wondered where my Needhams had gone," grumbled Doctor Bart. "I thought Maggie had nabbed them."

"Nice!" Maggie added jocularly. "Blame your mother-in-law for stealing your special chocolates."

"Well, Hannah's feast is certainly better than bread crumbs," said Nick. "And if we're lucky, someone will find evidence of Hansel and his two Gretels before the wildlife gobbles it up."

The woodsman turned to Doctor Bart. "You're in charge of the command center, Doc. Bring the volunteers up to speed and keep checking in with each search team. Don't send out any new team unless you have a good lead on where to send them." Nick didn't say it aloud, but the main reason he wanted Doctor Bart at the command center was in the event one of the children was injured. They needed the level-headed physician close at hand, not tramping through the woods.

Doctor Bart patted the yellow-lined pad of paper upon which he was jotting down notes. "Don't worry, I'll keep track of everything, just like a regular dispatcher."

"Good man. Also, you searchers—take your water bottles and wear suitable clothing and footwear. Any questions?"

"Seems like a solid plan," said Ryan. "But you haven't mentioned what you'll be doing."

Nick, who was sitting at the head of the long banquet table around which they were all gathered, now rose to his feet. "I'm heading off down the trail behind the church. I can cover the distance faster than any of you. I'll check the Toad Stools and the Millett Rock, and then run the length of the Sovereign Woods trail. If I find the kids, I'll bring them back here. If I don't find them, I'll meet everyone at the turnoff to the Millett Rock. We can implement Plan B from there."

"What's Plam B?" asked his father.

"I don't know yet, Dad," Nick admitted honestly. "But I don't expect to need it. Don't worry if I'm not back by the time you meet up at the turnoff. That means I'm hot on the kids' trail or I've found them."

Sabine, inclined forward in her chair and grasped his untucked shirt tail. "Can't I follow you, Nick? I won't have anything to do once I contact the Fire Department."

"Oh, yes you will, darling. You have a very important job. You're going to ring the church bell—and keep ringing it every fifteen minutes—until the kids and all the searchers are back."

"Ring the bell? Why?"

"Because that bell can be heard for miles around. The other day I heard it clearly down to my house. If any of you get lost," Nick directed the searchers, "head toward the sound of the bell."

"But won't the kids hear the bell and realize we're looking for them?" worried Rebecca.

"I hope so," Nick replied. "Right about now—after eight hours on the lam—Tad, Hope and Jana are tired, thirsty, confused, sad, and very, very lonely. When they hear the bell, they'll know help is on the way."

Nick slipped out the back door of the banquet hall, which opened behind the church near the access to the Sovereign Woods trail. As he hiked down over the hill, he heard the slamming of truck doors as the volunteer firefighters began to arrive. In the distance Nick discerned an approaching siren, no doubt the county deputies. By the time he reached the bridge over Black Brook, Sabine was ringing the bell. The uplifting sound of the Revere bell reverberated throughout the valley.

He quickly investigated the area around both ends of the wooden bridge. Nick had not expected to find evidence that the children had been there, nor did he. Likewise, the Toad Stools had not been visited by the kids nor anyone else recently.

Nick hurried southward into the cool shade of the tree-lined trail. The local Scouts troop had recently added a thin layer of pine mulch to the path, which emitted a pleasant astringent scent. He was glad to see the woodchips because the fresh ground covering would make it easier for him to track the children—if he could only pick up their trail!

Soon he reached the turnoffs to the Millett Rock and the trail leading up to the Russell homestead. A few steps up the trail to the east assured him that—as he suspected—the three kids had followed the old woods road down from Rebecca's house to the main trail. Nick could see where the children had trudged through the tall grass in the overgrown trail. But where had they gone from here?

He thought he saw disturbances in the pine mulch suggesting the runaways headed south down the main trail toward Maggie's house. But he didn't feel confident enough to pass by the Millett Rock without giving that site a once over. He hastened to the popular picnic spot and scouted around. Uncovering no evidence of the youngsters, he backtracked to the main trail.

Nick moved down the chip-strewn trail, accompanied by the dulcet tones of the church bell. Shortly, he spied drag marks in the mulch, suggesting one of the children had begun dragging his or her backpack. Two hundred yards further he picked a purple hair ribbon from a spruce bough that encroached upon the trail. Jana! He remembered his niece had been wearing purple ribbons on her pigtails at the bell rededication ceremony.

Nick felt a rush of love for his niece and her friends. The tempo of his heart picked up. He was gaining on them!

He cautioned himself, however, against becoming overconfident. The eight-hour headstart of the runaways would take him some time to make up. And just because the evidence showed they were on the main trail, didn't mean they stayed on the main trail. The three, knowing they would be followed, might have hooked off into the woods. Nick forced himself to slow his stride.

He continued to follow the drag mark in the mulch, eyes constantly roving over the wildflowers and grasses that crowded the trail edge, searching for other clues. He paused once, upon hearing a rustling noise beside the trail during the interim when Sabine wasn't ringing the bell. But the culprit turned out to be an excitable chipmunk hiding in a pile of dead leaves. The chipmunk, realizing it had been discovered, let loose a volley of high-pitched "chips" and ran up a nearby oak tree.

At the intersection of the trail to his home, Nick paused. The drag mark he was following indicated the children had continued southward, but how far ahead they might be he had no idea. Should he keep going? Or should he stop and equip himself for a search that might well extend into the evening? The day was still warm, but he knew that in less than two hours the evening dew would fall. When the sun set, his search would not only be in the dark, but also in the chilly dampness of the lowland bordering the swamp.

Nick decided to take the prudent course. He would stop at his house and pick up a water bottle, headlamp, and sweatshirt. In two minutes, he was striding up the herb-lined stone walkway that led to his house. He spotted Gerald sitting on his small east-facing porch. The youth hopped up from the willow rocker as Nick approached, and waited for him to reach the house.

Nick felt badly, but he was going to have to fob the boy off. "I'm sorry, Gerald, I haven't got time now for a math lesson." In addition to reading lessons, he had been schooling Gerald on math, science, and history, hoping to get the youth into school next month.

The boy jumped down from the deck and followed Nick into the kitchen. "I ain't wantin' no lesson. I'm here to confess. I think I done wrong."

"Later, Gerald. I really don't have time." Nick placed his aluminum water bottle in the sink and began forcefully pumping the well pump handle.

"I heared the bell, Nick. You lookin' for them kids?"

"Yes, I'm looking for the kids. Who told you the children were missing?"

"They did."

Nick released the handle, thinking he must have misheard the boy because of the noisy pump. "Who told you?"

"Them three kids did. I seen 'em on the trail below the Millett Rock. Hope said they was runnin' away so the boy's Ma wouldn't have to build the solar farm."

Nick clasped the youth by his bony shoulders. "Do you know where they are?" he demanded.

"Told ya, that's why I'm here! I think I done wrong 'n sartin 'tis I'm tryin' to do right!"

"What did you do wrong?"

"I showed them kids my deer trail through the swamp."

"Holy heck, Gerald! You're still using that swamp trail? After I specifically told you not to?"

Gerald hung his head. "Not after today I ain't, I 'spect"

"That's right—you ain't!" Nick turned the boy around so that he faced the kitchen door. He capped his water bottle, picked up his sweatshirt from the back of a chair, and grabbed his headlamp from a peg on the wall. "Let's go, hotshot! Take me to this infamous swamp trail. But if anything's happened to those kids, you're going to be in big trouble!"

"Oh, sartin I know that!"

In fifteen minutes, they reached the turnoff to Gerald's swamp trail. The youth pushed aside several of the swamp maple's branches, whose flaming red leaves had effectively screened the entrance to the deer trail. "Here ya go."

Nick glanced up the winding deer trail, and then at the branches the boy was holding out of the way. He shook his head. "How did you ever find this trail, Gerald? I had no idea it was here!"

The boy shrugged. "T'warn't hard. I seen a deer go in here one day 'n I follered it."

Nick moved in front of the tree, holding the branches back so that Gerald could pass ahead of him. "This is where you left the kids?"

"Yep. I told 'em to stay on the trail." The youth ventured in eight or ten steps. "Hey-ho! Now, why did them kids go thatta way? That ain't the trail." He shook his head in disgust.

Sure enough, the children had clearly veered off into the bowels of the swamp. "Why the heck did you leave them, Gerald? They're just little kids!"

Gerald, stung by Nick's angry outburst, hung his head in shame.

Nick shoved the youth aside and took over the lead. He tramped forward several minutes in stony silence, before recollecting that Gerald was himself still a child. A wave of remorse washed over the woodsman. He turned and threw his arm around the red-headed shadow that trod closely upon his heels, almost knocking the boy over. "Sorry, Gerald," Nick said, steadying him. "You did the right thing bringing me here. It was very brave of you to tell me the truth, and I might never have found the kids otherwise."

"We ain't found 'em yet," Gerald pointed out.

"No, but we will. Look, here's a shoe." Nick leaned over and fished from a small puddle of brown muck a filthy little sneaker. He suspected the pink shoe belonged to Jana. He handed the dirty sneaker to Gerald. "Rinse this off for me, please." Nick turned and surveyed the expansive swamp ahead. "How far can she get with only one sneaker?" he mused.

Not far, as it turned out. Two hundred yards west along the trodden-down trail left by the runaways, Nick spotted the three children perched like sunning turtles upon a fallen log. They had reached the edge of a beaver pond and could go no farther without getting wet.

"There's Nick!" cried Tad, seeing the woodsman stomping toward them over the hummocks of swamp grass.

"And Gerald!" added Hope. She waved affectionately at the youth.

"They ain't runnin'," Gerald whispered loudly to Nick, as they approached the youngsters.

Tad overhearing Gerald's remark, scoffed. "We've been waiting for you to find us." The nine-year-old smiled up at the woodsman. "We knew you was coming, Nick. We heard the bell." Sure enough, the sound of the church bell floated down upon the breeze, mingling with the chattering of the birds in the swamp.

Nick discerned with relief that the three were unhurt and unfazed by their day-long adventure. Not wanting to let the children know how worried he had been, he greeted the runaways a broad smile. "Did you have a good picnic?"

Tad nodded vehemently. "We ate all the Needhams!"

"And the cookies," added Hope. "They were very good."

Nick chuckled. "I'll bet you ate those! How many carrots sticks and apples did you eat?"

"Not many," the boy admitted.

"I lost my shoe," said Jana, holding up her dirty stockinged right foot to show her uncle.

Gerald proudly dangled the clean shoe. "Found 'er!"

"Thank you, Mr. Gerald."

Nick gave one of Jana's pigtails a light tug. "We found your hair ribbon, too."

Jana's little hand went up to feel for the missing ribbon. "Thank you, Uncle Nick."

"Who's ready to go home?" Nick inquired in a hearty voice, the tone of which suggested he would brook no dissent. He needn't have worried, however.

"Me!" cried the three children in unison.

Nick laughed. "OK, let's rock 'n roll." He hoisted up his niece and settled her onto his broad shoulders "Hang onto my neck," he directed Jana. "Careful, don't knock my headlamp off. Get her pack, will you, Gerald?"

The youth obligingly shouldered Jana's pack. Unprompted, Gerald also retrieved Hope's backpack by the handle. "Want me to carry this for ya, Hope?" he asked the girl.

"Oh, thank you, Gerald! That would be very nice. I'll bring my blankie." Hope gathered up her small cotton blanket from the atop the log and draped it over her shoulders. She reached out with her little hand and took hold of Gerald's rough mitt. "Can I walk with you? I'm tired."

"You surely can!"

Tad, feeling the first stirrings of jealousy in his young breast, glared at the other boy. "I can carry my own pack," he said proudly.

Nick fought back another chuckle. Tad's behavior reminded him of a ticked-off partridge whose nest the woodsman had once invaded. If Tad didn't take care, he thought, the boy might have some competition for his three neighborhood girlfriends!

"Good for you, Tad," said Nick. "Now, let's get this show on the road."

By the time the motley crew reached the turnoff to the Millett Rock, where the other searchers were already gathered, Nick was also carrying Tad's pack. The boy had struggled bravely with the weight of the hatchet and other equipment, but his short legs—and general fatigue from the day—had kept him lagging behind. So, Nick had relieved Tad of his burden.

"There's Daddy!" cried Hope, upon spying in the gloaming the familiar figure of her tall father. She let go of Gerald's hand and flew into her father's outstretched arms.

Ryan scooped up his daughter and pressed her to his heart. "We thought you were lost!"

"Oh, no, Daddy. We weren't lost. We were waiting for you to find us."

"Consider yerself found, Miss Minor," said Leland, affectionately chucking his granddaughter under her chin.

Maggie hurried to Nick's side and lovingly squeezed her granddaughter's plump knee. "Are you alright, Pumpkin?"

Jana nodded an affirmation. "Yes, Grammie."

"What happened to your shoe?"

"I lost it, but Gerald found it. We saw a beaver, Grammie. He slapped his tail on the water. It was very loud."

"Oh, my!"

"We saw a bird on stilts, too," interjected Tad, who was suddenly energetic enough to hop around on one foot.

Duncan took the fatherless boy by the hand. "Your mother is up at the church getting us something to eat, Tad. Are you hungry?" he asked.

"Sort of. Are there anymore Needhams?"

"A bird on stilts?" Maggie repeated, in feigned amazement to the boy. "That's very special. I'm not sure I've ever seen that, Tad."

"It was a heron, Grammie," said Jana.

Leland's ears perked up. "You don't say! What kind o' shitpoke was it?"

"Ahem," Duncan coughed. "We don't call them that—Jana's parents prefer child-appropriate terminology."

"Wal, I cain't call the bird by its rightful name if I don't know what kind o' shitpoke 'twas," Leland pointed out.

The other adults laughed. Leland scratched his head, wondering what the joke was.

Suddenly, Maggie's two-way radio went off. "That's your Daddy checking in, Pumpkin." She brought the radio up to her mouth and clicked on the button. "You can tell Sabine to stop ringing the bell—we've found them! Everybody is A-OK!"

It was dusk by the time they reached the church. The venerable building was ablaze with light, inside and out. Sabine had also switched on the new spotlights the firemen had installed in the bell tower, turning the old church into a living, beaming beacon of hope. Soon, the runaways were in the banquet hall in their mother's arms, regaling them with their adventures. Several firemen, the game warden, and a sheriff's deputy crowded around the three youngsters listening to the recounting of their experiences, which tales soon matured to incredible proportions.

Nick, who was sitting with another group of family and friends at an adjoining table, generously extolled Gerald's role in the rescue. "I might not have found the kids if it wasn't for him," he concluded.

"Aw, shucks," Gerald said, embarrassed. "'Twarn't nuthin'."

"Goodness!" exclaimed Rebecca, who had overheard both his and Nick's remarks. She leaped up and threw her arms around the ungainly youth, giving him a big squeeze. "It certainly *is* something! I'm forever in your debt, Gerald, for bringing Tad and the girls safely home."

Robinson Crockett, the solar farm developer, who was there with his fiancée, bent his head close to Nora's ear. "I stand corrected. The kid was worth twenty dollars."

Nora smiled smugly. "I told you so."

Stephen and Nadine Danforth proudly observed the exchange between their grandson and Rebecca. "We aim to get Gerald into regular school this fall," spoke up Stephen. "Walden's been givin' him lessons."

"We've put in for custody, Rebecca," Nadine added. "Primary physical custody—with the court, you know."

"Good for you!" Rebecca exclaimed. "Well, Gerald, you just come by my house anytime, I'll give you lessons, too. And I know the kids would love to see you. Maybe you can teach them some things in return?"

"Oh, I surely can, ma'am," Gerald assured the widow, recollecting with disdain how the runaways had been unable to follow an obvious deer trail.

After everyone had refreshed themselves with sandwiches, lemonade, coffee, and cookies, Maggie suggested a singalong. A murmur of approval passed through the crowd, and a wave of people gravitated across the hall, into the nave of the church.

"Who's going to play the piano?" Duncan asked, upon realizing that their regular pianist, Courtney Gilpin, was not one of the bustling, cheerful group clustered around the piano.

"I will," said Rebecca, stepping forward.

Maggie clapped her hands in delight. "Of course! It will be just like old times at the old Russell homestead."

Nick put his arm around Sabine's waist and gave her a fond squeeze. "Happy?"

"You know it!" The young minister raised her arms in exultation. "Let's make a joyful noise to the Lord, friends!"

Few things exceed the beauty of an August evening in Maine. Fireflies twinkle in the twilight. The air is as soft as moss. Night crickets tune up their wings, issuing a diminutive Haydn concerto. But this particular evening was the most beautiful of all in Sovereign because the lost children had been found.

Soon, dulcet piano notes diffused from a window, which one of the firemen had thrown open to partake of the refreshment of the night air. Inside, Rebecca's fingers traveled over the ivories, finding her way as happily as a child finds her way across stepping stones in a brook. A distinguishable melody shortly ensued.

Sabine, recognizing the prelude, felt her eyes fill with joyful tears. It was "Now the Day Is Over," Wendell's favorite song! She allowed the music to enter her being, melding with the immense gratitude she felt that the children had been found safe; the townspeople had come together; and that she had been right to place her trust in Nick. She silently prayed the Bible verse that had inspired the song: "Stay with us, Lord, for it is nearly evening; the day is almost over."

The young minister closed her eyes. She opened her mouth, and the words sprang forth from her heart: "*Now the day is over, night is drawing nigh,*" she sang.

Duncan, also recognizing the introductory notes to the song, accompanied Sabine's soprano with his baritone: "*Shadows of the evening, steal across the sky.*" Nick, who had learned the song after Sabine told him the history of her name, immediately joined them both with his deep bass.

And then they were all singing the sublime ballad by Sabine Baring-Gould, the nineteenth century Anglican priest and hymn writer for whom Sabine had been named. For the first time since the death of Wendell Russell in January, the heart and soul of Sovereign was once again whole.

Chapter 33

Conclusion

Before we depart Sovereign, Maine, we need to tie up a few loose ends. Since this might be our last visit to the pastoral little town it is not enough to simply conclude: "And they all lived happily ever after." (Although they did.)

Miss Crump's memorial service was held the Saturday after the lost children had been found. Sabine asked Maggie to co-officiate at the service—and Duncan offered a prayer and recited the traditional 23rd Psalm graveside—and so the centenarian was buried with full ecumenical Christian fanfare. During the open-mike segment of the service at the church several townspeople stepped forward to share how the elderly woman had touched their lives. Many locals who had struggled financially over the years spoke of Miss Crump's generosity. "She pretended to be an old Scrooge," said Nadine Danforth, "but she was a real softy at heart." In my opinion, however, the best eulogy for Miss Crump (and one she would have preferred) was that offered by little Jana upon hearing of the elderly lady's demise: "She was good to her chickens."

Miss Crump had no living relatives—she had outlasted her two unmarried siblings. The reading of the will was held Saturday after the committal service at Miss Crump's modest wood-framed home situated across from the entrance to her gravel pit. Ryan MacDonald, Miss Crump's attorney, invited Maggie and Duncan, Doctor Bart and Nellie, and Hannah and Henry Trow to be present when he opened and read her will.

"I don't know why I'm here," said Maggie, who with Duncan was first to arrive, followed closely by Henry and Hannah. Maggie settled into the cushioned wicker rocker by the south-facing window in the tiny kitchen. "I'm ashamed to admit, I only began calling upon Miss Crump a few years ago." One of Miss Crump's cats immediately jumped up into the minister's lap and began to purr.

Duncan appropriated the padded chrome chair across from where the attorney was seated at the red, fifty's dinette table. "Maybe she wanted you here so you could repent your sins?"

"Hush, you!" Maggie scolded her husband.

"Who's tending Miss Crump's chickens?" Henry asked the lawyer, as he helped Hannah into one of the other dinette chairs before taking the last seat himself.

"Leland," Ryan replied. "He's been coming over every day."

Hannah set her leather purse down on the patterned linoleum floor. "What will happen to the chickens?"

"Well, that's up to the new owner. You can ask him— or her—in a few minutes."

Doctor Bart and Nellie entered, and Maggie immediately pushed the cat out of her lap and stood up. "Sit here, dear," she directed her daughter. "I don't need to sit."

"Take my seat, Maggie," said Duncan, who moved back to lean against the neat Formica countertop, where Doctor Bart shortly joined him.

Nellie gratefully waddled to the rocking chair and sank down. "Thanks, Mom. Oh, I see! This chair comes with a built-in cat." The cat, however, not finding any available space in the pregnant woman's lap, toppled off in disgust. Nellie laughed. "Sorry, kitty! There isn't room for three of us here."

Maggie surveyed the tidy kitchen. "Remember when Leland joked that Miss Crump brought her chickens into the house at night?"

"I remember," said Doctor Bart. "That was at the May Breakfast."

"Well, I certainly don't see any evidence she did. Not unless Leland has added housekeeping to his other chores."

Ryan unfolded the deceased lady's will and pressed the stiff pages against the tabletop. "If I may remind you, my wife suggested at the time that provocative piece of information might be one of her father's tarradiddles." He glanced around at the little group of friends. "Shall we begin? I'm not going to read every word. Since I'm her executor, I'll just go over the disposition of her estate."

Miss Crump had left Hannah a 24-carat gold Wedgewood cameo necklace, a family heirloom, which Hannah had always admired. She also left Henry matching gold and blue Wedgewood cufflinks, which had belonged to her grandfather.

The button Miss Crump had recently given to young Hope MacDonald was fashioned from a pink Maine tourmaline crystal mined a half century earlier at Mt. Mica in Paris, Maine by Frank Perham. In her will, the childless spinster gave the other two tourmaline buttons from her hand-knit gray sweater to Jana and Alice Rose, and recommended the gems be made into necklaces for the three to remember her by. She also gave her gold-plated letter opener to Tad.

To Maggie, the centenarian bequeathed her family Bible. Ryan retrieved the ancient Bible from the bedroom and set the heavy book on the table in front of the minister. "I'm surprised she remembered!" Maggie exclaimed. "On one of my first visits to her, I admired this Bible—it's even more beautiful than the one we have at church."

"Helen might have been old, but there was nothing wrong with her mind," said Hannah. "She never forgot anything."

Duncan, who had expected nothing, was surprised to discover Miss Crump had willed him her rare copy of the Thomas Boston classic, *The Crook in the Lot*. He carefully opened the cover of the fragile, leather-bound booklet of sermons. "Next to the Bible, this was her favorite book," he said, deeply touched. "I remember once at church she asked me if I'd ever read *The Crook in the Lot*—the crook was Boston's term for a physical affliction, like a perpetual thorn in one's side—and I said I did in seminary, but hadn't lately. She told me she read from it every night. She mentioned how much Boston's sermons about his personal suffering helped her learn to accept her own physical pain."

A hush fell over the kitchen. "We don't ever know what someone else is going through, do we?" said Maggie. "More shame on me for not visiting Miss Crump more often."

Ryan shuffled the pages of the will. "There are a few financial bequests, too. A modest donation to the Sovereign Union Church, to the Ladies Auxiliary, and to the Corn Shop Museum. That's it."

"What about Metcalf and I?" asked Nellie, her curiosity piqued. "Why are we here?"

Doctor Bart chuckled. "I'm almost afraid to find out what Miss Crump left me. Probably a chicken, like she did the first time I treated her at the clinic."

Ryan sat back in his chair and burst into hearty laughter. "Not just one chicken, Doc—but ALL of them!"

Metcalf grinned. "I knew it! Well, I do like fresh eggs."

Nellie leaned forward in the rocker. "And me?"

"She left you this, Nellie," the attorney replied. He got up and placed a small plastic object in the young woman's hand.

Nellie examined the red-and-white gadget. "What *is* this thing?"

"That, Nellie, is a tally counter. And I'm glad you're sitting in the rocking chair, because that's the perfect spot by the window to count the loads of gravel being hauled from your gravel pit."

"My *what?*"

"Your gravel pit. Miss Crump left you and Doctor Bart the remainder of her estate—house, furnishings, land, stocks, bonds, chickens—and the largest gravel pit in Waldo County."

Nellie burst into tears. "The clinic! Oh, bless her! Miss Crump knew how much we needed money to keep the doors open!"

A flushed and shocked Doctor Bart ran his hand through his strawberry-blond curls, lately tinged with white due to overwork and financial stress. "Is this true?" he demanded of the attorney.

Ryan held up the will. "It's all here in black and white, Doc. And couldn't happen to a more deserving couple, in my opinion."

"Hear, hear!" said Henry. He pounded the table so hard the cat skedaddled and Miss Crump's chicken and rooster salt-and-pepper shakers jumped.

And that's how Nellie and Doctor Bart were able to keep the lights on at the free Songbird Medical Clinic for many, many years. Their baby was born two weeks later. To Maggie's initial dismay, the child was another girl. "We'll never even the odd of the neighborhood children at this rate," she grumbled to her husband. As soon as the minister peeked at the baby's face, however, she pronounced her infant granddaughter perfect in every way.

Nellie and Doctor Bart named their daughter Helen Mae, after their never-to-be forgotten benefactress, Miss Crump. They rented her house out to a newcomer in town, and Doctor Bart built a small display case to hold the plastic tally counter, some sand from the gravel pit, and a photograph of the centenarian. Nobody had really ever needed to keep track of the truckloads of gravel coming from the pit—Miss Crump always trusted her drivers—she had just enjoyed pretending to keep a close eye on them.

As it turned out, Maggie needn't have worried about the boy-girl ratio in the neighborhood. Before school began that fall, a family, which included three young boys, bought the Worthen place on the corner of the Russell Hill Road and Route 9. In addition, Stephen and Nadine Danforth were awarded primary physical custody of their grandson and Gerald went to live with them. Rebecca made good her grateful promise to the boy to give him lessons and Gerald sauntered down to the old Russell homestead every day in August when she was watching the neighborhood kids.

Rebecca had no sooner begun to teach Gerald geography, however, when Alice Rose MacDonald—the eleven-year-old termagant—adopted the youth as her personal project. Her parents discovered (to their relief) that Alice hadn't caused trouble because she was mean-hearted, but simply because she was bored. A bright child, Alice now made it her mission to get Gerald into Jana's class at school that fall. You would have laughed to see the ungainly youth meekly accepting the scolding and prompting of the skinny younger girl. Between them all— Nick, Rebecca, Alice Rose, and Gerald's grandparents— they did get him into second grade. But word is, Gerald won't stay there long. Every afternoon he gets off the bus at Scotch Broom Acres, where Alice continues to tutor and torment him.

What about the proposed solar farm, you ask? About a week before school started, residents were invited to attend an information session. There, they learned that Nick had worked out a Grand Compromise between the parties involved, with the help of Ryan and Henry Trow. Come to find out, Rebecca never needed the income from leasing all 300 acres of Wendell's woodlot to Robinson Crockett. Without giving much thought to the potential consequences, her doting husband—worried about the welfare of his wife and child in the event of his death— had understandably wanted the most for her and Tad. Rebecca calculated that the income from leasing 100 acres would be enough to comfortably keep the two of them, but she had not wanted to break her contract—the one Wendell approved but never signed—with the solar farm developer. With Nick's help, she didn't need to.

Nick had heard Henry's outburst at the special Town Meeting, "Hell, I want a solar farm, then!" and had taken the retired history professor at his word. Thus, instead of losing out, Robinson Crockett had gained a new client for the other half of his solar farm. Rebecca's half was installed first, upon some of her fallow back fields (unseen from the road) and a small section of woodlot (nowhere near Wendell's prize stand of pines). Prior to the building of the solar farm on Henry's land, though, the retired history professor gifted all of his real estate but ten acres around his house to the town of Sovereign.

"That's a mighty big passel of money you're leaving on the table," said John Woods, the First Selectman, when he met with Henry in his office before the information session. "Sure you want to do this?"

Henry gruffly waved away the selectmen's concerns. "Hannah and I don't need the money, John. UNH pays me a hefty pension. Put the income from the solar farm to good use—like lowering the real estate tax on my house." He shifted uncomfortably in the old duct-taped office chair. "And while you're at it, replace these damned antediluvian chairs!"

Leland Gorse soon fell into his comfortable old habit of dropping into the old Russell homestead around mealtime. He became a grandfather figure for Tad and a true friend to Rebecca. Heartily ashamed of his role in putting Stephen Danforth up to telling the widow to go back to Boston and take Robinson Crockett with her, he visited the house one day not long after the children had been found. When Leland walked into the kitchen, Rebecca burst into tears and flung herself into the octogenarian's arms. "Oh, I still miss him!" she cried, sobbing on the woodchopper's shoulder. "Ayuh, me, too," Leland admitted, consoling the widow as best he could. "Ain't nobody gonna forget Wendell, dear. But I reckon we can git by this soft patch—if we stick together."

In a similar penitent spirit, one afternoon Nick walked over to Maggie's house to apologize to his father. He found Duncan at the kitchen table, attempting to balance the checkbook. "Maybe I should let Maggie take this dang thing over?" Duncan mused, looking up at his son.

Nick pulled up a chair. "Do you think that's wise? You know math isn't her strong suit."

"No, but perhaps it's time I stopped trying to be wise? All my life I've trod the straight and narrow path—what harm would it do if I kick the traces and let loose a little?"

Nick laid his arm on the table and leaned forward earnestly. "Kicking the traces is not a good idea, Dad. Then you'd be like me, and look how I've turned out! That's why I'm here—to apologize for everything. I'm sorry for letting my ego run rampant; for picking a fight with our friends; for jeopardizing the lives of the kids; and for not being honest with you and Maggie. If you only knew how sorry I am!"

Duncan took his son by the hand. "I do know how sorry you are," he warmly assured Nick. "And I'm heartily sick over my share in the breakdown of our relationship. But you know what they say? 'These are things that bring men together and make them know each other better'," he quoted.

Nick sat back and gave his beard a thoughtful tug. "Thomas Boston?" he guessed.

"Nope," Duncan said with a wink. "Stonewall Jackson."

"Get out!"

"I kid you not. You know, son, someday, I'd love to tell you about your grandfather," he continued. "He was a very gifted man. You remind me a lot of him. I want you to know, I'm very proud of you."

With the help of clerical friends in high places, Maggie and Duncan were able to get Nick matriculated into Harvard Divinity School that fall. His three-year course of study would be grueling—and Nick had some catching up to do—but his years of reading every book in Maggie's office library helped prepare him for divinity school.

Alas for Sabine! She was unable to finish out her one-year contract as interim minister for the Sovereign Union Church. When Nick returned to town during January break, she and Nick were wed. Her mother flew in from Alaska to officiate at the marriage ceremony, with the assistance of Maggie and Duncan. Sabine was hired as the youth pastor of a Methodist church in Boston, and there she and Nick will reside until he has completed his coursework. There is no doubt they plan to return to Sovereign, though. For her wedding gift to them, Rebecca gave Nick and Sabine Wendell's prize stand of pine trees. One day in the not too distant future Nick will have his pastorate in their forest cathedral.

"Happy?" Nick asked his bride, as they snowshoed out to the pine grove one last time before departing for Boston. The January sun splashed twinkling blue glitter across a fresh dusting of snow.

"You know it!"

He dropped a kiss on her frosty red nose. "Now, about that slap …?"

Sabine hid her face in her thick woolen mittens. "Oh, don't remind me!"

"But I want to remind you, darling—and thank you—because that is the moment in which I truly saw the light of God's unconditional love. I want you to promise me that if I ever forget myself again …"

"Oh, don't worry, soon-to-be Pastor Faulkner," she interrupted him. "Your loving wife won't let you forget yourself." A soft thud of snow falling from a pine bough was the only sound to be heard in the woods as they kissed.

During the three years that Nick and Sabine would be away, his sister and her fiancée planned to occupy Nick's house in the Sovereign Woods. It was a sight to see Rob teaching Nora how to use the hand pump and the wringer washing machine, but in no time at all she was an adept.

"You amaze me," Rob said to her one day, as he watched Nora bring an armful of frozen clothes in from the clothesline and stand his jeans in a corner to thaw. He had sold his company to a larger solar farm developer (making a tidy profit) and now worked for Revision Energy, an employee-owned company out of Montville. "I honestly didn't think you'd be able to tough it out here."

Nora pooh-poohed him. "Hey, if Nicky can do it, so can I!"

"Does that mean we can build a house like this?" Rob asked hopefully.

"Not on your life!"

Back at Maggie's house, after the newlyweds departed for Boston, Duncan tossed another piece of rock maple into the living room woodstove. "You don't mind going back to work?" he asked his wife, who was reading comfortably on the couch in front of the fire.

Maggie put her finger in the page to mark her place. "Not in the least. I never knew how much I loved being pastor here until I wasn't anymore. I don't ever intend to retire. Do you think the board will let me work parttime when Sabine comes back?"

"Probably. But what about that book you're going to write?"

"Oh, I'll be too busy for that! I have two granddaughters, now, you know. I never really cared about that book anyway," she added. "The sabbatical was just a way for me to test out retirement."

"What's the verdict?"

"I don't like it."

Duncan sat down beside his wife on the couch. He removed the book from Maggie's hand and placed the novel on the coffee table. He threw his arm over his wife's shoulders and pulled her close. "You know, I think I finally figured out why you were so mad at Leland last spring when he dug up that yellow moccasin."

"Duncan! Don't tell me you've been ruminating on that for eight months? You've got too much time on your hands, dear. You need something else to do besides balance the checkbook."

"I've already taken over the cemeteries," Duncan reminded her. Upon Frank Whitehouse's retirement that fall, the retired Presbyterian minister had volunteered to become town sexton, a thankless position often difficult to fill.

"True, but there isn't much to do in the cemeteries in winter. OK, I'll bite. Why do you think I was mad at Leland?"

"Because as a young child you were uprooted from your family's home in Winslow. Seeing him dig up that yellow lady's slipper subconsciously reminded you of your negative childhood experience."

"Ouch! That one hits pretty close to the bone. So, you think you've got me all figured out?"

"Am I wrong?"

Maggie pushed him away and reached for her novel. "I haven't thought about it, nor do I intend to."

"OK, have it your way, dear," Duncan remarked. "You usually do." He recollected with wry amusement the ridiculous costume she had dressed him up in for the rededication of the bell. "And as my old buddy Leland would say," he continued, "I don't much mind."

Maggie was delighted to learn in the spring that the town had enrolled Henry's woodlot in the Maine Audubon program, Forestry for Maine Birds. The town forester would now manage the woods for the preservation and propagation of songbirds, as well as other wildlife. In May, the local scout troop that maintained the trail—utilizing town funds from the solar farm lease—put up interpretive signs throughout the Sovereign Woods, highlighting unusual trees and plants for the edification of hikers and picnic goers. Much to Maggie's disgust, however, the scouts widened the path Leland had hacked out to Nick's secret patch of yellow moccasins, where they added a sign explaining the botany of lady's slipper orchids. Twenty-four hours later a smaller second sign was posted anonymously—a crude, hand-painted sign—that read: DON'T DIG THE FLOWERS!

The End

Acknowledgements

I have always loved the Sabine-Baring Gould song, *Now the Day Is Over*, which our father used to sing to us kids at night. So, my first homage must go to the Anglican priest who penned these beautiful lyrics. (Although Baring-Gould also wrote the music to accompany his hymn, the music later created by Sir Joseph Barnby has become the most popular version of the song.) I'd also like to take the opportunity to credit the nineteenth century Norway (Maine) author, Dr. Osgood N. Bradbury, for my sketch of Duncan conversing with Frank Whitehouse, the Sovereign sexton, in the cemetery before Memorial weekend. I borrowed Bradbury's poignant vignette in which he described his visit to Norway Pine Grove Cemetery one day, where he spoke with Jonathan Whitehouse while the sexton was digging a grave. Many of the heart-felt words I put into Frank Whitehouse's mouth came from the Norway sexton's in real life. I'd also like to acknowledge the poet Hamish Mcmillan, whose sublime poem, "sea of longing," Nick quotes to Sabine at the end of Chapter 31.

Another creative spirit I'd like to recognize and gratefully thank is my long-time editor John Goldfine of Swanville, Maine. Over the course of many books of mine that he has edited, John has helped me become a better writer. If, as a young person, I'd ever had an editor like John, I might have written another ten books! John is so even-handed offering suggestions that he never crimps my style (or tries to impose upon it). Nor does he ever make me feel anything but grateful. (We writers tend to be a sensitive group.) In addition, the personal comments he adds as an aside are often the highlight of my day. I don't know how he does it, but John manages to be funny, curmudgeonly, inspiring, helpful, honest, and provocative—all at the same time. As a result of his personal asides, I think I know more about John than I do many of my friends, yet—incredibly—we've never met in person, although we live only 25 miles apart. Maybe I'll motor down to Swanville one of these days and look for John with his dogs and horses.

I'd also like to thank my cousin Adeline Wixson, who (along with John) read the chapters of *Now the Day Is Over* as I wrote them. She is a longtime fan and supporter of my Sovereign Series and so Adeline's immediate feedback was incredibly helpful. What was most interesting to me as a writer, however, was that early in the novel Adeline took a dislike to Sabine, while on the other hand John found Nick self-important and obnoxious. Their competing aversions to these characters forced me to work harder as writer to try—by the end of the book—to redeem Nick (in John's eyes) and Sabine (in Adeline's). Did I succeed? You, dear reader, will have to answer that question for yourself. I love both characters, despite their flaws.

New Hampshire artist Peter Harris deserves my deepest gratitude, also. Peter created the covers for my five previous *Sovereign Series* novels (as well as some of my non-fiction books), and so I was thrilled when Peter said he would step out of retirement to create the cover for *Now the Day Is Over*. Peter's book jackets add a spirit of unity to this collection of Maine novels. He often says more in one image than I say in 10,000 words!

I'd like to credit my loving husband Stanley Luce for putting up with me during the hours I spent so much time in Sovereign. He even managed to cook a few meals so that I could keep writing. They were pretty good dinners, too!

Finally, I'm grateful to all my fans—especially those of you who have been with me since *Hens and Chickens*—who encouraged me to continue writing about the little town of Sovereign, Maine. Without you, none of this would have been possible. Thank you.

Jen Wixson
Troy, Maine
December 25, 2025

Books by Jennifer Wixson

Fiction – _The Sovereign Series_
Hens and Chickens – Book 1
Peas, Beans & Corn – Book 2
The Songbird of Sovereign – Book 3
The Minister's Daughter – Book 4
Maggie's Dilemma – Book 5
Now the Day Is Over – Book 6

Non-fiction
Learning to SOAR!
Under the Apple Tree
A History of the Crocket Family of Crockett's Ridge, Norway Maine
"Into the Maine …" One Maine Family's Quest for Land, 1630-1830

About the Author

Maine writer, retired farmer, and former Quaker minister Jennifer Wixson lives and writes from her home in Troy. She and her husband garden, renovate old houses, and produce maple products. Jennifer is the author of *The Sovereign Series*, six novels set in the good-hearted town of Sovereign, Maine. She has also written several non-fiction books.